Ring Around the Sun: And Other Stories

Isaac Asimov was born in Russia near Smolensk in 1920. He was brought to the United States by his parents three years later and grew up in Brooklyn. He graduated from Columbia University in chemistry and after a short spell in the Army, gained his doctorate in 1949 and qualified as an instructor in biochemistry at Boston University School of Medicine, where he became Associate Professor in 1955. He retired to full-time authorship in 1958 while retaining his connection with the University. His first story 'Marooned Off Vesta' appeared in 1939 in *Amazing Stories*. Asimov became a regular contributor to the leading SF magazines of the day including *Astounding*, *Astonishing Stories*, *Super Science Stories* and *Galaxy*. He won the Hugo Award four times and the Nebula Award once. With nearly five hundred books to his credit and several hundred articles, Asimov's output was prolific by any standards.

Isaac Asimov died in 1992 at the age of 72.

BY THE SAME AUTHOR

ROBOT STORIES AND NOVELS
I, Robot
The Rest of the Robots
The Complete Robot
The Caves of Steel
The Naked Sun
The Robots of Dawn
Robots and Empire

THE GALACTIC EMPIRE NOVELS
The Currents of Space
The Stars, Like Dust
Pebble in the Sky

The End of Eternity

THE FOUNDATION SAGA
Prelude to Foundation
Forward the Foundation
Foundation
Foundation and Empire
Second Foundation
Foundation's Edge
Foundation and Earth

SHORT STORY COLLECTIONS
The Complete Stories:
Living Space: And Other Stories
Nightfall: And Other Stories
The Martian Way: And Other Stories
The Bicentennial Man: And Other Stories
Mother Earth: And Other Stories
Gold: The Final Science Fiction Collection
Magic: The Final Fantasy Collection

ISAAC ASIMOV

Ring Around the Sun:
And Other Stories

THE COMPLETE STORIES

HARPER
Voyager

Harper*Voyager*
An imprint of HarperCollins*Publishers* Ltd
1 London Bridge Street
London SE1 9GF

www.harpercollins.co.uk

HarperCollins*Publishers*
Macken House, 39/40 Mayor Street Upper,
Dublin 1, D01 C9W8, Ireland

This paperback edition 2024
1

A catalogue record for this book is available from the British Library.

ISBN: 978-0-00-867244-7

This book is set in Janson Text LT Std by HarperCollins*Publishers* India

Printed and bound in the UK using 100%
renewable electricity at CPI Group (UK) Ltd

MIX
Paper | Supporting
responsible forestry
FSC™ C007454

This book contains FSC™ certified paper and other controlled
sources to ensure responsible forest management.

For more information visit: www.harpercollins.co.uk/green

Contents

Marooned Off Vesta

'Will you please stop walking up and down like that?' said Warren Moore from the couch. 'It won't do any of us any good. Think of our blessings; we're airtight, aren't we?'

Mark Brandon whirled and ground his teeth at him. 'I'm glad you feel happy about that,' he spat out viciously. 'Of course, you don't know that our air supply will last only three days.' He resumed his interrupted stride with a defiant air.

Moore yawned and stretched, assumed a more comfortable position, and replied, 'Expending all that energy will only use it up faster. Why don't you take a hint from Mike here? He's taking it easy.'

'Mike' was Michael Shea, late a member of the crew of the *Silver Queen*. His short, squat body was resting on the only chair in the room and his feet were on the only table. He looked up as his name was mentioned, his mouth widening in a twisted grin.

'You've got to expect things like this to happen sometimes,' he said. 'Bucking the asteroids is risky business. We should've taken the hop. It takes longer, but it's the only safe way. But no, the captain wanted to make the schedule; he *would* go through' – Mike spat disgustedly – 'and here we are.'

'What's the "hop"?' asked Brandon.

'Oh, I take it that friend Mike means that we should have avoided the asteroid belt by plotting a course outside the plane of the ecliptic,' answered Moore. 'That's it, isn't it, Mike?'

Mike hesitated and then replied cautiously, 'Yeah – I guess that's it.'

Moore smiled blandly and continued, 'Well, I wouldn't blame Captain Crane too much. The repulsion screen must have failed five minutes before that chunk of granite barged into us. That's not his fault, though of course we ought to have steered clear instead of relying on the screen.' He shook his head meditatively. 'The *Silver Queen* just went to pieces. It's really miraculously lucky that this part of the ship remained intact, and what's more, airtight.'

'You've got a funny idea of luck, Warren,' said Brandon. 'Always have, for as long as I've known you. Here we are in a tenth part of a spaceship, comprising only three *whole* rooms, with air for three days, and no prospect of being alive after that, and you have the infernal gall to prate about luck.'

'Compared to the others who died instantly when the asteroid struck, yes,' was Moore's answer.

'You think so, eh? Well, let me tell you that instant death isn't so bad compared with what we're going to have to go through. Suffocation is a damned unpleasant way of dying.'

'We may find a way out,' Moore suggested hopefully.

'Why not face facts!' Brandon's face was flushed and his voice trembled. 'We're done, I tell you! Through!'

Mike glanced from one to the other doubtfully and then coughed to attract their attention. 'Well, gents, seeing that we're all in the same fix, I guess there's no use hogging things.' He drew a small bottle out of his pocket that was filled with a greenish liquid. 'Grade A Jabra this is. I ain't too proud to share and share alike.'

Brandon exhibited the first signs of pleasure for over a day. 'Martian Jabra water. Why didn't you say so before?'

But as he reached for it, a firm hand clamped down upon his wrist. He looked up into the calm blue eyes of Warren Moore.

'Don't be a fool,' said Moore, 'there isn't enough to keep us drunk for three days. What do you want to do? Go on a tear now and then die cold sober? Let's save this for the last six hours when the air gets stuffy and breathing hurts – then we'll finish the bottle among us and never *know* when the end comes, or *care*.'

Brandon's hand fell away reluctantly. 'Damn it, Warren, you'd bleed ice if you were cut. How can you think straight at a time like this?' He motioned to Mike and the bottle was once more stowed away. Brandon walked to the porthole and gazed out.

Moore approached and placed a kindly arm over the shoulders of the younger man. 'Why take it so hard, man?' he asked. 'You can't last at this rate. Inside of twenty-four hours you'll be a madman if you keep this up.'

There was no answer. Brandon stared bitterly at the globe that filled almost the entire porthole, so Moore continued, 'Watching Vesta won't do you any good either.'

Mike Shea lumbered up to the porthole. 'We'd be safe if we were only down there on Vesta. There're people there. How far away are we?'

'Not more than three or four hundred miles judging from its apparent size,' answered Moore. 'You must remember that it is only two hundred miles in diameter.'

'Three hundred miles from salvation,' murmured Brandon, 'and we might as well be a million. If there were only a way to get ourselves out of the orbit this rotten fragment adopted. You know, manage to give ourselves a push so as to start falling. There'd be no danger of crashing if we did, because that midget hasn't got enough gravity to crush a cream puff.'

'It has enough to keep us in the orbit,' retorted Brandon. 'It must have picked us up while we were lying unconscious after the crash. Wish it had come closer; we might have been able to land on it.'

'Funny place, Vesta,' observed Mike Shea. 'I was down there two-three times. What a dump! It's all covered with some stuff like snow, only it ain't snow. I forget what they call it.'

'Frozen carbon dioxide?' prompted Moore.

'Yeah, dry ice, that carbon stuff, that's it. They say that's what makes Vesta so shiny.'

'Of course! That would give it a high albedo.'

Mike cocked a suspicious eye at Moore and decided to let it pass. 'It's hard to see anything down there on account of the snow, but if you look close' – he pointed – 'you can see a sort of gray smudge. I thing that's Bennett's dome. That's where they keep the observatory. And there is Calorn's dome up there. That's a fuel station, that is. There're plenty more, too, only I don't see them.'

He hesitated and then turned to Moore. 'Listen, boss, I've been thinking. Wouldn't they be looking for us as soon as they hear about the crash? And wouldn't we be easy to find from Vesta, seeing we're so close?'

Moore shook his head, 'No, Mike, they won't be looking for us. No one's going to find out about the crash until the *Silver Queen* fails to turn up on schedule. You see, when the asteroid hit, we didn't have time to send out an SOS' – he sighed – 'and they won't find us down there at Vesta, either. We're so small that even at our distance they couldn't see us unless they knew what they were looking for, and exactly where to look.'

'Hmm.' Mike's forehead was corrugated in deep thought. 'Then we've got to get to Vesta before three days are up.'

'You've got the gist of the matter, Mike. Now, if we only knew how to go about it, eh?'

Brandon suddenly exploded, 'Will you two stop this infernal chitter-chatter and do something? For God's sake, do something.'

Moore shrugged his shoulders and without answer returned to the couch. He lounged at ease, apparently carefree, but there was the tiniest crease between his eyes which bespoke concentration.

There was no doubt about it; they *were* in a bad spot. He reviewed the events of the preceding day for perhaps the twentieth time.

After the asteroid had struck, tearing the ship apart, he'd gone out like a light; for how long he didn't know, his own watch being broken and no other timepiece available. When he came to, he found himself, along with Mark Brandon, who shared his room, and Mike Shea, a member of the crew, sole occupants of all that was left of the *Silver Queen*.

This remnant was now careening in an orbit about Vesta. At present, things were fairly comfortable. There was a food supply that would last a week. Likewise there was a regional Gravitator under the room that kept them at normal weight and would continue to do so for an indefinite time, certainly for longer than the air would last. The lighting system was less satisfactory but had held on so far.

There was no doubt, however, where the joker in the pack lay. Three days' air! Not that there weren't other disheartening features. There was no heating system – though it would take a long time for the ship to radiate enough heat into the vacuum of space to render them too uncomfortable. Far more important was the fact that their part of the ship had neither a means of communication nor a propulsive mechanism. Moore sighed. One fuel jet in working order would fix everything, for one blast in the right direction would send them safely to Vesta.

The crease between his eyes deepened. What was to be done? They had but one spacesuit among them, one heat ray, and one detonator. That was the sum total of space appliances after a thorough search of the accessible parts of the ship. A pretty hopeless mess, that.

Moore shrugged, rose, and drew himself a glass of water. He swallowed it mechanically, still deep in thought, when an idea struck him. He glanced curiously at the empty cup in his hand.

'Say, Mike,' he said, 'what kind of water supply have we? Funny that I never thought of that before.'

Mike's eyes opened to their fullest extent in an expression of ludicrous surprise. 'Didn't you know, boss?'

'Know *what?*' asked Moore impatiently.

'We've got all the water there was.' He waved his hand in an all-inclusive gesture. He paused, but as Moore's expression showed nothing but total mystification, he elaborated, 'Don't you see? We've got the main tank, the place where all the water for the whole ship was stored.' He pointed to one of the walls.

'Do you mean to say that there's a tank full of water adjoining us?'

Mike nodded vigorously, 'Yep! Cubic vat a hundred feet each way. And she's three-quarters full.'

Moore was astonished. 'Seven hundred and fifty thousand cubic feet of water.' Then suddenly: 'Why hasn't it run out through the broken pipes?'

'It only has one main outlet, which runs down the corridor just outside this room. I was fixing that main when the asteroid hit and had to shut it off. After I came to I opened the pipe leading to our faucet, but that's the only outlet open now.'

'Oh.' Moore had a curious feeling way down deep inside. An idea had half-formed in his brain, but for the life of him he could not drag it into the light of day. He knew only that there was something in what he had just heard that had some important meaning but he just could not place his finger on it.

Brandon, meanwhile, had been listening to Shea in silence, and now he emitted a short, humorless laugh. 'Fate seems to be having its fill of fun with us, I see. First, it puts us within arm's reach of a place of safety and then sees to it that we have no way of getting there.

'Then she provides us with a week's food, three days' air, and *a year's supply of water*. A year's supply, do you hear me? Enough water to drink and to gargle and to wash and to take baths in and – and to do anything else we want. Water – damn the water!'

'Oh, take a less serious view, Mark,' said Moore in an attempt to break the younger man's melancholy. 'Pretend we're a satellite of Vesta – which we are. We have our own period of revolution and of rotation. We have an equator and an axis. Our "north pole" is located somewhere toward the top of the porthole, pointing toward Vesta, and our "south" sticks out away from Vesta through the water tank somewhere. Well, as a satellite, we have an atmosphere, and now, you see, we have a newly discovered ocean.

'And seriously, we're not so badly off. For the three days our atmosphere will last, we can eat double rations and drink ourselves soggy. Hell, we have water enough to throw away—'

The idea which had been half-formed before suddenly sprang to maturity and was nailed. The careless gesture with which he had accompanied the last remark was frozen in mid-air. His mouth closed with a snap and his head came up with a jerk.

But Brandon, immersed in his own thoughts, noticed nothing of Moore's strange actions. 'Why don't you complete the analogy to a satellite,' he sneered, 'or do you, as a Professional Optimist, ignore any and all disagreeable facts? If *I* were you, I'd continue this way.' Here he imitated Moore's voice: 'The satellite is at present habitable and inhabited but, due to the approaching depletion of its atmosphere in three days, is expected to become a dead world.

'Well, why don't you answer? Why do you persist in making a joke out of this? Can't you see— *What's the matter?*'

The last was a surprised exclamation and certainly Moore's actions did merit surprise. He had risen suddenly and, after giving himself a smart rap on the forehead, remained stiff and silent, staring into the far distance with gradually narrowing eyelids. Brandon and Mike Shea watched him in speechless astonishment.

Suddenly Moore burst out, 'Ha! I've got it. Why didn't I think of it before?' His exclamations degenerated into the unintelligible.

Mike drew out the Jabra bottle with a significant look, but Moore waved it away impatiently. Whereupon Brandon, without any warning, lashed out with his right, catching the surprised Moore flush on the jaw and toppling him.

Moore groaned and rubbed his chin. Somewhat indignant, he asked, 'What was the reason for that?'

'Stand up and I'll do it again,' shouted Brandon, 'I can't stand it anymore. I'm sick and tired of being preached at, and having to listen to your Pollyanna talk. *You're* the one that's going daffy.'

'Daffy, nothing! Just a little overexcited, that's all. Listen, for God's sake. I think I know a way—'

Brandon glared at him balefully. 'Oh, you do, do you? Raise our hopes with some silly scheme and then find it doesn't work. I won't take it, do you hear? I'll find a real use for the water – drown you – and save some of the air besides.'

Moore lost his temper. 'Listen, Mark, you're out of this. I'm going through alone. I don't need your help and I don't want it. If you're that sure of dying and that afraid, why not have the agony over? We've got one heat ray and one detonator, both reliable weapons. Take your choice and kill yourself. Shea and I won't interfere.' Brandon's lip curled in a last weak gesture of defiance and then suddenly he capitulated, completely and abjectly. 'All right, Warren, I'm with you. I-I guess I didn't quite know what I was doing. I don't feel well, Warren. I-I—'

'Aw, that's all right, boy.' Moore was genuinely sorry for him. 'Take it easy. I know how you feel. It's got me too. But you mustn't give in to it. Fight it, or you'll go stark, raving mad. Now you just try and get some sleep and leave everything to me. Things will turn out right yet.'

Brandon, pressing a hand to an aching forehead, stumbled to the couch and tumbled down. Silent sobs shook his frame while Moore and Shea remained in embarrassed silence nearby.

At last Moore nudged Mike. 'Come on,' he whispered, 'let's get busy. We're going places. Airlock five is at the end of the corridor, isn't it?' Shea nodded and Moore continued, 'Is it airtight?'

'Well,' said Shea after some thought, 'the inner door is, of course, but I don't know anything about the outer one. For all I know it may be a sieve. You see, when I tested the wall for airtightness, I didn't dare open the inner door, because if there was anything wrong with the outer one – blooey!' The accompanying gesture was very expressive.

'Then it's up to us to find out about that outer door right now. I've got to get outside some way and we'll just have to take chances. Where's the spacesuit?'

He grabbed the lone suit from its place in the cupboard, threw it over his shoulder and led the way into the long corridor that ran down the side of the room. He passed closed doors behind whose airtight barriers were what once had been passenger quarters but which were now merely cavities, open to space. At the end of the corridor was the tight-fitting door of Airlock 5.

Moore stopped and surveyed it appraisingly. 'Looks all right,' he observed, 'but of course you can't tell what's outside. God, I hope it'll work.' He frowned. 'Of course we could use the entire corridor as an airlock, with the door to our room as the inner door and this as the outer door, but that would mean the loss of half our air supply. We can't afford that – yet.'

He turned to Shea. 'All right, now. The indicator shows that the lock was last used for entrance, so it should be full of air. Open the door the tiniest crack, and if there's a hissing noise, shut it quick.'

'Here goes,' and the lever moved one notch. The mechanism had been severely shaken up during the shock of the crash and its former noiseless workings had given way to a harsh, rasping sound, but it was still in commission. A thin black line appeared on the left-hand side of the lock, marking where the door had slid a fraction of an inch on the runners.

There was no hiss! Moore's look of anxiety faded somewhat. He took a small pasteboard from his pocket and held it against the crack. If air were leaking, that card should have held there, pushed by the escaping gas. It fell to the floor.

Mike Shea stuck a forefinger in his mouth and then put it against the crack. 'Thank the Lord,' he breathed, 'not a sign of a draft.'

'Good, good. Open it wider. Go ahead.'

Another notch and the crack opened farther. And still no draft. Slowly, ever so slowly, notch by notch, it creaked its way wider and wider. The two men held their breaths, afraid that while not actually punctured, the outer door might have been so weakened as to give way any moment. But it held! Moore was jubilant as he wormed into the spacesuit.

'Things are going fine so far, Mike,' he said. 'You sit down right here and wait for me. I don't know how long I'll take, but I'll be back. Where's the heat ray? Have you got it?'

Shea held out the ray and asked, 'But what are you going to do? I'd sort of like to know.'

Moore paused as he was about to buckle on the helmet. 'Did you hear me say inside that we had water enough to throw away? Well, I've been thinking it over and that's not such a bad idea. I'm going to throw it away.' With no other explanation, he stepped into the lock, leaving behind him a very puzzled Mike Shea.

It was with a pounding heart that Moore waited for the outer door to open. His plan was an extraordinarily simple one, but it might not be easy to carry out.

There was a sound of creaking gears and scraping ratchets. Air sighed away to nothingness. The door before him slid open a few inches and stuck. Moore's heart sank as for a moment he thought it would not open at all, but after a few preliminary jerks and rattles the barrier slid the rest of the way.

He clicked on the magnetic grapple and very cautiously put a foot out into space. Clumsily he groped his way out to the side of the ship. He had never been outside a ship in open space before and a vast dread overtook him as he clung there, flylike, to his precarious perch. For a moment dizziness overcame him.

He closed his eyes and for five minutes hung there, clutching the smooth sides of what had once been the *Silver Queen*. The magnetic grapple held him firm and when he opened his eyes once more he found his self-confidence in a measure returned.

He gazed about him. For the first time since the crash he saw the stars instead of the vision of Vesta which their porthole afforded. Eagerly he searched the skies for the little blue-white speck that was Earth. It had often amused him that Earth should always be the first object sought by space travelers when star-gazing, but the humor of the situation did not strike him now. However, his search was in vain. From where he lay, Earth was invisible. It, as well as the Sun, must be hidden behind Vesta.

Still, there was much else that he could not help but note. Jupiter was off to the left, a brilliant globe the size of a small pea to the naked eye. Moore observed two of its attendant satellites. Saturn was visible too, as a brilliant planet of some negative magnitude, rivaling Venus as seen from Earth.

Moore had expected that a goodly number of asteroids would be visible – marooned as they were in the asteroid belt – but space seemed surprisingly empty. Once he thought he could see a hurtling body pass within a few miles, but so fast had the impression come and gone that he could not swear that it was not fancy.

And then, of course, there was Vesta. Almost directly below him it loomed like a balloon filling a quarter of the sky. It floated steadily, snowy white, and Moore gazed at it with earnest longing. A good hard kick against the side of the ship, he thought, might start him falling toward Vesta. He *might* land safely and get help for the others. But the chance was too great that he would merely take on a new orbit about Vesta. No, it would have to be better than that.

This reminded him that he had no time to lose. He scanned the side of the ship, looking for the water tank, but all he could see was a jungle of jutting walls, jagged, crumbling, and pointed. He hesitated. Evidently the only thing to do was to make for the lighted porthole to their room and proceed to the tank from there.

Carefully he dragged himself along the wall of the ship. Not five yards from the lock the smoothness stopped abruptly. There was a yawning cavity which Moore recognized as having once been the room adjoining the corridor at the far end. He shuddered. Suppose he were to come across a bloated dead body in one of those rooms. He had known most of the passengers, many of them personally. But he overcame his squeamishness and forced himself to continue his precarious journey toward its goal.

And here he encountered his first practical difficulty. The room itself was made of non-ferrous material in many parts. The magnetic grapple was intended for use only on outer hulls and was useless throughout much of the ship's interior. Moore had forgotten this when suddenly he found himself floating down an incline, his grapple out of use. He gasped and clutched at a nearby projection. Slowly he pulled himself back to safety.

He lay for a moment, almost breathless. Theoretically he should be weightless out here in space – Vesta's influence being negligible – but the regional Gravitator under his room was working. Without the balance of the other Gravitators, it tended to place him under variable and suddenly shifting stresses as he kept changing his position. For his magnetic grapple to let go suddenly might mean being jerked away from the ship altogether. And then what?

Evidently this was going to be even more difficult than he had thought.

He inched forward in a crawl, testing each spot to see if the grapple would hold. Sometimes he had to make long, circuitous journeys to gain a few feet's headway and at other times he was forced to scramble and slip across small patches of non-ferrous material. And always there was that tiring pull of the Gravitator, continually changing directions as he progressed, setting horizontal floors and vertical walls at queer and almost haphazard angles.

Carefully he investigated all objects, that he came across. But it was a barren search, Loose articles, chairs, tables had been jerked away at the first shock, probably, and now were independent bodies of the Solar System. He did manage, however, to pick up a small field glass and fountain pen. These he placed in his pocket. They were valueless under present conditions, but somehow they seemed to make more real this macabre trip across the sides of a dead ship.

For fifteen minutes, twenty, half an hour, he labored slowly toward where he thought the porthole should be. Sweat poured down into his eyes and rendered his hair a matted mass. His muscles were beginning to ache under the unaccustomed strain. His mind, already strained by the ordeal of the previous day, was beginning to waver, to play him tricks.

The crawl began to seem eternal, something that had always existed and would exist forever. The object of the journey, that for which he was striving, seemed unimportant; he only knew that it was necessary to move. The time, one hour back, when he had been with Brandon and Shea, seemed hazy and lost in the far past. That more normal time, two days' age, wholly forgotten.

Only the jagged walls before him, only the vital necessity of getting at some uncertain destination existed in his spinning brain. Grasping, straining, pulling. Feeling for the iron alloy. Up and into gaping holes that were rooms and then out again. Feel and pull – feel and pull – and – a light.

Moore stopped. Had he not been glued to the wall he would have fallen. Somehow that light seemed to clear things. It was the porthole; not the many dark, staring ones he had passed, but alive and alight. Behind it was Brandon. A deep breath and he felt better, his mind cleared.

And now his way lay plain before him. Toward that spark of life he crept. Nearer, and nearer, and nearer until he could touch it. He was there!

His eyes drank in the familiar room. God knows that it hadn't any happy associations in his mind, but it was something real, something almost natural. Brandon slept on the couch. His face was worn and lined but a smile passed over it now and then.

Moore raised his fist to knock. He felt the urgent desire to talk with someone, if only by sign language; yet at the last instant he refrained. Perhaps the kid was dreaming of home. He was young and sensitive and had suffered much. Let him sleep. Time enough to wake him when – and if – his idea had been carried through.

He located the wall within the room behind which lay the water tank and then tried to spot it from the outside. Now it was not difficult; its rear wall stood out prominently. Moore marveled, for it seemed a miracle that it had escaped puncture. Perhaps the Fates had not been so ironic after all.

Passage to it was easy though it was on the other side of the fragment. What was once a corridor led almost directly to it. Once when the *Silver Queen* had been whole, that corridor had been level and horizontal, but now, under the unbalanced pull of the regional gravitator, it seemed more of a steep incline than anything else. And yet it made the path simple. Since it was of uniform beryl-steel, Moore found no trouble holding on as he wormed up the twenty-odd feet to the water supply.

And now the crisis – the last stage – had been reached. He felt that he ought to rest first, but his excitement grew rapidly in intensity. It was either now or bust. He pulled himself out to the bottom-center of the tank. There, resting on the small ledge formed by the floor of the corridor that had once extended on that side of the tank, he began operations.

'It's a pity that the main pipe is pointing in the wrong direction,' he muttered. 'It would have saved me a lot of trouble had it been right. As it is . . .' He sighed and bent to his work. The heat ray was adjusted to maximum concentration and the invisible emanations focused at a spot perhaps a foot above the floor of the tank.

Gradually the effect of the excitatory beam upon the molecules of the wall became noticeable. A spot the size of a dime began shining faintly at the point of focus of the ray gun. It wavered uncertainly, now dimming, now brightening, as Moore strove to steady his tired arm. He propped it on the ledge and achieved better results as the tiny circle of radiation brightened.

Slowly the color ascended the spectrum. The dark, angry red that had first appeared lightened to a cherry color. As the heat continued pouring in, the brightness seemed to ripple out in widening areas, like a target made of successively deepening tints of red. The wall for a distance of some feet from the focal point was becoming uncomfortably hot even though it did not glow and Moore found it necessary to refrain from touching it with the metal of his suit.

Moore cursed steadily, for the ledge itself was also growing hot. It seemed that only imprecations could soothe him. And as the melting wall began to radiate heat in its own right, the chief object of his maledictions were the spacesuit manufacturers. Why didn't they build a suit that could keep heat *out* as well as keep it *in?*

But what Brandon called Professional Optimism crept up. With the salt tang of perspiration in his mouth, he kept consoling himself,

'It could be worse, I suppose. At least, the two inches of wall here don't present too much of a barrier. Suppose the tank had been built flush against the outer hull. Whew! Imagine trying to melt through a foot of this.' He gritted his teeth and kept on.

The spot of brightness was now flickering into the orange-yellow and Moore knew that the melting point of the beryl-steel alloy would soon be reached. He found himself forced to watch the spot only at widely spaced intervals and then only for fleeting moments.

Evidently it would have to be done quickly if it were to be done at all. The heat ray had not been fully loaded in the first place, and, pouring out energy at maximum as it had been doing for almost ten minutes now, must be approaching exhaustion. Yet the wall was just barely passing the plastic stage. In a fever of impatience, Moore jammed the muzzle of the gun directly at the center of the spot, drawing it back speedily.

A deep depression formed in the soft metal, but a puncture had not been formed. However, Moore was satisfied. He was almost there now. Had there been air between himself and the wall, he would undoubtedly have heard the gurgling and the hissing of the steaming water within. The pressure was building up. How long would the weakened wall endure?

Then, so suddenly that Moore did not realize it for a few moments, he was through. A tiny fissure formed at the bottom of that little pit made by the ray gun and in less time than it takes to imagine, the churning water within had its way.

The soft, liquid metal at that spot puffed out, sticking out raggedly around a pea-sized hole. And from that hole there came a hissing and a roaring. A cloud of steam emerged and enveloped Moore.

Through the mist he could see the steam condense almost immediately to ice droplets and saw these icy pellets shrink rapidly into nothingness.

For fifteen minutes he watched the steam shoot out.

Then he became aware of a gentle pressure pushing him away from the ship. A savage joy welled up within him as he realized that this was the effect of acceleration on the ship's part. His own inertia was holding him back.

That meant his work had been finished – and successfully. That stream of water was substituting for the rocket blast.

He started back.

If the horrors and dangers of the journey to the tank had been great, those of the way back should have been greater. He was infinitely more tired, his aching eyes were all but blind, and added to the crazy pull of the Gravitator was the force induced by the varying acceleration of the ship. But whatever his labors to return, they did not bother him. In later time, he never even remembered the heart-breaking trip.

How he managed to negotiate the distance in safety he did not know. Most of the time he was lost in a haze of happiness, scarcely realizing the actualities of the situation. His mind was filled with one thought only – to get back quickly, to tell the happy news of their escape.

Suddenly he found himself before the airlock. He hardly grasped the fact that it *was* the airlock. He almost did not understand why he pressed the signal button. Some instinct told him it was the thing to do.

Mike Shea was waiting. There was a creak and a rumble and the outer door started opening, caught, and stopped at the same place as before, but once again it managed to slide the rest of the way. It closed behind Moore, then the inner door opened and he stumbled into Shea's arms.

As in a dream he felt himself half-pulled, half-carried down the corridor to the room. His suit was ripped off. A hot, burning liquid stung his throat. Moore gagged, swallowed, and felt better. Shea pocketed the Jabra bottle once more.

The blurred, shifting images of Brandon and Shea before him steadied and became solid. Moore wiped the perspiration from his face with a trembling hand and essayed a weak smile.

'Wait,' protested Brandon, 'don't say anything. You look half-dead. Rest, will you!'

But Moore shook his head. In a hoarse, cracked voice he narrated as well as he could the events of the past two hours. The tale was incoherent, scarcely intelligible but marvelously impressive. The two listeners scarcely breathed during the recital.

'You mean,' stammered Brandon, 'that the water spout is pushing us toward Vesta, like a rocket exhaust?'

'Exactly – same thing as – rocket exhaust,' panted Moore. 'Action and reaction. Is located – on side opposite Vesta – hence pushing us toward Vesta.'

Shea was dancing before the porthole. 'He's right, Brandon, me boy. You can make out Bennett's dome as clear as day. We're getting there, we're getting there.'

Moore felt himself recovering. 'We're approaching in spiral path on account of original orbit. We'll land in five or six hours probably. The water will last for quite a long while and the pressure is still great, since the water issues as steam.'

'Steam – at the low temperature of space?' Brandon was surprised.

'Steam – at the low pressure of space!' corrected Moore. 'The boiling point of water falls with the pressure. It is very low indeed in a vacuum. Even ice has a vapor pressure sufficient to sublime.'

He smiled. 'As a matter of fact, it freezes and boils at the same time. I watched it.' A short pause, then, 'Well, how do you feel now, Brandon? Much better, eh?'

Brandon reddened and his face fell. He groped vainly for words for a few moments. Finally he said in a half-whisper, 'You know, I must have acted like a damn fool and a coward at first. I-I guess I don't deserve all this after going to pieces and letting the burden of our escape rest on your shoulders.

'I wish you'd beat me up, or something, for punching you before. It'd make me feel better. I mean it.' And he really did seem to mean it.

Moore gave him an affectionate push. 'Forget it. You'll never know how near I came to breaking down myself.' He raised his voice in order to drown out any further apologies on Brandon's part, 'Hey,

Mike, stop staring out of that porthole and bring over that Jabra bottle.'

Mike obeyed with alacrity, bringing with him three Plexatron units to be used as makeshift cups. Moore filled each precisely to the brim. He was going to be drunk with a vengeance.

'Gentlemen,' he said solemnly, 'a toast.' The three raised the mugs in unison, 'Gentlemen, I give you the year's supply of good old H_2O *we used to have.*'

The Callistan Menace

'Damn Jupiter!' growled Ambrose Whitefield viciously, and I nodded agreement.

'I've been on the Jovian satellite run,' I said, 'for fifteen years and I've heard those two words spoken maybe a million times. It's probably the most sincere curse in the Solar System.'

Our watch at the controls of the scoutship *Ceres* had just been relieved and we descended the two levels to our room with dragging steps.

'Damn Jupiter – and damn it again,' insisted Whitefield morosely. 'It's too big for the System. It stays out there behind us and pulls and pulls and *pulls!* We've got to keep the Atomos firing all the way. We've got to check our course – completely – every hour. No relaxation, no coasting, no taking it easy! Nothing but the rottenest kind of work.'

There were tiny beads of perspiration on his forehead and he swabbed at them with the back of his hand. He was a young fellow, scarcely thirty, and you could see in his eyes that he was nervous, and even a little frightened.

And it wasn't Jupiter that was bothering him, in spite of his profanity. Jupiter was the least of our worries. It was Callisto! It was that little moon which gleamed a pale blue upon our visiplates that made Whitefield sweat and that had spoiled four nights' sleep for me already. Callisto! Our destination!

Even old Mac Steeden, gray mustachioed veteran who, in his youth, had sailed with the great Peewee Wilson himself, went about his duties with an absent stare. Four days out – and ten days more ahead of us – and panic was reaching out with clammy fingers.

We were all brave enough in the ordinary course of events. The eight of us on the *Ceres* had faced the purple Lectronics and stabbing Disintos of pirates and rebels and the alien environments of half a dozen worlds. But it takes more than run-of-the-mill bravery to face the unknown; to face Callisto, the 'mystery world' of the Solar System.

One fact was known about Callisto – one grim, bare fact. Over a period of twenty-five years, seven ships, progressively better equipped, had landed – and never been heard from again. The Sunday supplements peopled the satellite with anything from super-dinosaurs to invisible ghosts of the fourth dimension, but that did not solve the mystery.

We were the eighth. We had a better ship than any of those preceding. We were the first to sport the newly-developed beryltungsten hull, twice as strong as the old steel shells. We possessed super-heavy armaments and the very latest Atomic Drive engines.

Still – we were only the eighth, and every man jack of us knew it.

Whitefield entered our quarters silently and flopped down upon his bunk. His fists were clenched under his chin and showed white at the knuckles. It seemed to me that he wasn't far from the breaking point. It was a case for careful diplomacy.

'What we need,' said I, 'is a good, stiff drink.'

'What we need,' he answered harshly, 'is a hell of a lot of good, stiff drinks.'

'Well, what's stopping us?'

He looked at me suspiciously, 'You know there isn't a drop of liquor aboard ship. It's against Navy regulations!'

'Sparkling green *Jabra* water,' I said slowly, letting the words drip from my mouth. 'Aged beneath the Martian deserts. Melted emerald juice. Bottles of it! Cases of it!'

'Where?'

'I know where. What do you say? A few drinks – just a few – will cheer us both up.'

For a moment, his eyes sparkled, and then they dulled again, 'What if the Captain finds out? He's a stickler for discipline, and on a trip like this, it's liable to cost us our rating.'

I winked and grinned, 'It's the Captain's own cache. He can't discipline us without cutting his own throat – the old hypocrite. He's the best damn Captain there ever was, but he likes his emerald water.'

Whitefield stared at me long and hard, 'All right. Lead me to it.'

We slipped down to the supply room, which was deserted, of course. The Captain and Steeden were at the controls; Brock and Charney were at the engines; and Harrigan and Tuley were snoring their fool heads off in their own room.

Moving as quietly as I could, through sheer habit, I pushed aside several crates of food tabs and slid open a hidden panel near the floor. I reached in and drew out a dusty bottle, which, in the dim light, sparkled a dull sea-green.

'Sit down,' I said, 'and make yourself comfortable.' I produced two tiny cups and filled them.

Whitefield sipped slowly and with every evidence of satisfaction. He downed his second at one gulp.

'How come you volunteered for this trip, anyway, Whitey?' I asked, 'You're a little green for a thing like this.'

He waved his hand, 'You know how it is. Things get dull after a while. I went in for zoology after getting out of college – big field since interplanetary travel – and had a nice comfortable position back on Ganymede. It was dull, though; I was bored blue. So I joined the Navy on an impulse, and on another I volunteered for this trip.' He sighed ruefully, 'I'm a little sorry I did.'

'That's not the way to take it, kid. I'm experienced and I know.

When you're panicky, you're as good as licked. Why, two months from now, we'll be back on Ganymede.'

'I'm not scared, if that's what you're thinking,' he exclaimed angrily. 'It's – it's,' there was a long pause in which he frowned at his third cupful. 'Well, I'm just worn out trying to imagine what the hell to expect. My imagination is working overtime and my nerves are rubbing raw.'

'Sure, sure,' I soothed, 'I'm not blaming you. It's that way with all of us, I guess. But you have to be careful. Why, I remember once on a Mars-Titan trip, we had—'

Whitefield interrupted what was one of my favorite yarns – and I could spin them as well as anyone in the service – with a jab in the ribs that knocked the breath out of me.

He put down his *Jabra* gingerly.

'Say, Jenkins,' he stuttered, 'I haven't downed enough liquor to be imagining things, have I?'

'That depends on what you imagined.'

'I could swear I saw something move somewhere in the pile of empty crates in the far corner.'

'That's a bad sign,' and I took another swig as I said it. 'Your nerves are going to your eyes and now they're going back on you. Ghosts, I suppose, or the Callistan menace looking us over in advance.'

'I saw it, I tell you. There's something alive there.' He edged towards me – his nerves were plenty shot – and for a moment, in the dim, shadowy light even I felt a bit choked up.

'You're crazy,' I said in a loud voice, and the echoes calmed me down a bit. I put down my empty cup and got up just a wee bit unsteadily. 'Let's go over and poke through the crates.'

Whitefield followed me and together we started shoving the light aluminum cubicles this way and that. Neither of us was quite one hundred percent sober and we made a fair amount of noise. Out of the corner of my eye, I could see Whitefield trying to move the case nearest the wall.

'This one isn't empty,' he grunted, as it lifted very slightly off the floor.

Muttering under his breath, he knocked off the cover and looked in. For a half second he just stared and then he backed away slowly. He tripped over something and fell into a sitting position, still gaping at the case.

I watched his actions with raised eyebrows, then glanced hastily at the case in question. The glance froze into a steady glare, and I emitted a hoarse yell that rattled off each of the four walls.

A boy was sticking his head out of the case – a red-haired dirty-faced kid of thirteen or thereabouts.

'Hello,' said the boy as he clambered out into the open. Neither of us found the strength to answer him, so he continued, 'I'm glad you found me. I was getting a cramp in my shoulder trying to curl up in there.'

Whitefield gulped audibly, 'Good God! A kid stowaway! And on a voyage to *Callisto*!'

'And we can't turn back,' I reminded in a stricken voice, 'without wrecking ourselves. The Jovian satellite run is *poison*.'

'Look here,' Whitefield turned on the kid in a sudden belligerence. 'Who are you, you young nut, and what are you doing here?'

The kid flinched. 'I'm Stanley Fields,' he answered, a bit scared. 'I'm from New Chicago on Ganymede. I-I ran away to space, like they do in books.' He paused and then asked brightly, 'Do you think we'll have a fight with pirates on this trip, mister?'

There was no doubt that the kid was filled to the brim with 'Dime Spacers'. I used to read them myself as a youngster.

'How about your parents?' asked Whitefield, grimly.

'Oh, all I got's an uncle. He won't care much, I guess.' He had gotten over his first uneasiness and stood grinning at us.

'Well, what's to be done?' said Whitefield, looking at me in complete helplessness.

I shrugged, 'Take him to the Captain. Let *him* worry.'

'And how will he take it?'

'Anyway he wants. It's not *our* fault. Besides, there's absolutely nothing to be done about the mess.'

And grabbing an arm apiece, we walked away, dragging the kid between us.

Captain Bartlett is a capable officer and one of the deadpan type that very rarely displays emotion. Consequently, on those few occasions when he does, it's like a Mercurian volcano in full eruption – and you haven't lived until you've seen one of those.

It was a case of the final straw. A satellite run is always wearing. The image of Callisto up ahead was harder on him than on any member of the crew. And now there was this kid stowaway.

It wasn't to be endured! For half an hour, the Captain shot off salvo after salvo of the very worst sort of profanity. He started with the sun and ran down the list of planets, satellites, asteroids, comets, to the very meteors themselves. He was starting on the nearer fixed stars, when he collapsed from sheer nervous exhaustion. He was so excited that he never thought to ask us what we were doing in the storeroom in the first place, and for that Whitefield and I were duly grateful.

But Captain Bartlett is no fool. Having purged his system of its nervous tension, he saw clearly that that which cannot be cured must be endured.

'Someone take him and wash him up,' he growled wearily, 'and keep him out of my sight for a while.' Then, softening a bit, he drew me towards him, 'Don't scare him by telling him where we're going. He's in a bad spot, the poor kid.'

When we left, the old soft-hearted fraud was sending through an emergency message to Ganymede trying to get in touch with the kid's uncle.

Of course, we didn't know it at the time, but that kid was a Godsend – a genuine stroke of Old Man Luck. He took our minds off Callisto. He gave us something else to think about. The tension, which at the end of four days had almost reached the breaking point, eased completely.

There was something refreshing in the kid's natural gayety; in his bright ingenuousness. He would meander about the ship asking the silliest kind of questions. He insisted on expecting pirates at any moment. And, most of all, he persisted in regarding each and every one of us as 'Dime Spacer' heroes.

That last flattered our egos, of course, and put us on our mettle. We vied with each other in chest-puffing and tale-telling, and old Mac Steeden, who in Stanley's eyes was a demi-god, broke the all-time record for plain and fancy lying.

I remember, particularly, the talk-fest we had on the seventh day out. We were just past the midpoint of the trip and were set to begin a cautious deceleration. All of us (except Harrigan and Tuley, who were at the engines) were sitting in the control room. Whitefield, with half an eye on the Mathematico, led off, and, as usual, talked zoology.

'It's a little slug-like thing,' he was saying, 'found only on Europa. It's called the Carolus Europis but we always referred to it as the Magnet Worm. It's about six inches long and has a sort of a slategray color – most disgusting thing you could imagine.

'We spent six months studying that worm, though, and I never saw old Mornikoff so excited about anything before. You see, it killed by some sort of magnetic field. You put the Magnet Worm at one end of the room and a caterpillar, say, at the other. You wait about five minutes and the caterpillar just curls up and dies.

'And the funny thing is this. It won't touch a frog – too big; but if you take that frog and put some sort of iron band about it, that Magnet Worm kills it just like that. That's why we know it's some type of magnetic field that does it – the presence of iron more than quadruples its strength.'

His story made quite an impression on us. Joe Brock's deep bass voice sounded, 'I'm damn glad those things are only four inches long, if what you say is right.'

Mac Steeden stretched and then pulled at his gray mustachios with exaggerated indifference, 'You call *that* worm unusual. It isn't a patch on some of the things I've seen in my day.' He shook his head slowly and reminiscently, and we knew we were in for a long and gruesome tale. Someone groaned hollowly, but Stanley brightened up the minute he saw the old veteran was in a story-telling mood.

Steeden noticed the kid's sparkling eyes, and addressed himself to the little fellow, 'I was with Peewee Wilson when it happened – you've heard of Peewee Wilson, haven't you?'

'Oh, yes,' Stanley's eyes fairly exuded hero-worship. 'I've read books about him. He was the greatest spacer there ever was.'

'You bet all the radium on Titan he was, kid. He wasn't any taller than you, and didn't scale much more than a hundred pounds, but he was worth five times his weight in Venusian Devils in any fight. And me and him were just like that. He never went anyplace but what I was with him. When the going was toughest it was always me that he turned to.'

He sighed lugubriously, 'I was with him to the very end. It was only a broken leg that kept me from going with him on his last voyage—'

He choked off suddenly and a chilly silence swept over all of us. Whitefield's face went gray, the Captain's mouth twisted in a funny sort of way, and I felt my heart skid all the way down to the soles of my feet.

No one spoke, but there was only one thought among the six of us. Peewee Wilson's last trip had been to Callisto. He had been the second – and had never returned. We were the eighth.

Stanley stared from one to the other of us in astonishment, but we all avoided his eyes.

It was Captain Bartlett that recovered first.

'Say, Steeden, you've got an old spacesuit of Peewee Wilson's, haven't you?' His voice was calm and steady but I could see that it took a great deal of effort to keep it so.

Steeden brightened and looked up. He had been chewing at the tips of his mustachios (he always did when nervous) and now they hung downwards in a bedraggled fashion.

'Sure thing, Captain. He gave it to me with his own hand, he did.

It was back in '23 when the new steel suits were just being put out. Peewee didn't have any more use for his old vitri-rubber contraption, so he let me have it – and I've kept it ever since. It's good luck for me.'

'Well, I was thinking that we might fix up that old suit for the boy here. No other suit'll fit him, and he needs one bad.'

The veteran's faded eyes hardened and he shook his head vigorously, 'No sir, Captain. No one touches that old suit. Peewee gave it to me himself. With his own hand! It's-it's *sacred*, that's what it is.'

The rest of us chimed in immediately upon the Captain's side but Steeden's obstinacy grew and hardened. Again and again he would repeat tonelessly, 'That old suit stays where it is.' And he would emphasize the statement with a blow of his gnarled fist.

We were about to give up, when Stanley, hitherto discreetly silent, took a hand.

'Please, Mr Steeden,' there was just the suspicion of a quaver in his voice. 'Please let me have it. I'll take good care of it. I'll bet if Peewee Wilson were alive today he'd say I could have it.' His blue eyes misted up and his lower lip trembled a bit. The kid was a perfect actor.

Steeden looked irresolute and took to biting his mustachio again, 'Well – oh, hell, you've *all* got it in for me. The kid can have it but don't expect me to fix it up! The rest of you can lose sleep – I wash my hands of it.'

And so Captain Bartlett killed two birds with one stone. He took our minds off Callisto at a time when the morale of the crew hung in the balance and he gave us something to think about for the remainder of the trip – for renovating that ancient relic of a suit was almost a week's job.

We worked over that antique with a concentration out of all proportion to the importance of the job. In its pettiness, we forgot the steadily growing orb of Callisto. We soldered every last crack and blister in that venerable suit. We patched the inside with close-meshed aluminium wire. We refurbished the tiny heating unit and installed new tungsten oxygen-containers.

Even the Captain was not above giving us a hand with the suit, and Steeden, after the first day, in spite of his tirade at the beginning, threw himself into the job with a will.

We finished it the day before the scheduled landing, and Stanley, when he tried it on, glowed with pride, while Steeden stood by, grinning and twirling his mustachio.

And as the days passed, the pale blue circle that was Callisto grew upon the visiplate until it took up most of the sky. The last day was an uneasy one. We went about our tasks abstractedly, and studiously avoided the sight of the hard, emotionless satellite ahead.

We dived – in a long, gradually contracting spiral. By this maneuvre, the Captain had hoped to gain some preliminary knowledge of the nature of the planet and its inhabitants, but the information gained was almost entirely negative. The large percentage of carbon dioxide present in the thin, cold atmosphere was congenial to plant life, so that vegetation was plentiful and diversified. However, the three percent oxygen content seemed to preclude the possibility of any animal life, other than the simplest and most sluggish species. Nor was there any evidence at all of cities or artificial structures of any kind.

Five times we circled Callisto before sighting a large lake, shaped something like a horse's head. It was towards that lake that we gently lowered ourselves, for the last message of the second expedition – Peewee Wilson's expedition – spoke of landing near such a lake. We were still half a mile in the air, when we located the gleaming metal ovoid that was the *Phobos*, and when we finally thumped softly on to the green stubble of vegetation, we were scarcely five hundred yards from the unfortunate craft.

'Strange,' muttered the Captain, after we had all congregated in the control room, waiting for further orders, 'there seems to be no evidence of any violence at all.'

It was true! The *Phobos* lay quietly, seemingly unharmed. Its old-fashioned steel hull glistened brightly in the yellow light of a gibbous Jupiter, for the scant oxygen of the atmosphere could make no rusty inroads upon its resistant exterior.

The Captain came out of a brown study and turned to Charney at the radio.

'Ganymede has answered?'

'Yes, sir. They wish us luck.' He said it simply, but a cold shiver ran down my spine.

Not a muscle of the Captain's face flickered. 'Have you tried to communicate with the *Phobos?*'

'No answer, sir.'

'Three of us will investigate the *Phobos*. Some of the answers, at least, should be there.'

'Matchsticks!' grunted Brock, stolidly.

The Captain nodded gravely.

He palmed eight matches, breaking three in half, and extended his arm towards us, without saying a word.

Charney stepped forward and drew first. It was broken and he stepped quietly towards the space-suit rack. Tuley followed and after him Harrigan and Whitefield. Then I, and I drew the second broken match. I grinned and followed Charney, and in thirty seconds, old Steeden himself joined us.

'The ship will be backing you fellows,' said the Captain quietly, as he shook our hands. 'If anything dangerous turns up, run for it. No heroics now, for we can't afford to lose men.'

We inspected our pocket Lectronics and left. We didn't know exactly what to expect and weren't sure but that our first steps on Callistan soil might not be our last, but none of us hesitated an instant. In the 'Dime Spacers,' courage is a very cheap commodity, but it is rather more expensive in real life. And it is with considerable pride that I recall the firm steps with which we three left the protection of the *Ceres*.

I looked back only once and caught a glimpse of Stanley's face pressed white against the thick glass of the porthole. Even from a distance, his excitement was only too apparent. Poor kid! For the last two days he had been convinced we were on our way to clean up a pirate stronghold and was almost dying with impatience for the fighting to begin. Of course, none of us cared to disillusion him.

The outer hull of the *Phobos* rose before us and overshadowed us with its might. The giant vessel lay in the dark green stubble, silent as death. One of the seven that had attempted and failed. And we were the eighth.

Charney broke the uneasy silence, 'What are these white smears on the hull?'

He put up a metal-encased finger and rubbed it along the steel plate. He withdrew it and gazed at the soft white pulp upon it. With an involuntary shudder of disgust, he scraped it off upon the coarse grass beneath.

'What do you think it is?'

The entire ship as far as we could see – except for that portion immediately next the ground – was besmeared by a thin layer of the pulpy substance. It looked like dried foam – like—

I said: 'It looks like slime left after a giant slug had come out of the lake and slithered over the ship.'

I wasn't serious in my statement, of course, but the other two cast hasty looks at the mirror-smooth lake in which Jupiter's image lay unruffied. Charney drew his hand Lectronic.

'Here!' cried Steeden, suddenly, his voice harsh and metallic as it came over the radio, 'that's no way to be talking. We've got to find some way of getting into the ship; there must be some break in its hull somewhere. You go around to the right, Charney, and you, Jenkins, to the left. I'll see if I can't get atop of this thing somehow.'

Eyeing the smoothly-round hull carefully, he drew back and jumped. On Callisto, of course, he weighed only twenty pounds or less, suit and all, so he rose upwards some thirty or forty feet. He slammed against the hull lightly, and as he started sliding downwards, he grabbed a rivet-head and scrambled to the top.

Waving a parting to Charney at this point, I left.

'Everything all right?' the Captain's voice sounded thinly in my ear.

'All O.K.,' I replied gruffly, 'so far.' And as I said so, the *Ceres* disappeared behind the convex bulge of the dead *Phobos* and I was entirely alone upon the mysterious moon.

I pursued my round silently thereafter. The spaceship's 'skin' was entirely unbroken except for the dark, staring portholes, the lowest of which were still well above my head. Once or twice I thought I could see Steeden scrambling monkey-like on top of the smooth hulk, but perhaps that was only fancy.

I reached the prow at last which was bathed in the full light of Jupiter. There, the lowest row of portholes were low enough to see into and as I passed from one to the other, I felt as if I were gazing into a shipful of spectres, for in the ghostly light all objects appeared only as flickering shadows.

It was the last window in the line that proved to be of sudden, overpowering interest. In the yellow rectangle of Jupiter-light stamped upon the floor, there sprawled what remained of a man. His clothes were draped about him loosely and his shirt was ridged as if the ribs below had moulded it into position. In the space between the open shirt collar and engineer's cap, there showed a grinning, eyeless skull. The cap, resting askew upon the smooth skullcase, seemed to add the last refinement of horror to the sight.

A shout in my ears caused my heart to leap. It was Steeden, exclaiming profanely somewhere above the ship. Almost at once, I caught sight of his ungainly steel-clad body slipping and sliding down the side of the ship.

We raced towards him in long, floating leaps and he waved us on, running ahead of us, towards the lake. At its very shores, he stopped and bent over some half-buried object. Two bounds brought us to him, and we saw that the object was a space-suited human, lying face downward. Over it was a thick layer of the same slimy smear that covered the *Phobos*.

'I caught sight of it from the heights of the ship,' said Steeden, somewhat breathlessly, as he turned the suited figure over.

What we saw caused all three of us to explode in a simultaneous cry. Through the glassy visor, there appeared a leprous countenance.

The features were putrescent, fallen apart, as if decay had set in and ceased because of the limited air supply. Here and there a bit of gray bone showed through. It was the most repulsive sight I have ever witnessed, though I have seen many almost as bad.

'My God!' Charney's voice was half a sob. 'They simply die and decay.' I told Steeden of the clothed skeleton I had seen through the porthole.

'Damn it, it's a puzzle,' growled Steeden, 'and the answer *must* be inside the *Phobos*.' There was a momentary silence, 'I tell you what. One of us can go back and get the Captain to dismount the Disintegrator. It ought to be light enough to handle on Callisto, and at low power, we can draw it fine enough to cut a hole without blowing the entire ship to kingdom come. You go, Jenkins. Charney and I will see if we can't find any more of the poor devils.'

I set off for the *Ceres* without further urging, covering the ground in space-devouring leaps. Three-quarters of the distance had been covered when a loud shout, ringing metallically in my ear, brought me to a skidding halt. I wheeled in dismay and remained petrified at the sight before my eyes.

The surface of the lake was broken into boiling foam, and from it there reared the fore-parts of what appeared to be giant caterpillars. They squirmed out upon land, dirty-gray bodies dripping slime and water. They were some four feet long, about one foot in thickness, and their method of locomotion was the slowest of oxygen-conserving crawls. Except for one stalky growth upon their forward end, the tip of which glowed a faint red, they were absolutely featureless.

Even as I watched, their numbers increased, until the shore became one heaving mass of sickly gray flesh.

Charney and Steeden were running towards the *Ceres*, but less than half the distance had been covered when they stumbled, their run slowing to a blind stagger. Even that ceased, and almost together they fell to their knees.

Charney's voice sounded faintly in my ear, 'Get help! My head is splitting. I can't move! I—' Both lay still now.

I started towards them automatically, but a sudden sharp pang just over my temples staggered me, and for a moment I stood confused.

Then I heard a sudden unearthly shout from Whitefield, 'Get back to the ship, Jenkinsl Get back! Get back!'

I turned to obey, for the pain had increased into a continuous tearing pain. I weaved and reeled as I approached the yawning air-lock, and I believe that I was at the point of collapse when I finally fell into it. After that, I can recall only a jumble for quite a period.

My next clear impression was of the control-room of the *Ceres*. Someone had dragged the suit off me, and I gazed about me in dismay at a scene of the utmost confusion. My brain was still some-what addled and Captain Bartlett as he leant over me appeared double.

'Do you know what those damnable creatures are?' He pointed outwards at the giant caterpillars.

I shook my head mutely.

'They're the great grand-daddies of the Magnet Worm White-field was telling us of once. Do you remember the Magnet Worm?'

I nodded, 'The one that kills by a magnetic field which is strength-ened by surrounding iron.'

'Damn it, yes,' cried Whitefield, interrupting suddenly. 'I'll swear to it. If it wasn't for the lucky chance that our hull is beryl-tungsten and not steel – like the *Phobos* and the rest – evcry last one of us would be unconscious by now and dead before long.'

'Then *that's* the Callistan menace.' My voice rose in sudden dismay, 'But what of Charney and Steeden?'

'They're sunk,' muttered the Captain grimly. 'Unconscious – maybe dead. Those filthy worms are crawling towards them and there's nothing we can do about it.' He ticked off the points on his fingers. 'We can't go after them in a spacesuit without signing our own death warrant – spacesuits are steel. No one can last there and back without one. We have no weapons with a beam fine enough to blast the Worms without scorching Charney and Steeden as well. I've thought of maneuvering the *Ceres* nearer and making a dash for it, but one can't handle a spaceship on planetary surfaces like that – not without cracking up. We—'

'In short,' I interrupted hollowly, 'we've got to stand here and watch them die.' He nodded and I turned away bitterly.

I felt a slight twitch upon my sleeve, and when I turned, it was to find Stanley's wide blue eyes staring up at me. In the excitement, I had forgotten about him, and now I regarded him bad-temperedly.

'What is it?' I snapped.

'Mr Jenkins,' his eyes were red, and I think he would have preferred pirates to Magnet Worms by a good deal, 'Mr Jenkins, maybe *I* could go and get Mr Charney and Mr Steeden.'

I sighed, and turned away.

'But, Mr Jenkins, I *could*. I heard what Mr Whitefield said, and *my* spacesuit isn't steel. It's vitri-rubber.'

'The kid's right,' whispered Whitefield slowly, when Stanley repeated his offer to the assembled men. 'The unstrengthened field doesn't harm us, that's evident. He'd be safe in a vitri-rubber suit.'

'But it's a wreck, that suit!' objected the Captain. 'I never really intended having the kid use it.' He ended raggedly and his manner was evidently irresolute.

'We can't leave Neal and Mac out there without trying, Captain,' said Brock stolidly.

The Captain made up his mind suddenly and became a whirlwind of action. He dived into the space-suit rack for the battered relic himself, and helped Stanley into it.

'Get Steeden first,' said the Captain, as he clipped shut the last bolt. 'He's older and has less resistance to the field. Good luck to you, kid, and if you can't make it, come back right away. Right away, do you hear me?'

Stanley sprawled at the first step, but life on Ganymede had inured him to below-normal gravities and he recovered quickly. There was no sign of hesitation, as he leaped towards the two prone figures, and we breathed easier. Evidently, the magnetic field was not affecting him yet.

He had one of the suited figures over his shoulders now and was proceeding back to the ship at an only slightly slower pace. As he dropped his burden inside the airlock, he waved an arm to us at the window and we waved back.

He had scarcely left, when we had Steeden inside. We ripped the spacesuit off him and laid him out, a gaunt pale figure, on the couch.

The Captain bent an ear to his chest and suddenly laughed aloud in sudden relief, 'The old geezer's still going strong.'

We crowded about happily at hearing that, all eager to place a finger upon his wrist and so assure ourselves of the life within him. His face twitched, and when a low, blurred voice suddenly whispered, 'So I said to Peewee, I said—' our last doubts were put to rest.

It was a sudden, sharp cry from Whitefield that drew us back to the window again, 'Somethings wrong with the kid.'

Stanley was half way back to the ship with his second burden, but he was staggering now – progressing erratically.

'It can't be,' whispered Whitefield, hoarsely, 'It can't be. The field *can't* be getting him!'

'God!' the Captain tore at his hair wildly, 'that damned antique has no radio. He can't tell us what's wrong.' He wrenched away suddenly. 'I'm going after him. Field or no field, I'm going to get him.'

'Hold on, Captain,' said Tuley, grabbing him by the arm, 'he may make it.'

Stanley was running again, but in a curious weaving fashion that made it quite plain, he didn't see where he was going. Two or three times he slipped and fell but each time he managed to scramble up again. He fell against the hull of the ship, at last, and felt wildly about for the yawning airlock. We shouted and prayed and sweated, but could help in no way.

And then he simply disappeared. He had come up against the lock and fallen inside.

We had them both inside in record time, and divested them of

their suits. Charney was alive, we saw that at a glance, and after that
we deserted him unceremoniously for Stanley. The blue of his face,
his swollen tongue, the line of fresh blood running from nose to chin
told its own story.

'The suit sprung a leak,' said Harrigan.

'Get away from him,' ordered the Captain, 'give him air.'

We waited. Finally, a soft moan from the kid betokened returning
consciousness and we all grinned in concert.

'Spunky little kid,' said the Captain. 'He traveled that last hundred yards on nerve and nothing else.' Then, again. 'Spunky little
kid. He's going to get a Naval Medal for this, if I have to give him
my own.'

Callisto was a shrinking blue ball on the televisor – an ordinary
unmysterious world. Stanley Fields, honorary Captain of the good
ship *Ceres*, thumbed his nose at it, protruding his tongue at the same
time. An inelegant gesture, but the symbol of Man's triumph over a
hostile Solar System.

Ring Around the Sun

Jimmy Turner was humming merrily, if a bit raucously, when he entered the reception room.

'Is Old Sourpuss in?' he asked, accompanying the question with a wink at which the pretty secretary blushed gratefully.

'He is; and waiting for you.' She motioned him towards the door on which was written in fat, black letters, 'Frank McCutcheon, General Manager, United Space Mail.'

Jim entered. 'Hello, Skipper, what now?'

'Oh, it's you, is it?' McCutcheon looked up from his desk, champing a foul-smelling stogie. 'Sit down.'

McCutcheon stared at him from under bushy gray eyebrows. 'Old Sourpuss,' as he was euphoniously known to all members of United Space Mail, had never been known to laugh within the memory of the oldest inmate, though rumor did have it that when a child he had smiled at the sight of his father falling out of an apple-tree. Right now his expression made the rumor appear exaggerated.

'Now, listen, Turner,' he barked, 'United Space Mail is inaugurating a new service and you're elected to blaze the trail.' Disregarding

Jimmy's grimace, he continued, 'From now on the Venerian mail is on an all-year-round basis.'

'What! I've always thought that it was ruinous from a financial standpoint to deliver the Venerian mail except when it was this side of the Sun.'

'Sure,' admitted McCutcheon, 'if we follow the ordinary routes. But we might cut straight across the system if we could only get near enough to the sun. That's where you come in! They've put out a new ship equipped to approach within twenty million miles of the sun and which will be able to remain at that distance indefinitely.'

Jimmy interrupted nervously, 'Wait a while, S— Mr McCutcheon, I don't quite follow. What kind of a ship is this?'

'How do you expect me to know? I'm no fugitive from a laboratory. From what they tell me, it emits some kind of a field that bends the radiations of the sun around the ship. Get it? It's all deflected. No heat reaches you. You can stay there forever and be cooler than in New York.'

'Oh, is that so?' Jimmy was skeptical. 'Has it been tested, or is that a little detail that has been left for me?'

'It's been tested, of course, but not under actual solar conditions.'
'Then it's out. I've done plenty for United, but this is the limit. I'm not crazy, *yet*.'

McCutcheon stiffened. 'Must I recall the oath you took upon entering the service, Turner? "Our flight through space—"'

'"—must ne'er be stopped by anything save death,"' finished Jimmy. 'I know that as well as you do and I also notice that it's very easy to quote that from a comfortable armchair. If you're that idealistic, you can do it yourself. It's still out, as far as I'm concerned. And if you want, you can kick me out. I can get other jobs just like that,' he snapped his fingers airily.

McCutcheon's voice dropped to a silky whisper. 'Now, now, Turner, don't be hasty. You haven't heard all I have to say yet. Roy Snead is to be your mate.'

'Huh! Snead! Why, that four-flusher wouldn't have the guts to take a job like this in a million years. Tell me some other fairy tale.'

'Well, as a matter of fact, he has already accepted. I thought you might accompany him, but I guess he was right. He insisted you'd back down. I thought at first you wouldn't.'

McCutcheon waved him away and bent his eyes unconcernedly on the report he had been scrutinizing at the time of Jimmy's entrance. Jimmy wheeled, hesitated, then returned.

'Wait a while, Mr McCutcheon; do you mean to say that Roy is actually going?' McCutcheon nodded, still apparently absorbed in other matters, and Jimmy exploded, 'Why, that low-down, spindle-shanked, dish-faced mug! So he thinks I'm too yellow to go! Well, I'll show him. I'll take the job and I'll put up ten dollars to a Venetian nickel that *he* gets sick at the last minute.'

'Good!' McCutcheon rose and shook hands, 'I thought you'd see reason. Major Wade has all the details. I think you leave in about six weeks and as I'm leaving for Venus tomorrow, you'll probably meet me there.'

Jimmy left, still boiling, and McCutcheon buzzed for the secretary. 'Oh, Miss Wilson, get Roy Snead on the 'visor.'

A few minutes' pause and then the red signal-light shone. The 'visor was clicked on and the dark-haired, dapper Snead appeared on the visi-plate.

'Hello, Snead,' McCutcheon growled. 'You lose that bet, Turner accepted that job. I thought he'd laugh himself sick when I told him you said he wouldn't go. Send over the twenty dollars, please.'

'Wait a while, Mr McCutcheon,' Snead's face was dark with fury, 'what's the idea of telling that punch-drunk imbecile I'm not going? You must have, you double-crosser. I'll be there all right, but you can put up another twenty and I'll bet he changes his mind *yet*. But *I'll* be there.' Roy Snead was still spluttering when McCutcheon clicked off.

The General Manager leaned back, threw away his mangled cigar, and lit a fresh one. His face remained sour, but there was a definite note of satisfaction in his tone when he said, 'Ha! I thought that would get them.'

It was a tired and sweaty pair that blasted the good ship *Helios* across Mercury's orbit. In spite of the perfunctory friendship enforced upon them by the weeks alone in space, Jimmy Turner and Roy Snead were scarcely on speaking terms. Add to this hidden hostility, the heat of the bloated sun and the torturing uncertainty of the final outcome of the trip and you have a miserable pair indeed.

Jimmy peered tiredly at the maze of dials confronting him, and, brushing a damp lock of hair from his eyes, grunted, 'What's the thermometer reading now, Roy?'

'One hundred twenty-five degrees Fahrenheit and still climbing,' was the growled response.

Jimmy cursed fluently, 'The cooling system is on at maximum, the ship's hull reflects 95% of the solar radiation, and it's still in the hundred twenties.' He paused. 'The gravometer indicates that we're still some thirty-five million miles from the Sun. Fifteen million miles to go before the Deflection Field becomes effective. The temperature will probably scale 150 yet. That's a sweet prospect! Check the desiccators. If the air isn't kept absolutely dry, we're not going to last long.'

'Within Mercury's orbit, think of it!' Snead's voice was husky. 'No one has ever been this close to the sun before. And we're going closer yet.'

'There have been many this close and closer,' reminded Jimmy, 'but *they* were out of control and landed *in* the sun. Friedländer, Debuc, Anton—' His voice trailed into a brooding silence.

Roy stirred uneasily. 'How effective is this Deflection Field anyway, Jimmy? Your cheerful thoughts aren't very soothing, you know.'

'Well, it's been tested under the harshest conditions laboratory technicians could devise. I've watched them. It's been bathed in radiation approximating the sun's at a distance of twenty million. The Field worked like a charm. The light was bent about it so that the ship became invisible. The men inside the ship claimed that every-thing outside became invisible and that no heat reached them. A funny thing, though, the Field will work only under certain radiation strengths.'

'Well, I wish it were over one way or the other,' Roy glowered. 'If Old Sourpuss is thinking of making this my regular run, well, he'll lose his ace pilot.'

'He'll lose his *two* ace pilots,' Jimmy corrected.

The two lapsed into silence and the *Helios* blasted on.

The temperature climbed: 130, 135, 140. Then, three days later, with the mercury quivering at 148, Roy announced that they were approaching the critical belt, the belt where the solar radiation reached sufficient intensity to energize the Field.

The two waited, minds at feverish concentration, pulses pounding.

'Will it happen suddenly?'

'I don't know. We'll have to wait.'

From the portholes, only the stars were visible. The sun, three times the size as seen from Earth, poured its blinding rays upon opaque metal, for on this specially designed ship, portholes closed automatically when struck by powerful radiation.

And then the stars began disappearing. Slowly, at first, the dim-mest faded – then the brighter ones: Polaris, Regulus, Arcturus, Sirius. Space was uniformly black.

'It's working,' breathed Jimmy. The words were scarcely out of his mouth, when the sunward portholes clicked open. The sun was gone!

'Ha! I feel cooler already,' Jimmy Turner was jubilant. 'Boy, it worked like a charm. You know, if they could adjust this Deflection Field to all radiation strengths, we would have perfected invisibil-ity. It would make a convenient war weapon.' He lit a cigarette and leaned back luxuriously.

'But meanwhile we're flying blind,' Roy insisted.

Jimmy grinned patronizingly, 'You needn't worry about that, Dishface. I've taken care of everything. We're in an orbit about the sun. In two weeks, we'll be on the opposite side and then I'll let the rockets blast and out of this band we go, zooming towards Venus.' He was very self-satisfied indeed.

'Just leave it to Jimmy "Brains" Turner. I'll have us through in two months, instead of the regulation six. You're with United's ace pilot, now.'

Roy laughed nastily. 'To listen to you, you'd think you did all the work. All you're doing is to run the ship on the course *I've* plotted. *You're* the mechanic; *I'm* the brains.'

'Oh, is that so? Any damn pilot-school rookie can plot a course. It takes a man to navigate one.'

'Well, that's your opinion. Who's paid more, though, the navigator or the course-plotter?'

Jimmy gulped on that one and Roy stalked triumphantly out of the pilot room. Unmindful of all this, the *Helios* blasted on.

For two days, all was serene; then, on the third day, Jimmy inspected the thermometer, scratched his head and looked worried. Roy entered, watched the proceedings and raised his eyebrows in surprise.

'Is anything wrong?' He bent over and read the height of the thin, red column. 'Just 100 degrees. That's nothing to look like a sick goat over. From your expression, I thought something had gone wrong with the Deflection Field and that it was rising again,' he turned away with an ostentatious yawn.

'Oh, shut up, you senseless ape,' Jimmy's foot lifted in a half-hearted attempt at a kick. 'I'd feel a lot better if the temperature were rising. This Deflection Field is working a lot too good for my liking.'

'Huh! What do you mean?'

'I'll explain, and if you listen carefully you *may* understand me. This ship is built like a vacuum bottle. It gains heat only with the greatest of difficulty and loses it likewise.' He paused and let his words sink in. 'At ordinary temperatures this ship is not supposed to lose more than two degrees a day if no outside sources of heat are supplied. Perhaps at the temperature at which we were, the loss might amount to five degrees a day. Do you get me?'

Roy's mouth was open wide and Jimmy continued. 'Now this blasted ship has lost fifty degrees in less than three days.'

'But that's impossible.'

'There it is.' Jimmy pointed ironically. 'I'll tell you what's wrong. It's that damn Field. It acts as a repulsive agent towards electromagnetic radiations and somehow is hastening the loss of heat of our ship.'

Roy sank into thought and did some rapid mental calculations. 'If what you say is true,' he said at length, 'we'll hit freezing point in five days and then spend a week in what amounts to winter weather.'

'That's right. Even allowing for the decrease in heat-loss as the temperature is lowered, we'll probably end up with the mercury anywhere between thirty and forty *below*.'

Roy gulped unhappily. 'And at twenty million miles away from the sun!'

'That isn't the worst,' Jimmy pointed out. 'This ship, like all others used for travel within the orbit of Mars, has no heating system. With the sun shining like fury and no way to lose heat except by ineffectual radiation, Mars and Venus space-ships have always specialized in cooling systems. We, for instance, have a very efficient refrigeration device.'

'We're in a devil of a fix, then. The same applies to our space suits.'

In spite of the still roasting temperature, the two were beginning to experience a few anticipatory chills.

'Say, I'm not going to stand this,' Roy burst out. 'I vote we get out of here right now and head for Eaith. They can't expect more of us.'

'Go ahead! You're the pilot. Can you plot a course at this distance from the sun and guarantee that we won't fall *into* the sun?'

'Hell! I hadn't thought of that.'

The two were at their wits' end. Communication via radio had been impossible ever since they had passed Mercury's orbit. The sun was at sunspot maximum and static had drowned out all attempts.

So they settled down to wait.

The next few days were taken up entirely with thermometer

watching, with a few minutes taken out here and there when one of the two happened to think of an unused malediction to hurl at the head of Mr Frank McCutcheon. Eating and sleeping were indulged in, but not enjoyed.

And meanwhile, the *Helios*, entirely unconcerned in the plight of its occupants, blasted on.

As Roy had predicted, the temperature passed the red line marked 'Freezing' towards the end of their seventh day in the Deflection Belt. The two were remarkably unhappy when this happened even though they had expected it.

Jimmy had drawn off about a hundred gallons of water from the tank. With this he had filled almost every vessel on board.

'It might,' he pointed out, 'save the pipes from bursting when the water freezes. And if they do, as is probable, it is just as well that we supply ourselves with plenty of available water. We have to stay here another week, you know.'

And on the next day, the eighth, the water froze. There were the buckets, overflowing with ice, standing chill and bluecold. The two gazed at them forlornly. Jimmy broke one open.

'Frozen solid,' he said bleakly and wrapped anothor sheet about himself.

It was hard to think of anything but the increasing cold now. Roy and Jimmy had requisitioned every sheet and blanket on the ship, after having put on three or four shirts and a like number of pairs of pants.

They kept in bed for as long as they were able, and when forced to move out, they huddled near the small oil-burner for warmth. Even this doubtful pleasure was soon denied them, for, as Jimmy remarked, 'the oil supply is extremely limited and we will need the burner to thaw out the water and food.'

Tempers were short and clashes frequent, but the common misery kept them from actually jumping on each other's throats. It was on the tenth day, however, that the two, united by a common hatred, suddenly became friends.

*

The temperature was hovering down near the zero point, making up its mind to descend into the minus regions. Jimmy was huddled in a corner thinking of the times back in New York when he had complained of the August heat and wondered how he could have done so. Roy, meanwhile, had manipulated numb fingers long enough to calculate that they would have to endure the coldness for exactly 6354 minutes more.

He regarded the figures with distaste and read them off to Jimmy. The latter scowled and grunted, 'The way I feel, I'm not going to last 54 minutes, let alone 6354.' Then, impatiently, 'I wish you could manage to think of some way of getting us out of this.'

'If we weren't so near the sun,' suggested Roy, 'we might start the rear blasts and hurry us up.'

'Yes, and if we landed *in* the sun, we'd be nice and warm. You're a big help!'

'Well, you're the one that calls himself "Brains" Turner. *You* think of something. The way you talk, you'd think all this was my fault.'

'It certainly is, you donkey in human clothing! My better judgment told me all along not to go on this fool trip. When McCutcheon proposed it, I refused pointblank. I knew better.' Jimmy was very bitter. 'So what happened? Like the fool you are, you accept and rush in where sensible men fear to tread. And then, of course, I naturally *had* to tag along.

'Why, do you know what I should have done,' Jimmy's voice ascended the scale, 'I should have let you go alone and freeze and then sat down by a roaring fire all by myself and gloated. That is, if I had known what was going to happen.'

A hurt and surprised look appeared on Roy's face. 'Is that so? So that's how it is! Well, all I can say is that you certainly have a genius for twisting facts, if for nothing else. The fact of the matter is that *you* were unutterably stupid enough to accept and *I* the poor fellow raked in by the force of circumstances.'

Jimmy's expression was one of the utmost disdain. 'Evidently the cold has driven you batty, though I admit it wouldn't take much to knock the little sense you possess out of you.'

'Listen,' Roy answered hotly. 'On October 10th, McCutcheon called me up on the 'visor and told me you had accepted and laughed at me for a yellow-belly for refusing to go. Do you deny that?'

'Yes, I do, and unconditionally. On October 10, Sourpuss told *me* that *you* had decided to go and had bet him that—'

Jimmy's voice faded away very suddenly and a shocked look spread over his face. 'Say – are you sure McCutcheon told you I had agreed to go?'

A chill, clammy feeling clutched at Roy's heart when he caught Jimmy's drift, a feeling that drowned out the numbness of the cold.

'Absolutely,' he answered, 'I'll swear to that. That's why I went.'

'But he told me you had accepted and that's why *I* went.' Jimmy felt very stupid all at once.

The two fell. into a protracted and ominous silence which was broken at length by Roy, who spoke in a voice that quivered with emotion.

'Jimmy, we've been the victims of a contemptible, dirty, low-down, doublecrossing trick.' His eyes dilated with fury. 'We've been cheated, robbed—' words failed him but he kept on uttering mean-ingless sounds, indicative mainly of devouring rage.

Jimmy was cooler, but none the less vindictive, 'You're right, Roy; McCutcheon has done us dirty. He has plumbed the depths of human iniquity. But we'll get even. When we get through in 6300 odd min-utes, we will have a score to settle with Mr McCutcheon.'

'What are we going to do?' Roy's eyes were filled with a blood-thirsty joy.

'On the spur of the moment, I suggest that we simply tear into him and rend him into tiny, little pieces.'

'Not gruesome enough. How about boiling him in oil?'

'That's reasonable, yes; but it might take too long. Let's give him a good old-fashioned beating – with brass knuckles.'

Roy rubbed his hands. 'We'll have lots of time to think up some really adequate measures. The dirty, God-forsaken, yellow-livered, leprous—' The rest verged fluently into the unprintable.

And for four more days, the temperature dove. It was on the fourteenth and last day that the mercury froze, the solid red shaft pointed its congealed finger at forty below.

On this terrible last day, they had lit the oil-burner, using their entire scanty supply of oil. Shivering and more than half frozen, they crouched close, attempting to extract every last drop of heat.

Jimmy had found a pair of ear-muffs several days before in some obscure corner, and it now changed hands at the end of every hour. Both sat buried under a small mountain of blankets, chafing chilled hands and feet. With every passing minute, their conversation, concerning McCutcheon almost exclusively, grew more vitriolic.

'Always quoting that triply-damned slogan of the Space Mail: 'Our flight through sp—' Jimmy choked with impotent fury.

'Yes, and always rubbing holes in chairs instead of coming out here and doing something like a man's work, the rotten so-and-so,' agreed Roy.

'Well, we're due to pass out of the deflection zone in two hours. Then three weeks and we'll be on Venus,' said Jimmy, sneezing. 'That can't be too soon for me,' answered Sneed, who had been sniffling for the last two days. 'I'm never taking another space trip except maybe the one that takes me back to Earth. After this, I make my living growing bananas in Central America. A fellow can be decently warm out there at least.'

'We might not get off Venus, after what we're going to do to McCutcheon.'

'No, you're right there. But that's all right. Venus is even warmer than Central America and that's all I care about,'

'We have no legal worries either,' Jimmy sneezed again. 'On Venus, life imprisonment's the limit for first-degree murder. A nice, warm, dry cell for the rest of my life. What could be sweeter?'

The second hand on the chronometer whirled at its even pace; the minutes ticked off. Roy's hands hovered lovingly over the lever that would set off the right rear blasts which would drive the *Helios* out away from the sun and from that terrible Deflection Zone.

And at last, 'Go!' shouted Jimmy eagerly. 'Let her blast!'

With a deep reverberating roar, the rockets fired. The *Helios* trembled from stem to stern. The pilots felt the acceleration press them back into their seats and were happy. In a matter of minutes, the sun would shine again and they would be warm, feel the blessed heat once more.

It happened before they were aware of it. There was a momentary flash of light and then a grinding and a click, as the sunward portholes closed.

'Look,' cried Roy, 'the stars! We're out of it!' He cast an ecstatically happy glance at the thermometer. 'Well, old boy, from now on we go up again.' He pulled the blankets about him closer, for the cold still lingered.

There were two men in Frank McCutcheon's office at the Venus branch of the United Space Mail: McCutcheon himself and the elderly, white-haired Zebulon Smith, inventor of the Deflection Field. Smith was talking.

'But, Mr McCutcheon, it is really of great importance that I learn exactly how my Deflection Field worked. Surely they have transmitted all possible information to you.'

McCutcheon's face was a study in dourness as he bit the edge off one of his two-for-five cigars and lit it.

'That, my dear Mr Smith,' he said, 'is exactly what they did not do. Ever since they have receded far enough from the sun to render communication possible, I have been sending requests for information regarding the practicability of the Field. They just refuse to answer. They say it worked and that they're alive and that they'll give the details when they reach Venus. That's all!'

Zebulon Smith sighed in disappointment. 'Isn't that a bit unusual; insubordination, so to speak? I thought they were required to be complete in their reports and to give any requested details.'

'So they are. But these are my ace pilots and rather temperamental. We have to extend some leeway. Besides, I tricked them into going on this trip, a very hazardous one, as you know, and so am inclined to be lenient.'

'Well, then, I suppose I must wait.'

'Oh, it won't be for long,' McCutcheon assured him. 'They're due today, and I assure you that as soon as I get in touch with them, I shall send you the full details. After all, they survived for two weeks at a distance of twenty million miles from the sun, so your invention is a success. That should satisfy you.'

Smith had scarcely left when McCutcheon's secretary entered with a puzzled frown on her face.

'Something is wrong with the two pilots of the *Helios*, Mr McCutcheon,' she informed him. 'I have just received a bulletin from Major Wade at Pallas City, where they landed. They have refused to attend the celebration prepared for them, but instead immediately chartered a rocket to come here, refusing to state the reason. When Major Wade tried to stop them, they became violent, he says.' She laid the communication down on his desk.

McCutcheon glanced at it perfunctorily. 'Hmm! They do seem confoundedly temperamental. Well, send them to me when they come. I'll snap them out of it.'

It was perhaps three hours later that the problem of the two misbehaving pilots again forced itself upon his mind, this time by a sudden commotion that had arisen in the reception room. He heard the deep angry tones of two men and then the shrill remonstrances of his secretary. Suddenly the door burst open and Jim Turner and Roy Snead strode in.

Roy coolly closed the door and planted his back against it.

'Don't let anyone disturb me until I'm through,' Jimmy told him.

'No one's getting through this door for a while,' Roy answered grimly, 'but remember, you promised to leave some for me.'

McCutcheon said nothing during all this, but when he saw Turner casually draw a pair of brass knuckles from his pocket and put them on with a determined air, he decided that it was time to call a halt to the comedy.

'Hello, boys,' he said, with a heartiness unusual in him. 'Glad to see you again. Take a seat.'

Jimmy ignored the offer. 'Have you anything to say, any last request, before I start operations?' He gritted his teeth with an unpleasant scraping noise.

'Well, if you put it that way,' said McCutcheon, 'I might ask exactly what this is all about – if I'm not being too unreasonable. Perhaps the Deflector was inefficient and you had a hot trip.'

The only answer to that was a loud snort from Roy and a cold stare on the part of Jimmy.

'First,' said the latter, 'what was the idea of that filthy, disgusting cheat you pulled on us?'

McCutcheon's eyebrows raised in surprise. 'Do you mean the little white lies I told you in order to get you to go? Why, that was nothing. Common business practice, that's all. Why, I pull worse things than that every day and people consider it just routine. Besides, what harm did it do you?'

'Tell him about our "pleasant trip," Jimmy,' urged Roy.

'That's exactly what I'm going to do,' was the response. He turned to McCutcheon and assumed a martyr-like air. 'First, on this blasted trip, we fried in a temperature that reached 150 but that was to be expected and we're not complaining; we were half Mercury's distance from the sun.

'But after that, we entered this zone where the light bends around us; incoming radiation sank to zero and we started losing heat and not just a degree a day the way we learned it in pilot school.' He paused to breathe a few novel curses he had just thought of, then continued.

'In three days, we were down to a hundred and in a week down to freezing. Then for one entire week, seven long days, we drove through our course at sub-freezing temperature. It was so cold the last day that the mercury froze.' Turner's voice rose till it cracked, and at the door, a fit of self-pity caused Roy to catch his breath with an audible gulp. McCutcheon remained inscrutable.

Jimmy continued. 'There we were without a heating system, in fact, no heat of any kind, not even any warm clothing. We froze, damn it; we had to thaw out our food and melt our water. We were stiff, couldn't move. It was hell, I tell you, in reverse temperature.' He paused, at a loss for words.

Roy Snead took up the burden. 'We were twenty million miles away from the sun and I had a case of frost-bitten ears. Frostbitten, I say.' He shook his fist viciously under McCutcheon's nose. 'And it was your fault. You tricked us into it! While we were freezing, we promised ourselves that we'd come back and get you and we're going to keep that promise.' He turned to Jimmy. 'Go ahead, start it, will you? We've wasted enough time.'

'Hold it, boys,' McCutcheon spoke at last. 'Let me get this straight. You mean to say that the Deflection Field worked so well that it kept all the radiation away and sucked out what heat there was in the ship in the first place?' Jimmy grunted a curt assent.

'And you froze for a week because of that?' McCutcheon continued. Again the grunt.

And then a very strange and unusual thing happened. McCutcheon, 'Old Sourpuss,' the man without the 'risus' muscle, smiled. He actually bared his teeth in a grin. And what's more, the grin grew wider and wider until finally a rusty, long-unused chuckle was heard louder and louder, until it developed into a full-fledged laugh, and the laugh into a bellow. In one stentorian burst, McCutcheon made up for a lifetime of sour gloom.

The walls reverberated, the windowpanes rattled, and still the Homeric laughter continued. Roy and Jimmy stood open-mouthed, entirely non-plussed. A puzzled bookkeeper thrust his head inside the door in a fit of temerity and remained frozen in his tracks. Others crowded about the door, conversing in awed whispers. *McCutcheon had laughed!*

Gradually, the risibilities of the old General Manager subsided. He ended in a fit of choking and finally turned a purple face towards his ace pilots, whose surprise had long since given way to indignation.

'Boys,' he told them, 'that was the best joke I ever heard. You can consider your pay doubled, both of you.' He was still grinning away like clockwork and had developed a beautiful case of hiccoughs.

The two pilots were left cold at the handsome proposal. 'What's so killingly funny?' Jimmy wanted to know, 'I don't see anything to laugh at, myself.'

McCutcheon's voice dripped honey, 'Now, fellows, before I left I gave each of you several mimeographed sheets containing special instructions. What happened to them?'

There was sudden embarrassment in the air.

'I don't know. I must have mislaid mine,' gulped Roy.

'I never looked at mine; I forgot about it.' Jimmy was genuinely dismayed.

'You see,' exclaimed McCutcheon triumphantly, 'It was all the fault of your own stupidity.'

'How do you figure that out?' Jimmy wanted to know. 'Major Wade told us all we had to know about the ship, and besides, I guess there's nothing *you* could tell us about running one.'

'Oh, isn't there? Wade evidently forgot to inform you of one minor point which you would have found on my instructions. The strength of the Deflection Field was *adjustable*. It happened to be set at maximum strength when you started, that's all.' He was now beginning to chuckle faintly once more. 'Now, if you had taken the trouble to read the sheets, you would have known that a simple movement of a small lever,' he made the appropriate gesture with his thumb, 'would have weakened the Field any desired amount and allowed as much radiation to leak through as was wanted.'

And now the chuckle was becoming louder. 'And you froze for a week because you didn't have the brains to pull a lever. And then you ace pilots come here and blame *me*. What a laugh!' and off he went again while a pair of very sheepish young men glanced askance at each other.

When McCutcheon came around to normal, Jimmy and Roy were gone.

Down in an alley adjoining the building, a little ten year-old boy watched, with open mouth and intense absorption, two young men who were engaged in the strange and rather startling occupation of kicking each other alternately. They were vicious kicks, too!

The Magnificent Possession

Walter Sills reflected now, as he had reflected often before, that life was hard and joyless. He surveyed his dingy chemical laboratory and grinned cynically – working in a dirty hole of a place, living on occasional ore analyses that barely paid for absolutely indispensable equipment, while others, not half his worth perhaps, were working for big industrial concerns and taking life easy.

He looked out the window at the Hudson River, ruddied in the flame of the dying sun, and wondered moodily whether these last experiments would finally bring him the fame and success he was after, or if they were merely some more false alarms.

The unlocked door creaked open a crack and the cheerful face of Eugene Taylor burst into view. Sills waved and Taylor's body followed his head and entered the laboratory.

'Hello, old soak,' came the loud and carefree hail. 'How go things?' Sills shook his head at the other's exuberance. 'I wish I had your foolish outlook on life, Gene. For your information, things are bad. I need money, and the more I need it, the less I have.'

'Well, I haven't any money either, have I?' demanded Taylor. 'But why worry about it? You're fifty, and worry hasn't got you anything except a bald head. I'm thirty, and I want to keep my beautiful brown hair.'

The chemist grinned. 'I'll get my money yet, Gene. Just leave it to me.'

'Your new ideas shaping out well?'

'Are they? I haven't told you much about it, have I? Well, come here and I'll show you what progress I've made.'

Taylor followed Sills to a small table, on which stood a rack of testtubes, in one of which was about half an inch of a shiny metallic substance.

'Sodium-mercury mixture, or sodium amalgam, as it is called,' explained Sills pointing to it.

He took a bottle labeled 'Ammonium Chloride Sol.' from the shelf and poured a little into the tube. Immediately the sodium amalgam began changing into a loosely-packed, spongy substance.

'That,' observed Sills, 'is ammonium amalgam. The ammonium radical (NH_4) acts as a metal here and combines with mercury.' He waited for the action to go to completion and then poured off the supernatant liquid.

'Ammonium amalgam isn't very stable,' he informed Taylor, 'so I'll have to work fast.' He grasped a flask of straw-colored, pleasant-smelling liquid and filled the test-tube with it. Upon shaking, the loosely-packed ammonium amalgam vanished and in its stead a small drop of metallic liquid rolled about the bottom.

Taylor gazed at the test-tube, open-mouthed. 'What happened?'

'This liquid is a complex derivative of hydrazine which I've discovered and named Ammonaline. I haven't worked out its formula yet, but that doesn't matter. The point about it is that it has the property of dissolving the ammonium out of the amalgam. Those few drops at the bottom are pure mercury; the ammonium is in solution.'

Taylor remained unresponsive and Sills waxed enthusiastic. 'Don't you see the implications? I've gone half way towards isolating pure ammonium, a thing which has never been done before! Once accomplished it means fame, success, the Nobel Prize, and who knows what else.'

'Wow!' Taylor's gaze became more respectful. 'That yellow stuff doesn't look so important to me.' He snatched for it, but Sills withheld it.

'I haven't finished, by any means, Gene. I've got to get it in its free metallic state, and I can't do that so far. Every time I try to evaporate the Ammonaline, the ammonium breaks down to everlasting ammonia and hydrogen . . . But I'll get it – I'll get it!'

Two weeks later, the epilogue to the previous scene was enacted. Taylor received a hurried and emphatic call from his chemist friend and appeared at the laboratory in a flurry of anticipation.

'You've got it?'

'I've got it – and it's bigger than I thought! There's millions in it, really,' Sills' eyes shone with rapture.

'I've been working from the wrong angle up to now,' he explained. 'Heating the solvent always broke down the dissolved ammonium, so I separated it out by freezing. It works the same way as brine, which, when frozen slowly, freezes into fresh ice, the salt crystallizing out. Luckily, the Ammonaline freezes at 18 degrees Centigrade and doesn't require much cooling.'

He pointed dramatically to a small beaker, inside a glass-walled case. The beaker contained pale, straw-colored, needle-like crystals and, covering the top of this, a thin layer of a dullish, yellow substance.

'Why the case?' asked Taylor.

'I've got it filled with argon to keep the ammonium (which is the yellow substance on top of the Ammonaline) pure. It is so active that it will react with anything else but a helium-type gas.'

Taylor marveled and pounded his complacently-smiling friend on the back.

'Wait, Gene, the best is yet to come.'

Taylor was led to the other end of the room and Sills' trembling finger pointed out another airtight case containing a lump of metal of a gleaming, yellow that sparkled and glistened.

'That, my friend, is ammonium oxide ($NH_{42}O$), formed by passing *absolutely dry* air over free ammonium metal. It is perfectly inert (the sealed case contains quite a bit of chlorine, for instance, and yet there is no reaction). It can be made as cheaply as aluminum, if not more so, and yet it looks more like gold than gold does itself. Do you see the possibilities?'

'Do I?' exploded Taylor. 'It will sweep the country. You can have ammonium jewelry, and ammonium-plated table-ware, and a million other things. Then again, who knows how many countless industrial applications it may have? You're rich, Walt – you're rich!'

'*We're* rich,' corrected Sills gently. He moved towards the telephone, 'The newspapers are going to hear of this. I'm going to begin to cash in on fame right now.'

Taylor frowned, 'Maybe you'd better keep it a secret, Walt.'

'Oh, I'm not breathing a hint as to the process. I'll just give them the general idea. Besides, we're safe; the patent application is in Washington right now.'

But Sills was wrong! The article in the paper ushered in a very, very hectic two days for the two of them.

J. Throgmorton Bankhead is what is commonly known as a 'captain of industry.' As head of the Acme Chromium and Silver Plating Corporation he no doubt deserved the title; but to his patient and long-suffering wife, he was merely a dyspeptic and grouchy husband, especially at the breakfast table . . . and he was at the breakfast table now.

Rustling his morning paper angrily, he sputtered between bites of buttered toast, 'This man is ruining the country.' He pointed aghast at big, black headlines. 'I said before and I'll say again that the man is as crazy as a bedbug. He won't be satisfied . . .'

'Joseph, please,' pleaded his wife, 'you're getting purple in the face. Remember your high blood pressure. You know the doctor told you to stop reading the news from Washington if it annoys you so. Now, listen dear, about the cook. She's . . .'

'The doctor's a damn fool, and so are you,' shouted J. Throgmorton Bankhead. 'I'll read all the news I please and get purple in the face too, if I want to.'

He raised the cup of coffee to his mouth and took a critical sip. While he did so, his eyes fell upon a more insignificant headline towards the bottom of the page: 'Savant Discovers Gold Substitute.' The coffee cup remained in the air while he scanned the article quickly. 'This new metal,' it ran in part, 'is claimed by its discoverer to be far superior to chromium, nickel, or silver for cheap and beautiful jewelry. "The twenty-dollar-a-week clerk," said Professor Sills, "will eat off ammonium plate more impressive in appearance than the gold plate of the Indian Nabob." There is no . . .'

But J. Throgmorton Bankhead had stopped reading. Visions of a ruined Acme Chromium and Silver Plating Corporation danced before his eyes; and as they danced, the cup of coffee dropped from his hand, and splashed hot liquid over his trousers.

His wife rose to her feet in alarm, 'What is it, Joseph; what is it?'

'Nothing,' Bankhead shouted. 'Nothing. For God's sake, go away, will you?'

He strode angrily out of the room, leaving his wife to search the paper for anything that could have disturbed him.

'Bob's Tavern' on Fifteenth Street is usually pretty well filled at all times, but on the morning we are speaking of, it was empty except for four or five rather poorly-dressed men who clustered about the portly and dignified form of Peter Q. Hornswoggle, eminent ex-Congressman.

Peter Q. Hornswoggle was, as usual, speaking fluently. His subject, again as usual, concerned the life of a Congressman.

'I remember a case in point,' he was saying, 'when that same argument was brought up in the House, and which I answered as follows: "The eminent gentleman from Nevada in his statements overlooks one very important aspect of the problem. He does not realize that it is to the interest of the entire nation that the apple-parers of this country be attended to promptly; for, gentlemen, on the welfare of the apple-parers depends the future of the entire fruit industry and on the fruit-industry is based the entire economy of this great and glorious nation, the United States of America."'

Hornswoggle paused, swallowed half a pint of beer at once, and then smiled in triumph, 'I have no hesitation in saying, gentlemen, that at that statement, the entire House burst into wild and tumultuous applause.'

One of the assembled listeners shook his head slowly and marveled.

'It must be great to be able to spiel like that, Senator. You musta been a sensation.'

'Yeah,' agreed the bartender, 'it's a dirty shame you were beat last election.'

The ex-Congressman winced and in a very dignified tone began, 'I have been reliably informed that the use of bribery in that campaign reached unprecedented prop . . .' His voice died away suddenly as he caught sight of a certain article in the newspaper of one of his listeners. He snatched at it and read it through in silence and thereupon his eyes gleamed with a sudden idea.

'My friends,' he said turning to them again, 'I find I must leave you. There is pressing work that *must* be done immediately at City Hall.' He leant over to whisper to the bar-keeper, 'You haven't got twenty-five cents, have you? I find I left my wallet in the Mayor's office by mistake. I will surely repay you tomorrow.'

Clutching the quarter, reluctantly given, Peter Q. Hornswoggle left.

In a small and dimly lit room somewhere in the lower reaches of First Avenue, Michael Maguire, known to the police by the far more euphonious name of Mike the Slug, cleaned his trusty revolver and hummed a tuneless song. The door opened a crack and Mike looked up.

'That you, Slappy?'

'Yeh,' a short, wizened person sidled in, 'I brung ya de evenin sheet. De cops are still tinkin' Bragoni pulled de job.'

'Yeh? That's good.' He bent unconcernedly over the revolver. 'Anything else doing?'

'Naw! Some dippy dame killed herself, but dat's all.'

He tossed the newspaper to Mike and left. Mike leaned back and flipped the pages in a bored manner.

A headline attracted his eye and he read the short article that followed. Having finished, he threw aside the paper, lit a cigarette, and did some heavy thinking. Then he opened the door.

'Hey, Slappy, c'mere. There's a job that's got to be done.'

Walter Sills was happy, deliriously so. He walked about his laboratory king of all he surveyed, strutting like a peacock, basking in his new-found glory. Eugene Taylor sat and watched him, scarcely less happy himself.

'How does it feel to be famous?' Taylor wanted to know.

'Like a million dollars; and that's what I'm going to sell the secret of ammonium metal for. It's the fat of the land for me from now on.'

'You leave the practical details to me, Walt. I'm getting in touch with Staples of Eagle Steel today. You'll get a decent price from him.'

The bell rang, and Sills jumped. He ran to open the door.

'Is this the home of Walter Sills?' The large, scowling visitor gazed about him superciliously.

'Yes, I'm Sills. Do you wish to see me?'

'Yes. My name is J. Throgmorton Bankhead and I represent the Acme Chromium and Silver Plating Corporation. I would like to have a moment's discussion with you.'

'Come right in. Come right in! This is Eugene Taylor, my associate. You may speak freely before him.'

'Very well.' Bankhead seated himself heavily. 'I suppose you surmise the reason for my visit.'

'I take it that you have read of the new ammonium metal in the papers.'

'That's right. I have come to see whether there is any truth in the story and to buy your process if there is.'

'You can see for yourself, sir,' Sills led the magnate to where the argon-filled container of the few grams of pure ammonium were. 'That is the metal. Over here to the right, I've got the oxide, an oxide which is more metallic than the metal itself, strangely enough. It is the oxide that is what the papers call "substitute gold".'

Bankhead's face showed not an atom of the sinking feeling within him as he viewed the oxide with dismay. 'Take it out in the open,' he said, 'and let's see it.'

Sills shook his head. 'I can't, Mr Bankhead. Those are the first samples of ammonium and ammonium-oxide that ever existed. They're museum pieces. I can easily make more for you, if you wish.'

'You'll have to, if you expect me to sink my money in it. You satisfy me and I'll be willing to buy your patent for as much as – oh, say a thousand dollars.'

'A thousand dollars!' exclaimed Sills and Taylor together.

'A very fair price, gentlemen.'

'A million would be more like it,' shouted Taylor in an outraged tone. 'This discovery is a goldmine.'

'A million, indeed! You are dreaming, gentlemen. The fact of the matter is that my company has been on the track of ammonium for years now, and we are just at the point of solving the problem. Unfortunately you beat us by a week or so, and so I wish to buy up your patent in order to save my company a great deal of annoyance. You realize, of course, that if you refuse my price, I could just go ahead and manufacture the metal, using my own process.'

'We'll sue if you do,' said Taylor.

'Have you got the money for a long, protracted, and expensive – lawsuit?' Bankhead smiled nastily. 'I have, you know. To prove, however, that I am not unreasonable, I will make the price two thousand.'

'You've heard our price,' answered Taylor stonily, 'and we have nothing further to say.'

'All right, gentlemen,' Bankhead walked towards the door, 'think it over. You'll see it my way, I'm sure.'

He opened the door and revealed the symmetrical form of Peter Q. Hornswoggle bent in rapt concentration at the keyhole. Bankhead sneered audibly and the ex-Congressman jumped to his feet in consternation, bowing rapidly two or three times, for want of anything better to do.

The financier passed by disdainfully and Hornswoggle entered, slammed the door behind him, and faced the two bewildered friends.

'That man, my dear sirs, is a malefactor of great wealth, an economic royalist. He is the type of predatory interest that is the ruination of this country. You did quite right in refusing his offer.' He placed his hand on his ample chest and smiled at them benignantly.

'Who the devil are you?' rasped Taylor, suddenly recovering from his initial surprise.

'I?' Hornswoggle was taken aback. 'Why – er – I am Peter Quintus Hornswoggle. Surely you know me. I was in the House of Representatives last year.'

'Never heard of you. What do you want?'

'Why, bless me! I read in the papers of your wonderful discovery and have come to place my services at your feet.'

'What services?'

'Well, after all, you two are not men of the world. With your new invention, you are prey for every self-seeking unscrupulous person that comes along – like Bankhead, for instance. Now, a practical man of affairs, such as I, one with experience of the world, would be of inestimable use to you. I could handle your affairs, attend to details, see that—'

'All for nothing, of course, eh?' Taylor asked, sardonically.

Hornswoggle coughed convulsively. 'Well, naturally, I thought that a small interest in your discovery might fittingly be assigned to me.'

Sills, who had remained silent during all this, rose to his feet suddenly. 'Get out of here! Did you hear me? Get out, before I call the police.'

'Now, Professor Sills, pray don't get excited,' Hornswoggle retreated towards the door which Taylor held open for him. He passed out, still protesting, and swore softly to himself when the door slammed in his face.

Sills sank wearily into the nearest chair. 'What are we to do, Gene? He offers only two thousand. A week ago that would have been beyond anything I could have hoped for, but now—'

'Forget it. The fellow was only bluffing. Listen, I'm going right now to call on Staples. We'll sell to him for what we can get (it ought to be plenty) and then if there's any trouble with Bankhead – well, that's Staples' worry.' He patted the other on the shoulder. 'Our troubles are practically over.'

Unfortunately, however, Taylor was wrong; their troubles were only beginning.

Across the street, a furtive figure, with beady eyes peering from upturned coat-collar, surveyed the house carefully. A curious policeman might have identified him as 'Slappy' Egan if he had bothered to look, but no one did and 'Slappy' remained unmolested.

'Cripes,' he muttered to himself, 'dis is gonna be a cinch. De whole woiks on the bottom floor, back window can be jimmied wid a toot'pick, no alarms, no nuttin'.' He chuckled and walked away.

Nor was 'Slappy' alone with his ideas. Peter Q. Hornswoggle, as he walked away, found strange thoughts wandering through his massive cranium – thoughts which involved a certain amount of unorthodox action.

And J. Throgmorton Bankhead was likewise active. Belonging to that virile class known as 'go-getters' and being not at all scrupulous as to how he 'go-got,' and certainly not intending to pay a million dollars for the secret of Ammonium, he found it necessary to call on a certain one of his acquaintances.

This acquaintance, while a very useful one, was a bit unsavory, and

Bankhead found it advisable to be very careful and cautious while visiting him. However, the conversation that ensued ended in a pleasing manner for both of them.

Walter Sills snapped out of an uneasy sleep with startled suddenness. He listened anxiously for a while and then leaned over and nudged Taylor. He was rewarded by a few incoherent snuffles.

'Gene, Gene, wake up! Come on, get up!'

'Eh? What is it? What are you bothering—'

'Shut up! Listen, do you hear it?'

'I don't hear anything. Leave me alone, will you?'

Sills put his finger on his lips, and the other quieted. There was a distinct shuffling noise down below, in the laboratory.

Taylor's eyes widened and sleep left them entirely. 'Burglars!' he whispered.

The two crept out of bed, donned bathrobe and slippers, and tiptoed to the door. Taylor had a revolver and took the lead in descending the stairs.

They had traversed perhaps half the flight, when there was a sudden, surprised shout from below, followed by a series of loud, threshing noises. This continued for a few moments and then there was a loud crash of glassware.

'My ammonium!' cried Sills in a stricken voice and rushed headlong down the stairs evading Taylor's clutching arms.

The chemist burst into the laboratory, followed closely by his cursing associate, and clicked the lights on. Two struggling figures blinked owlishly in the sudden illumination, and separated.

Taylor's gun covered them. 'Well, isn't this nice,' he said.

One of the two lurched to his feet from amid a tangle of broken beakers and flasks, and, nursing a cut on his wrist, bent his portly body in a still dignified bow. It was Peter Q. Hornswoggle.

'No doubt,' he said, eyeing the unwavering firearm nervously, 'the circumstances seem suspicious, but I can explain very easily. You see, in spite of the very rough treatment I received after having made my reasonable proposal, I still felt a great deal of kindly interest in you two.

'Therefore, being a man of the world, and knowing the iniquities of mankind, I just decided to keep an eye on your house tonight, for I saw you had neglected to take precautions against house-breakers. Judge my surprise to see this distardly creature,' he pointed to the flat-nosed, plug-ugly, who still remained on the floor in a daze, 'creeping in at the back window.

'Immediately, I risked life and limb in following the criminal, attempting desperately to save your great discovery. I really feel I deserve great credit for what I have done. I'm sure you will feel that I am a valuable person to deal with and reconsider your answers to my earlier proposals.'

Taylor listened to all this with a cynical smile. 'You can certainly lie fluently, can't you P.Q.?'

He would have continued at greater length and with greater forcefulness had not the other burglar suddenly raised his voice in loud protest. 'Cripes, boss, dis fat slob here is only tryin' to get me in bad. I'm just followin' orders, boss. A fellow hired me to come in here and rifle the safe and I'm just oinin' a bit o' honest money. Just plain safe-crackin', boss, I ain't out to hurt no one.

'Den, just as I was gettin' down to de job – warmin' up, so to say – in crawls dis little guy wid a chisel and blowtorch and makes for de safe. Well, naturally, I don't like no competition, so I lays for him and then—'

But Hornswoggle had drawn himself up in icy hauteur. 'It remains to be seen whether the word of a gangster is to be taken before the word of one, who, I may truthfully say, was, in his time, one of the most eminent members of the great—'

'Quiet, both of you,' shouted Taylor, waving the gun threateningly. 'I'm calling the police and you can annoy *them* with your stories. Say, Walt, is everything all right?'

'I think so!' Sills returned from his inspection of the laboratory. 'They only knocked over empty glassware. Everything else is unharmed.'

'That's good,' Taylor began, and then choked in dismay.

From the hallway, a cool individual, hat drawn well over his eyes, entered. A revolver, expertly handled, changed the situation considerably.

'O. K.,' he grunted at Taylor, 'drop the gat!' The other's weapon slipped from reluctant fingers and hit the floor with a clank.

The new menace surveyed the four others with a sardonic glance. 'Well! So there were two others trying to beat me to it. This seems to be a very popular place.'

Sills and Taylor stared stupidly, while Hornswoggle's teeth chattered energetically. The first mobster moved back uneasily, muttering as he did so, 'For Pete's sake, it's Mike the Slug.'

'Yeah,' Mike rasped, 'Mike the Slug. There's lots of guys who know me and who know I ain't afraid to pull the trigger anytime I feel like. Come on, Baldy, hand over the works. You know – the stuff about your fake gold. Come on, before I count five.'

Sills moved slowly toward the old safe in the corner. Mike stepped back carelessly to give him room, and in so doing, his coat sleeve brushed against a shelf. A small vial of sodium sulphate solution tottered and fell.

With sudden inspiration, Sills yelled, 'My God, watch out! It's nitroglycerine!'

The vial hit the floor with a smashing tinkle of broken glass, and involuntarily, Mike yelled and jumped in wild dismay. And as he did so, Taylor crashed into him with a beautiful flying tackle. At the same time, Sills lunged for Taylor's fallen weapon to cover the other two. For this, however, there was no longer need. At the very beginning of the confusion, both had faded hurriedly into the night from whence they came.

Taylor and Mike the Slug rolled round and round the laboratory floor, locked in desperate struggle while Sills hopped over and about them, praying for a moment of comparative quiet that he might bring the revolver into sharp and sudden contact with the gangster's skull.

But no such moment came. Suddenly Mike lunged, caught Taylor stunningly under the chin, and jerked free. Sills yelled in consternation and pulled the trigger at the fleeing figure. The shot was wild and Mike escaped unharmed. Sills made no attempt to follow.

A sluicing stream of cold water brought Taylor back to his senses. He shook his head dazedly as he surveyed the surrounding shambles.

'Whew!' he said, 'What a night!'

Sills groaned, 'What are we going to do now, Gene? Our very lives are in danger. I never thought of the possibility of thieves, or I would never have told of the discovery to the newspapers.'

'Oh, well, the harm's done; no use weeping over it. Now, listen, the first thing we have to do now is to get back to sleep. They won't bother us again tonight. Tomorrow you'll go to the bank and put the papers outlining the details of the process in the vault (which you should have done long ago). Staples will be here at 3 p.m.; we'll close the deal, and then, at last, we'll live happily ever after.'

The chemist shook his head dolefully. 'Ammonium has certainly proved to be very upsetting so far. I almost wish I had never heard of it. I'd almost rather be back doing ore analysis.'

As Walter Sills rattled cross-town towards his bank, he found no reason to change his wish. Even the comforting and homely jiggling of his ancient and battered automobile failed to cheer him. From a life characterized by peaceful monotony, he had entered a period of bedlam, and he was not at all satisfied with the change.

'Riches, like poverty, has its own peculiar problems,' he remarked sententiously to himself as he braked the car before the two-story, marble edifice that was the bank. He stepped out carefully, stretched his cramped legs, and headed for the revolving door.

He didn't get there right away, though. Two husky specimens of the human race stepped up, one at each side, and Sills felt a very hard object pressing with painful intensity against his ribs. He opened his mouth involuntarily, and was rewarded by an icy voice in his ears,

'Quiet, Baldy, or you'll get what you deserve for the damn trick you pulled on me last night.'

Sills shivered and subsided. He recognized Mike the Slug's voice very easily.

'Where's the details?' asked Mike, 'and make it quick.'

'Inside jacket pocket,' croaked Sills tremulously.

Mike's companion passed his hand dexterously into the indicated pocket and flicked out three or four folded sheets of foolscap.

'Dat it, Mike?'

A hasty appraisal and a nod, 'Yeh, we got it. All right, Baldy, on your way!' A sudden shove and the two gangsters jumped into their car and drove away rapidly, while the chemist sprawled on the sidewalk. Kindly hands raised him up.

'It's all right,' he managed to gasp. 'I just tripped, that's all. I'm not hurt.' He found himself alone again, passed into the bank, and dropped into the nearest bench, in near-collapse. There was no doubt about it; the new life was not for him.

But he should have been prepared for it. Taylor had foreseen a possibility of this sort of thing happening. He, himself, had thought a car had been trailing him. Yet, in his surprise and fright, he had almost ruined everything.

He shrugged his thin shoulders and, taking off his hat, abstracted a few folded sheets of paper from the sweatband. It was the work of five minutes to deposit them in a vault, and see the immensely strong steel door swing shut. He felt relieved.

'I wonder what they'll do,' he muttered to himself on the way home, 'when they try to follow the instructions on the paper they *did* get.' He pursed his lips and shook his head. 'If they do, there's going to be one heck of an explosion.'

Sills arrived home to find three policemen pacing leisurely up and down the sidewalk in front of the house.

'Police guard,' explained Taylor shortly, 'so that we have no more trouble like last night.'

The chemist related the events at the bank and Taylor nodded grimly. 'Well, it's checkmate for them now. Staples will be here in two hours, and until then the police will take care of things. Afterwards,' he shrugged, 'it will be Staples' affair.'

'Listen, Gene,' the chemist put in suddenly, 'I'm worried about the ammonium. I haven't tested its plating abilities and those are the most important things, you know. What if Staples comes, and we find that all we have is pigeon milk.'

'Hmm,' Taylor stroked his chin, 'you're right there. But I'll tell you what we can do. Before Staples comes, let's plate something – a spoon, suppose – for our own satisfaction.'

'It's really very annoying,' Sills complained fretfully. 'If it weren't for these troublesome hooligans, we wouldn't have to proceed in this slipshod and unscientific manner.'

'Well, let's eat dinner first.'

After the mid-day meal, they began. The apparatus was set up in feverish haste, In a cubic vat, a foot each way, a saturated solution of Ammonaline was poured. An old, battered spoon was the cathode and a mass of ammonium amalgam (separated from the rest of the solution by a perforated glass partition) was the anode. Three batteries in series provided the current.

Sills explained animatedly, 'It works on the same principle as ordinary copper plating. The ammonium ion, once the electric current is run through, is attracted to the cathode, which is in the spoon. Ordinarily it would break up, being unstable, but this is not the case when it is dissolved in Ammonaline. This Ammonaline is itself very slightly ionized and oxygen is given off at the anode.

'This much I know from theory. Let us see what happens in practice.'

He closed the key while Taylor watched with breathless interest. For a moment, no effect was visible. Taylor looked disappointed.

Then Sills grasped his sleeve. 'See!' he hissed. 'Watch the anode!'

Sure enough, bubbles of gas were slowly forming upon the spongy ammonium amalgam. They shifted their attention to the spoon.

Gradually, they noticed a change. The metallic appearance became dulled, the silver color slowly losing its whiteness. A layer of distinct, if dull, yellow was being built up. For fifteen minutes, the current ran and then Sills broke the circuit with a contented sigh.

'It plates perfectly,' he said.

'Good! Take it out! Let's see it!'

'What?' Sills was aghast. 'Take it out! Why, that's pure ammonium. If I were to expose it to ordinary air, the water vapor would dissolve it to NH_4OH in no time. We can't do that.'

He dragged a rather bulky piece of apparatus to the table. 'This,' he said, 'is a compressed-air container. I run it through calcium chloride dryers and then bubble the perfectly dry oxygen (safely diluted with four times its own volume of nitrogen) directly into the solvent.'

He introduced the nozzle into the solution just beneath the spoon and turned on a slow stream of air. It worked like magic. With almost lightning speed, the yellow coating began to glitter and gleam, to shine with almost ethereal beauty.

The two men watched it with beating heart and panting breath. Sills shut the air off, and for a while they watched the wonderful spoon and said nothing.

Then Taylor whispered hoarsely, 'Take it out. Let me feel it! My God! – it's beautiful!'

With reverent awe, Sills approached the spoon, grasped it with forceps, and withdrew it from the surrounding liquid.

What followed immediately after that can never be fully described. Later on, when excited newspaper reporters pressed them unmercifully, neither Taylor nor Sills had the least recollection of the happenings of the next few minutes.

What happened was that the moment the ammonium-plated spoon was exposed to open air, the most horrible odor ever conceived assailed their nostrils! An odor that cannot be described, a terrible broth of Hell that plunged the room into sheer, horrible nightmare.

With one strangled gasp, Sills dropped the spoon. Both were

coughing and retching, tearing wildly at their throats and mouths, yelling, weeping, sneezing!

Taylor pounced upon the spoon and looked about wildly. The odor grew steadily more powerful and their wild exertions to escape it had already succeeded in wrecking the laboratory and had upset the vat of Ammonaline. There was only one thing to do, and Sills did it. The spoon went flying out the open window in the middle of Twelfth Avenue. It hit the sidewalk right at the feet of one of the policemen, but Taylor didn't care.

'Take off your clothes. We'll have to burn them,' Sills was gasping. 'Then spray something over the laboratory – anything with a strong smell. Burn sulphur. Get some liquid Bromine.'

Both were tearing at their clothes in distraction when they realized that someone had walked in through the unlocked door. The bell had rung, but neither had heard it. It was Staples, six-foot, lion-maned Steel King.

One step into the hall ruined his dignity utterly. He collapsed in one tearing sob and Twelfth Avenue was treated to the spectacle of an elderly, richly-dressed gentleman tearing uptown as fast as his feet would carry him, shedding as much of his clothes as he dared while doing so.

The spoon continued its deadly work. The three policemen had long since retired in abject rout, and now to the numbed and tortured senses of the two innocent and suffering causes of the entire mess came a roaring and confused shouting from the street.

Men and women were pouring out of the neighboring houses, horses were bolting. Fire engines clanged down the street, only to be abandoned by their riders. Squadrons of police came – and left.

Sills and Taylor finally gave up, and clad only in trousers, ran pell-mell for the Hudson. They did not stop until they found themselves neck-deep in water, with blessed, pure air above them.

Taylor turned bewildered eyes to Sills. 'But how could it emit that horrible odor? You said it was stable and stable solids have no odors. It takes vapor for that, doesn't it?'

'Have you ever smelled musk?' groaned Sills. 'It will give off an aroma for an indefinite period without losing any appreciable weight. We've come up against something like that.'

The two ruminated in silence for a while, wincing whenever the wind brought a vagrant waft of Ammonium vapor to them, and then Taylor said in a low voice, 'When they finally trace the trouble to the spoon, and find out who made it, I'm afraid we'll be sued – or maybe thrown in jail.'

Sills' face lengthened. 'I wish I'd never seen the damned stuff! It's brought nothing but trouble.' His tortured spirit gave way and he sobbed loudly.

Taylor patted him on the back mournfully. 'It's not as bad as all that, of course. The discovery will make you famous and you'll be able to demand your own price, working at any industrial lab in the country. Then, too, you're a cinch to win the Nobel Prize.'

'That's right,' Sills smiled again, 'and I may find a way to counter-act the odor, too. I hope so.'

'I hope so, too,' said Taylor feelingly. 'Let's go back. I think they've managed to remove the spoon by now.'

Trends

John Harman was sitting at his desk, brooding, when I entered the office that day. It had become, a common sight, by then, to see him staring out at the Hudson, head in hand, a scowl contorting his face – all too common. It seemed unfair for the little bantam to be eating his heart out like that day after day, when by rights he should have been receiving the praise and adulation of the world.

I flopped down into a chair. 'Did you see the editorial in today's *Clarion*, boss?'

He turned weary, bloodshot eyes to me. 'No, I haven't. What do they say? Are they calling the vengeance of God down upon me again?' His voice dripped with bitter sarcasm.

'They're going a little farther *now*, boss,' I answered. 'Listen to this:

'"Tomorrow is the day of John Harman's attempt at profaning the heavens. Tomorrow, in defiance of world opinion and world conscience, this man will defy God.

"It is not given to man to go wheresoever ambition and desire lead him. There are things forever denied him, and aspiring to the stars is one of these. Like Eve, John Harman wishes to eat of the forbidden fruit, and like Eve he will suffer due punishment therefor.

"But it is not enough, this mere talk. If we allow him thus to brook the vengeance of God, the trespass is mankind's and not Harman's alone. In allowing him to carry out his evil designs, we make ourselves accessory to the crime, and Divine vengeance will fall on all alike.

"It is, therefore, essential that immediate steps be taken to prevent Harman from taking off in his so-called rocketship tomorrow. The government in refusing to take such steps may force violent action. If it will make no move to confiscate the rocketship, or to imprison Harman, our emaged citizenry may have to take matters into their own hands—'''

Harman sprang from his seat in a rage and, snatching the paper from my hands, threw it into the corner furiously. 'It's an open call to a lynching,' he raved. 'Look at this!'

He cast five or six envelopes in my direction. One glance sufficed to tell what they were.

'More death threats?' I asked.

'Yes, exactly that. I've had to arrange for another increase in the police patrol outside the building and for a motorcycle police escort when I cross the river to the testing ground tomorrow.'

He marched up and down the room with agitated stride. 'I don't know what to do, Clifford. I've worked on the *Prometheus* almost ten years. I've slaved, spent a fortune of money, given up all that makes life worth while – and for what? So that a bunch of fool revivalists can whip up public sentiment against me until my very life isn't safe.'

'You're in advance of the times, boss,' I shrugged my shoulders in a resigned gesture which made him whirl upon me in a fury.

'What do you mean "in advance of the times"? This is 1973. The world has been ready for space travel for half a century now. Fifty years ago, people were talking, dreaming of the day when man could free himself of Earth and plumb the depths of space. For fifty years, science has inched toward this goal, and now . . . now I finally have it, and behold! You say the world is not ready for me.'

'The '20s and '30s were years of anarchy, decadence, and misrule, if you remember your history,' I reminded him gently. 'You cannot accept them as criteria.'

'I know, I know. You're going to tell me of the First War of 1914, and the Second of 1940. It's an old story to me; my father fought in the Second and my grandfather in the First. Nevertheless, those were the days when science *flourished*. Men were not afraid then; somehow they dreamed and dared. There was no such thing as conservatism when it came to matters mechanical and scientific. No theory was too radical to advance, no discovery too revolutionary to publish. Today, dry rot has seized the world when a great vision, such as space travel, is hailed as "defiance of God".'

His head sank slowly down, and he turned away to hide his trembling lips and the tears in his eyes. Then he suddenly straightened again, eyes blazing: 'But I'll show them. I'm going through with it, in spite of Hell, Heaven and Earth. I've put too much into it to quit now.'

'Take it easy, boss,' I advised. 'This isn't going to do you any good tomorrow, when you get into that ship. Your chances of coming out alive aren't too good now, so what will they be if you start out worn to pieces with excitement and worry?'

'You're right. Let's not think of it any more. Where's Shelton?'

'Over at the Institute arranging for the special photographic plates to be sent us.'

'He's been gone a long time, hasn't he?'

'Not especially; but listen, boss, there's something wrong with him. I don't like him.'

'Poppycock! He's been with me two years, and I have no complaints.'

'All right.' I spread my hands in resignation. 'If you won't listen to me, you won't. Just the same I caught him reading one of those infernal pamphlets Otis Eldredge puts out. You know the kind:

"Beware, O mankind, for judgment draws near. Punishment for your sins is at hand. Repent and be saved." And all the rest of the time-honoured junk.'

Harman snorted in disgust. 'Cheap tub-thumping revivalist! I suppose the world will never outgrow his type – not while sufficient morons exist. Still you can't condemn Shelton just because he reads it. I've read them myself on occasion.'

'He *says* he picked it up on the sidewalk and read it in "idle curiosity", but I'm pretty sure that I saw him take it out of his wallet. Besides, he goes to church every Sunday.'

'Is *that* a crime? Everyone does, nowadays!'

'Yes, but not to the Twentieth Century Evangelical Society. That's Eldredge's.'

That jolted Harman. Evidently, it was the first he had heard of it. 'Say, that *is* something, isn't it? We'll have to keep an eye on him, then.'

But after that, things started to happen, and we forgot all about Shelton – until it was too late.

There was nothing much left to do that last day before the test, and I wandered into the next room, where I went over Harman's final report to the Institute. It was my job to correct any errors or mistakes that crept in, but I'm afraid I wasn't very thorough. To tell the truth, I couldn't concentrate. Every few minutes, I'd fall into a brown study.

It seemed queer, all this fuss over a space travel. When Harman had first announced the approaching perfection of the *Prometheus*, some six months before, scientific circles had been jubilant. Of course, they were cautious in their statements and qualified everything they said, but there was real enthusiasm.

However, the masses didn't take it that way. It seems strange, perhaps, to you of the twenty-first century, but perhaps we should have expected it in those days of '73. People weren't very progressive then. For years there had been a swing toward religion, and when the churches came out unanimously against Harman's rocket – well, there you were.

At first, the opposition confined itself *to* the churches and we thought it might play itself out. But it didn't. The papers got hold of it, and literally spread the gospel. Poor Harman became an anathema to the world in a remarkably short time, and then his troubles began.

He received death threats, and warnings of divine vengeance every day. He couldn't walk the streets in safety. Dozens of sects, to none of which he belonged – he was one of the very rare free-thinkers of the day, which was another count against him – excommunicated him and placed him under special interdict. And, worst of all, Otis Eldredge and his Evangelical Society began stirring up the populace.

Eldredge was a queer character – one of those geniuses, in their way, that arise every so often. Gifted with a golden tongue and a sulphurous vocabulary, he could fairly hypnotize a crowd. Twenty thousand people were so much putty in his hands, could he only bring them within earshot. And for four months, he thundered against Harman; for four months, a pouring stream of denunciation rolled forth in oratorical frenzy. And for four months, the temper of the world rose.

But Harman was not to be daunted. In his tiny, five-foot-two body, he had enough spirit for five six-footers. The more the wolves howled, the firmer he held his ground. With almost divine – his enemies said, diabolical – obstinacy, he refused to yield an inch. Yet his outward firmness was to me, who knew him, but an imperfect concealment of the great sorrow and bitter disappointment within.

The ring of the doorbell interrupted my thoughts at that point and brought me to my feet in surprise. Visitors were very few those days.

I looked out the window and saw a tall, portly figure talking with Police Sergeant Cassidy. I recognized him at once as Howard Winstead, head of the Institute. Harman was hurrying out to greet him, and after a short exchange of phrases, the two entered the office. I followed them in, being rather curious as to what could have brought Winstead, who was more politician than scientist, here.

Winstead didn't seem very comfortable, at first; not his usual suave self. He avoided Harman's eyes in an embarrassed manner and mumbled a few conventionalities concerning the weather. Then he came to the point with direct, undiplomatic bluntness.

'John,' he said, 'how about postponing the trial for a time?'

'You really mean abandoning it altogether, don't you? Well, I won't, and that's final.'

Winstead lifted his hand. 'Wait now, John, don't get excited. Let me state my case. I know the Institute agreed to give you a free hand, and I know that you paid at least half the expenses out of your own pocket, but you can't go through with it.'

'Oh, can't I, though?' Harman snorted derisively.

'Now listen, John, you know your science, but you don't know your human nature, and I do. This is not the world of the "Mad Decades", whether you realize it or not. There have been profound changes since 1940.' He swung into what was evidently a carefully prepared speech.

'After the First World War, you know, the world as a whole swung away from religion and toward freedom from convention. People were disgusted and disillusioned, cynical and sophisticated. Eldredge calls them "wicked and sinful". In spite of that, science flourished – some say it always fares best in such an unconventional period. From *its* standpoint it was a "Golden Age".'

'However, you know the political and economic history of the period. It was a time of political chaos and international anarchy; a suicidal, brainless, insane period – and it culminated in the Second World War. And just as the First War led to a period of sophistication, so the Second initiated a return to religion.

'People were disgusted with the "Mad Decades". They had had enough of it, and feared, beyond all else, a return to it. To remove that possibility, they put the ways of those decades behind them. Their motives, you see, were understandable and laudable. All the freedom, all the sophistication, all the lack of convention were gone – swept away clean. We are living now in a second Victorian age; and naturally so, because human history goes by swings of the pendulum and this is the swing toward religion and convention.

'One thing only is left over since those days of half a century ago. That one thing is the respect of humanity for science. We have prohibition; smoking for women is outlawed; cosmetics are forbidden; low dresses and short skirts are unheard of; divorce is frowned upon. But science has not been confined – *as yet*.

'It behoves science, then, to be circumspect, to refrain from arousing the people. It will be very easy to make them believe – and Otis Eldredge has come perilously close to doing it in some of his speeches – that it was science that brought about the horrors of the Second World War. Science outstripped culture, they will say, technology outstripped sociology, and it was that unbalance that came so near to destroying the world. Somehow, I am inclined to believe they are not so far wrong, at that.

'But do you know what would happen, if it ever *did* come to that? Scientific research may be forbidden; or, if they don't go that far, it will certainly be so strictly regulated as to stifle in its own decay. It will be a calamity from which humanity would not recover for a millennium.

'And it is your trial flight that may precipitate all this. You are arousing the public to a stage where it will be difficult to calm them. I warn you, John. The consequences will be on your head.'

There was absolute silence for a moment and then Harman forced a smile. 'Come, Howard, you're letting yourself be frightened by shadows on the wall. Are you trying to tell me that it is your serious belief that the world as a whole is ready to plunge into a second Dark Ages? After all, the intelligent men are on the side of science, aren't they?'

'If they are, there aren't many of them left from what I see.' Winstead drew a pipe from his pocket and filled it slowly with tobacco as he continued: 'Eldredge formed a League of the Righteous two months ago – they call it the L. R. – and it has grown unbelievably. *Twenty million is its membership in the United States alone.* Eldredge boasts that after the next election Congress will be his; and there seems to be more truth than bluff in that. Already there has been strenuous lobbying in favour of a bill outlawing rocket experiments, and laws of that type have been enacted in Poland, Portugal and Rumania. Yes, John, we are perilously close to open persecution of science.' He was smoking now in rapid, nervous puffs.

'But if I succeed, Howard, if I succeed! What then?'

'Bah! You know the chances for that. Your own estimate gives you only one chance in ten of coming out alive.'

'What does that signify? The next experimenter will learn by my mistakes, and the odds will improve. That's the scientific method.'

'The mob doesn't know anything about the scientific method; and they don't want to know. Well, what do you say? Will you call it off?'

Harman sprang to his feet, his chair tumbling over with a crash. 'Do you know what you ask? Do you want me to give up my life's work, my dream, just like that? Do you think I'm going to sit back and wait for your *dear* public to become benevolent? Do you think they'll change in *my* lifetime?

'Here's my answer: I have an inalienable right to pursue knowledge. Science has an inalienable right to progress and develop without interference. The world, in interfering with me, is wrong; I am right. And it shall go hard; but I *will not* abandon my rights.'

Winstead shook his head sorrowfully. 'You're wrong, John, when you speak of "inalienable" rights. What you call a "right" is merely a *privilege, generally agreed upon*. What society accepts, is right; what it does not, is wrong.'

'Would your friend, Eldredge, agree to such a definition of his "righteousness"?' questioned Harman bitterly.

'No, he would not, but that's irrelevant. Take the case of those African tribes who used to be cannibals. They were brought up as cannibals, have the long tradition of cannibalism, and their society accepts the practice. To *them*, cannibalism is *right*, and why shouldn't it be? So you see how relative the whole notion is, and how inane your conception of "inalienable" rights to perform experiments is.'

'You know, Howard, you missed your calling when you didn't become a lawyer.' Harman was really growing angry. 'You've been

bringing out every moth-eaten argument you can think of. For God's
sake, man, are you trying to pretend that it is a crime to refuse to run
with the crowd? Do you stand for absolute uniformity, ordinariness,
orthodoxy, commonplaceness? Science would die far sooner under
the programme you outline than under governmental prohibition.'

Harman stood up and pointed an accusing finger at the other.
'You're betraying science and the tradition of those glorious rebels:
Galileo, Darwin, Einstein and their kind. My rocket leaves tomorrow
on schedule in spite of you and every other stuffed shirt in the United
States. That's that, and I refuse to listen to you any longer. So you can
just get out.'

The head of the Institute, red in the face, turned to me. 'You're
my witness, young man, that I warned this obstinate nitwit, this . . .
this hare-brained fanatic.' He spluttered a bit, and then strode out,
the picture of fiery indignation.

Harman turned to me when he had gone: 'Well, what do *you*
think? I suppose you agree with him.'

There was only one possible answer and I made it: 'You're not
paying me to do anything else but follow orders, boss. I'm sticking
with you.'

Just then Shelton came in and Harman packed us both off to go
over the calculations of the orbit of flight for the umpteenth time,
while he himself went off to bed.

The next day, July 15th, dawned in matchless splendor, and
Harman, Shelton, and myself were in an almost gay mood as we
crossed the Hudson to where the *Prometheus* – surrounded by an
adequate police guard – lay in gleaming grandeur.

Around it, roped off at an apparently safe distance, rolled a crowd
of gigantic proportions. Most of them were hostile, raucously so. In
fact, for one fleeting moment, as our motorcycle police escort parted
the crowds for us, the shouts and imprecations that reached our ears
almost convinced me that we should have listened to Winstead.

But Harman paid no attention to them at all, after one supercilious sneer at a shout of: 'There goes John Harman, son of Belial.'

Calmly, he directed us about our task of inspection. I tested the foot-thick outer walls and the air locks for leaks, then made sure the air purifier worked. Shelton checked up on the repellent screen and the fuel tanks. Finally, Harman tried on the clumsy spacesuit, found it suitable, and announced himself ready.

The crowd stirred. Upon a hastily erected platform of wooden planks piled in confusion by some in the mob, there rose up a strik-ing figure. Tall and lean; with thin, ascetic countenance; deep-set, burning eyes, peering and half closed; a thick, white mane crowning all – it was Otis Eldredge. The crowd recognized him at once and many cheered. Enthusiasm waxed and soon the entire turbulent mass of people shouted themselves hoarse over him.

He raised a hand for silence, turned to Harman, who regarded him with surprise and distaste, and pointed a long, bony finger at him:

'John Harman, son of the devil, spawn of Satan, you are here for an evil purpose. You are about to set out upon a blasphemous attempt to pierce the veil beyond which man is forbidden to go. You are tast-ing of the forbidden fruit of Eden and beware that you taste not of the fruits of sin.'

The crowd cheered him to the echo and he continued: 'The finger of God is upon you, John Harman. He shall not allow His works to be defiled. You die today, John Harman.' His voice rose in intensity and his last words were uttered in truly prophet-like fervor.

Harman turned away in disdain. In a loud, clear voice, he addressed the police sergeant: 'Is there any way, officer, of removing these spec-tators. The trial flight may be attended by some destruction because of the rocket blasts, and they're crowding too close.'

The policeman answered in a crisp, unfriendly tone: 'If you're afraid of being mobbed, say so, Mr Harman. You don't have to worry, though, we'll hold them back. And as for danger – from *that* contrap-tion—' He sniffed loudly in the direction of the *Prometheus*, evoking a torrent of jeers and yells.

Harman said nothing further, but climbed into the ship in silence.

And when he did so, a queer sort of stillness fell over the mob; a palpable tension. There was no attempt at rushing the ship, an attempt I had thought inevitable. On the contrary, Otis Eldredge himself shouted to everyone to move back.

'Leave the sinner to his sins,' he shouted. '"Vengeance is mine," saith the Lord.'

As the moment approached, Shelton nudged me. 'Let's get out of here,' he whispered in a strained voice. 'Those rocket blasts are poison.' Saying this, he broke into a run, beckoning anxiously for me to follow.

We had not yet reached the fringes of the crowd when there was a terrific roar behind me. A wave of heated air swept over me. There was the frightening hiss of some speeding object past my ear, and I was thrown violently to the ground. For a few moments I lay dazed, my ears ringing and my head reeling.

When I staggered drunkenly to my feet again, it was to view a dreadful sight. Evidently, the entire fuel supply of the *Prometheus* had exploded at once, and where it had lain a moment ago there was now only a yawning hole. The ground was strewn with wreckage. The cries of the hurt were heartrending, and the mangled bodies – but I won't try to describe those.

A weak groan at my feet attracted my attention. One look, and I gasped in horror, for it was Shelton, the back of his head a bloody mass.

'I did it.' His voice was hoarse and triumphant but withal so low that I could scarcely hear it. 'I did it. I broke open the liquid-oxygen compartments and when the spark went through the acetylide mixture the whole cursed thing exploded.' He gasped a bit and tried to move but failed. 'A piece of wreckage must have hit me, but I don't care. I'll die knowing that—'

His voice was nothing more than a rasping rattle, and on his face was the ecstatic look of martyr. He died then, and I could not find it in my heart to condemn him.

It was then I first thought of Harman. Ambulances from Manhattan and from Jersey City were on the scene, and one had sped to a wooden patch some five hundred yards distant, where, caught in the treetops, lay a splintered fragment of the *Prometheus'* forward compartment. I limped there as fast as I could, but they had dragged out Harman and clanged away long before I could reach them.

After that, I didn't stay. The disorganized crowd had no thought but for the dead and wounded *now*, but when they recovered, and bent their thoughts to revenge, my life would not be worth a straw. I followed the dictates of the better part of valour and quietly disappeared.

The next week was a hectic one for me. During that time, I lay in hiding at the home of a friend, for it would have been more than my life was worth to allow myself to be seen and recognized. Harman, himself, lay in a Jersey City hospital, with nothing more than superficial cuts and bruises – thanks to the backward force of the explosion and the saving clump of trees which cushioned the fall of the *Prometheus*. It was on him that the brunt of the world's wrath fell.

New York, and the rest of the world also, just about went crazy. Every last paper in the city came out with gigantic headlines, '28 Killed, 73 Wounded – the Price of Sin,' printed in blood-red letters. The editorials howled for Harman's life, demanding he be arrested and tried for first-degree murder.

The dreaded cry of 'Lynch him!' was raised throughout the five boroughs, and milling thousands crossed the river and converged on Jersey City. At their head was Otis Eldredge, both legs in splints, addressing the crowd from an open automobile as they marched. It was a veritable army.

Mayor Carson of Jersey City called out every available policeman and phoned frantically to Trenton for the State militia. New York clamped down on every bridge and tunnel leaving the city – but not till after many thousands had left.

There were pitched battles on the Jersey coast that sixteenth of July. The vastly outnumbered police clubbed indiscriminately but were gradually pushed back and back. Mounties rode down upon the mob relentlessly but were swallowed up and pulled down by sheer force of numbers. Not until tear gas was used, did the crowd halt – and even then they did not retreat.

The next day, martial law was declared, and the State militia entered Jersey City. That was the end for the lynchers. Eldredge was called to confer with the mayor, and after the conference ordered his followers to disperse.

In a statement to the newspapers, Mayor Carson said: 'John Harman must needs suffer for his crime, but it is essential that he do so legally. Justice must take its course, and the State of New Jersey will take all necessary measures.'

By the end of the week, normality of a sort had returned and Harman slipped out of the public spotlight. Two more weeks and there was scarcely a word about him in the newspapers, excepting such casual references to him in the discussion of the new Zittman antirocketry bill that had just passed both houses of Congress by unanimous votes.

Yet he remained in the hospital still. No legal action had been taken against him, but it began to appear that a sort of indefinite imprisonment 'for his own protection' might be his eventual fate. Therefore, I bestirred myself to action.

Temple Hospital is situated in a lonely and outlying district of Jersey City, and on a dark, moonless night I experienced no difficulty at all in invading the grounds unobserved. With a facility that surprised me, I sneaked in through a basement window, slugged a sleepy intern into insensibility and proceeded to Room 15E, which was listed in the books as Harman's.

'Who's there?' Harman's surprised shout was music in my ears.

'Sh! Quiet! It's I, Cliff McKenny.'

'You! What are you doing here?'

'Trying to get you out. If I don't, you're liable to stay here the rest of your life. Come on, let's go.'

I was hustling him into his clothes while we were speaking, and in no time at all we were sneaking down the corridor. We were out safely and into my waiting car before Harman collected his scattered wits sufficiently to begin asking questions.

'What's happened since that day?' was the first question. 'I don't remember a thing after starting the rocket blasts until I woke up in the hospital.'

'Didn't they tell you anything?'

'Not a damn thing,' he swore. 'I asked until I was hoarse.'

So I told him the whole story from the explosion on. His eyes were wide with shocked surprise when I told of the dead and wounded, and filled with wild rage when he heard of Shelton's treachery. The story of the riots and attempted lynching evoked a muffled curse from between set lips.

'Of course, the papers howled "murder",' I concluded, 'but they couldn't pin *that* on you. They tried manslaughter, but there were too many eye-witnesses that had heard your request for the removal of the crowd and the police sergeant's absolute refusal to do so. That, of course, absolved you from all blame. The police sergeant himself died in the explosion, and they couldn't make him the goat.

'Still, with Eldredge yelling for your hide, you're never safe. It would be best to leave while able.'

Harman nodded his head in agreement, 'Eldredge survived the explosion, did he?'

'Yes, worse luck. He broke both legs, but it takes more than that to shut his mouth.'

Another week had passed before I reached our future haven – my uncle's farm in Minnesota. There, in a lonely and out-of-the-way rural community, we stayed while the hullabaloo over Harman's disappearance gradually died down and the perfunctory search for us faded away. The search, by the way, was short indeed, for the authorities seemed more relieved than concerned over the disappearance.

Peace and quiet did wonders with Harman. In six months he seemed a new man – quite ready to consider a second attempt at space travel.

Not all the misfortunes in the world could stop him, it seemed, once he had his heart set on something.

'My mistake the first time,' he told me one winter's day, 'lay in announcing the experiment. I should have taken the temper of the people into account, as Winstead said. This time, however' – he rubbed his hands and gazed thoughtfully into the distance – 'I'll steal a march on them. The experiment will be performed in secrecy – absolute secrecy.'

I laughed grimly, 'It would have to be. Do you know that all future experiment in rocketry, even entirely theoretical research is a crime punishable by death?'

'Are you afraid, then?'

'Of course not, boss. I'm merely stating a fact. And here's another plain fact. We two can't build a ship all by ourselves, you know.'

'I've thought of that and figured a way out, Cliff. What's more, I can take care of the money angle, too, You'll have to do some traveling, though.

'First, you'll have to go to Chicago and look up the firm of Roberts & Scranton and withdraw everything that's left of my father's inheritance, which,' he added in a rueful aside, 'is more than half gone on the first ship. Then, locate as many of the old crowd as you can: Harry Jenkins, Joe O'Brien, Neil Stanton – all of them. And get back as quickly as you can. I am tired of delay.'

Two days later, I left for Chicago. Obtaining my uncle's consent to the entire business was a simple affair. 'Might as well be strung up for a herd of sheep as for a lamb,' he grunted, 'so go ahead. I'm in enough of a mess now and can afford a bit more, I guess.'

It took quite a bit of traveling and even more smooth talk and persuasion before I managed to get four men to come: the three mentioned by Harman and one other, a Saul Simonoff. With that skeleton force and with the half million still left Harman out of the reputed millions left him by his father, we began work.

The building of the *New Prometheus* is a story in itself – a long story of five years of discouragement and insecurity. Little by little, buying girders in Chicago, beryl-steel plates in New York, a vanadium cell in San Francisco, miscellaneous items in scattered corners of the nation, we constructed the sister ship to the ill-fated *Prometheus*.

The difficulties in the way were all but insuperable. To prevent drawing suspicion down upon us, we had to spread our purchases over periods of time, and to see to it, as well, that the orders were made out to various places. For this we required the co-operation of various friends, who, to be sure, did not know at the time for exactly what purpose the purchases were being used.

We had to synthesize our own fuel, ten tons of it, and that was perhaps the hardest job of all; certainly it took the most time. And finally, as Harman's money dwindled, we came up against our biggest problem – the necessity of economizing. From the beginning we had known that we could never make the *New Prometheus* as large or as elaborate as the first ship had been, but it soon developed that we would have to reduce its equipment to a point perilously close to the danger line. The repulsion screen was barely satisfactory and all attempts at radio communication were perforce abandoned.

And as we labored through the years, there in the backwoods of northern Minnesota, the world moved on, and Winstead's prophecies proved to have hit amazingly near the mark.

The events of those five years – from 1973 to 1978 – are well known to the schoolboys of today, the period being the climax of what we now call the 'Neo-Victorian Age.' The happenings of those years seem well-nigh unbelievable as we look back upon them now.

The outlawing of all research on space travel came in the very beginning, but was a bare start compared to the antiscientific measures taken in the ensuing years. The next congressional elections, those of 1974, resulted in a Congress in which Eldredge controlled the House and held the balance of power in the Senate.

Hence, no time was lost. At the first session of the ninety-third Congress, the famous Stonely-Carter bill was passed. It established the Federal Scientific Research Investigatory Bureau – the FSRIB – which was given full power to pass on the legality of all research in the country. Every laboratory, industrial or scholastic, was required to file information, in advance, on all projected research before this new bureau, which could, and did, ban absolutely all such as it disapproved of.

The inevitable appeal to the supreme court came on November 9, 1974, in the case of Westly vs. Simmons, in which Joseph Westly of Stanford upheld his right to continue his investigations on atomic power on the grounds that the Stonley-Carter act was unconstitutional.

How we five, isolated amid the snowdrifts of the Middle West, followed that case! We had all the Minneapolis and St. Paul papers sent to us – always reaching us two days late – and devoured every word of print concerning it. For the two months of suspense work ceased entirely on the *New Prometheus*.

It was rumoured at first that the court would declare the act unconstitutional, and monster parades were held in every large town against this eventuality. The League of the Righteous brought its powerful influence to bear – and even the supreme court submitted. It was five to four for constitutionality. *Science strangled by the vote of one man.*

And it was strangled beyond a doubt. The members of the bureau were Eldredge men, heart and soul, and nothing that would not have immediate industrial use was passed.

'Science has gone too far,' said Eldredge in a famous speech at about that time. 'We must halt it indefinitely, and allow the world to catch up. Only through that and trust in God may we hope to achieve universal and permanent prosperity.'

But this was one of Eldredge's last statements. He had never fully recovered from the broken legs he received that fateful day in July of '73, and his strenuous life since then had strained his constitution past the breaking point. On February 2, 1976, he passed away amid a burst of mourning unequaled since Lincoln's assassination.

His death had no immediate effect on the course of events. The rules of the FSRIB grew, in fact, in stringency as the years passed. So starved and choked did science become, that once more colleges found themselves forced to reinstate philosophy and the classics as the chief studies – and at that the student body fell to the lowest point since the beginning of the twentieth century.

These conditions prevailed more or less throughout the civilized world, reaching even lower depths in England, and perhaps least depressing in Germany, which was the last to fall under the 'Neo-Victorian' influence.

The nadir of science came in the spring of 1978, a bare month before the completion of the *New Prometheus*, with the passing of the 'Easter Edict' – it was issued the day before Easter. By it, *all* independent research or experimentation was absolutely forbidden.

The FSRIB thereafter reserved the right to allow only such research as it *specifically requested*.

John Harman and I stood before the gleaming metal of the *New Prometheus* that Easter Sunday; I in the deepest gloom, and he in an almost jovial mood.

'Well, Clifford, my boy,' said he, 'the last ton of fuel, a few polishing touches, and I am ready for my second attempt. This time there will be no Sheltons among us.' He hummed a hymn. That was all the radio played those days, and even we rebels sang them from sheer frequency of repetition.

I grunted sourly: 'It's no use, boss. Ten to one, you end up somewhere in space, and even if you come back, you'll most likely be hung by the neck. We can't win.' My head shook dolefully from side to side.

'Bah! This state of affairs can't last, Cliff.'

'I think it will. Winstead was right that time. The pendulum swings, and since 1945 it's been swinging against us. We're ahead of the times – or behind them.'

'Don't speak of that fool, Winstead. You're making the same mistake he did. Trends are things of centuries and millenniums, not years or decades. For five hundred years we have been moving toward science. You can't reverse that in thirty years.'

'Then what are we doing?' I asked sarcastically.

'We're going through a momentary reaction following a period of too-rapid advance in the Mad Decades. Just such a reaction took place in the Romantic Age – the first Victorian Period – following the too-rapid advance of the eighteenth-century Age of Reason.'

'Do you really think so?' I was shaken by his evident self-assurance.

'Of course. This period has a perfect analogy in the spasmodic "revivals" that used to hit the small towns in America's Bible Belt a century or so ago. For a week, perhaps everyone would get religion, and virtue would reign triumphant. Then, one by one, they would backslide and the Devil would resume his sway.

'In fact, there are symptoms of backsliding even now. The L.R. has indulged in one squabble after another since Eldredge's death. There have been half a dozen schisms already. The very extremities to which those in power are going are helping us, for the country is rapidly tiring of it.'

And that ended the argument – I in total defeat, as usual.

A month later, the *New Prometheus* was complete. It was nowhere near as glittering and as beautiful as the original, and bore many a trace of makeshift workmanship, but we were proud of it – proud and triumphant.

'I'm going to try again, men' – Harman's voice was husky, and his little frame vibrant with happiness – 'and I may not make it, but for that I don't care.' His eyes shone in anticipation. 'I'll be shooting through the void at last, and the dream of mankind will come true. Out around the Moon and back; the first *to* see the other side. It's worth the chance.'

'You won't have fuel enough *to* land on the Moon, boss, which is a pity,' I said.

At that a pessimistic whisper ran through the little group surrounding him, to which he paid no attention.

'Goodbye,' he said. 'I'll be seeing you.' And with a cheerful grin he climbed into the ship.

Fifteen minutes later, the five of us sat about the living-room table, frowning, lost in thought, eyes gazing out of the building at the spot where a burned section of soil marked the spot where a few minutes earlier the *New Prometheus* had lain.

Simonoff voiced the thought that was in the mind of each one of us: 'Maybe it would be better for him *not* to come back. He won't be treated very well if he does, I think.' And we all nodded in gloomy assent.

How foolish that prediction seems to me now from the hindsight of three decades.

The rest of the story is really not mine, for I did not see Harman again until a month after his eventful trip ended in a safe landing. It was almost thirty-six hours after the take-off that a screaming projectile shot its way over Washington and buried itself in the mud just across the Potomac.

Investigators were at the scene of the landing within fififteen minutes, and in another fifteen minutes the police were there, for it was found that the projectile was a *rocketship*. They stared in involuntary awe at the tired, disheveled man who staggered out in near-collapse.

There was utter silence while he shook his *fist* at the staring spectators and shouted: 'Go ahead, hang me, fools. But I've reached the Moon, and you can't hang *that*. Get the FSRIB. Maybe they'll declare the flight illegal and, therefore, nonexistent.' He laughed weakly and suddenly collapsed.

Someone shouted: 'Take him to a hospital. He's sick.' In stiff unconsciousness Harman was bundled into a police car and carried away, while the police formed a guard about the rocketship.

Government officials arrived and investigated the ship, read the log, inspected the drawings and photographs he had taken of the Moon, and finally departed in silence. The crowd grew and the word spread that a man had reached the Moon.

Curiously enough, there was little resentment of the fact. Men were impressed and awed; the crowd whispered and cast inquisitive glances at the dim crescent of Luna, scarcely seen in the bright sunlight. Over all, an uneasy pall of silence, the silence of indecision, lay.

Then, at the hospital, Harman revealed his identity, and the fickle world went wild. Even Harman himself was stunned in surprise at the rapid change in the world's temper. It seemed almost incredible, and yet it was true. Secret discontent, combined with a heroic tale of man against overwhelming odds – the sort of tale that had stirred man's soul since the beginning of time – served to sweep everyone into an ever-swelling current of anti-Victorianism. And Eldredge was dead – no other could replace him.

I saw Harman at the hospital shortly after that. He was propped up and still half buried with papers, telegrams and letters. He grinned at me and nodded. 'Well, Cliff,' he whispered, 'the pendulum swung back again.'

The Weapon too Dreadful to Use

Karl Frantor found the prospect a terribly dismal one. From low-hanging clouds, fell eternal misty rain; squat, rubbery vegetation with its dull, reddish-brown color stretched away in all directions. Now and then a Hop-scotch Bird fluttered wildly above them, emitting plaintive squawks as it went.

Karl turned his head to gaze at the tiny dome of *Aphrodopolis*, largest city on Venus.

'God,' he muttered, 'even the dome is better than this awful world out here.' He pulled the rubberized fabric of his coat closer about him. 'I'll be glad to get back to Earth again.'

He turned to the slight figure of Antil, the Venusian, 'When are we coming to the ruins, Antil?'

There was no answer and Karl noticed the tear that rolled down the Venusian's green, puckered cheeks. Another glistened in the large, lemur-like eyes; soft, incredibly beautiful eyes.

The Earthman's voice softened. 'Sorry, Antil, I didn't mean to say anything against Venus.'

Antil turned his green face toward Karl, 'It was not that, my friend. Naturally, you would not find much to admire in an alien world. I, however, love Venus, and I weep because I am overcome with its beauty.' The words came fluently but with the inevitable distortion caused by vocal cords unfitted for harsh languages.

'I know it seems incomprehensible to you,' Antil continued, 'but to me Venus is a paradise, a golden land – I cannot express my feelings for it properly.'

'Yet there are some that say only Earthmen can love.' Karl's sympathy was strong and sincere.

The Venusian shook his head sadly. 'There is much besides the capacity to feel emotion that your people deny us.'

Karl changed the subject hurriedly. 'Tell me, Antil, doesn't Venus present a dull aspect even to you? You've been to Earth and should know. How can this eternity of brown and gray compare to the living, warm colors of Earth?'

'It is far more beautiful to me. You forget that my color sense is so enormously different from yours.* How can I explain the beauties, the wealth of color in which this landscape abounds?' He fell silent, lost in the wonders he spoke of, while to the Terrestrial the deadly, melancholy gray remained unchanged.

'Someday,' Antil's voice came as from a person in a dream, 'Venus will once more belong to the Venusians. The Earthlings shall no longer rule us, and the glory of our ancestors shall return to us.'

Karl laughed. 'Come, now, Antil, you speak like a member of the Green Bands, that are giving the government so much trouble. I thought you didn't believe in violence.'

'I don't, Karl,' Antil's eyes were grave and rather frightened, 'but the extremists are gaining power, and I fear the worst. And if – if open rebellion against Earth breaks out, I *must* join them.'

'But you disagree with them.'

'Yes, of course,' he shrugged his shoulders, a gesture he had learned

---

* The Venusian eye can distinguish between two tints, the wavelengths of which differ by as little as five Angstrom units. They see thousands of colors to which Earthmen are blind. –Author.

from Earthmen, 'we can gain nothing by violence. There are five billion of you and scarcely a hundred million of us. You have resources and weapons while we have none. It would be a fool's venture, and even should we win, we might leave such a heritage of hatred that there could never be peace among our two planets.'

'Then why join them?'

'Because I am a Venusian.'

The Earthman burst into laughter again. 'Patriotism, it seems, is as irrational on Venus as on Earth. But come, let us proceed to the ruins of your ancient city. Are we nearly there?'

'Yes,' answered Antil, 'it's a matter of little more than an Earth mile now. Remember, however, that you are to disturb nothing. The ruins of *Ash-taz-zor* are sacred to us, as the sole existing remnant of the time when we, too, were a great race, rather than the degenerate remains of one.'

They walked on in silence, slogging through the soft earth beneath, dodging the writhing roots of the Snaketree, and giving the occasional Tumbling Vines they passed a wide berth.

It was Antil who resumed the conversation.

'Poor Venus.' His quiet, wistful voice was sad. 'Fifty years ago the Earthman came with promises of peace and plenty – and we believed. We showed them the emerald mines and the *juju* weed and their eyes glittered with desire. More and more came, and their arrogance grew. And now—'

'It's too bad, Antil,' Karl said, 'but you really feel too strongly about it.'

'Too strongly! Are we allowed to vote? Have we any representation at all in the Venusian Provincial Congress? Aren't there laws against Venusians riding in the same stratocars as Earthlings, or eating in the same hotel, or living in the same house? Are not all colleges closed to us? Aren't the best and most fertile parts of the planet pre-empted by Earthlings? Are there any rights *at all* that Terrestrials allow us upon our *own* planet?'

'What you say is perfectly true, and I deplore it. But similar conditions once existed on Earth with regard to certain so-called "inferior races", and in time, all those disabilities were removed until today total equality reigns. Remember, too, that the intelligent people of Earth are on your side. Have I, for instance, ever displayed any prejudice against a Venusian?'

'No, Karl, you know you haven't. But how many intelligent men are there? On Earth, it took long and weary millennia, filled with war and suffering, before equality was established. What if Venus refuses to wait those millennia?'

Karl frowned, 'You're right, of course, but you must wait. What else can you do?'

'I don't know – I don't know,' Antil's voice trailed into silence. Suddenly, Karl wished he hadn't started on this trip to the ruins of mysterious *Ash-taz-zor*. The maddeningly monotonous terrain, the just grievances of Antil had served to depress him greatly. He was about to call the whole thing off when the Venusian raised his webbed fingers to point out a mound of earth ahead.

'That's the entrance,' he said; '*Ash-taz-zor* has been buried under the soil for uncounted thousands of years, and only Venusians know of it. You're the first Earthman ever to see it.'

'I shall keep it absolutely secret, Antil. I have promised.'

'Come, then.'

Antil brushed aside the lush vegetation to reveal a narrow entrance between two boulders and beckoned to Karl to follow. Into a narrow, damp corridor they crept. Antil drew from his pouch a small Atomite lamp, which cast its pearly white glow upon walls of dripping stone.

'These corridors and burrows,' he said, 'were dug three centuries ago by our ancestors who considered the city a holy place. Of late, however, we have neglected it. I was the first to visit it in a long, long time. Perhaps that is another sign of our degeneracy.'

For over a hundred yards they walked on straight ahead; then the corridors flared out into a lofty dome. Karl gasped at the view before him. There were the remains of buildings, architectural marvels unrivaled on Earth since the days of Periclean Athens. But all lay in shattered ruins, so that only a hint of the city's magnificence remained.

Antil led the way across the open space and plunged into another burrow that twisted its way for half a mile through soil and rock. Here and there, side-corridors branched off, and once or twice Karl caught glimpses of ruined structures. He would have investigated had not Antil kept him on the path.

Again they emerged, this time before a low, sprawling building constructed of a smooth, green stone. Its right wing was utterly smashed, but the rest seemed scarcely touched.

The Venusian's eyes shone; his slight form straightened with pride. 'This is what corresponds to a modern museum of arts and sciences. In this you shall see the past greatness and culture of Venus.'

With high excitement, Karl entered – the first Earthman ever to see these ancient achievements. The interior, he found, was divided into a series of deep alcoves, branching out from the long central colonnade. The ceiling was one great painting that showed dimly in the light of the Atomite lamp.

Lost in wonder, the Earthman wandered through the alcoves. There was an extraordinary sense of strangeness to the sculptures and paintings about him, an unearthliness that doubled their beauty.

Karl realized that he missed something vital in Venusian art simply because of the lack of common ground between his own culture and theirs, but he could appreciate the technical excellence of the work. Especially, did he admire the color-work of the paintings which went far beyond anything he had ever seen on Earth. Cracked, faded, and scaling though they were, there was a blending and a harmony about them that was superb.

'What wouldn't Michelangelo have given,' he said to Antil, 'to have the marvellous color perception of the Venusian eye.'

Antil inflated his chest with happiness. 'Every race has its own attributes. I have often wished *my* ears could distinguish the slight tones and pitches of sound the way it is said Earthmen can. Perhaps

I would then be able to understand what it is that is so pleasing about your Terrestrial music. As it is, its noise is dreadfully monotonous to me.'

They passed on, and every minute Karl's opinion of Venusian culture mounted higher. There were long, narrow strips of thin metal, bound together, covered with the lines and ovals of Venusian script – thousands upon thousands of them. In them, Karl knew, might lie such secrets as the scientists of Earth would give half their lives to know.

Then, when Antil pointed out a tiny, six-inch-high affair, and said that, according to the inscription, it was some type of atomic converter with an efficiency several times any of the current Terrestrial models, Karl exploded.

'Why don't you reveal these secrets to Earth? If they only knew your accomplishments in ages past, Venusians would occupy a far higher place than they do now.'

'They would make use of our knowledge of former days, yes,' Antil replied bitterly, 'but they would never release their stranglehold on Venus and its people. I hope you are not forgetting your promise of absolute secrecy.'

'No, I'll keep quiet, but I think you're making a mistake.'

'I think not,' Antil turned to leave the alcove, but Karl called to him to wait.

'Aren't we going into this little room here?' he asked.

Antil whirled, eyes staring, 'Room? What room are you talking about? There's no room here.'

Karl's eyebrows shot up in surprise as he mutely pointed out the narrow crack that extended half way up the rear wall.

The Venusian muttered something beneath his breath and fell to his knees, delicate fingers probing the crack.

'Help me, Karl. This door was never meant to be opened, I think. At least there is no record of its being here, and I know the ruins of *Ash-taz-zor* perhaps better than any other of my people.'

The two pushed against the section of the wall, which gave backward with groaning reluctance for a short distance, then yielded suddenly so as to catapult them into the tiny, almost empty cubicle beyond. They regained their feet and stared about.

The Earthman pointed out broken, ragged rust-streaks on the floor, and along the line where door joined wall. 'Your people seem to have sealed this room up pretty effectively. Only the rust of eons broke the bonds. You'd think they had some sort of secret stored here.'

Antil shook his green head. 'There was no evidence of a door last time I was here. However—' he raised the Atomite lamp up high and surveyed the room rapidly, 'there doesn't seem to be anything here, anyway.'

He was right. Aside from a nondescript oblong chest that squatted on six stubby legs, the place contained only unbelievable quantities of dust and the musty, almost suffocating smell of long-shut-up tombs.

Karl approached the chest, tried to move it from the corner where it stood. It didn't budge, but the cover slipped under his pressing fingers.

'The cover's removable, Antil. Look!' He pointed to a shallow compartment within, which contained a square slab of some glassy substance and five six-inch-long cylinders resembling fountain-pens.

Antil shrieked with delight when he saw these objects and for the first time since Karl knew him, lapsed into sibilant Venusian gibberish. He removed the glassy slab and inspected it closely. Karl, his curiosity aroused, did likewise. It was covered with closely-spaced, varicolored dots, but there seemed no reason for Antil's extreme glee.

'What is it, Antil?'

'It is a complete document in our ancient ceremonial language. Up to now we have never had more than disjointed fragments. This is a great find.'

'Can you decipher it?' Karl regarded the object with more respect.

'I think I can. It is a dead language and I know little more than a smattering. You see, it is a color language. Each word is designated by a combination of two, and sometimes three, colored dots. The colors are finely differentiated, though, and a Terrestrial, even if he had the key to the language, would have to use a spectroscope to read it.'

'Can you work on it now?'

'I think so, Karl. The Atomite lamp approximates normal daylight very closely, and I ought to have no trouble with it. However, it may take me quite a time; so perhaps you'd better continue your investigation. There's no danger of your getting lost, provided you remain inside this building.'

Karl left, taking a second Atomite lamp with him, left Antil, the Venusian, bent over the ancient manuscript, deciphering it slowly and painfully.

Two hours passed before the Earthman returned; but when he did, Antil had scarcely changed his position. Yet, now, there was a look of honor on the Venusian's face that had not been there before. The 'color' message lay at his feet, disregarded. The noisy entrance of the Earthman made no impression upon him. As if ossified, he sat in unmoving, staring fright.

Karl jumped to his side. 'Antil, Antil, what's wrong?'

Antil's head turned slowly, as though moving through viscous liquid, and his eyes gazed unseeingly at his friend. Karl grasped the other's thin shoulders and shook him unmercifully.

The Venusian came to his senses. Writhing out of Karl's grasp he sprang to his feet. From the desk in the corner he removed the five cylindrical objects, handling them with a queer sort of reluctance, placing them in his pouch. There, likewise, did he put the slab he had deciphered.

Having done this, he replaced the cover on the chest and motioned Karl out of the room. 'We must go now. Already we have stayed too long.' His voice had an odd, frightened tone about it that made the Earthman uncomfortable.

Silently, they retraced their steps until once more they stood upon the soaked surface of Venus. It was still day, but twilight was near. Karl felt a growing hunger. They would need to hurry if they expected to reach *Aphrodopolis* before the coming of night. Karl turned up the collar of his slicker, pulled his rubberized cap low over his forehead and set out.

Mile after mile passed by and the domed city once more rose upon the gray horizon. The Earthman chewed at damp ham sandwiches, wished fervently for the comfortable dryness of *Aphrodopolis*. Through it all, the normally friendly Venusian maintained a stony silence, vouchsafing not so much as a glance upon his companion.

Karl accepted this philosophically. He had a far higher regard for Venusians than the great majority of Earthmen, but even he experienced a faint disdain for the ultra-emotional character of Antil and his kind. This brooding silence was but a manifestation of feelings that in Karl would perhaps have resulted in no more than a sigh or a frown. Realizing this, Antil's mood scarcely affected him.

Yet the memory of the haunting fright in Antil's eyes aroused a faint unease. It had come after the translation of that queer slab. What secret could have been revealed in that message by those scientific progenitors of the Venusians?

It was with some diffidence that Karl finally persuaded himself to ask, 'What did the slab say, Antil? It must be interesting, I judge, considering that you've taken it with you.'

Antil's reply was simply a sign to hurry, and the Venusian thereupon plunged into the gathering darkness with redoubled speed. Karl was puzzled and rather hurt. He made no further attempt at conversation for the duration of the trip.

When they reached *Aphrodopolis*, however, the Venusian broke his silence. His puckered face, drawn and haggard, turned to Karl with the expression of one who has come to a painful decision.

'Karl,' he said, 'we have been friends, so I wish to give you a bit of friendly advice. You are going to leave for Earth next week. I know your father is high in the councils of the Planetary President. You yourself will probably be a personage of importance in the not-too-distant future. Since this is so, I beg you earnestly to use every atom of your influence to a moderation of Earth's attitude toward Venus. I, in my turn, being a hereditary noble of the largest tribe on Venus, shall do my utmost to repress all attempts at violence.'

The other frowned. 'There seems to be something behind all this. I don't get it at all. What are you trying to say?'

'Just this. Unless conditions are bettered – and soon – Venus will rise in revolt. In that case, I will have no choice but to place my services at her feet, and then Venus will no longer be defenceless.'

These words served only to amuse the Earthman. 'Come, Antil, Your patriotism is admirable, and your grievances justified, but melodrama and chauvinism don't go with me. I am, above all, a realist.'

There was a terrible earnestness in the Venusians voice. 'Believe me, Karl, when I say nothing is more real than what I tell you now. In case of a Venusian revolt, I cannot vouch for Earth's safety.'

'Earth's safety!' The enormity of this stunned Karl.

'Yes,' continued Antil, 'for I may be forced to destroy Earth. There you have it.' With this, he wheeled and plunged into the underbrush on the way back to the little Venusian village outside the great dome.

Five years passed – years of turbulent unrest, and Venus stirred in its sleep like an awakening volcano. The short-sighted Terrestrial masters of *Aphrodopolis*, *Venusia*, and other domed cities cheerfully disregarded all danger signals. When they thought of the little green Venusians at all, it was with a disdainful grimace as if to say, 'Oh, THOSE things!'

But 'those things' were finally pushed beyond endurance, and the nationalistic Green Bands became increasingly vociferous with every passing day. Then, on one gray day, not unlike the gray days preceding, crowds of natives swarmed upon the cities in organized rebellion.

The smaller domes, caught by surprise, succumbed. In rapid succession *New Washington*, *Mount Vulcan*, and *St. Denis* were taken, together with the entire eastern continent. Before the reeling Terrestrials realized what was happening, half of Venus was no longer theirs.

Earth, shocked and stunned by this sudden emergency – which, of course, should have been foreseen – sent arms and supplies to the inhabitants of the remaining beleaguered towns and began to equip a great space fleet for the recovery of the lost territory.

Earth was annoyed but not frightened, knowing that ground lost by surprise could easily be regained at leisure, and that ground not now lost would never be lost. Or such, at least, was the belief.

Imagine, then, the stupefaction of Earth's leaders as no pause came in the Venusian advance. *Venusia City* had been amply stocked with weapons and food; her outer defences were up, the men at their posts. A tiny army of naked, unarmed natives approached and demanded unconditional surrender. *Venusia* refused haughtily, and the messages to Earth were mirthful in their references to the unarmed natives who had become so recklessly flushed with success.

Then, suddenly, no more messages were received, and the natives took over *Venusia*.

The events at *Venusia* were duplicated, over and over again, at what should have been impregnable fortresses. Even *Aphrodopolis* itself, with half a million population, fell to a pitiful five hundred Venusians. This, in spite of the fact that every weapon known to Earth was available to the defenders.

The Terrestrial Government suppressed the facts, and Earth itself remained unsuspecting of the strange events on Venus; but in the inner councils, statesmen frowned as they listened to the strange words of Karl Frantor, son of the Minister of Education.

Jan Heersen, Minister of War, rose in anger at the conclusion of the report.

'Do you wish us to take seriously the random statement of a half-mad Greenie and make our peace with Venus on its own terms? That is definitely and absolutely impossible. What those damned beasts need is the mailed fist. Our fleet will blast them out of the Universe, and it is time that it were done.'

'The blasting may not be so simple, Heersen,' said the gray-haired, elder Frantor, rushing to his son's defence. 'There are many of us who have all along claimed that the Government policy toward the Venusians was all wrong. Who knows what means of attack they have found and what, in revenge, they will do with it?'

'Fairy Tales!' exclaimed Heersen. 'You treat the Greenies as if they were people. They're animals and should be thankful for the benefits of civilization we brought them. Remember, we're treating them much better than some of our own Earth races were treated in our early history, the Red Indians for example.'

Karl Frantor burst in once more in an agitated voice. 'We must investigate, sirs! Antil's threat is too serious to disregard, no matter how silly it sounds – and in the light of the Venusian conquests, it sounds anything but silly. I propose that you send me with Admiral von Blumdorff, as a sort of envoy. Let me get to the bottom of this before we attack them.'

The saturnine Earth President, Jules Debuc, spoke now for the first time. 'Frantor's proposal is reasonable, at least. It shall be done. Are there any objections?'

There were none, though Heersen scowled and snorted angrily. Thus, a week later, Karl Frantor accompanied the space armada of Earth when it set off for the inner planet.

It was a strange Venus that greeted Karl after his five years' absence. It was still its old soaking self, its old dreary, monotony of white and gray, its scattering of domed cities – and yet how different.

Where before the haughty Terrestrials had moved in disdainful splendor among the cowering Venusians, now the natives maintained undisputed sway. *Aphrodopolis* was a native city entirely, and in the office of the former governor sat Antil.

Karl eyed him doubtfully, scarcely knowing what to say. 'I rather thought you might be king-pin,' he managed at length. 'You, the pacifist.'

'The choice was not mine. It was that of circumstance,' Antil replied. 'But you! I did not expect *you* to be your planet's spokesman.'

'It was to me that you made your silly threat years ago, and so it is I who was most pessimistic concerning your rebellion. I come, you see, but not unaccompanied.' His hand motioned vaguely upward, where spaceships lazed motionless and threatening.

'You come to menace me?'

'No! To hear your aims and your terms.'

'That is easily accomplished. Venus demands its independence and we promise friendship, together with free and unrestricted trade.'

'And you expect us to accept all that without a struggle.'

'I hope you do – for Earth's own sake.'

Karl scowled and threw himself back in his chair in annoyance, 'For God's sake, Antil, the time for mysterious hints and bogies has passed. Show your hand. How did you overcome *Aphrodopolis* and the other cities so easily?'

'We were forced to it, Karl. We did not desire it.' Antil's voice was shrill with agitation. 'They would not accept our fair terms of surrender and began to shoot their Tonite guns. We – we had to use the – the weapon. We had to kill most of them afterward – out of mercy.'

'I don't follow. What weapon are you talking about?'

'Do you remember that time in the ruins of *Ash-taz-zor*, Karl? The hidden room; the ancient inscription; the five little rods.'

Karl nodded somberly. 'I thought so, but I wasn't sure.'

'It was a horrible weapon, Karl.' Antil hurried on as if the mere thought of it were not to be endured. 'The ancients discovered it – but never used it. They hid it instead, and why they did not destroy it, I can't imagine. I wish they had destroyed it; I really do. But they didn't and I found it and I must use it – for the good of Venus.'

His voice sank to a whisper, but with a manifest effort he nerved himself to the task of explanation. 'The little harmless rods you saw then, Karl were capable of producing a force field of some unknown nature (the ancients wisely refused to be explicit there) which has the power of disconnecting brain from mind.'

'What?' Karl stared in open-mouthed surprise. 'What *are* you talking about?'

'Why, you must know that the brain is merely the *seat* of the mind, and not the mind itself. The nature of "mind" is a mystery, unknown even to our ancients; but whatever it is, it uses the brain as its intermediary to the world of matter.'

'I see. And your weapon divorces mind from brain – renders mind helpless – a space-pilot without his controls.'

Antil nodded solemnly. 'Have you ever seen a decerebrated animal?' he asked suddenly.

'Why, yes, a dog – in my bio course back in college.'

'Come, then, I will show you a decerebrated human.'

Karl followed the Venusian to an elevator. As he shot downward to the lowest level – the prison level – his mind was in a turmoil. Torn between horror and fury, he had alternate impulses of unreasoning desire to escape and almost insuperable yearnings to slay the Venusian at his side. In a daze, he left the cubicle and followed Antil down a gloomy corridor, winding its way between rows of tiny, barred cells.

'There.' Antil's voice roused Karl as would a sudden stream of cold water. He followed the pointing webbed hand and stared in fascinated revulsion at the human figure revealed.

It was human, undoubtedly, in form – but inhuman, nevertheless. It (Karl could not imagine it as 'he') sat dumbly on the floor, large staring eyes never leaving the blank wall before him. Eyes that were empty of soul, loose lips from which saliva drooled, fingers that moved aimlessly. Nauseated, Karl turned his head hastily.

'He is not exactly decerebrated.' Antil's voice was low. 'Organically, his brain is perfect and unharmed. It is merely disconnected.'

'How does it live, Antil? Why doesn't it die?'

'Because the autonomic system is untouched. Stand him up and he will remain balanced. Push him and he will regain his balance. His heart beats. He breathes. If you put food in his mouth, he will swallow, though he would die of starvation before performing the voluntary act of eating food that has been placed before him. It is life – of a sort; but it were better dead, for the disconnection is permanent.'

'It is horrible – horrible.'

'It is worse than you think. I feel convinced that somewhere within the shell of humanity, the mind, unharmed, still exists. Imprisoned helplessly in a body it cannot control, what must be that mind's torture?'

Karl stiffened suddenly. 'You shan't overcome Earth by sheer unspeakable brutality. It is an unbelievably cruel weapon but no more deadly than any of a dozen of ours. You shall pay for this.'

'Please, Karl, you have no conception of one-millionth of the deadliness of the "Disconnection Field". The Field is independent of space, and perhaps of time, too, so that its range can be extended almost indefinitely. Do you know that it required merely one discharge of the weapon to render every warm-blooded creature in *Aphrodopolis* helpless?' Antil's voice rose tensely. 'Do you know that I am able to bathe ALL EARTH in the Field – to render all your teeming billions the duplicate of that dead-alive hulk in there AT ONE STROKE.'

Karl did not recognize his own voice as he rasped, 'Fiend! Are you the only one who knows the secret of this damnable Field?'

Antil burst into a hollow laugh, 'Yes, Karl, the blame rests on me, alone. Yet killing me will not help. If I die, there are others who know where to find the inscription, others who have not my sympathy for Earth. I am perfectly safe from you, Karl for my death would be the end of your world.'

The Earthman was broken – utterly. Not a fragment of doubt as to the Venusian's power was left within him. 'I yield,' he muttered, 'I yield. What shall I tell my people?'

'Tell them of my terms, and of what I could do if I wished.'

Karl shrank from the Venusian as if his very touch was death, 'I will tell them that.'

'Tell them also, that Venus is not vindictive. We do not wish to use our weapon, for it is too dreadful to use. If they will give us our independence on our own terms, and allow us certain wise precautions against future re-enslavement, we will hurl each of our five guns and the explanatory inscription explaining it into the sun.'

The Terrestrial's voice did not change from its toneless whisper.
'I will tell them that.'

Admiral von Blumdorff was as Prussian as his name, and his military code was the simple one of brute force. So it was quite natural that his reactions to Karl's report were explosive in their sarcastic derision.

'You forsaken fool,' he raved at the young man. 'This is what comes of talk, of words, of tomfoolery. You *dare* come back to me with this old-wives' tale of mysterious weapons, of untold force. Without any proof at all, you accept all that this damned Greenie tells you at absolute face value, and surrender abjectly. Couldn't *you* threaten, couldn't *you* bluff, couldn't *you* lie?'

'He didn't threaten, bluff, or lie,' Karl answered warmly. 'What he said was the gospel truth. If you had seen the decerebrated man—'

'Bah! That is the most inexcusable part of the whole cursed business. To exhibit a lunatic to you, some perfectly normal mental defective, and to say, "This is our weapon!" and for you to accept that without question! Did they do anything but talk? Did they demonstrate the weapon? Did they even show it to you?'

'Naturally not. The weapon is deadly. They're not going to kill a Venusian to satisfy me. As for showing me the weapon – well, would *you* show your ace-in-the-hole to the enemy? Now you answer *me* a few questions. Why is Antil so cocksure of himself? How did he conquer all Venus so easily?'

'I can't explain it I admit, but does that prove that *theirs* is the correct explanation? Anyhow, I'm sick of this talk. We're attacking now, and to hell with theories. I'll face them with Tonite projectiles and you can watch their bluff backfire in their ugly faces.'

'But, Admiral, you *must* communicate my report to the President.'

'I will – after I blow *Aphrodopolis* into kingdom come.'

He turned on the central broadcasting unit. 'Attention, all ships! Battle formation! We dive at *Aphrodopolis* with all Tonites blasting in fifteen minutes.' Then he turned to the orderly. 'Have Captain

Larsen inform *Aphrodopolis* that they have fifteen minutes to hoist the white flag.'

The minutes that ticked by after that were tense and nervewracking for Karl Frantor. He sat in bent silence, head buried in his hands and the faint click of the chronometer at the end of every minute sounded like a thunder-clap in his ears. He counted those clicks in a mumbling whisper – 8-9-10. God!

Only five minutes to certain death! Or *was* it certain death? Was von Blumdorff right? Were the Venusians putting over a daring bluff?

An orderly catapulted into the room and saluted. 'The Greenies have just answered, sir.'

'Well,' von Blumdorff leaned forward eagerly.

'They say, "Urgently request fleet not to attack. If done, we shall not be responsible for the consequences."'

'Is that all?' came the outraged shout.

'Yes, sir.'

The Admiral burst into a sulphurous stream of profanity. 'Why, the infernal gall of them,' he shouted. 'They dare bluff to the very end.'

And as he finished, the fifteenth minute clicked off, and the mighty armada burst into motion. In streaking, orderly flight they shot down toward the cloudy shroud of the second planet. Von Blumdorff grinned in a grisly appreciation of the awesome view spread over the televisor – until the mathematically precise battle formation suddenly broke.

The Admiral stared and rubbed his eyes. The entire further half of the fleet had suddenly gone crazy. First, the ships wavered; then they veered and shot off at mad angles.

Then calls came in from the sane half of the fleet – reports that the left wing had ceased to respond to radio.

The attack on *Aphrodopolis* was immediately disrupted as the order went out to capture the ships that had run amok. Von Blumdorff stamped up and down and tore his hair. Karl Frantor cried out dully, 'It is their weapon,' and lapsed back into his former silence.

From *Aphrodopolis* came no word at all.

For two solid hours the remnant of the Terrestrial fleet battled their own ships. Following the aimless courses of the stricken vessels, they approached and grappled. Bound together then by rigid force, rocket blasts were applied until the insane flight of the others had been balanced and stopped. Fully twenty of the fleet were never caught; some continuing on some orbit about the sun, some shooting off into unknown space, a few crashing down to Venus.

When the remaining ships of the left wing were boarded, the unsuspecting boarding parties stopped short in horror. *Seventy-five staring witless shells of humanity in each ship.* Not a single *human* being left.

Some of the first to enter screamed in horror and fled ina panic. Others merely retched and turned away their eyes. One officer took in the situation at a glance, calmly drew his Atomo-pistol and rayed every decerebrate in sight.

Admiral von Blumdorff was a stricken man; a pitiful, limp wreck of his former proud and blustering self, when he heard the worst. One of the decerebrates was brought to him, and he reeled back.

Karl Frantor gazed at him with red-rimmed eyes, 'Well, Admiral are you satisfied?'

But the Admiral made no answer. He drew his gun, and before anyone could stop him, shot himself through the head.

Once again Karl Frantor stood before a meeting of the President and his Cabinet, before a dispirited, frightened group of men. His report was definite and left no doubt as to the course that must now be followed.

President Debuc stared at the decerebrate brought in as an exhibit. 'We are finished,' he said. 'We must surrender unconditionally, throw ourselves upon their mercy. But someday—' his eyes kindled in retribution.

'No, Mr President!' Karl's voice rang out, 'there shall be no someday. We must give the Venusians their simple due – liberty and independence. Bygones must be bygones – our dead have but paid for the half-century of Venusian slavery. After this, there must be a new order in the Solar System – the birth of a new day.'

The President lowered his head in thought and then raised it again. 'You are right,' he answered with decision; 'there shall be no thought of revenge.'

Two months later the peace treaty was signed and Venus became what it has remained ever since – an independent and sovereign power. And with the signing of the treaty, a whirling speck shot out toward the sun. It was the weapon too dreadful to use.

Black Friar of the Flame

Russell Tymball's eyes were filled with gloomy satisfaction as they gazed at the blackened ruins of what had been a cruiser of the Lhasinuic Fleet a few hours before. The twisted girders, scattered in all directions, were ample witness of the terrific force of the crash.

The pudgy Earthman re-entered his own sleek Strato-rocket and waited. Fingers twisted a long cigar aimlessly for minutes before lighting it. Through the up-drifting smoke, his eyes narrowed and he remained lost in thought.

He came to his feet at the sound of a cautious hail. Two men darted in with one last fugitive glance behind them. The door closed softly, and one stepped immediately to the controls. The desolate desert landscape was far beneath them almost at once, and the silver prow of the Strato-rocket pointed for the ancient metropolis of New York.

Minutes passed before Tymball spoke, 'All clear?'

The man at the controls nodded. 'Not a tyrant ship about. It's quite evident the "Grahul" had not been able to radio for help.'

'You have the dispatch?' the other asked eagerly.

'We found it easily enough. It is unharmed.'

'We also found,' said the second man bitterly, 'one other thing – the last report of Sidi Peller.'

For a moment, Tymball's round face softened and something almost like pain entered his expression. And then it hardened again, 'He died! But it was for Earth, and so it was not death. It was martyrdom!'

Silence, and then sadly, 'Let me see the report, Petri.'

He took the single, folded sheet handed him and held it before him. Slowly, he read aloud:

'On September 4, made successful entry into "Grahul" cruiser of the tyrant fleet. Maintained self in hiding during passage from Pluto to Earth. On September 5, located dispatch in question and assumed possession. Have just shorted rocket jets. Am sealing this report in with dispatch. Long live Earth!'

Tymball's voice was strangely moved as he read the last word. 'The Lhasinuic tyrants have never martyrized a greater man than Sidi Peller. But we'll be repaid, and with interest. The Human Race is not quite decadent yet.'

Petri stared out the window. 'How did Peller do it all? One man – to stow away successfully upon a cruiser of the fleet and in the face of the entire crew to steal the dispatch and wreck the fleet. How was it done? And we'll never know; except for the bare facts in his report.'

'He had his orders,' said Willums, as he locked controls and turned about. 'I carried them to him on Pluto myself. Get the dispatch! Wreck the "Grahul" in the Gobi! He did it! That's all!' He shrugged his shoulders wearily.

The atmosphere of depression deepened until Tymball himself broke it with a growl. 'Forget it. Did you take care of everything at the wreck?'

The other two nodded in unison. Petri's voice was businesslike, 'All traces of Peller were removed and de-atomized. They will never detect the presence of a Human among the wreckage. The document itself was replaced by the prepared copy, and carefully burnt beyond recognition. It was even impregnated with silver salts to the exact amount contained in the official seal of the Tyrant Emperor. I'll stake my head that no Lhasinu will suspect that the crash was no accident or that the dispatch was not destroyed by it.'

'Good! They won't locate the wreck for twenty-four hours at least. It's an airtight job. Let me have the dispatch now.'

He fondled the metalloid container almost with reverence. It was blackened and twisted, still faintly warm. And then with a savage twist of the wrist, he tore off the lid.

The document that he lifted out unrolled with a rustling sound. At the lower left hand corner was the huge silver seal of the Lhasinuic Emperor himself – the tyrant, who from Vega, ruled one third of the Galaxy. It was addressed to the Viceroy of Sol.

The three Earthmen regaided the fine print solemnly. The harshly angular Lhasinuic script glinted redly in the rays of the setting sun.

'Was I right?' whispered Tymball.

'As always,' assented Petri.

Night did not really fall. The sky's black-purple deepened ever so slightly and the stars brightened imperceptibly, but aside from that the stratosphere did not differentiate between the absence and the presence of the sun.

'Have you decided upon the next step?' asked Willums, hesitantly.

'Yes – long ago. I'm going to visit Paul Kane tomorrow, with this,' and he indicated the dispatch.

'*Loara* Paul Kane!' cried Petri.

'That – that *Loarist!*' came simultaneously from Willums.

'The Loarist,' agreed Tymball. 'He is our man!'

'Say rather that he is the lackey of the Lhasinu,' ground out Willums. 'Kane – the head of Loarism – consequently the head of the traitor Humans who preach submission to the Lhasinu.'

'That's right,' Petri was pale but more calm. 'The Lhasinu are our known enemies and are to be met in fair fight – but the Loarists are vermin. Great Space! I would rather throw myself on the mercy of the tyrant Viceroy himself than have anything to do with those snuffling students of ancient history, who praise the ancient glory of Earth and encompass its present degradation.'

'You judge too harshly.' There was the trace of a smile about Tymball's lips. 'I have had dealings with this leader of Loarism before. Oh—' he checked the cries of startled dismay that rose, 'I was quite discreet about it. Even you two didn't know, and, as you see, Kane has not yet betrayed me. I failed in those dealings, but I learned a little bit. Listen to me!'

Petri and Willums edged nearer, and Tymball continued in crisp, matter-of-fact tones, 'The first Galactic Drive of the Lhasinu ended two thousand years ago just after the capture of Earth. Since then, the aggression has not been resumed, and the independent Human Planets of the Galaxy are quite satisfied at the maintenance of the status quo. They are too divided among themselves to welcome a return of the struggle. Loarism itself is only interested in its own survival against the encroachments of newer ways of thought, and it is no great moment to them whether Lhasinu or Human rules Earth as long as Loarism itself prospers. As a matter of fact, we – the Nationalists – are perhaps a greater danger to them in that respect than the Lhasinu.'

Willums smiled grimly, 'I'll say we are.'

'Then, granting that, it is natural that Loarism assume the role of appeasement. Yet, if it were to their interests, they would join us at a second's notice. And this,' he slapped the document before him, 'is what will convince them where their interests lie.'

The other two were silent.

Tymball continued, 'Our time is short. Not more than three years, perhaps not more than two. And yet you know what the chances of success for a rebellion today are.'

'We'd do it,' snarled Petri, and then in a muffled tone, 'if the only Lhasinu we had to deal with were those of Earth.'

'Exactly. But they can call upon Vega for help, and we can call upon no one. No one of the Human Planets would stir in our defense, any more than they did five hundred years ago. And that's why we must have Loarism on our side.'

'And what did Loarism do five hundred years ago during the Bloody Rebellion?' asked Willums, bitter hatred in his voice. 'They abandoned us to save their own precious hides.'

'We are in no position to remember that,' said Tymball. 'We will have their help now – and then, when all is over, our reckoning with them—'

Willums returned to the controls, 'New York in fifteen minutes!' And then, 'But I still don't like it. What can those filthy Loarists *do?* Dried out husks fit for nothing but treason and platitudes!'

'They are the last unifying force of Humanity,' answered Tymball. 'Weak enough now and helpless enough, but Earth's only chance.'

They were slanting downwards now into the thicker, lower atmosphere, and the whistling of the air as it streamed past them became shriller in pitch. Willums fired the braking rockets as they pierced a gray layer of clouds. There upon the horizon was the great diffuse glow of New York City.

'See that our passes are in perfect order for the Lhasinuic inspection and hide the document. They won't search us, anyway.'

Loara Paul Kane leaned back in his ornate chair. The slender fingers of one hand played with the ivory paperweight upon his desk. His eyes avoided those of the smaller, rounder man before him, and his voice, as he spoke, took on solemn inflections.

'I cannot risk shielding you longer, Tymball. I have done so until now because of the bond of common Humanity between us, but—' his voice trailed away.

'But?' prompted Tymball.

Kane's fingers turned his paperweight over and over. 'The Lhasinu are growing harsher this past year. They are almost arrogant.' He looked up suddenly. 'I am not quite a free agent, you know, and haven't the influence and power you seem to think I have.'

His eyes dropped again, and a troubled note entered his voice, 'The Lhasinu suspect. They are beginning to detect the workings of a tightly-knit conspiracy underground, and we cannot afford to become entangled in it.'

'I know. If necessary, you are quite willing to sacrifice us as your predecessor sacrificed the patriots five centuries ago. Once again, Loarism shall play its noble part.'

'What good are your rebellions?' came the weary reply. 'Are the Lhasinu so much more terrible than the oligarchy of Humans that rules Santanni or the dictator that rules Trantor? If the Lhasinu are not Human, they are at least intelligent. Loarism must live at peace with the rulers.'

And now Tymball smiled. There was no humor in it – rather mocking irony, and from his sleeve, he drew forth a small card.

'You think so, do you? Here, read this. It is a reduced photostat of – no, don't touch it – read it as *I* hold it, and—'

His further remarks were drowned in the sudden hoarse cry from the other. Kane's face twisted alarmingly into a mask of horror, as he snatched desperately at the reproduction held out to him.

'Where did you get this?' He scarcely recognized his own voice.

'What odds? I have it, haven't I? And yet it cost the life of a brave man, and a ship of His Reptilian Eminence's navy. I believe you can see that there is no doubt as to the genuineness of this.'

'No – no!' Kane put a shaking hand to his forehead. 'That is the Emperor's signature and seal. It is impossible to forge them.'

'You see, Excellency,' there was sarcasm in the title, 'the renewal of the Galactic Drive is a matter of two years – or three – in the future. The first step in the drive comes within the year – and it is concerning that first step,' his voice took on a poisonous sweetness, 'that this order has been issued to the Viceroy.'

'Let me think a second. Let me think.' Kane dropped into his chair.

'Is there the necessity?' cried Tymball, remorselessly. 'This is nothing but the fulfillment of my prediction of six months ago, to which you would not listen. Earth, as a Human world, is to be destroyed; its population scattered in groups throughout the Lhasinuic portions of the Galaxy; every trace of Human occupancy destroyed.'

'But Earth! Earth, the home of the Human Race; the beginning of our civilization.'

'Exactly! Loarism is dying and the destruction of Earth will kill it. And with Loarism gone, the last unifying force is destroyed, and the human planets, invincible when united, shall be wiped out, one by one, in the Second Galactic Drive. Unless—'

The other's voice was toneless.

'I know what you're going to say.'

'No more than I said before. Humanity must unite, and can do so only about Loarism. It must have a Cause for which to fight, and that Cause must be the liberation of Earth. *I* shall fire the spark here on Earth and *you* must convert the Human portion of the Galaxy into a powder-keg.'

'You wish a Total War – a Galactic Crusade,' Kane spoke in a whisper, 'yet who should know better than I that a Total War has been impossible for these thousand years.' He laughed suddenly, harshly, 'Do you know how weak Loarism is today?'

'Nothing is so weak that it cannot be strengthened. Although Loarism has weakened since its great days during the First Galactic Drive, you still have your organization and your discipline; the best in the Galaxy. And your leaders are, as a whole, capable men, I must say that for you. A thoroughly centralized group of capable men, working desperately, can do much. It *must* do much, for it has no choice.'

'Leave me,' said Kane, brokenly, 'I can do no more now. I must think.' His voice trailed away, but one finger pointed toward the door.

'What good are thoughts?' cried Tymball, irritably. 'We need deeds!' And with that, he left.

The night had been a horrible one for Kane. His face was pale and drawn; his eyes hollow and feverishly brilliant. Yet he spoke loudly and firmly.

'We are allies, Tymball.'

Tymball smiled bleakly, took Kane's outstretched hand for a

moment, and dropped it, 'By necessity, Excellency, only. I am not your friend.'

'Nor I yours. Yet we may work together. My initial orders have gone out and the Central Council will ratify them. In that direction, at least, I anticipate no trouble.'

'How quickly may I expect results?'

'Who knows? Loarism still has its facilities for propaganda. There are still those who will listen from respect and others from fear, and still others from the mere force of the propaganda itself. But who can say? Humanity has slept, and Loarism as well. There is little anti-Lhasinuic feeling, and it will be hard to drum it up out of nothing.'

'Hate is never hard to drum up,' and Tymball's moon-face seemed oddly harsh. 'Emotionalism! Propaganda! Frank and unscrupulous opportunism! And even in its weakened state, Loarism is rich. The masses may be corrupted by words, but those in high places, the important ones, will require a bit of the yellow metal.'

Kane waved a weary hand, 'You preach nothing new. That line of dishonor was Human policy far back in the misty dawn of history when only this poor Earth was Human and even *it* split into waning segments.' Then, bitterly, 'To think that we must return to the tactics of that barbarous age.'

The conspirator shrugged his shoulders cynically, 'Do you know any better?'

'And even so, with all that foulness, we may yet fail.'

'Not if our plans are well-laid.'

Loara Paul Kane rose to his feet and his hands clenched before him, 'Fool! You and your plans! Your subtle, secret, snaky, tortuous plans! Do you think that conspiracy is rebellion, or rebellion, victory? What can you do? You can ferret out information and dig quietly at the roots, but you can't lead a rebellion. I can organize and prepare, but I can't lead a rebellion.'

Tymball winced, 'Preparation – perfect preparation—'

'—is nothing, I tell you. You can have every chemical ingredient necessary, and all the proper conditions, and yet there may be no reaction. In psychology – particularly mob psychology – as in chemistry, one must have a catalyst.'

'What in space do you mean?'

'Can *you* lead a rebellion?' cried Kane. 'A crusade is a war of emotion. Can *you* control the emotions? Why, you conspirator, you could not stand the light of open warfare an instant. Can I lead the rebellion? I, old and a man of peace? Then who is to be the leader, the psychological catalyst, that can take the dull worthless clay of your precious "preparation" and breathe life into it?'

Russell Tymball's jaw muscles quivered, 'Defeatism! So soon?'

The answer was harsh, 'No! Realism!'

There was angry silence and Tymball turned on his heel and left.

It was midnight, ship time, and the evening's festivities were reaching their high point. The grand salon of the superliner *Flaming Nova* was filled with whirling, laughing, glittering figures, growing more convivial as the night wore on.

'This reminds me of the triply-damned affairs my wife makes me attend back on Lacto,' muttered Sammel Maronni to his companion. 'I thought I'd be getting away from some of it, at least out here in hyperspace, but evidently I didn't.' He groaned softly and gazed at the assemblage with a faintly disapproving stare.

Maronni was dressed in the peak of fashion, from purple head-sash to sky-blue sandals, and looked exceedingly uncomfortable. His portly figure was crammed into a brilliantly red and terribly tight tunic and the occasional jerks at his wide belt showed that he was only too conscious of its ill fit.

His companion, taller and slimmer, bore his spotless white uniform with an ease born of long experience, and his imposing figure contrasted strongly with the slightly ridiculous appearance of Sammel Maronni.

The Lactonian exporter was conscious of this fact. 'Blast it, Drake, you've got one fine job here. You dress like a nob and do nothing but look pleasant and answer salutes. How much do you get paid, anyway?'

'Not enough.' Captain Drake lifted one gray eyebrow and stared quizzically at the Lactonian. 'I wish *you* had my job for a week or so. You'd sing mighty small after that. If you think taking care of fat dowager damsels and curly-headed society snobs is a bed of roses, you're welcome to it.' He muttered viciously to himself for a moment and then bowed politely to a bejeweled harridan who simpered past. 'It's what's grayed my hair and furrowed my brow, by Rigel.'

Maronni drew a long *Karen* smoke out of his waist-pouch and lit up luxuriously. He blew a cloud of apple-green smoke into the Captain's face and smiled impishly.

'I've never heard the man yet who didn't knock his own job, even when it was the pushover yours is, you hoary old fraud. Ah, if I'm not mistaken, the gorgeous Ylen Surat is bearing down upon us.'

'Oh, pink devils of Sirius! I'm afraid to look. Is that old hag actually moving in our direction?'

'She certainly is – and aren't you the lucky one! She's one of the richest women on Santanni and a widow, too. The uniform gets them, I suppose. What a pity I'm married.'

Captain Drake twisted his face into a most frightful grimace, 'I hope a chandelier falls on her.'

And with that he turned, his expression metamorphosed into one of bland delight in an instant, 'Why, Madam Surat, I thought I'd never get the chance to see you tonight.'

Ylen Surat, for whom the age of sixty was past experience, giggled girlishly, 'Be still, you old flirt, or you'll make me forget that I've come here to scold you.'

'Nothing is wrong, I hope?' Drake felt a sinking of the heart. He had had previous experience with Madam Surat's complaints. Things usually *were* wrong.

'A great deal is wrong. I've just been told that in fifty hours, we shall land on Earth – if that's the way you pronounce the word.'

'Perfectly correct,' answered Captain Drake, a bit more at ease.

'But it wasn't listed as a stop when we boarded.'

'No, it wasn't. But then, you see, it's quite a routine affair. We leave ten hours after landing.'

'But this is insupportable. It will delay me an entire day. It is necessary for me to reach Santanni within the week, and days are precious. Now, I've never heard of Earth. My guide book,' she extracted a leather-covered volume from her reticule and flipped its pages angrily, 'doesn't even mention the place. No one, I feel sure, has any interest in a halt there. If you persist in wasting the passengers' time in a perfectly useless stop, I shall take it up with the president of the line. I'll remind you that I have some little influence back home.'

Captain Drake sighed inaudibly. It had not been the first time he had been reminded of Ylen Surat's 'little influence.' 'My dear madam, you are right, entirely right, perfectly right – but I can do nothing. All ships on the Sirius, Alpha Centauri, and 61 Cygni lines must stop at Earth. It is by interstellar agreement, and even the president of the line, no matter how stimulated he may be by your argument, could do nothing.'

'Besides,' interrupted Maronni, who thought it time to come to the aid of the beleaguered captain, 'I believe that we have two passengers who are actually headed for Earth.'

'That's right. I had forgotten.' Captain Drake's face brightened a bit. 'There! We have concrete reason for the stop as well.'

'Two passengers out of over fifteen hundred! Reason, indeed!'

'You are unfair,' said Maronni, lightly. 'After all, it was on Earth that the Human race originated. You know that, I suppose?'

Ylen Surat lifted patently false eyebrows, 'Did we?'

The blank look on her face twisted to one of disdain, 'Oh, well, that was all thousands and thousands of years ago. It doesn't matter any more.'

'It does to the Loarists and the two who wish to land are Loarists.'

'Do you mean to say,' sneered the widow, 'that there are still people in this enlightened age who go about studying "our ancient culture". Isn't that what they're always talking about?'

'That's what Filip Sanat is always talking about,' laughed Maronni. 'He gave me a long sermon only a few days ago on that very subject. And it was interesting, too. There was a lot to what he said.'

He nodded lightly and continued, 'He's got a good head on him, that Filip Sanat. He might have made a good scientist or businessman.'

'Speak of meteors and hear them whizz,' said the Captain, suddenly, and nodded his head to the right.

'Well!' gasped Maronni. 'There he is. But – but what in space is he doing *here?*'

Filip Sanat *did* make a rather incongruous picture as he stood framed in the far doorway. His long, dark purple tunic – mark of the Loarist – was a sombre splotch upon an otherwise gay scene. His grave eyes turned toward Maronni and he lifted his hand in immediate recognition.

Astonished dancers made way automatically as he passed, staring at him long and cmiously afterwards. One could hear the wake of whispering that he left in his path. Filip Sanat, however, took no notice of this. Eyes fixed stonily ahead of him and expression stolidly immobile, he reached Captain Drake, Sammel Maronni, and Ylen Surat.

Filip Sanat greeted the two men warmly and then, in response to an introduction, bowed gravely to the widow, who regarded him with surprise and open disdain.

'Pardon me for disturbing you, Captain Drake,' said the young man, in a low tone. 'I only want to know at what time we are leaving hyper-space.'

The captain yanked out a corpulent pocket-chroma. 'An hour from now. Not more.'

'And we shall then be—?'

'Just outside the orbit of Planet IX.'

'That would be Pluto. Sol will then be in sight as we enter normal space?'

'If you're looking in the right direction, it will be toward the prow of the ship.'

'Thank you,' Filip Sanat made as if to depart, but Maronni detained him.

'Hold on there, Filip, you're not going to leave us, are you? I'm sure Madam Surat here is fairly dying to ask you several questions. She has displayed great interest in Loarism.' There was more than the suspicion of a twinkle in the Lactonian's eye.

Filip Sanat turned politely to the widow, who, taken aback for the moment, remained speechless, and then recovered.

'Tell me, young man,' she burst forth, 'are there really still people like you left? —Loarists, I mean.'

Filip Sanat started and stared quite rudely at his questioner, but did not lose his tongue. With calm distinctness, he said, 'There are still people left who try to maintain the culture and way of life of ancient Earth.'

Captain Drake could not forbear a tiny bit of irony, 'Even down to the culture of the Lhasinuic masters?'

Ylen Surat uttered a stifled scream, 'Do you mean to say Earth is a Lhasinuic world? Is it? Is it?' Her voice rose to a frightened squeak.

'Why, certainly,' answered the puzzled captain, sorry that he had spoken. 'Didn't you know?'

'Captain,' there was hysteria in the woman's voice. 'You *must* not land. If you do, I shall make trouble – plenty of trouble. I will *not* be exposed to hordes of those terrible Lhasinu – those awful reptiles from Vega.'

'You need not fear, Madam Surat,' observed Filip Sanat, coldly. 'The vast majority of Earth's population is very much human. It is only the one percent that rules that is Lhasinuic.'

'Oh—' A pause, and then, in a wounded manner, 'Well, I don't think Earth can be so important, if it is not even ruled by Humans. Loarism indeed! Silly waste of time, I call it!'

Sanat's face flushed suddenly, and for a moment he seemed to struggle vainly for speech. When he did speak, it was in an agitated tone, 'You have a very superficial view. The fact that the Lhasinu control Earth has nothing to do with the fundamental problem of Loarism which—'

He turned on his heel and left.

Sammel Maronni drew a long breath as he watched the retreating figure. 'You hit him in a sore spot, Madam Surat, I never saw him squirm away from an argument or an attempt at an explanation in that way before.'

'He's not a bad looking chap,' said Captain Drake.

Maronni chuckled, 'Not by a long shot. We're from the same planet, that young fellow and I. He's a typical Lactonian, like me.'

The widow cleared her throat grumpily, 'Oh, let us change the subject by all means. That person seems to have cast a shadow over the entire room. Why do they wear those awful purple robes? So unstylish!'

Loara Broos Porin glanced up as his young acolyte entered.

'Well?'

'In less than forty-five minutes, Loara Broos.'

And throwing himself into a chair, Sanat leaned a flushed and frowning face upon one balled fist.

Porin regarded the other with an affectionate smile, 'Have you been arguing with Sammel Maronni again, Filip?'

'No, not exactly.' He jerked himself upright. 'But what's the use, Loara Broos? There, on the upper level, are hundreds of Humans, thoughtless, gaily dressed, laughing, frolicking; and there outside is Earth, disregarded. Only we two of the entire ship's company are stopping there to view the world of our ancient days.'

His eyes avoided those of the older man and his voice took on a bitter tinge, 'And once thousands of Humans from every corner of the Galaxy landed on Earth every day. The great days of Loarism are over.'

Loara Broos laughed. One would not have thought such a hearty laugh to be in his spindly figure. 'That is at least the hundredth time I have heard that said by you. Foolish! The day will come when Earth will once more be remembered. People will yet again flock. By the thousands and millions they'll come.'

'No! It is over!'

'Bah! The croaking prophets of doom have said that over and over again through history. They have yet to prove themselves right.'

'This time they will.' Sanat's eyes blazed suddenly, 'Do you know why? It is because Earth is profaned by the reptile conquerors. A woman has just said to me – a vain, stupid, shallow woman – that "I don't think Earth can be so important if it is not even ruled by Humans." She said what billions must say unconsciously, and I hadn't the words to refute her. It was one argument I couldn't answer.'

'And what would your solution be, Filip? Come, have you thought it out?'

'Drive them from Earth! Make it a Human planet once more! We fought them once during the First Galactic Drive two thousand years ago, and stopped them when it seemed as if they might absorb the Galaxy. Let us make a Second Drive of our own and hurl them back to Vega.'

Porin sighed and shook his head, 'You young hothead! There never was a young Loarist who didn't eat fire on the subject. You'll outgrow it. You'll outgrow it.'

'Look, my boy!' Loara Broos arose and grasped the other by the shoulders, 'Man and Lhasinu have intelligence, and are the *only* two intelligent races of the Galaxy. They are brothers in mind and spirit. Be at peace with them. Don't hate; it is the most unreasoning emotion. Instead, strive to understand.'

Filip Sanat stared stonily at the ground and made no indication that he heard. His mentor clicked his tongue in gentle rebuke.

'Well, when you are older, you will understand. Now, forget all this, Filip. Remember that the ambition of every real Laorist is about to be fulfilled for you. In two days, we shall reach Earth and its soil shall be under your feet. Isn't that enough to make you happy? Just think! When you return, you shall be awarded the title "Loara". You shall be one who has visited Earth. The golden sun will be pinned to your shoulder.'

Porin's hand crept to the staring yellow orb upon his own tunic, mute witness of his three previous visits to Earth.

'Loara Filip Sanat,' said Sanat slowly, eyes glistening. 'Loara Filip Sanat. It has a wonderful sound, hasn't it? And only a little ways off.'

'Now, then, you feel better. But come, in a few moments we shall leave hyper-space and we will see Sol.'

Already, even as he spoke, the thick, choking cloak of hyper-stuff that clung so closely to the sides of the *Flaming Nova* was going through those curious changes that marked the beginning of the shift to normal space. The blackness lightened a bit and concentric rings of various shades of gray chased each other across the port-view with gradually hastening speed. It was a weird and beautiful optical illusion that science has never succeeded in explaining.

Porin clicked off the lights in the room, and the two sat quietly in the dark, watching the feeble phosphorescence of the racing ripples as they sped into a blur. Then, with a terrifying silent suddenness, the whole shucture of hyper-stuff seemed to burst apart in a whirling madhouse of brilliant color. And then all was peaceful again. The stars sparkled quietly, against the curved backdrop of normal space.

And up in the corner of the port blazed the brightest spark of the sky with a luminous yellow flame that lit up the faces of the two men into pale, waxen masks. It was Sol!

The birth-star of Man was so distant that it lacked a perceptible disc, yet it was incomparably the brightest object to be seen. In its feeble yellow light, the two remained in quiet thought, and Filip Sanat grew calmer.

In two days, the *Flaming Nova* landed on Earth.

Filip Sanat forgot the delicious thrill that had seized him at the moment when his sandals first came into contact with the firm green sod of Earth, when he caught his first glimpse of a Lhasinuic official.

They seemed actually *human* – or humanoid, at least.

At first glance, the predominantly Manlike characteristics drowned out all else. The body plan differed in no essential from Man's. The four-limbed, bipedal body; the middling-well proportioned arms and legs; the well-defined neck, were all astonishingly in evidence. It was only after a few minutes that the smaller details marking the difference between the two races were noticed at all.

Chief of these were the scales covering the head and a thick line down the backbone, halfway to the hips. The face itself, with its flat, broad, thinly-scaled nose and lidless eyes was rather repulsive, but in no way bestial. Their clothes were few and simple, and their speech quite pleasant to the ear. And, what was most important, there was no masking the intelligence that showed forth in their dark, luminous eyes.

Porin noted Sanat's surprise at this first glimpse of the Vegan reptiles with every sign of satisfaction.

'You see,' he remarked, 'their appearance is not at all monstrous. Why should hate exist between Human and Lhasinu, then?'

Sanat didn't answer. Of course, his old friend was right. The word 'Lhasinu' had so long been coupled with the words 'alien' and 'monster' in his mind, that against all knowledge and reason, he had subconsciously expected to see some weird life-form.

Yet, overlying the foolish feeling this realization induced was the same haunting hate that clung closely to him, growing to fury as they passed inspection by an over-bearing English-speaking Lhasinu.

The next morning, the two left for New York, the largest city of the planet. In the historic lore of the unbelievably ancient metropolis, Sanat forgot for a day the troubles of the Galaxy outside. It was a great moment for him when he finally stood before a towering structure and said to himself, '*This* is the Memorial.'

The Memorial was Earth's greatest monument, dedicated to the birthplace of the Human race, and this was Wednesday, the day of the week when two men 'guarded the Flame.' Two men, alone in the Memorial, watched over the flickering yellow fire that symbolized Human courage and Human initiative – and Porin had already arranged that the choice should fall that day upon himself and Sanat, as being two newly-arrived Loarists.

And so, in the fading twilight, the two sat alone in the spacious Flame Room of the Memorial. In the murky semi-darkness, lit only by the fitful glare of a dancing yellow flame, a quiet peace descended upon them.

There was something about the brooding aura of the place that wiped all mental disturbance clean away. There was something about the wavering shadows as they weaved through the pillars of the long colonnade on either side, that cast a hypnotic spell

Gradually, he fell into a half doze, and out of sleepy eyes regarded the Flame intently, until it became a living being of light weaving a dim, silent figure beside him.

But tiny sounds are sufficient to disturb a reverie, especially when contrasted with a hitherto deep silence. Sanat stiffened suddenly, and grasped Porin's elbow in a fierce grip.

'Listen,' he hissed the warning quietly.

Porin started violently out of a peaceful day-dream, regarded his young companion with uneasy intentness, then, without a word, trumpeted one ear. The silence was thicker than ever – also a tangible cloak. Then the faintest possible scraping of feet upon marble, far off. A low whisper, down at the limits of audibility, and then silence again.

'What is it?' he asked bewilderedly of Sanat, who had already risen to his feet.

'Lhasinu!' ground out Sanat, face a mask of hate-filled indignation.

'Impossible!' Porin strove to keep his voice coldly steady, but it trembled in spite of itself. 'It would be an unheard-of event. We are just imagining things, now. Our nerves are rubbed raw by this silence, that is all. Perhaps it is some official of the Memorial.'

'After sunset, on Wednesday?' came Sanat's strident voice. 'That is as illegal as the entrance of Lhasinuic lizards, and far more unlikely. It is my duty as a Guardian of the Flame to investigate this.'

He made as if to walk toward the shadowed door, and Porin caught his wrist fearfully, 'Don't Filip. Let us forget this until sunrise.

One can never tell what will happen. What can you do, even supposing that Lhasinu have entered the Memorial? If you—'

But Sanat was no longer listening. Roughly, he shook off the other's desperate grasp, 'Stay here! The Flame must be guarded. I shall be back soon.'

He was already half way across the wide, marble-floored hall. Cautiously, he approached the glass-paned door to the dark, twisting staircase that circled its way upwards through the twilit gloom into the desert recesses of the tower.

Slipping off his sandals, he crept up the stairs, casting one last look back toward the softly luminous Flame, and toward the nervous, frightened figure standing beside it.

The two Lhasinu stared about them in the pearly light of the Atomo lamp.

'Dreary old place,' said Threg Ban Sola. His wrist camera clicked three times. 'Take down a few of those books on the walls. They'll serve as additional proof.'

'Do you think we ought to,' asked Cor Wen Hasta. 'These Human apes may miss them.'

'Let them!' came the cool response. 'What can they do? Here, sit down!' He flicked a hasty glance upon his chronometer. 'We'll get fifty credits for every minute we stay, so we might as well pile up enough to last us for a while.'

'Pirat For is a fool. What made him think we wouldn't take the bet?'

'I think,' said Ban Sola, 'he's heard about the soldier torn to pieces last year for looting a European museum. The Humans didn't like it, though Loarism is filthy rich, Vega knows. The Humans were disciplined, of course, but the soldier was dead. Anyway, what Pirat For doesn't know is that the Memorial is deserted Wednesdays. This is going to cost him money.'

'Fifty credits a minute. And it's been seven minutes now.'

'Three hundred and fifty credits. Sit down. We'll play a game of cards and watch our money mount.'

Threg Ban Sola drew forth a worn pack of cards from his pouch which, though they were typically and essentially Lhasinuic, bore unmistakable traces of their Human derivation.

'Put the Atomo-light on the table and I'll sit between it and the window,' he continued peremptorily, shuffling the cards as he spoke. 'Hah! I'll warrant no Lhasinu ever gamed in such an atmosphere. Why, it will triple the zest of the play.'

Cor Wen Hasta seated himself, and then rose again, 'Did you hear anything?' He stared into the shadows beyond the half-open door.

'No,' Ban Sola frowned and continued shuffling. 'You're not getting nervous, are you?'

'Of course not. Still, if they *were* to catch us here in this blasted tower, it might not be pleasant.'

'Not a chance. The shadows are making you jumpy.' He dealt the hands.

'Do you know,' said Wen Hasta, studying his cards carefully, 'it wouldn't be so nice if the Viceroy were to get wind of this, either. I imagine he wouldn't deal lightly with offenders of the Loarists, as a matter of policy. Back on Sirius, where I served before I was shifted, the scum—'

'Scum, all right,' grunted Ban Sola. 'They breed like flies and fight each other like mad bulls. Look at the creatures!' He turned his cards downward and grew argumentative. 'I mean, look at them scientifically and impartially. What are they? Only mammals! Mammals that can think, in a way; but mammals just the same. That's all.'

'I know. Did you ever visit one of the Human worlds?'

Ban Sola smiled, 'I may, pretty soon.'

'Furlough?' Wen Hasta registered polite astonishment.

'Furlough, my scales. With my ship! And with guns shooting!'

'What do you mean?' There was a sudden glint in Wen Hasta's eyes.

Ban Sola's grin grew mysterious. 'This isn't supposed to be known, even among us officers, but you know how things leak out.'

Wen Hasta nodded, 'I know.' Both had lowered their voices instinctively.

'Well. The Second Drive will be on, now, any time.'

'No!'

'Fact! And we're starting right here. By Vega, the Viceregal Palace is buzzing with nothing else. Some of the officers have even started a lottery on the exact date of the first move. I've got a hundred credits at twenty to one myself. But then, I drew only to the nearest week. You can get a hundred and fifty to one, if you're nervy enough to pick a particular day.'

'But why here on this Galaxy-forsaken planet?'

'Strategy on the part of the Home Office.' Ban Sola leaned forward. 'The position we're in now has us facing a numerically superior enemy hopelessly divided amongst itself. If we can keep them so, we can take them over one by one. The Human Worlds would just naturally rather cut their own throats than co-operate with each other.'

Wen Hasta grinned agreement, 'That's typical mammalian behavior for you. Evolution must have laughed when she gave a brain to an ape.'

'But Earth has particular significance. It's the center of Loarism, because the Humans originated here. It corresponds to our own Vegan system.'

'Do you mean that? But you couldn't! This little two-by-four flyspeck?'

'That's what they say. I wasn't here at the time, so I wouldn't know. But anyway, if we can destroy Earth, we can destroy Loarism, which is centered here. It was Loarism, the historians say, that united the Worlds against us at the end of the First Drive. No Loarism; the last fear of enemy unification is gone; and victory is easy.'

'Damned clever! How are we going to go about it?'

'Well, the word is that they're going to pack up every last Human on Earth and scatter them through the subject worlds. Then we can remove everything else on Earth that smells of the Mammals and make it an entirely Lhasinuic world.'

'But when?'

'We don't know; hence the lottery. But no one has placed his bet at a period more than two years in the future.'

'Hurrah for Vega! I'll give you two to one I riddle a Human cruiser before you do, when the time comes.'

'Done,' cried Ban Sola. 'I'll put up fifty credits.'

They rose to touch fists in token and Wen Hasta grinned at his chronometer, 'Another minute and we'll have an even thousand credits coming to us. Poor Pirat For. He'll groan. Let's go now; more would be extortionate.'

There was low laughter as the two Lhasinu left, long cloaks swishing softly behind them. They did not notice the slightly darker shadow hugging the wall at the head of the stairs, though they almost brushed it as they passed. Nor did they sense the burning eyes focused upon them as they descended noiselessly.

Loara Broos Porin jerked to his feet with a sob of relief as he saw the figure of Filip Sanat stumble across the hall toward him. He ran to him eagerly, grasping both hands tightly.

'What kept you, Filip? You don't know what wild thoughts have passed through my head this past hour. If you had been gone another five minutes, I would have gone mad for sheer suspense and uncertainty. But what's wrong?'

It took several moments for Loara Broos' wild relief to subside sufficiently to note the other's trembling hands, his disheveled hair, his feverishly-glinting eyes; but when it did, all his fears returned.

He watched Sanat in dismay, scarcely daring to press his question for fear of the answer. But Sanat needed no urging. In short, jerky sentences he related the conversation he had overheard and his last words trailed into a despairing silence.

Loara Broos' pallor was almost frightening, and twice he tried to talk with no success other than a few hoarse gasps. Then, finally, 'But it is the death of Loarism! What is to be done?'

Filip Sanat laughed, as men laugh when they are at last convinced that nothing remains to laugh at. 'What *can* be done? Can we inform the Central Council? You know only too well how helpless they are. The various Human governments? You can imagine how effective *those* divided fools would be.'

'But it can't be true! It simply can't be!'

Sanat remained silent for seconds, and then his face twisted agonizedly and in a voice thick with passion, he shouted, 'I won't have it! Do you hear? It shan't be! I'll stop it!'

It was easy to see that he had lost control of himself; that wild emotion was driving him. Porin, large drops of perspiration on his brow, grasped him about the waist, 'Sit down, Filip, sit down! Are you going crazy?'

'No!' With a sudden push, he sent Porin stumbling backwards into a sitting position, while the Flame wavered and flickered madly in the rush of air, 'I'm going sane. The time for idealism and compromise and subservience is gone! The time for force has come! We will fight and, by Space, we will win!'

He was leaving the room at a dead run.

Porin limped after, 'Filip! Filip!' He stopped at the doorway in frightened despair: He could go no further. Though the Heavens fell, someone must guard the Flame.

But – but what was Filip Sanat going to do? And through Porin's tortured mind flickered visions of a certain night, five hundred years before, when a careless word, a blow, a shot, had lit a fire over Earth that was finally drowned in Human blood.

Loara Paul Kane was alone that night. The inner office was empty; the dim, blue light upon the severely simple desk the only illumination in the room. His thin face was bathed in the ghastly light, and his chin buried musingly between his hands.

And then there was a crashing interruption as the door was flung open and a disheveled Russell Tymball knocked off the restraining hands of half a dozen men and catapulted in. Kane whirled in dismay at the intrusion and one hand flew up to his throat as his eyes widened in apprehension. His face was one startled question.

Tymball waved his arm in a quieting gesture. 'It's all right. Just let me catch my breath.' He wheezed a bit and seated himself gently before continuing, 'Your catalyst has turned up, Loara Paul – and guess where. Here on Earth! Here in New York! Not half a mile from where we're sitting now!'

Loara Paul Kane eyed Tymball narrowly, 'Are you mad?'

'Not so you can notice it. I'll tell you about it, if you don't mind turning on a light or two. You look like a ghost in the blue.' The room whitened under the glare of Atomos, and Tymball continued, 'Femi and I were returning from the meeting. We were passing the Memorial when it happened, and you can thank Fate for the lucky coincidence that led us to the right spot at the right moment.

'As we passed, a figure shot out the side entrance, jumped on the marble steps in front, and shouted, "Men of Earth!" Everyone turned to look – you know how filled Memorial Sector is at eleven – and inside of two seconds, he had a crowd.'

'Who was the speaker, and what was he doing inside the Memorial? This is Wednesday night, you know.'

'Why,' Tymball paused to consider, 'now that you mention it, he must have been one of the two Guardians. He was a Loarist – you couldn't mistake the tunic. He wasn't Terrestrial, either!'

'Did he wear the yellow orb?'

'No.'

'Then I know who he was. He's Porin's young friend. Go ahead.'

'There he stood!' Tymball was warming to his task. 'He was some twenty feet above street level. You have no idea what an impressive figure he made with the glare of the Luxites lighting his face. He was handsome, but not in an athletic, brawny way. He was the ascetic type, if you know what I mean. Pale, thin face, burning eyes, long, brown hair.

'And when he spoke! It's no use describing it; in order to appreciate it really, you would have to hear him. He began telling the crowd of the Lhasinuic designs; shouting what *I* had been whispering. Evidently, he had gotten them from a good source, for he went into details – and how he put them! He made them sound real and frightening. He frightened *me* with them; had me standing there scared blue at what he was saying; and as for the crowd, after the second sentence, they were hypnotized. Every one of them had had "Lhasinuic Menace" drilled into them over and over again, but this was the first time they listened – actually *listened*.

'Then he began damning the Lhasinu. He rang the changes on their bestiality, their perfidy, their criminality – only he had a vocabulary that raked them into the lowest mud of a Venusian ocean. And every time he let loose with an epithet, the crowd stood upon its hind legs and let out a roar. It began to sound like a catechism. "Shall we allow this to go on?" cried he. "Never!" yelled the crowd. "Must we yield?" "Never!" "Shall we resist?" "To the end!" "Down with the Lhasinu," he shouted. "Kill them!" they howled.

'I howled as loud as any of them – forgot myself entirely.

'I don't know how long it lasted before Lhasinuic guards began closing in. The crowd turned on them, with the Loarist urging them on. Did you ever hear a mob yell for blood? No? It's the most awful sound you can imagine. The guards thought so, too, for one look at what was before them made them turn and run for their lives, in spite of the fact that they were armed. The mob had grown into a matter of thousands and thousands by then.

'But in two minutes, the alarm siren sounded – for the first time in a hundred years. I came to my senses at last and made for the Loarist, who had not stopped his tirade a moment. It was plain that we couldn't let him fall into the hands of the Lhasinu.

'The rest is pretty much of a mixup. Squadrons of motorized police were charging down on us, but somehow, Femi and I managed between the two of us to grab the Loarist, slip out, and bring him here. I have him in the outer room, gagged and tied, to keep him quiet.'

During all the last half of the narrative, Kane had paced the floor nervously, pausing every once in a while in deep consideration. Little fleeks of blood appeared on his lower lip.

'You don't think,' he asked, 'that the riot will get out of hand? A premature explosion—'

Tymball shook his head vigorously, 'They're mopping up already. Once the young fellow disappearnd, the crowd lost its spirit, anyway.'

'There will be many killed or hurt, but— Well, bring in the young firebrand.' Kane seated himself behind his desk and composed his face into a semblance of tranquility.

Filip Sanat was in sad shape as he kneeled before his superior. His tunic was in tatters, and his face scratched and bloody, but the fire of determination shone as brilliantly as ever in his fierce eyes. Russell Tymball regarded him breathlessly as though the previous hour's magic still lingered.

Kane extended his arm gently, 'I have heard of your wild escapade, my boy. What was it that impelled you to do so foolish an act? It might very well have cost you your life, to say nothing of the lives of thousands of others.'

For the second time that night, Sanat repeated the conversation he had overheard – dramatically and in the minutest detail.

'Just so, just so,' said Kane, with a grim smile, upon the conclusion of the tale, 'and did you think we knew nothing of this? For a long time we have been preparing against this danger, and you have come near to upsetting all our carefully laid plans. By your premature appeal, you might have worked irreparable harm to our cause.'

Filip Sanat reddened, 'Pardon my inexperienced enthusiasm—'

'Exactly,' exclaimed Kane. 'Yet, properly directed, you might be of great aid to us. Your oratory and youthful fire might work wonders if well managed. Would you be willing to dedicate yourself to the task?'

Sanat's eyes flashed, 'Need you ask?'

Loara Paul Kane laughed and cast a jubilant side-glance at Russell Tymball, 'You'll do. In two days, you shall leave for the outer stars. With you, will go several of my own men. And now, you are tired. You will be taken to where you may wash and treat your cuts. Then, you had better sleep, for you shall need your strength in the days to come.'

'But – but Loara Broos Porin – my companion at the Flame?'

'I shall send a messenger to the Memorial immediately. He will tell Loara Broos of your safety and serve as the second Guardian for the remainder of the night. Go, now!'

But even as Sanat, relieved and deliriously happy, rose to go, Russell Tymball leaped from his chair and grasped the older Loarist's wrist in a convulsive grip.

'Great Space! Listen!'

The shrill, keening whine that pierced to the inner sanctum of Kane's offices told its own story. Kane's face turned haggard.

'It's martial law!'

Tymball's very lips had turned bloodless, 'We lost out, after all. They're using tonight's disturbance to strike the first blow. They're after Sanat, and they'll have him. A mouse couldn't get through the cordon they're going to throw about the city now.'

'But they mustn't have him.' Kane's eyes glittered. 'We'll take him to the Memorial by the Passageway. They won't dare violate the Memorial.'

'They have done it once already,' came Sanat's impassioned cry. 'I won't hide from the lizards. Let us fight.'

'Quiet,' said Kane, 'and follow silently.'

A panel in the wall had slid aside, and toward it Kane motioned.

And as the panel closed noiselessly behind them, leaving them in the cold glow of a pocket Atomo lamp, Tymball muttered softly, 'If they are ready, even the Memorial will yield no protection.'

New York was in ferment. The Lhasinuic garrison had mustered its full strength and placed it in a state of siege. No one might enter. No one might leave. Through the key avenues, rolled the ground cars of the army, while overhead poised the Strata-cars that guarded the airways.

The Human population stirred restlessly. They percolated through the streets, gathering in little knots that broke up at the approach of the Lhasinu. The spell of Sanat lingered, and here and there frowning men exchanged angry whispers.

The atmosphere crackled with tension.

The Viceroy of New York realized that as he sat behind his desk in the Palace, which raised its spires upon Washington Heights. He stared out the window at the Hudson River, flowing darkly beneath, and addressed the uniformed Lhasinu before him.

'There must be positive action, Captain. You are right in that. And yet, if possible, an outright break must be avoided. We are woefully undermanned and we haven't more than five third-rate war-vessels on the entire planet.'

'It is not our strength but their own fear that keeps them help-less, Excellency. Their spirit has been thoroughly broken in these last centuries. The rabble would break before a single unit of Guards-men. That is precisely the reason why we must strike hard now. The population has reared and they must feel the whip immediately. The Second Drive may as well begin tonight.'

'Yes,' the Viceroy grimaced wryly. 'We are caught off-stride, but the – er – rabble-rouser must be made an example of. You have him, of course.'

The captain smiled grimly, 'No. The Human dog had powerful friends. He is a Loarist, you know. Kane—'

'Is Kane standing against us?' Two red spots burnt over the Vice-roy's eyes. 'The fool presumes! The troops are to arrest the rebel in spite of him – and him, too, if he objects.'

'Excellency!' the captain's voice rang metallically. 'We have reason to believe the rebel may be skulking in the Memorial.'

The Viceroy half-rose to his feet. He scowled in indecision and seated himself once more, 'The Memorial! That presents difficulties!'

'Not necessarily!'

'There are some things those Humans won't stand.' His voice trailed off uncertainly.

The Captain spoke decisively, 'The nettle seized firmly does not sting. Quickly done – a criminal could be dragged from the Hall of the Flame itself – and we kill Loarism at a stroke. There could be no struggle after that supreme defiance.'

'By Vega! Blast me, if you're not right. Good! Storm the Memorial!'

The Captain bowed stiffly, turned on his heel, and left the Palace.

Filip Sanat re-entered the Hall of Flame, thin face set angrily, 'The entire Sector is patrolled by the lizards. All avenues of approach to the Memorial have been shut off.'

Russell Tymball rubbed his jaw, 'Oh, they're not fools. They've treed us, and the Memorial won't stop them. As a matter of fact, they may have decided to make this The Day.'

Filip frowned and his voice was thickly furious, 'And we're to wait here, are we? Better to die fighting, than to die hiding.'

'Better not to die at all, Filip,' responded Tymball quietly.

There was a moment of silence. Loara Paul Kane sat staring at his fingers.

Finally, he said, 'If you were to give the signal to strike now, Tymball, how long could you hold out?'

'Until Lhasinuic reinforcements could arrive in sufficient numbers to crush us. The Terrestrial garrison, including the entire Solar Patrol, is not enough to stop us. Without outside help, we can fight effectively for six months at the very least. Unfortunately it's out of the question.' His composure was unruffled.

'Why is it out of the question?'

And his face reddened suddenly, as he sprang angrily to his feet, 'Because you can't just push buttons. The Lhasinu are weak. My men know that, but Earth doesn't. The lizards have one weapon, fear! We can't defeat them, unless the populace is with us, at least passively.' His mouth twisted, 'You don't know the practical difficulties involved. Ten years, now, I've been planning, working, trying. I have an army; and a respectable fleet in the Appalachians. I could set the wheels in motion in all five continents simultaneously. But what good would it do? It would be useless. If I had New York, now – if I were able to prove to the rest of Earth that the Lhasinu were not invincible.'

'If I could banish fear from the hearts of Humans?' said Kane softly.

'I would have New York by dawn. But it would take a miracle.'

'Perhaps! Do you think you can get through the cordon and reach your men?'

'I could if I had to. What are you going to do?'

'You will know when it happens.' Kane was smiling fiercely. 'And when it does happen, strike!'

There was a Tonite gun in Tymball's hand suddenly, as he backed away. His plump face was not at all gentle, 'I'll take a chance, Kane. Goodbye!'

The captain strode up the deserted marble steps of the Memorial arrogantly. He was flanked on each side by an armed adjutant.

He paused an instant before the huge double-door that loomed up before him and stared at the slender pillars that soared gracefully upwards at its sides.

There was faint sarcasm in his smile, 'Impressive, all this, isn't it?'

'Yes, Captain!' was the double reply.

'And mysteriously dark, too, except for the dim yellow of their Flame. You see its light?' He pointed toward the stained glass of the bottom windows, which glinted flickeringly.

'Yes, Captain!'

'It's dark, and mysterious, and impressive – and it is about to fall in ruins.' He laughed, and suddenly brought the butt end of his saber down upon the metal carvings on the door in a clanging salvo.

It echoed through the emptiness within and sounded hollowly in the night, but there was no answer.

The adjutant at his left raised his televisor to his ear and caught the faint words issuing therefrom. He saluted, 'Captain, the Humans are crowding into the sector.'

The captain sneered, 'Let them! Order the guns placed in

readiness and aimed along the avenues. Any Human attempting to pass the cordon is to be rayed mercilessly.'

His barked command was murmured into the televisor, and a hundred yards beyond, Lhasinuic Guardsmen put guns in order and aimed them carefully. A low, inchoate murmur went up – a murmur of fear. Men pressed back.

'If the door does not open,' said the captain, grimly, 'it is to be broken down.' He raised his saber again, and again there was the thunder of metal on metal.

Slowly, noiselessly, the door yawned wide, and the captain recognized the stem, purple-clad figure that stood before him.

'Who disturbs the Memorial on the night of the Guarding of the Flame?' demanded Loara Paul Kane solemnly.

'Very dramatic, Kane. Stand aside!'

'Back!' The words rang out loudly and clearly. 'The Memorial may not be approached by the Lhasinu.'

'Yield us our prisoner, and we leave. Refuse, and we will take him by force.'

'The Memorial yields no prisoner. It is inviolate. You may not enter.'

'Make way!'

'Stand back!'

The Lhasinu growled throatily and became aware of a dim roaring. The streets about him were empty, but a block away in every direction was the thin line of Lhasinuic troops, stationed at their guns, and beyond were the Humans. They were massed in noisy thickness and the whites of their faces shone palely in the Chromolights.

'What,' gritted the captain to himself, 'do the scum yet snarl?' His tough skin ridged at the jaws and the scales upon his head uptilted sharply. He turned to the adjutant with the televisor. 'Order a round over their heads.'

The night was split in two by the purple blasts of energy and the Lhasinu laughed aloud at the silence that followed.

He turned to Kane, who remained standing upon the threshold.

'So you see that if you expect help from your people, you will be disappointed. The next round will be aimed at head level. If you think that bluff, try me!'

Teeth clicked together sharply, 'Make way!' A Tonite was leveled in his hand, and thumb was firm upon the trigger.

Loara Paul Kane retreated slowly, eyes upon the gun. The captain followed. And as he did so, the inner door of the anteroom swung open and the Hall of the Flame stood revealed. In the sudden draft, the Flame staggered, and at the sight of it, there came a huge shout from the distant spectators.

Kane turned toward it, face raised upwards. The motion of one of his hands was all but imperceptible.

And the Flame suddenly changed. It steadied and roared up to the vaulted ceiling, a blazing shaft fifty feet high. Loara Paul Kane's hand moved again, and as it did so, the Flame turned carmine. The color deepened and the crimson light of that flaming pillar streamed out into the city and turned the Memorial's windows into staring, bloody eyes.

Long seconds passed, while the captain froze in bewilderment; while the distant mass of Humanity fell into awed silence.

And then there was a confused murmur, which strengthened and grew and split itself into one vast shout.

'*Down with the Lhasinu!*'

There was the purple flash of a Tonite from somewhere high above, and the captain came to life an instant too late. Caught squarely, he bent slowly to his death; cold, reptilian face a mask of contempt to the last.

Russell Tymball brought down his gun and smiled sardonically, 'A perfect target against the Flame. Good for Kane! The changing of the Flame was just the emotion-stirring thing we needed. Let's go!'

From the roof of Kane's dwelling he aimed down upon the Lhasinu below. And as he did, all Hell erupted. Men mushroomed from the very ground, it seemed, weapons in hand. Tonites blazed from every side, before the startled Lhasinu could spring to their triggers.

And when they did so, it was too late, for the mob, white-hot with flaring rage, broke its bounds. Someone shrieked, 'Kill the lizards!' and the cry was taken up in one roaring ululation that swelled to the sky.

Like a many-headed monster, the stream of Humanity surged forward, weaponless. Hundreds withered under the belated fury of the defending guns, and tens of thousands scrambled over the corpses, charging to the very muzzles.

The Lhasinu never wavered. Their ranks thinned steadily under the deadly sharp-shooting of the Tymballists, and those that remained were caught by the Human flood that surged over them and tore them to horrible death.

The Memorial sector gleamed in the crimson of the bloody Flame and echoed to the agony of the dying, and the shrieking fury of the triumphant.

It was the first battle of the Great Rebellion, but it was not really a battle, or even madness. It was concentrated anarchy.

Throughout the city, from the tip of Long Island to the mid-Jersey flatlands, rebels sprang from nowhere and Lhasinu went to their death. And as quickly as Tymball's orders spread to raise the snipers, so did the news of the changing of the Flame speed from mouth to mouth and grow in the telling. All New York heaved, and poured its separate lives into the single giant crucible of the 'mob.'

It was uncontrollable, unanswerable, irresistible. The Tymballists followed helplessly where it led, all efforts at direction hopeless from the start.

Like a mighty river, it lashed its way through the metropolis, and where it passed no living Lhasinu remained.

The sun of that fateful morning arose to find the masters of Earth occupying a shrinking circle in upper Manhattan. With the cool courage of born soldiers, they linked arms and withstood the charging, shrieking millions. Slowly, they backed away; each building a skirmish; each block a desperate battle, They split into isolated groups; defending first a building, and then its upper stories, and finally its roof.

With the noonday sun boiling down, only the Palace itself remained. Its last desperate stand held the Humans at bay. The withering circle of fire about it paved the grounds with blackened bodies. The Viceroy himself from his throneroom directed the defense; his own hand upon the butt of a semi-portable.

And then, when the mob had finally come to a pause, Tymball seized his opportunity and took the lead. Heavy guns clanked to the front. Atomos and delta-rays, from the rebel stock and from the stores captured the previous night, pointed their death-laden muzzles at the Palace.

Gun answered gun, and the first organized battle of machines flared into desperate fury. Tymball was an omnipresent figure, shouting, directing, leaping from gun-emplacement to gun-emplacement, firing his own hand Tonite defiantly at the Palace.

Under a barrage of the heaviest fire, the Humans charged once more and pierced to the walls as the defenders fell back. An Atomo projectile smashed its way into the central tower and there was a sudden inferno of fire.

That blaze was the funeral pyre of the last of the Lhasinu in New York. The blackening walls of the palace crumbled in, in one vast crash; but to the very last, room blazing about him, face horribly cut, the Viceroy stood his ground, aiming into the thick of the besieging force. And when his semi-portable expended the last dregs of its power and expired, he heaved it out the window in a last futile gesture of defiance, and plunged into the burning Hell at his back.

Above the Palace grounds at sunset, with a yet-roaring furnace as the background, there floated the green flag of independent Earth.

New York was once more Human.

Russell Tymball was a sorry figure when he entered the Memorial once more that night. Clothes in tatters, and bloody from head to foot from the undressed cut on his cheek, he surveyed the carnage about him with sated eyes.

Volunteer squads, occupied in removing the dead and tending to the wounded had not yet succeeded in making more than a dent in the deadly work of the rebellion.

The Memorial was an improvised hospital. There were few wounded, for energy weapons deal death; and of these few, almost none slightly. It was a scene of indescribable confusion, and the moans of the hurt and dying mingled horribly with the distant yells of celebrating war-drunk survivors.

Loara Paul Kane pushed through the crowding attendants to Tymball.

'Tell me; is it over?' His face was haggard.

'The beginning is. The Terrestrial Flag flies over the ruins of the Palace.'

'It was horrible! The day has – has—' He shuddered and closed his eyes, 'If I had known in advance, I would rather have seen Earth dehumanized and Loarism destroyed.'

'Yes, it was bad. But the results might have been much more dearly bought, and yet have remained cheap at the price. Where's Sanat?'

'In the courtyard – helping with the wounded. We all are. It – it—' Again his voice failed him.

There was impatience in Tymball's eyes, and he shrugged weary shoulders, 'I'm not a callous monster, but it had to be done, and as yet it is only the beginning. Today's events mean little. The uprising has taken place over most of Earth, but without the fanatic enthusiasm of the rebellion in New York. The Lhasinu aren't defeated, or anywhere near defeated; make no mistake about that. Even now the Solar Guard is flashing to Earth, and the forces on the outer planets are being called back. In no time at all, the entire Lhasinuic Empire will converge upon Earth and the reckoning will be a terrible and bloody one. We must have help!'

He grasped Kane by the shoulders and shook him roughly. 'Do

you understand? We must have help! Even here in New York the first flush of victory will fade by tomorrow. *We must have help!*'

'I know,' said Kane tonelessly. 'I'll get Sanat and he can leave today.' He sighed, 'If today's action was any criterion of his power as a catalyst, we may expect great events.'

Sanat climbed into the little two-man cruiser half an hour later and took his seat beside Petri at the controls.

He extended his hand to Kane a last time, 'When I come back it will be with a navy behind me.'

Kane grasped the young man's hand tightly, 'We depend upon you, Filip.' He paused and said slowly, 'Good luck, Loara Filip Sanat!'

Sanat flushed with pleasure at the title as he resumed his seat once more. Petri waved and Tymball called out, 'Watch out for the Solar Guard!'

The airlock clanged shut, and then, with a coughing roar, the pygmy cruiser was off into the heavens.

Tymball followed it to where it dwindled into a speck and less and then turned to Kane, 'All is now in the hands of Fate. And, Kane, just how was that Changing of the Flame worked? Don't tell me the Flame turned red of itself.'

Kane shook his head slowly, 'No! That carmine blaze was the result of opening a hidden pocket of strontium salts, originally placed there to impress the Lhasinu in case of need. The rest was chemistry.'

Tymball laughed grimly, 'You mean the rest was mob psychology! And the Lhasinu, I think, were impressed – and *how!*'

Space itself gave no warning, but the mass-detector buzzed. It buzzed peremptorily and insistently. Petri stiffened in his seat and said, 'We're in none of the meteor zones.'

Filip Sanat held his breath as the other turned the knob that rotated the peri-rotor. The star-field in the 'visor shifted with slow dignity, and then they saw it.

It glinted in the sun like half a tiny, orange football, and Petri growled, 'If they've spotted us, we're sunk.'

'Lhasinuic ship?'

'Ship? That's no *ship!* That's a fifty-thousand ton battle cruiser! What in the Galaxy it's doing here, I don't know. Tymball said the Patrol had made for Earth.'

Sanat's voice was calm, 'That one hasn't. Can we outrace it?'

'Fat chance!' Petri's fist clenched white on the G-stick. 'They're coming closer.'

The words might have been a signal. The audiomitter jiggled and the harsh Lhasinuic voice started from a whisper and rose to stridence as the radio beam sharpened, 'Fire reverse motors and prepare for boarding!'

Petri released the controls and shot a look at Sanat, 'I'm only the chauffeur. What do you want to do? We haven't the chance of a meteor against the sun – but if you like the gamble—'

'Well,' said Sanat, simply, 'we're not going to surrender, are we?'

The other grinned, as the decelerating rockets blasted, 'Not bad for a Loarist! Can you shoot a mounted Tonite?'

'I've never tried!'

'Well, then, learn how. Grab that little wheel over there and keep your eye on the small 'visor above. See anything?' Speed was steadily dropping and the enemy ship was approaching.

'Just stars!'

'All right, rotate the wheel – go ahead, further. Try the other direction. Do you see the ship now?'

'Yes! There it is.'

'Good! Now center it. Get it where the hairlines cross, and for the sake of Sol, keep it there. Now I'm going to turn toward the lizard scum,' siderockets blasted as he spoke, 'and you keep it centered.'

The Lhasinuic ship was bloating steadily, and Petri's voice descended to a tense whisper, 'I'm dropping our screen and lunging directly at her. It's a gamble. If they're sufficiently startled, they may drop *their* screen and shoot; and if they shoot in a hurry, they may miss.'

Sanat nodded silently.

'Now the second you see the purple flash of the Tonite, pull back on the wheel. Pull back *hard;* and pull back *fast.* If you're the tiniest trifle late, we're through.' He shrugged, 'It's a gamble!'

With that, he slammed the G-stick forward hard and shouted, 'Keep it centered!'

Acceleration pushed Sanat back gaspingly, and the wheel in his sweating hands responded reluctantly to pressure. The orange football wobbled at the center of the 'visor. He could feel his hands trembling, and that didn't help any. Eyes winced with tension.

The Lhasinuic ship was swelling terribly now, and then, from its prow, a purple sword leaped toward them. Sanat closed his eyes and jerked backwards.

He kept his eyes closed and waited. There was no sound.

He opened them and started to his feet; for Petri, arms akimbo, was laughing down upon him.

'A beginner's own luck,' he laughed. 'Never held a gun before in his life and knocks out a heavy cruiser in as pretty a pink as I ever saw.'

'I hit it?' gasped Sanat.

'Not on the button, but you did disable it. That's good enough. And now, just as soon as we get far enough away from the sun, we're going into hyperspace.'

The tall, purple-clad figure standing by the central portview gazed longingly at the silent globe without. It was Earth, huge, gibbous, glorious.

Perhaps his thoughts were just a trifle bitter as he considered the six-month period that had just passed. It had begun with a novablaze. Enthusiasm kindled to white heat and spread, leaping the stellar gulfs from planet to planet as fast as the hyper-atomic beam. Squabbling governments, sudden putty before the outraged clamoring of their peoples, outfitted fleets. Enemies of centuries made sudden peace and flew under the same green flag of Earth.

Perhaps it would have been too much to expect this love-feast to continue. While it did the Humans were irresistible. One fleet was not two parsecs from Vega itself; another had captured Luna and hovered one light-second above the Earth, where Tymball's ragged revolutionaries still held on doggedly.

Filip Sanat sighed and turned at the sound of a step. White-haired Ion Smitt of the Lactonian contingent entered.

'Your face tells the story,' said Sanat.

Smitt shook his head, 'It seems hopeless.'

Sanat turned away again, 'Did you know that we've gotten word from Tymball today? They're fighting on what they can filch from the Lhasinu. The lizards have captured Buenos Aires, and all South America seems likely to go under their heel. They're disheartened – the Tymballists – and disgusted, and I am, too.' He whirled suddenly, 'You say that our new needle-ships insure victory. Then, why don't we attack?'

'Well, for one thing,' the grizzled soldier planted one booted leg on the chair next to him, 'the reinforcements from Santanni are not coming.'

Sanat started, 'I thought they were on their way. What happened?'

'The Santannian government has decided its fleet is required for home defense.' A wry smile accompanied his words.

'What home defense? Why, the Lhasinu are five hundred parsecs away from them.'

Smitt shrugged, 'An excuse is an excuse and need not make sense. I didn't say that was the real reason.'

Sanat brushed his hair back and his fingers strayed to the yellow sun upon his shoulder, 'Even so! We could still fight, with over a hundred ships. The enemy outnumbers us two to one, but with the needle ships and with Lunar Base at our backs and the rebels harass-ing them in the rear—' He fell into a brooding reverie.

'You won't get them to fight, Filip. The Trantorian squadron favors retreat.' His voice was suddenly savage, 'Of the entire fleet, I can trust only the twenty ships of my own squadron – the Lactonian. Oh, Filip, you don't know the dirt of it – you never have known.

You've won the people to the Cause, but you've never won the governments. Popular opinion forced them in, but now that they are in, they're in only for what they can get.'

'I can't believe that, Smitt. With victory in their grasp—'

'Victory? Victory for whom? It is exactly over that bone that the planets are squabbling. At a secret convention of the nations, Santanni demanded control of all the Lhasinuic worlds of the Sirius sector – none of which have been recognized as yet – and was refused. Ah, you didn't know that. Consequently, she decides that she must take care of her home defense, and withdraws her various squadrons.'

Filip Sanat turned away in pain, but Ion Smitt's voice hammered on, hard, unmerciful.

'And then Trantor realizes that she hates and fears Santanni more than ever she did the Lhasinu and any day now she will withdraw *her* fleet to refrain from crippling them while her enemy's ships remain quietly and safely in port. The Human nations are falling apart,' the soldier's fist came down upon the table, 'like rotten cloth. It was a fool's dream to think that the selfish idiot could ever unite for any worthy purpose long.'

Sanat's eyes were suddenly calculating slits, 'Wait a while! Things will yet work out all right, if we can only manage to seize control of Earth. Earth is the key to the whole situation.' His fingers drummed upon the table edge. 'Its capture would provide the vital spark. It would drum up Human enthusiasm, now lagging, to the boiling point, and the Governments – well, they would either have to ride the wave, or be dashed to pieces.'

'I know that. If we fought today, you have a soldier's word we'd be on Earth tomorrow. They realize it, too, but they won't fight.'

'Then – then they must be *made* to fight. The only way they can be made to fight is to leave no alternative. They won't fight now, because they can reheat whenever they wish, but if—'

He suddenly looked up, face aglow, 'You know, I haven't been out of the Loarist tunic in years. Do you suppose your clothes will fit me?'

Ion Smitt looked down upon his ample girth and grinned, 'Well, they might not fit you, but they'll cover you all right. What are you thinking of doing?'

'I'll tell you. It's a terrible chance, but— Relay the following orders immediately to the Lunar Base garrison—'

The admiral of the Lhasinuic Solar squadron was a war-scarred veteran who hated two things above all else: Humans and civilians. The combination, in the person of the tall, slender Human in illfitted clothing, put a scowl of dislike upon his face.

Sanat wriggled in the grasp of the two Lhasinuic soldiers. 'Tell them to let go,' he cried in the Vegan tongue. 'I am unarmed.'

'Speak,' ordered the admiral in English. 'They do not understand your language.' Then, in Lhasinuic to the soldiers, 'Shoot when I give the word.'

Sanat subsided, 'I came to discuss terms.'

'I judged as much when you hoisted the white flag. Yet you come in a one-man cruiser from the night side of your own fleet, like a fugitive. Surely, you cannot speak for your fleet.'

'I speak for myself.'

'Then I give you one minute. If I am not interested by the end of that time, you will be shot.' His expression was stony.

Sanat tried once more to free himself, with little success. His captors tightened their grips.

'Your situation,' said the Earthman, 'is this. You can't attack the Human squadron as long as they control Lunar Base, without serious damage to your own fleet, and you can't risk that with a hostile Earth behind you. At the same time, I happen to know that the order from Vega is to drive the Humans from the Solar System at all costs, and that the Emperor dislikes failures.'

'You have ten seconds left,' said the admiral, but tell-tale red spots appeared above his eyes.

'All right, then,' came the hurried response, 'how's this? What if I offer you the entire Human Fleet caught in a trap?'

There was silence. Sanat went on, 'What if I show you how you can take over Lunar Base, and surround the Humans?'

'Go on!' It was the first sign of interest the admiral had permitted himself.

'I am in command of one of the squadrons and I have certain powers. If you'll agree to our terms, we can have the Base deserted within twelve hours. Two ships,' the Human raised two fingers impressively, 'will take it.'

'Interesting,' said the Lhasinu, slowly, 'but your motive? What is your reason for doing this?'

Sanat thrust out a surly under-lip, 'That would not interest you. I have been ill-treated and deprived of my rights. Besides,' his eyes glittered, 'Humanity's is a lost cause, anyway. For this I shall expect payment – ample payment. Swear to that, and the fleet is yours.'

The admiral glared his contempt. 'There is a Lhasinuic proverb: The Human is steadfast in nothing but his treachery. Arrange your treason, and I shall repay. I swear by the word of a Lhasinuic soldier. You may return to your ships.'

With a motion, he dismissed the soldiers and then stopped them at the doorway, 'But remember, I risk two ships. They mean little as far as my fleet's strength is concerned, but, nevertheless, if harm comes to a Lhasinuic head through Human treachery—' The scales on his head were stiffly erect and Sanat's eyes dropped beneath the other's cold stare.

For a long while, the admiral sat alone and motionless. Then he spat. 'This Human filth! It is a disgrace even to fight them!'

The Flagship of the Human fleet lazed one hundred miles above Luna, and within it the captains of the Squadrons sat about the table and listened to Ion Smitt's shouted indictment.

'—I tell you your actions amount to treason. The battle off Vega is progressing, and if the Lhasinu win, their Solar squadron will be strengthened to the point where we must retreat. And if the Humans win, our treachery here exposes their Bank and renders the victory worthless. We can win, I tell you. With these new needle-ships—'

The sleepy-eyed Trantorian leader spoke up. 'The needle-ships have never been tried before. We cannot risk a major battle on an experiment, when the odds are against us.'

'That wasn't your original view, Porcut. You – yes, and the rest of you as well – are a cowardly traitor. Cowards! Cravens!'

A chair crashed backwards as one arose in anger and others followed. Loara Filip Sanat, from his vantage-point at the central port, from where he watched the bleak landscape of Luna below with devouring concentration, turned in alarm. But Jem Porcut raised a gnarled hand for order.

'Let's stop fencing,' he said. 'I represent Trantor, and I take orders only from her. We have eleven ships here, and Space knows how many at Vega. How many has Santanni got? None! Why is she keeping them at home? Perhaps to take advantage of Trantor's preoccupation. Is there anyone who hasn't heard of her designs against us? We're not going to destroy our ships here for her benefit. Trantor will not fight! My division leaves tomorrow! Under the circumstances, the Lhasinu will be glad to let us go in peace.'

Another spoke up, 'And Poritta, too. The treaty of Draconis has hung like neutronium around our neck these twenty years. The imperialist planets refuse revision, and we will not fight a war which is to their interests only.'

One after another, surly exclamations dinned the perpetual refrain, 'Our interests are against it! We will not fight!'

And suddenly, Loara Filip Sanat smiled. He had turned away from Luna and laughed at the snarling arguers.

'Sirs,' he said, 'no one is leaving.'

Ion Smitt sighed with relief and sank back in his chair.

'Who will stop us?' asked Porcut with disdain.

'The Lhasinu! They have just taken Lunar Base and we are surrounded.'

The room was a babble of dismay. Shouting confusion held sway and then one roared above the rest, 'What of the garrison?'

'The garrison had destroyed the fortifications and evacuated hours before the Lhasinu took over. The enemy met with no resistance.'

The silence that followed was much more terrifying than the cries that had preceded. 'Treason,' whispered someone.

'Who is at the bottom of this?' One by one they approached Sanat. Fists clenched. Faces Bushed. 'Who did this?'

'I did,' said Sanat, calmly.

A moment of stunned disbelief. 'Dog!' 'Pig of a Loaristl' 'Tear his guts out!'

And then they shrank back at the pair of Tonite guns that appeared in Ion Smitt's fists. The burly Lactonian stepped before the younger man.

'I was in on this, too,' he snarled. 'You'll *have* to fight now. It is necessary to fight fire with fire sometimes, and Sanat fought treason with treason.'

Jem Porcut regarded his knuckles carefully and suddenly chuckled, 'Well, we can't wriggle out now, so we might as well fight. Except for orders, I wouldn't mind taking a crack at the damn lizards.'

The reluctant pause was followed by shamefaced shouts – proof-positive of the willingness of the rest.

In two hours, the Lhasinuic demand for surrender had been scornfully rejected and the hundred ships of the Human squadron spread outwards on the expanding surface of an imaginary sphere – the standard defense formation of a surrounded fleet – and the Battle for Earth was on.

A space-battle between approximately equal forces resembles in almost every detail a gigantic fencing match in which controlled shafts of deadly radiation are the rapiers and impermeable walls of etheric inertia are the shields.

The two forces advance to battle and maneuver for position. Then the pale purple of a Tonite beam lashes out in a blaze of fury against the screen of an enemy ship, and in so doing, its own screen is forced to blink out. For that one instant it is vulnerable and is a perfect target for an enemy ray, which, when loosed, renders *its* ship open to attack for the moment. In widening circles, it spreads. Each unit of the fleet, combining speed of mechanism with speed of human reaction, attempts to slip through at the crucial moment and yet maintain its own safety.

Loara Filip Sanat knew all this and more. Since his encounter with the battle cruiser on the way out from Earth, he had studied space war, and now, as the battle fleets fell into line, he felt his very fingers twitch for action.

He turned and said to Smitt, 'I'm going down to the big guns.'

Smitt's eye was on the grand 'visor, his hand on the etherwave sender, 'Go ahead, if you wish, but don't get in the way.'

Sanat smiled. The captain's private elevator carried him to the gun levels, and from there it was five hundred feet through an orderly mob of gunners and engineers to Tonite One. Space is at a premium in a battleship. Sanat could feel the crampedness of the room in which individual Humans dove-tailed their work smoothly to create the gigantic machine that was a giant dreadnaught.

He mounted the six steep steps to Tonite One and motioned the gunner away. The gunner hesitated; his eye fell upon the purple tunic, and then he saluted and backed reluctantly down the steps.

Sanat turned to the co-ordinator at the gun's visiplate, 'Do you mind working with me? My speed of reaction has been tested and grouped 1–A. I have my rating card, if you'd care to see it.'

The co-ordinator flushed and stammered, 'No, *sir!* It's an honor to work with you, sir.'

The amplifying system thundered, 'To your stations!' and a deep silence fell, in which the cold purr of machinery sounded its ominous note.

Sanat spoke to the co-ordinator in a whisper, 'This gun covers a full quadrant of space, doesn't it?'

'Yes, sir.'

'Good, see if you can locate a dreadnaught with the sign of a double sun in partial eclipse.'

There was a long silence. The co-ordinator's sensitive hands were on the Wheel, delicate pressure turning it this way and that, so that the field in view on the visiplate shifted. Keen eyes scanned the ordered array of enemy ships.

'There it is,' he said. 'Why, it's the flagship.'

'Exactly! Center that ship!'

As the Wheel turned, the space-field reeled, and the enemy flagship wobbled toward the point where the hairlines crossed. The pressure of the co-ordinator's fingers became lighter and more expert.

'Centered!' he said. Where the hairlines crossed the tiny oval globe remained impaled.

'Keep it that way!' ordered Sanat, grimly. 'Don't lose it for a second as long as it stays in our quadrant. The enemy admiral is on that ship and we're going to get him, you and I.'

The ships were getting within range of each other and Sanat felt tense. He knew it was going to be close – very close. The Humans had the edge in speed, but the Lhasinu were two to one in numbers.

A flickering beam shot out, another, ten more.

There was a sudden blinding flash of purple intensity!

'First hit,' breathed Sanat. He relaxed. One of the enemy ships drifted off helplessly, its stern a mass of fused and glowing metal.

The opposing ships were not at close grips. Shots were being exchanged at blinding speed. Twice, a purple beam showed at the extreme limits of the visiplate and Sanat realized with a queer sort of shiver down his spine that it was one of the adjacent Tonites of their own ship that was firing.

The fencing match was approaching a climax. Two flashes blazed into being, almost simultaneously, and Sanat groaned. One of the two had been a Human ship. And three times there came that disquieting hum as Atomo-engines in the lower level shot into high gear – and that meant that an enemy beam directed at their own ship had been stopped by the screen.

And, always, the co-ordinator kept the enemy flagship centered. An hour passed; an hour in which six Lhasinu and four Human ships had been whiffed to destruction; an hour in which the Wheel turned fractions of a degree this way, that way; in which it swiveled on its universal socket mere hairlines in half a dozen directions.

Sweat matted the co-ordinator's hair and got into his eyes; his fingers half-lost all sensation, but that flagship never left the ominous spot where the hairlines crossed.

And Sanat watched; finger on trigger – watched – and waited.

Twice the flagship had glowed into purple luminosity, its guns blazing and its defensive screen down; and twice Sanat's finger had quivered on the trigger and refrained. He hadn't been quick enough.

And then Sanat rammed it home and rose to his feet tensely. The co-ordinator yelled and dropped the Wheel.

In a gigantic funeral pyre of purple-hued energy, the flagship with the Lhasinuic Admiral inside had ceased to exist.

Sanat laughed. His hand went out, and the co-ordinator's came to meet it in a firm grasp of triumph.

But the triumph did not last long enough for the co-ordinator to speak the first jubilant words that were welling up in his throat, for the visiplate burst into a purple bombshell as five Human ships detonated simultaneously at the touch of deadly energy shafts.

The amplifiers thundered, 'Up screens! Cease firing! Ease into Needle formation!'

Sanat felt the deadly pall of uncertainty squeeze his throat. He knew what had happened. The Lhasinu had finally managed to set up their big guns on Lunar Base; big guns with three times the range of even the largest ship guns – big guns that could pick off Human ships with no fear of reprisal.

And so the fencing match was over, and the real battle was to start. But it was to be a real battle of a type never before fought, and Sanat knew that that was the thought in every man's mind. He could see it in their grim expressions and feel it in their silence.

It might work! And it might not!

*

The Earth squadron had resumed its spherical formation and drifted slowly outwards, its offensive batteries silent. The Lhasinu swept in for the kill. Cut off from power supply as the Earthmen were, and unable to retaliate with the gigantic guns of the Lunar batteries commanding near-by space, it seemed only a matter of time before either surrender or annihilation.

The enemy Tonite beams lashed out in continuous blasts of energy, and tortured screens on Human ships sparked and fluoresced under the harsh whips of radiation.

Sanat could hear the buzz of the Atomo-engines rise to a protesting squeal. Against his will, his eye flicked to the energy gauge, and the quivering needle sank as he watched, moving down the dial at perceptible speed.

The co-ordinator licked dry lips, 'Do you think we'll make it, sir?'

'Certainly!' Sanat was far from feeling his expressed confidence. 'We need hold out for an hour – provided they don't fall back.'

And the Lhasinu didn't. To have fallen back would have meant a thinning of the lines, with a possible breakthrough and escape on the part of the Humans.

The Human ships were down to crawling speed – scarcely above a hundred miles an hour. Idling along, they crept up the purple beams of energy, the imaginary sphere increasing in size, the distance between the opposing forces ever narrowing.

But inside the ship, the gauge-needle was dropping rapidly, and Sanat's heart dropped with it. He crossed the gunlevel to where hard-bitten soldiers waited at a gigantic and gleaming lever, in anticipation of an order that had to come soon – or never.

The distance between opponents was now only a matter of one or two miles – almost contact from the viewpoint of space warfare – and then that order shot over the shielded etheric beams from ship to ship.

It reverberated through the gun level:

'Out needles!'

A score of hands reached for the lever, Sanat's among them, and jerked downwards. Majestically, the lever bent in a curving arc to the floor and as it did so, there was a vast scraping noise and a sharp thud that shook the ship.

The dreadnaught had become a 'needle ship!'

At the prow, a section of armor plate had slid aside and a glittering shaft of metal had lunged outward viciously. One hundred feet long, it narrowed gracefully from a base ten feet in diameter to a needle-sharp diamond point. In the sunlight, the chrome-steel of the shaft gleamed in flaming splendor.

And every other ship of the Human squadron was likewise equipped. Each had become ten, fifteen, twenty, fifty thousand tons of driving rapier.

Swordfish of space!

Somewhere in the Lhasinuic fleet, frantic orders must have been issued. Against this oldest of all naval tactics – old even in the dim dawn of history when rival triremes had maneuvered and rammed each other to destruction with pointed prows – the super-modern equipment of a space-fleet has no defense.

Sanat forced his way to the visiplate and strapped himself into an anti-acceleration seat, and he felt the springs absorb the backward jerk as the ship sprang into sudden acceleration.

He didn't bother with that, though. He wanted to watch the battle! There wasn't one here, nor anywhere in the Galaxy, that risked what he did. They risked only their lives; and he risked a dream that he had, almost single-handed, created out of nothing.

He had taken an apathetic Galaxy and driven it into revolt against the reptile. He had taken an Earth on the point of destruction and dragged it from the brink, almost unaided. A Human victory would be a victory for Loara Filip Sanat and no one else.

He, and Earth, and the Galaxy were now lumped into one and thrown into the scale. And against it was weighed the outcome of this last battle, a battle hopelessly lost by his own purposeful treachery, unless the needles won.

And if they lost, the gigantic defeat – the ruin of Humanity – was also his.

The Lhasinuic ships were jumping aside, but not fast enough. While they were slowly gathering momentum and drifting away, the Human ships had cut the distance by three-quarters. On the screen, a Lhasinuic ship had grown to colossal proportions. Its purple whip of energy had gone out as every ounce of power had gone into a mankilling attempt at rapid acceleration.

And nevertheless its image grew and the shining point that could be seen at the lower end of the screen aimed like a glittering javelin at its heart.

Sanat felt he could not bear the tension. Five minutes and he would take his place as the Galaxy's greatest hero – or its greatest traitor! There was a horrible, unbearable pounding of blood in his temples.

Then it came.

Contact!!

The screen went wild in a chaotic fury of twisted metal. The anti-acceleration seats shrieked as springs absorbed the shock. Things cleared slowly. The screenview veered wildly as the ship slowly steadied. The ship's needle had broken, the jagged stump twisted awry, but the enemy vessel it had pierced was a gutted wreck.

Sanat held his breath as he scanned space. It was a vast sea of wrecked ships, and on the outskirts tattered remnants of the enemy were in flight, with Human ships in pursuit.

There was the sound of colossal cheering behind him and a pair of strong hands on his shoulders.

He turned. It was Smitt – Smitt, the veteran of five wars, with tears in his eyes.

'Filip,' he said, 'we've won. We've just received word from Vega. The Lhasinuic Home Fleet has been smashed – and also with the needles. The war is over, and we've won. *You've* won, Filip! *You!*'

His grip was painful, but Loara Filip Sanat did not mind that. For a single, ecstatic moment, he stood motionless, face transfigured.

Earth was free! Humanity was saved!

Half-Breed

Jefferson Scanlon wiped a perspiring brow and took a deep breath. With trembling finger, he reached for the switch – and changed his mind. His latest model, representing over three months of solid work, was very nearly his last hope. A good part of the fifteen thousand dollars he had been able to borrow was in it. And now the closing of a switch would show whether he won or lost.

Scanlon cursed himself for a coward and grasped the switch firmly. He snapped it down and fucked it open again with one swift movement. And nothing happened – his eyes, strain though they might, caught no flash of surging power. The pit of his stomach froze, and he closed the switch again, savagely, and left it closed. Nothing happened: the machine, again, was a failure.

He buried his aching head in his hands, and groaned. 'Oh, God! It should work – it should. My math is right and I've produced the fields I want. By every law of science, those fields should crack the atom.' He arose, opening the useless switch, and paced the floor in deep thought.

His theory was right. His equipment was cut neatly to the pattern of his equations. If the theory was right, the equipment must be wrong. But the equipment was right, so the theory must . . . 'I'm getting out of here before I go crazy,' he said to the four walls.

He snatched his hat and coat from the peg behind the door and was out of the house in a whirlwind of motion, slamming the door behind him in a gust of fury.

Atomic power. Atomic power! *Atomic power!*

The two words repeated themselves over and over again, singing a monotonous, maddening song in his brain. A siren song! It was luring him to destruction; for this dream he had given up a safe and comfortable professorship at M.I.T. For it, he had become a middle-aged man at thirty – the first flush of youth long gone – an apparent failure.

And now his money was vanishing rapidly. If the love of money is the root of all evil, the need of money is most certainly the root of all despair. Scanlon smiled a little at the thought – rather neat.

Of course, there were the beautiful prospects in store if he could ever bridge the gap he had found between theory and practice. The whole world would be his – Mars too, and even the unvisited planets. All his. All he had to do was to find out what was wrong with his mathematics – no, he'd checked that, it was in the equipment. Although— He groaned aloud once more.

The gloomy train of his thoughts was broken as he suddenly became aware of a tumult of boyish shouts not far off. Scanlon frowned. He hated noise especially when he was in the dumps.

The shouts became louder and dissolved into scraps of words, 'Get him, Johnny!' 'Whee – look at him run!'

A dozen boys careened out from behind a large frame building, not two hundred yards away, and ran pell-mell in Scanlon's general direction.

In spite of himself, Scanlon regarded the yelling group curiously. They were chasing something or other, with the heartless glee of children. In the dimness he couldn't make out just what it was. He screened his eyes and squinted. A sudden motion and a lone figure disengaged itself from the crowd and ran frantically.

Scanlon almost dropped his solacing pipe in astonishment, for the fugitive was a Tweenie – an Earth-Mars half-breed. There was no mistaking that brush of wiry, dead-white hair that rose stiffly in all directions like porcupine-quills. Scanlon marveled – what was one of *those* things doing outside an asylum?

The boys had caught up with the Tweenie again, and the fugitive was lost to sight. The yells increased in volume, Scanlon, shocked, saw a heavy board rise and fall with a thud. A profound sense of the enormity of his own actions in standing idly by while a helpless creature was being hounded by a crew of gamins came to him, and before he quite realized it he was charging down upon them, fists waving threateningly in the air.

'Scat, you heathens! Get out of here before I—' the point of his foot came into violent contact with the seat of the nearest hoodlum, and his arms sent two more tumbling.

The entrance of the new force changed the situation considerably. Boys, whatever their superiority in numbers, have an instinctive fear of adults – especially such a shouting, ferocious adult as Scanlon appeared to be. In less time than it took Scanlon to realize it they were gone, and he was left alone with the Tweenie, who lay halfprone, and who between panting sobs cast fearful and uncertain glances at his deliverer.

'Are you hurt?' asked Scanlon gruffly.

'No, sir.' The Tweenie rose unsteadily, his high silver crest of hair swaying incongruously. 'I twisted my ankle a bit, but I can walk. I'll go now. Thank you very much for helping me.'

'Hold on! Wait!' Scanlon's voice was much softer, for it dawned on him that the Tweenie, though almost full-grown, was incredibly gaunt; that his clothes were a mere mass of dirty rags; and that there was a heart-rending look of utter weariness on his thin face.

'Here,' he said, as the Tweenie turned towards him again, 'are you hungry?'

The Tweenie's face twisted as though he were fighting a battle within himself. When he spoke it was in a low, embarrassed voice. 'Yes – I am, a little.'

'You look it. Come with me to my house,' he jerked a thumb over his shoulder. 'You ought to eat. Looks like you can do with a wash and a change of clothes, too.' He turned and led the way.

He didn't speak again until he had opened his front door and entered the hall. 'I think you'd better take a bath first, boy. There's the bathroom. Hurry into it and lock the door before Beulah sees you.'

His admonition came too late. A sudden, startled gasp caused Scanlon to whirl about, the picture of guilt, and the Tweenie *to* shrink backwards into the shadow of a hat-rack.

Beulah, Scanlon's housekeeper, scurried towards them, her mild face aflame with indignation and her short, plump body exuding exasperation at every pore.

'Jefferson Scanlon! Jefferson!' She glared at the Tweenie with shocked disgust. 'How can you bring such a thing into this house! Have you lost your sense of morals?'

The poor Tweenie was washed away with the flow of her anger, but Scanlon, after his first momentary panic, collected himself. 'Come come, Beulah. This isn't like you. Here's a poor fellow-creature, starved, tired, beaten by a crowd of boys, and you have no pity for him. I'm really disappointed in you, Beulah.'

'Disappointed!' sniffed the housekeeper, though touched. 'Because of *that* disgraceful thing. He should be in an institution where they keep such monsters!'

'All right, we'll talk about it later. Go ahead, boy, take your bath. And, Beulah, see if you can't rustle up some old clothes of mine.'

With a last look of disapproval, Beulah flounced out of the room.

'Don't mind her, boy,' Scanlon said when she left. 'She was my nurse once and she still has a sort of proprietary interest in me. She won't harm you. Go take your bath.'

The Tweenie was a different person altogether when he finally seated himself at the dining-room table. Now that the layer of grime was removed, there was something quite handsome about his thin face, and his high, clear forehead gave him a markedly intellectual look. His hair still stood erect, a foot tall, in spite of the moistening it had received. In the light its brilliant whiteness took an imposing dignity, and to Scanlon it seemed to lose all ugliness.

'Do you like cold chicken?' asked Scanlon.

'Oh, *yes!*' enthusiastically.

'Then pitch in. And when you finish that, you can have more. Take anything on the table.'

The Tweenie's eyes glistened as he set his jaws to work; and, between the two of them, the table was bare in a few minutes.

'Well, now,' exclaimed Scanlon when the repast had reached its end, 'I think you might answer some questions now. What's your name?'

'They called me Max.'

'Ah! And your last name?'

The Tweenie shrugged his shoulders. 'They never called me anything but Max – when they spoke to me at all. I don't suppose a half-breed needs a name.' There was no mistaking the bitterness in his voice.

'But what were you doing running wild through the country? Why aren't you where you live?'

'I was in a home. Anything is better than being in a home – even the world outside, which I had never seen. Especially after Tom died.'

'Who was Tom, Max?' Scanlon spoke softly.

'He was the only other one like me. He was younger – fifteen – but he died.' He looked up from the table, fury in his eyes. '*They* killed him, Mr Scanlon. He was such a young fellow, and so friendly. He couldn't stand being alone the way I could. He needed friends and fun, and – all he had was me. No one else would speak to him, because he was a half-breed. And when he died I couldn't stand it anymore either. I left.'

'They meant to be kind, Max. You shouldn't have done that. You're not like other people; they don't understand you. And they must have done something for you. You talk as though you've had some education.'

'I could attend classes, all right,' he assented gloomily. 'But I had to sit in a corner away from all the others. They let me read all I wanted, though, and I'm thankful for *that*.'

'Well, there you are, Max. You weren't so badly off, were you?'

Max lifted his head and stared at the other suspiciously. 'You're not going to send me back, are you?' He half rose, as though ready for instant flight.

Scanlon coughed uneasily. 'Of course, if you don't want to go back I won't make you. But it would be the best thing for you.'

'It wouldn't!' Max cried vehemently.

'Well, have it your own way. Anyway, I think you'd better go to sleep now. You need it. We'll talk in the morning.'

He led the still suspicious Tweenie up to the second floor, and pointed out a small bedroom. 'That's yours for the night. I'll be in the next room later on, and if you need anything just shout.' He turned to leave, then thought of something. 'But remember, you mustn't try to run away during the night.'

'Word of honor. I won't.'

Scanlon retired thoughtfully to the room he called his study. He lit a dim lamp and seated himself in a worn armchair. For ten minutes he sat without moving, and for the first time in six years thought about something besides his dream of atomic power.

A quiet knock sounded, and at his grunted acknowledgment Beulah entered. She was frowning, her lips pursed. She planted herself firmly before him.

'Oh, Jefferson! To think that you should do this! If your dear mother knew . . .'

'Sit down, Beulah,' Scanlon waved at another chair, 'and don't worry about my mother. She wouldn't have minded.'

'No. Your father was a good-hearted simpleton, too. You're just like him, Jefferson. First you spend all your money on silly machines that might blow the house up any day – and now you pick up that awful creature from the streets . . . Tell me, Jefferson,' there was a solemn and fearful pause, 'are you thinking of *keeping* it?'

Scanlon smiled moodily. 'I think I am, Beulah. I can't very well do anything else.'

A week later Scanlon was in his workshop. During the night before, his brain, rested by the change in the monotony brought about by the presence of Max, had thought of a possible solution to the puzzle of why his machine wouldn't work. Perhaps some of the parts were defective, he thought. Even a very slight flaw in some of the parts could render the machine inoperative.

He plunged into work ardently. At the end of half an hour the machine lay scattered on his workbench, and Scanlon was sitting on a high stool, eying it disconsolately.

He scarcely heard the door softly open and close. It wasn't until the intruder had coughed twice that the absorbed inventor realized another was present.

'Oh – it's Max.' His abstracted gaze gave way to recognition. 'Did you want to see me?'

'If you're busy I can wait, Mr Scanlon.' The week had not removed his shyness. 'But there were a lot of books in my room . . .'

'Books? Oh, I'll have them cleaned out, if you don't want them. I don't suppose you do – they're mostly textbooks, as I remember. A bit too advanced for you just now.'

'Oh, it's not too difficult,' Max assured him. He pointed to a book he was carrying. 'I just wanted you *to* explain a bit here in Quantum Mechanics. There's some math with Integral Calculus that I don't quite understand. It bothers me. Here – wait till I find it.'

He ruffied the pages, but stopped suddenly as he became aware of his surroundings. 'Oh say – are you breaking up your model?'

The question brought the hard facts back to Scanlon at a bound. He smiled bitterly. 'No, not yet. I just thought there might be something wrong with the insulation or the connections that kept it from functioning. There isn't – I've made a mistake somewhere.'

'That's too bad, Mr Scanlon.' The Tweenie's smooth brow wrinkled mournfully.

'The worst of it is that I can't imagine what's wrong. I'm positive the theory's perfect – I've checked every way I can. I've gone over the mathematics time and time again, and each time it says the same thing. Space-distortion fields of such and such an intensity will smash the atom to smithereens. Only they don't.'

'May I see the equations?'

Scanlon gazed at his ward quizzically, but could see nothing in his face other than the most serious interest. He shrugged his shoulders. 'There they are – under that ream of yellow paper on the desk. I don't know if you can read them, though. I've been too lazy to type them out, and my handwriting is pretty bad.'

Max scrutinized them carefully and flipped the sheets one by one. 'It's a bit over my head, I guess.'

The inventor smiled a little. 'I rather thought they would be, Max.'

He looked around the littered room, and a sudden sense of anger came over him. Why wouldn't the thing work? Abruptly he got up and snatched his coat. 'I'm going out of here, Max,' he said. 'Tell Beulah not to make me anything hot for lunch. It would be cold before I got back.'

It was afternoon when he opened the front door, and hunger was sharp enough to prevent him from realizing with a puzzled start that someone was at work in his laboratory. There came to his ears a sharp buzzing sound followed by a momentary silence and then again the buzz which this time merged into a sharp crackling that lasted an instant and was gone.

He bounded down the hall and threw open the laboratory door. The sight that met his eyes froze him into an attitude of sheer astonishment – stunned incomprehension.

Slowly, he understood the message of his senses. His precious atomic motor had been put together again, but this time in a manner so strange as to be senseless, for even his trained eye could see no reasonable relationship among the various parts.

He wondered stupidly if it were a nightmare or a practical joke, and then everything became clear to him at one bound, for there at the other end of the room was the unmistakable sight of a brush of silver hair protruding from above a bench, swaying gently from side to side as the hidden owner of the brush moved.

'Max!' shouted the distraught inventor, in tones of fury. Evidently the foolish boy had allowed his interest to inveigle him into idle and dangerous experiments.

At the sound, Max lifted a pale face which upon the sight of his guardian turned a dull red. He approached Scanlon with reluctant steps.

'What have you done?' cried Scanlon, staring about him angrily. 'Do you know what you've been playing with? There's enough juice running through this thing to electrocute you twice over.'

'I'm sorry, Mr Scanlon. I had a rather silly idea about all this when I looked over the equations, but I was afraid to say anything because you know so much more than I do. After you went away, I couldn't resist the temptation to try it out, though I didn't intend to go this far. I thought I'd have it apart again before you came back.'

There was a silence that lasted a long time. When Scanlon spoke again, his voice was curiously mild, 'Well, what have you done?'

'You won't be angry?'

'It's a little too late for that. You couldn't have made it much worse, anyway.'

'Well, I noticed here in your equations,' he extracted one sheet and then another and pointed, 'that whenever the expression representing the space-distortion fields occurs, it is always referred to as a function of x^2 plus y^2 plus z^2. Since the fields, as far as I could see, were always referred to as constants, that would give you the equation of a sphere.'

Scanlon nodded, 'I noticed that, but it has nothing to do with the problem.'

'Well, *I* thought it might indicate the necessary *arrangement* of the individual fields, so I disconnected the distorters and hooked them up again in a sphere.'

The inventor's mouth fell open. The mysterious rearrangement of his device seemed clear now – and what was more, eminently sensible.

'Does it work?' he asked.

'I'm not quite sure. The parts haven't been made to fit this arrangement so that it's only a rough set-up at best. Then there's the constant error—'

'But does it *work?* Close the switch, damn it!' Scanlon was all fire and impatience once more.

'All right, stand back. I cut the power to one-tenth normal so we won't get more output than we can handle.'

He closed the switch slowly, and at the moment of contact, a glowing ball of blue-white flame leaped into being from the recesses of the central quartz chamber. Scanlon screened his eyes automatically, and sought the output gauge. The needle was climbing steadily and did not stop until it was pressing the upper limit. The flame burned continuously, releasing no heat seemingly, though beside its light, more intensely brilliant than a magnesium flare, the electric lights faded into dingy yellowness.

Max opened the switch once more and the ball of flame reddened and died, leaving the room comparatively dark and red. The output gauge sank to zero once more and Scanlon felt his knees give beneath him as he sprawled onto a chair.

He fastened his gaze on the flustered Tweenie and in that look there was respect and awe, and something more, too, for there was *fear*. Never before had he really realized that the Tweenie was not of Earth or Mars but a member of a race apart. He noticed the difference now, not in the comparatively minor physical changes, but in the profound and searching mental gulf that he only now comprehended.

'Atomic power!' he croaked hoarsely. 'And solved by a boy, not yet twenty years old.'

Max's confusion was painful, 'You did all the real work, Mr Scanlon, years and years of it. I just happened to notice a little detail that you might have caught yourself the next day.' His voice died before the fixed and steady stare of the inventor.

'Atomic power – the greatest achievement of man so far, and we actually have it, we two.'

Both – guardian and ward – seemed awed at the grandeur and power of the thing they had created.

And in that moment the age of Electricity died.

Jefferson Scanlon sucked at his pipe contentedly. Outside, the snow was falling and the chill of winter was in the air, but inside, in the comfortable warmth, Scanlon sat and smoked and smiled to himself. Across the way, Beulah, likewise quietly happy, hummed softly in time to clicking knitting needles, stopping only occasionally as her fingers flew through an unusually intricate portion of the pattern. In the corner next the window sat Max, occupied in his usual pastime of reading, and Scanlon reflected with faint surprise that of late Max had confined his reading to light novels.

Much had happened since that well-remembered day over a year ago. For one thing, Scanlon was now a world-famous and world-adored scientist, and it would have been strange had he not been sufficiently human to be proud of it. Secondly, and scarcely less important, atomic power was remaking the world.

Scanlon thanked all the powers that were, over and over again, for the fact that war was a thing of two centuries past, for otherwise atomic power would have been the final ruination of civilization. As it was, the coalition of World Powers that now controlled the great force of Atomic Power proved it a real blessing and were introducing it into Man's life in the slow, gradual stages necessary to prevent economic upheaval.

Already, interplanetary travel had been revolutionized. From hazardous gambles, trips to Mars and Venus had become holiday jaunts to be negotiated in a third of the previous time, and trips to the outer planets were at last feasible.

Scanlon settled back further in his chair, and pondered once more upon the only fly in his wonderful pot of ointment. Max had refused all credit; stormily and violently refused to have his name as much as mentioned. The injustice of it galled Scanlon, but aside from a vague mention of 'capable assistants' he had said nothing; and the thought of it still made him feel an ace of a cad.

A sharp explosive noise brought him out of his reverie and he turned startled eyes towards Max, who had suddenly closed his book with a peevish slap.

'Hello,' exclaimed Scanlon, 'and what's wrong now?'

Max tossed the book aside and stood up, his underlip thrust out in a pout, 'I'm lonely, that's all.'

Scanlon's face fell, and he felt at an uncomfortable loss for words. 'I guess I know that, Max,' he said softly, at length. 'I'm sorry for you, but the conditions – are so—'

Max relented, and brightening up, placed an affectionate arm about his foster-father's shoulder, 'I didn't mean it that way, you know. It's just – well, I can't say it but it's that – you get to wishing you had someone your own age to talk to – someone of your own kind.'

Beulah looked up and bestowed a penetrating glance upon the young Tweenie but said nothing.

Scanlon considered, 'You're right, son, in a way. A friend and companion is the best thing a fellow can have, and I'm afraid Beulah and I don't qualify in that respect. One of your own kind, as you say, would be the ideal solution, but that's a tough proposition.' He rubbed his nose with one finger and gazed at the ceiling thoughtfully.

Max opened his mouth as if he were going to say something more, but changed his mind and turned pink for no evident reason. Then he muttered, barely loud enough for Scanlon to hear, 'I'm being silly!' With an abrupt turn he marched out of the room, banging the door loudly as he left.

The older man gazed after him with undisguised surprise, 'Well! What a funny way to act. What's got into him lately, anyway?'

Beulah halted the nimbly-leaping needles long enough to remark acidly, 'Men are born fools and blind into the bargain.'

'Is that so?' was the somewhat nettled response, 'And do *you* know what's biting him?'

'I certainly do. It's as plain as that terrible tie you're wearing. I've seen it for months now. Poor fellow!'

Scanlon shook his head, 'You're speaking in riddles, Beulah.'

The housekeeper laid her knitting aside and glanced at the inventor wearily, 'It's very simple. The boy is twenty. He needs company.'

'But that's just what he said. Is *that* your marvelous penetration?'

'Good lord, Jefferson. Has it been so long since you were twenty yourself? Do you mean to say that you honestly think he's referring to *male* company?'

'Oh,' said Scanlon, and then brightening suddenly, 'Oh!' He giggled in an inane manner.

'Well, what are you going to do about it?'

'Why – why, nothing. What *can* be done?'

'That's a fine way to speak of your ward, when you're rich enough to buy five hundred orphan asylums from basement to roof and never miss the money. It should be the easiest thing in the world to find a likely-looking young lady Tweenie to keep him company.'

Scanlon gazed at her, a look of intense horror on his face, 'Are you serious, Beulah? Are you trying to suggest that I go shopping for a female Tweenie for Max? Why – why, what do I know about women – especially Tweenie women. I don't know his standards. I'm liable to pick one he'll consider an ugly hag.'

'Don't raise silly objections, Jefferson. Outside of the hair, they're the same in looks as anyone else, and I'll leave it to you to pick a pretty one. There never was a bachelor old and crabbed enough not to be able to do *that*.'

'No! I won't do it. Of all the horrible ideas—'

'Jefferson! You're his guardian. You owe it to him.'

The words struck the inventor forcibly, 'I owe it to him,' he repeated. 'You're right there, more right than you know.' He sighed, 'I guess it's got to be done.'

Scanlon shifted uneasily from one trembling foot to the other under the piercing stare of the vinegar-faced official, whose name-board proclaimed in large letters – Miss Martin, Superintendent.

'Sit down, sir,' she said sourly. 'What do you wish?'

Scanlon cleared his throat. He had lost count of the asylums visited up to now and the task was rapidly becoming too much for him. He made a mental vow that this would be the last – either they would have a Tweenie of the proper sex, age, and appearance or he would throw up the whole thing as a bad job.

'I have come to see,' he began, in a carefully-prepared, but stammered speech, 'if there are any Twee— Martian half-breeds in your asylum. It is—'

'We have three,' interrupted the superintendent sharply.

'Any females?' asked Scanlon, eagerly.

'*All* females,' she replied, and her eye glittered with disapproving suspicion.

'Oh, good. Do you mind if I see them. It is—'

Miss Martin's cold glance did not waver, 'Pardon me, but before we go any further, I would like to know whether you're thinking of adopting a half-breed.'

'I *would* like to take out guardianship papers if I am suited. Is that so very unusual?'

'It certainly is,' was the prompt retort. 'You understand that in any such case, we must first make a thorough investigation of the family's status, both financial and social. It is the opinion of the government that these creatures are better off under state supervision, and adoption would be a difficult matter.'

'I know, madam, I know. I've had practical experience in this matter about fifteen months ago. I believe I can give you satisfaction as to my financial and social status without much trouble. My name is Jefferson Scanlon—'

'Jefferson Scanlon!' her exclamation was half a scream. In a trice, her face expanded into a servile smile, 'Why of course. I should have recognized you from the many pictures I've seen of you. How stupid of me. Pray do not trouble yourself with any further references. I'm sure that in your case,' this with a particularly genial expression, 'no red tape need be necessary.'

She sounded a desk-bell furiously. 'Bring down Madeline and the two little ones as soon as you can,' she snapped at the frightened maid who answered. 'Have them cleaned up and warn them to be on their best behavior.'

With this, she turned to Scanlon once more, 'It will not take long, Mr Scanlon. It is really such a great honor to have you here with us, and I am so ashamed at my abrupt treatment of you earlier. At first I didn't recognize you, though I saw immediately that you were some-one of importance.'

If Scanlon had been upset by the superintendent's former harsh haughtiness, he was entirely unnerved by her effusive geniality. He wiped his profusely-perspiring brow time and time again, answering in incoherent monosyllables the vivacious questions put to him. It was just as he had come to the wild decision of taking to his heels and escaping from the she-dragon by flight that the maid announced the three Tweenies and saved the situation.

Scanlon surveyed the three half-breeds with interest and sudden satisfaction. Two were mere children, perhaps ten years of age, but the third, some eighteen years old, was eligible from every point of view.

Her slight form was lithe and graceful even in the quiet attitude of wait-ing that she had assumed, and Scanlon, 'dried-up, dyed-in-the-wool bachelor' though he was, could not restrain a light nod of approval.

Her face was certainly what Beulah would call 'likely-looking' and her eyes, now bent towards the floor in shy confusion, were of a deep blue, which seemed a great point to Scanlon.

Even her strange hair was beautiful. It was only moderately high, not nearly the size of Max's lordly male crest, and its silky-white sheen caught the sunbeams and sent them back in glistening highlights. The two little ones grasped the skirt of their elder companion with tight grips and regarded the two adults in wide-eyed fright which increased as time passed.

'I believe, Miss Martin, that the young lady will do,' remarked Scanlon. 'She is exactly what I had in mind. Could you tell me how soon guardianship papers could be drawn up?'

'I could have them ready for you tomorrow, Mr Scanlon. In an unusual case such as yours, I could easily make special arrangements.'

'Thank you. I shall be back then—' he was interrupted by a loud sniffle. One of the little Tweenies could stand it no longer and had burst into tears, followed soon by the other.

'Madeline,' cried Miss Martin to the eighteen-year-old. 'Please keep Rose and Blanche quiet. This is an abominable exhibition.'

Scanlon intervened. It seemed to him that Madeline was rather pale and though she smiled and soothed the youngsters he was certain that there were tears in her eyes.

'Perhaps,' he suggested, 'the young lady has no wish to leave the institution. Of course, I wouldn't think of taking her on any but a purely voluntary basis.'

Miss Martin smiled superciliously, 'She won't make any trouble.' She turned to the young girl, 'You've heard of the great Jefferson Scanlon, haven't you?'

'Ye-es, Miss Martin,' replied the girl, in a low voice.

'Let me handle this, Miss Martin,' urged Scanlon. 'Tell me, girl, would you really prefer to stay here?'

'Oh, no,' she replied earnestly, 'I would be very glad to leave, though,' with an apprehensive glance at Miss Martin, 'I have been very well treated here. But you see – what's to be done with the two little ones? I'm all they have, and if I left, they – they—'

She broke down and snatched them to her with a sudden, fierce grip, 'I don't want to leave them, sir!' She kissed each softly, 'Don't cry, children. I won't leave you. They won't take me away.'

Scanlon swallowed with difficulty and groped for a handkerchief with which to blow his nose. Miss Martin gazed on with disapproving hauteur.

'Don't mind the silly thing, Mr Scanlon,' said she. 'I believe I can have everything ready by tomorrow noon.'

'Have ready guardianship papers for all three,' was the gruff reply.

'What? All three? Are you serious?'

'Certainly. I can do it if I wish, can't I?' he shouted.

'Why, of course, but—'

Scanlon left precipitately, leaving both Madeline and Miss Martin petrified, the latter with utter stupefaction, the former in a sudden upsurge of happiness. Even the ten-year-olds sensed the change in affairs and subsided into occasional sobs.

Beulah's surprise, when she met them at the airport and saw three Tweenies where she had expected one, is not to be described. But, on the whole, the surprise was a pleasant one, for little Rose and Blanche took to the elderly housekeeper immediately. Their first greeting was to bestow great, moist kisses upon Beulah's lined cheeks at which she glowed with joy and kissed them in turn.

With Madeline she was enchanted, whispering to Scanlon that he knew a little more about such matters than he pretended.

'If she had decent hair,' whispered Scanlon in reply, 'I'd marry her myself. That I would,' and he smiled in great self-satisfaction.

The arrival at home in mid-afternoon was the occasion of great excitement on the part of the two oldsters. Scanlon inveigled Max into accompanying him on a long walk together in the woods, and when the unsuspecting Max left, puzzled but willing, Beulah busied herself with setting the three newcomers at their ease.

They were shown over the house from top to bottom, the rooms assigned to them being indicated. Beulah prattled away continuously, joking and chaffing, until the Tweenies had lost all their shyness and felt as if they had known her forever.

Then, as the winter evening approached, she turned to Madeline rather abruptly and said, 'It's getting late. Do you want to come downstairs with me and help prepare supper for the men?'

Madeline was taken aback, 'The *men*. Is there, then, someone besides Mr Scanlon?'

'Oh, yes. There's Max. You haven't seen him yet.'

'Is Max a relation of yours?'

'No, child. He's another of Mr Scanlon's wards.'

'Oh, I see.' She blushed and her hand rose involuntarily to her hair.

Beulah saw in a moment the thoughts passing through her head and added in a softer voice, 'Don't worry, dear. He won't mind your being a Tweenie. He'll be *glad* to see you.'

It turned out, though, that 'glad' was an entirely inadequate adjective when applied to Max's emotions at the first sight of Madeline.

He tramped into the house in advance of Scanlon, taking off his overcoat and stamping the snow off his shoes as he did so.

'Oh, boy,' he cried at the half-frozen inventor who followed him in, 'why you were so anxious to saunter about on a freezer like today I don't know.' He sniffed the air appreciatively, 'Ah, do I smell lamb chops?' and he made for the dining-room in double-quick time.

It was at the threshold that he stopped suddenly, and gasped for air as if in the last throes of suffocation. Scanlon slipped by and sat down.

'Come on,' he said, enjoying the other's brick-red visage. 'Sit down. We have company today. This is Madeline and this is Rose and this is Blanche. And this,' he turned to the seated girls and noted with satisfaction that Madeline's pink face was turning a fixed glance of confusion upon the plate before her, 'is my ward, Max.'

'How do you do,' murmured Max, eyes like saucers, 'I'm pleased to meet you.'

Rose and Blanche shouted cheery greetings in reply but Madeline only raised her eyes fleetingly and then dropped them again.

The meal was a singularly quiet one. Max, though he had complained of a ravenous hunger all afternoon, allowed his chop and mashed potatoes to die of cold before him, while Madeline played with her food as if she did not know what it was there for. Scanlon and Beulah ate quietly and well, exchanging sly glances between bites.

Scanlon sneaked off after dinner, for he rightly felt that the more tactful touch of a woman was needed in these matters, and when Beulah joined him in his study some hours later, he saw at a glance that he had been correct.

'I've broken the ice,' she said happily, 'they're telling each other their life histories now and are getting along wonderfully. They're still afraid of each other, though, and insist on sitting at opposite ends of the room, but that'll wear off – and pretty quickly, too.'

'It's a fine match, Beulah, eh?'

'A finer one I've never seen. And little Rose and Blanche are angels. I've just put them to bed.'

There was a short silence, and then Beulah continued softly, 'That was the only time you were right and I was wrong – that time you first brought Max into the house and I objected – but that one time makes up for everything else. You are a credit to your dear mother, Jefferson.'

Scanlon nodded soberly, 'I wish I could make all Tweenies on earth so happy. It would be such a simple thing. If we treated them like humans instead of like criminals and gave them homes built especially for them and calculated especially for their happiness—'

'Well, why don't *you* do it?' interrupted Beulah.

Scanlon turned a serious eye upon the old housekeeper, 'That's exactly what I was leading up to.' His voice lapsed into a dreamy murmur, 'Just think. A town of Tweenies – run by them and for them – with its own governing officials and its own schools and its own public utilities. A little world within a world where the Tweenie can consider himself a human being – instead of a freak surrounded and looked down upon by endless multitudes of pure-bloods.'

He reached for his pipe and filled it slowly, 'The world owes a debt to *one* Tweenie which it can never repay – and I owe it to him as well. I'm going to do it. I'm going to create Tweenietown.'

That night he did not go to sleep. The stars turned in their grand circles and paled at last. The gray of dawn came and grew, but still Scanlon sat unmoving – dreaming and planning.

At eighty, age sat lightly upon Jefferson Scanlon's head. The spring was gone from his step, the sturdy straightness from his shoulders, but his robust health had not failed him, and his mind, beneath the shock of hair, now as white as any Tweenie's, still worked with undiminished vigor.

A happy life is not an aging one, and for forty years now, Scanlon had watched Tweenietown grow, and in the watching, had found happiness.

He could see it now stretched before him like a large, beautiful painting as he gazed out the window. A little gem of a town with a population of slightly more than a thousand, nestling amid three hundred square miles of fertile Ohio land.

Neat and sturdy houses, wide, clean streets, parks, theaters, schools, stores – a model town, bespeaking decades of intelligent effort and co-operation.

The door opened behind him and he recognized the soft step without needing to turn, 'Is that you, Madeline?'

'Yes, father,' for by no other title was he known to any inhabitant of Tweenietown. 'Max is returning with Mr Johanson.'

'That's good,' he gazed at Madeline tenderly. 'We've seen Tweenietown grow since those days long ago, haven't we?'

Madeline nodded and sighed.

'Don't sigh, dear. It's been well worth the years we've given to it. If only Beulah had lived to see it now.'

He shook his head as he thought of the old housekeeper, dead now a quarter of a century.

'Don't think such sad thoughts,' admonished Madeline in her turn. 'Here comes Mr Johanson. Remember it's the fortieth anniversary and a happy day; not a sad one.'

Charles B. Johanson was what is known as a 'shrewd' man. That is, he was an intelligent, far-seeing person, comparatively well-versed in the sciences, but one who was wont to put these good qualities into practice only in order to advance his own interest. Consequently, he went far in politics and was the first appointee to the newly created Cabinet post of Science and Technology.

It was the first official act of his to visit the world's greatest scientist and inventor, Jefferson Scanlon, who, in his old age, still had no peer in the number of useful inventions turned over to the government every year. Tweenietown was a considerable surprise to him. It was known rather vaguely in the outside world that the town existed, and it was considered a hobby of the old scientist – a harmless eccentricity. Johanson found it a well-worked-out project of sinister connotations.

His attitude, however, when he entered Scanlon's room in company with his erstwhile guide, Max, was one of frank geniality, concealing well certain thoughts that swept through his mind.

'Ah, Johanson,' greeted Scanlon, 'you're back. What do you think of all this?' his arm made a wide sweep.

'It is surprising – something marvelous to behold,' Johanson assured him.

Scanlon chuckled, 'Glad to hear it. We have a population of 1154 now and growing every day. You've seen what we've done already but it's nothing to what we are going to do in the future – even after my death. However, there is something I wish to see done *before* I die and for that I'll need your help.'

'And that is?' questioned the Secretary of Science and Technology guardedly.

'Just this. That you sponsor measures giving these Tweenies, these so long despised half-breeds, full equality, political, legal, economic, social, with Terrestrials and Martians.'

Johanson hesitated, 'It would be difficult. There is a certain amount of perhaps understandable prejudice against them, and until we can convince Earth that the Tweenies deserve equality—' he shook his head doubtfully.

'Deserve equality!' exclaimed Scanlon, vehemently, 'Why, they deserve more. I am *moderate* in my demands.' At these words, Max, sitting quietly in a corner, looked up and bit his lip, but said nothing as Scanlon continued, 'You don't know the true worth of these Tweenies. They combine the best of Earth and Mars. They possess the cold, analytical reasoning powers of the Martians together with the emotional drive and boundless energy of the Earthman. As far as intellect is concerned, they are your superior and mine, every one of them. I ask only equality.'

The Secretary siniled soothingly, 'Your zeal misleads you perhaps, my dear Scanlon.'

'It does not. Why do you suppose I turn out so many successful gadgets – like this gravitational shield I created a few years back. Do you think I could have done it without my Tweenie assistants? It was Max here,' Max dropped his eyes before the sudden piercing gaze of the Cabinet member, 'that put the final touch upon my discovery of atomic power itself.'

Scanlon threw caution to the winds, as he grew excited, 'Ask Professor Whitsun of Stanford and he'll tell you. He's a world authority on psychology and knows what he's talking about. He *studied* the Tweenie and he'll tell you that the Tweenie is the *coming* race of the Solar System, destined to take the supremacy away from us pure-bloods as inevitably as night follows day. Don't you think they deserve equality in that case?'

'Yes, I do think so – definitely,' replied Johanson. There was a strange glitter in his eyes, and a crooked smile upon his lips, 'This is of extreme importance, Scanlon. I shall attend to it immediately. So immediately, in fact, that I believe I had better leave in half an hour, to catch the 2:10 strato-car.'

Johanson had scarcely left, when Max approached Scanlon and blurted out with no preamble at all, 'There is something I have to show you, father – something you have not known about before.'

Scanlon stared in surprise, 'What do you mean?'

'Come with me, please, father. I shall explain.' His grave expression was almost frightening. Madeline joined the two at the door, and at a sign from Max, seemed to comprehend the situation. She said nothing but her eyes grew sad and the lines in her forehead seemed to deepen. In utter silence, the three entered the waiting Rocko-car and were sped across the town in the direction of the Hill o' the Woods. High over Lake Clare they shot to come down once more in the wooded patch at the foot of the hill.

A tall, burly Tweenie sprang to attention as the car landed, and started at the sight of Scanlon.

'Good afternoon, father,' he whispered respectfully, and cast a questioning glance at Max as he did so.

'Same to you, Emmanuel,' replied Scanlon absently. He suddenly became aware that before him was a cleverly-camouflaged opening that led into the very hill itself.

Max beckoned him to follow and led the way into the opening which after a hundred feet opened into an enormous man-made cavern. Scanlon halted in utter amazement, for before him were three giant space-ships, gleaming silvery-white and equipped, as he could plainly see, with the latest atomic power.

'I'm sorry, father,' said Max, 'that all this was done without your knowledge. It is the only case of the sort in the history of Tweenietown.' Scanlon scarcely seemed to hear, standing as if in a daze, and Max continued, 'The center one is the flagship – the *Jefferson Scanlon*. The one to the right is the *Beulah Goodkin* and the one to the left the *Madeline*.'

Scanlon snapped out of his bemusement, 'But what does this all mean and why the secrecy?'

'These ships have been lying ready for five years now, fully fuelled and provisioned, ready for instant take-off. Tonight, we blast away the side of the hill and shoot for Venus – tonight. We have not told you till now, for we did not wish to disturb your peace of mind with a misfortune we knew long ago to be inevitable. We had thought that perhaps,' his voice sank lower, 'its fulfillment might have been postponed until after you were no longer with us.'

'Speak out,' cried Scanlon suddenly. 'I want the full details. Why do you leave just as I feel sure I can obtain full equality for you?'

'Exactly,' answered Max, mournfully. 'Your words to Johanson swung the scale. As long as Earthmen and Martians merely thought us different and inferior, they despised us and tolerated us. You have told Johanson we were superior and would ultimately supplant Mankind. They have no alternative now but to hate us. There shall be no further toleration; of that I can assure you. We leave before the storm breaks.'

The old man's eyes widened as the truth of the other's statements became apparent to him, 'I see. I must get in touch with Johanson.

Perhaps, we can together correct that terrible mistake.' He clapped a hand to his forehead.

'Oh, Max,' interposed Madeline, tearfully, 'why don't you come to the point? We want you to come with us, father. In Venus, which is so sparsely settled, we can find a spot where we can develop unharmed for an unlimited time. We can establish our nation, free and untrammeled, powerful in our own right, no longer dependent on—'

Her voice died away and she gazed anxiously at Scanlon's face, now grown drawn and haggard. 'No,' he whispered, 'no! My place is here with my own kind. Go, my children, and establish your nation. In the end, your descendants shall rule the System. But I – I shall stay here.'

'Then I shall stay, too,' insisted Max. 'You are old and someone must care for you. I owe you my life a dozen times over.'

Scanlon shook his head firmly, 'I shall need no one. Dayton is not far. I shall be well taken care of there or anywhere else I go. You, Max, are needed by your race. You are their leader. Go!'

Scanlon wandered through the deserted streets of Tweenietown and tried to take a grip upon himself. It was hard. Yesterday, he had celebrated the fortieth anniversary of its founding—it had been at the peak of its prosperity. Today, it was a ghost town.

Yet, oddly enough, there was a spirit of exultation about him. His dream had shattered – but only to give way to a brighter dream. He had nourished foundlings and brought up a race in its youth and for that he was someday to be recognized as the founder of the *super-race*.

It was *his* creation that would someday rule the system. Atomic power – gravity nullifiers – all faded into insignificance. *This* was his real gift to the Universe.

This, he decided, was how a God must feel.

The Secret Sense

The lilting strains of a Strauss waltz filled the room. The music waxed and waned beneath the sensitive fingers of Lincoln Fields, and through half-closed eyes he could almost see whirling figures pirouetting about the waxed floor of some luxurious salon.

Music always affected him that way. It filled his mind with dreams of sheer beauty and transformed his room into a paradise of sound. His hands flickered over the piano in the last delicious combinations of tones and then slowed reluctantly to a halt.

He sighed and for a moment remained absolutely silent as if trying to extract the last essence of beauty from the dying echoes. Then he turned and smiled faintly at the other occupant of the room.

Garth Jan smiled in turn but said nothing. Garth had a great liking for Lincoln Fields, though little understanding. They were worlds apart – literally – for Garth hailed from the giant underground cities of Mars while Fields was the product of sprawling Terrestrial New York.

'How was that, Garth, old fellow?' questioned Fields doubtfully.

Garth shook his head. He spoke in his precise, painstaking manner, 'I listened attentively and can truly say that it was not unpleasant.

There is a certain rhythm, a cadence of sorts, which, indeed, is rather soothing. But beautiful? No!'

There was pity in Fields' eyes – pity almost painful in its intensity. The Martian met the gaze and understood all that it meant, yet there was no answering spark of envy. His bony giant figure remained doubled up in a chair that was too small for him and one thin leg swung leisurely back and forth.

Fields lunged out of his seat impetuously and grasped his companion by the arm. 'Here! Seat yourself on the bench.'

Garth obeyed genially. 'I see you want to carry out some little experiment.'

'You've guessed it. I've read scientific works which tried to explain all about the difference in sense-equipment between Earthman and Martian, but I never could quite grasp it all.'

He tapped the notes C and F in a single octave and glanced at the Martian inquiringly.

'If there's a difference,' said Garth doubtfully, 'it's a very slight one. If I were listening casually, I would certainly say you had hit the same note twice.'

The Earthman marveled. 'How's this?' He tapped C and G.

'I can hear the difference this time.'

'Well, I suppose all they say about your people is true. You poor fellows – to have such a crude sense of hearing. You don't know what you're missing.'

The Martian shrugged his shoulders fatalistically. 'One misses nothing that one has never possessed.'

Garth Jan broke the short silence that followed. 'Do you realize that this period of history is the first in which two intelligent races have been able to communicate with each other? The comparison of sense equipment is highly interesting – and rather broadens one's views on life.'

'That's right,' agreed the Earthman, 'though we seem to have all the advantage of the comparison. You know a Terrestrial biologist stated last month that he was amazed that a race so poorly equipped in the matter of sense-perception could develop so high a civilization as yours.'

'All is relative, Lincoln. What we have is sufficient for us.'

Fields felt a growing frustration within him. 'But if you only *knew*, Garth, if you only *knew* what you were missing.

'You've never seen the beauties of a sunset or of dancing fields of flowers. You can't admire the blue of the sky, the green of the grass, the yellow of ripe corn. To you the world consists of shades of dark and light.' He shuddered at the thought. 'You can't smell a flower or appreciate its delicate perfume. You can't even enjoy such a simple thing as a good, hearty meal. You can't taste nor smell nor see color. I pity you for your drab world.'

'What you say is meaningless, Lincoln. Waste no pity on me, for I am as happy as you.' He rose and reached for his cane – necessary in the greater gravitational field of Earth.

'You must not judge us with such easy superiority, you know.' That seemed to be the galling aspect of the matter. 'We do not boast of certain accomplishments of our race of which you know nothing.'

And then, as if heartily regretting his words, a wry grimace overspread his face, and he started for the door.

Fields sat puzzled and thoughtful for a moment, then jumped up and ran after the Martian, who was stumping his way towards the exit. He gripped Garth by the shoulder and insisted that he return.

'What did you mean by that last remark?'

The Martian turned his face away as if unable to face his questioner. 'Forget it, Lincoln. That was just a moment of indiscretion when your unsolicited pity got on my nerves.'

Fields gave him a sharp glance. 'It's true, isn't it? It's logical that Martians possess senses Earthmen do not, but it passes the bounds of reason that your people should want to keep it secret.'

'That is as it may be. But now that you've found me out through my own utter stupidity, you will perhaps agree to let it go no further?'

'Of course! I'll be as secret as the grave, though I'm darned if I can make anything of it. Tell me, of what nature is this secret sense of yours?'

Garth Jan shrugged listlessly. 'How can I explain? Can you define color to me, who cannot even conceive it?'

'I'm not asking for a definition. Tell me its uses. Please,' he gripped the other's shoulder, 'you might as well. I have given my promise of secrecy.'

The Martian sighed heavily. 'It won't do you much good. Would it satisfy you to know that if you were to show me two containers, each filled with a clear liquid, I could tell you at once whether either of the two were poisonous? Or, if you were to show me a copper wire, I could tell instantly whether an electric current were passing through it, even if it were as little as a thousandth of an ampere? Or I could tell you the temperature of any substance within three degrees of the true value even if you held it as much as five yards away? Or I could – well, I've said enough.'

'Is that all?' demanded Fields, with a disappointed cry. 'What more do you wish?'

'All you've described is very useful – but where is the beauty in it? Has this strange sense of yours no value to the spirit as well as to the body?'

Garth Jan made an impatient movement. 'Really, Lincoln, you talk foolishly. I have given you only that for which you asked – the uses I put this sense to. I certainly didn't attempt to explain its nature. Take your color sense. As far as I can see its only use is in making certain fine distinctions which I cannot. You can identify certain chemical solutions, for instance, by something you call color when I would be forced to run a chemical analysis. Where's the beauty in that?'

Fields opened his mouth to speak but the Martian motioned him testily into silence. 'I know. You're going to babble foolishness about sunsets or something. But what do you know of beauty? Have you ever known what it was to witness the beauty of the naked copper wires when an AC current is turned on? Have you sensed the delicate loveliness of induced currents set up in a solenoid when a magnet is passed through it? Have you ever attended a Martian *portwem?*'

Garth Jan's eyes had grown misty with the thoughts he was conjuring up, and Fields stared in utter amazement. The shoe was on the other foot now and his sense of superiority left him of a sudden.

'Every race has its own attributes,' he mumbled with a fatalism that had just a trace of hypocrisy in it, 'but I see no reason why you should keep it such a blasted secret. We Earthmen have kept no secrets from your race.'

'Don't accuse us of ingratitude,' cried Garth Jan vehemently. According to the Martian code of ethics, ingratitude was the supreme vice, and at the insinuation of that Garth's caution left him. 'We never act without reason, we Martians. And certainly it is not for our own sake that we hide this magnificent ability.'

The Earthman smiled mockingly. He was on the trail of something – he felt it in his bones – and the only way to get it out was to *tease* it out.

'No doubt there is some nobility behind it all. It is a strange attribute of your race that you can always find some altruistic motive for your actions.'

Garth Jan bit his lip angrily. 'You have no right to say that.' For a moment he thought of pleading worry over Fields' future peace of mind as a reason for silence, but the latter's mocking reference to 'altruism' had rendered that impossible. A feeling of anger crept over him gradually and that forced him to his decision.

There was no mistaking the note of frigid unfriendliness that entered his voice. 'I'll explain by analogy.' The Martian stared straight ahead of him as he spoke, eyes half-closed.

'You have told me that I live in a world that is composed merely of shades of light and dark. You try to describe a world of your own composed of infinite variety and beauty. I listen but care little concerning it. I have never known it and never can know it. One does not weep over the loss of what one has never owned.

'But – what if you were able to give me the ability to see color for five minutes? What if, for five minutes, I reveled in wonders undreamed of? What if, after those five minutes, I have to return it *forever?* Would those five minutes of paradise be worth a lifetime of regret afterwards – a lifetime of dissatisfaction because of my own shortcomings? Would it not have been the kinder act never to have told me of color in the first place and so have removed its ever-present temptation?'

Fields had risen to his feet during the last part of the Martians speech and his eyes opened wide in a wild surmise. 'Do you mean an Earthman could possess the Martian sense if so desired?'

'For five minutes in a lifetime,' Garth Jan's eyes grew dreamy, 'and in those five minutes sense—'

He came to a confused halt and glared angrily at his companion, 'You know more than is good for you. See that you don't forget your promise.'

He rose hastily and hobbled away as quickly as he could, leaning heavily upon the cane. Lincoln Fields made no move to stop him. He merely sat there and thought.

The great height of the cavern shrouded the roof in misty obscurity in which, at fixed intervals, there floated luminescent globes of radite. The air, heated by this subterranean volcanic stratum, wafted past gently. Before Lincoln Fields stretched the wide, paved avenue of the principal city of Mars, fading away into the distance.

He clumped awkwardly up to the entrance of the home of Garth Jan, the six-inch-thick layer of lead attached to each shoe a nuisance unending. Though it was still better than the uncontrollable bounding Earth muscles brought about in this lighter gravity.

The Martian was surprised to see his friend of six months ago but not altogether joyful. Fields was not slow to notice this but he merely smiled to himself. The opening formalities passed, the conventional remarks were made, and the two seated themselves.

Fields crushed the cigarette in the ash-tray and sat upright suddenly serious. 'I've come to ask for those five minutes you claim you can give me! May I have them?'

'Is that a rhetorical question? It certainly doesn't seem to require an answer.' Garth's tone was openly contemptuous.

The Earthman considered the other thoughtfully. 'Do you mind if I outline my position in a few words?'

The Martian smiled indifferently. 'It won't make any difference,' he said.

'I'll take my chance on that. The situation is this: I've been born and reared in the lap of luxury and have been most disgustingly spoiled. I've never yet had a reasonable desire that I have not been able to fulfill, and I don't know what it means *not* to get what I want. Do you see?'

There was no answer and he continued, 'I have found my happiness in beautiful sights, beautiful words, and beautiful sounds. I have made a cult of beauty. In a word, I am an aesthete.'

'Most interesting,' the Martian's stony expression did not change a whit, 'but what bearing has all this on the problem at hand?'

'Just this: You speak of a new form of beauty – a form unknown to me at present and entirely inconceivable even, but one which could be known if you so wished. The notion attracts me. It more than attracts me – it makes its demands of me. Again I remind you that when a notion begins to make demands of me, I yield – I always have.'

'You are not the master in this case,' reminded Garth Jan. 'It is crude of me to remind you of this, but you cannot force *me*, you know. Your words, in fact, are almost offensive in their implications.'

'I am glad you said that, for it allows me to be crude in my turn without offending my conscience.'

Garth Jan's only reply to this was a self-confident grimace.

'I make my demand of you,' said Fields, slowly, 'in the name of gratitude.'

'Gratitude?' the Martian started violently.

Fields grinned broadly, 'It's an appeal no honorable Martian can refuse – by your own ethics. You owe me gratitude, now, because it was through me you gained entrance into the houses of the greatest and most honorable men of Earth.'

'I know that,' Garth Jan flushed angrily. 'You are impolite to remind me of it.'

'I have no choice. You acknowledged the gratitude you owe me in actual words, back on Earth. I demand the chance to possess this mysterious sense you keep so secret – in the name of this acknowledged gratitude. Can you refuse now?'

'You know I can't,' was the gloomy response. 'I hesitated only for your own sake.'

The Martian rose and held out his hand gravely, 'You have me by the neck, Lincoln. It is done. Afterwards, though, I owe you nothing more. This will pay my debt of gratitude. Agreed?'

'Agreed!' The two shook hands and Lincoln Fields continued in an entirely different tone. 'We're still friends, though, aren't we? This little altercation won't spoil things?'

'I hope not. Come! Join me at the evening meal and we can discuss the time and place of your – er – five minutes.'

Lincoln Fields tried hard to down the faint nervousness that filled him as he waited in Garth Jan's private 'concert'-room. He felt a sudden desire to laugh as the thought came to him that he felt exactly as he usually did in a dentist's waiting room.

He lit his tenth cigarette, puffed twice and threw it away, 'You're doing this very elaborately, Garth.'

The Martian shrugged, 'You have only five minutes so I might as well see to it that they are put to the best possible use. You're going to "hear" part of a *portwem*, which is to our sense what a great symphony (is that the word?) is to sound.'

'Have we much longer to wait? The suspense, to be trite, is terrible.'

'We're waiting for Novi Lon, who is to play the *portwem*, and for Done Vol, my private physician. They'll be along soon.'

Fields wandered onto the low dais that occupied the center of the room and regarded the intricate mechanism thereupon with curious interest. The fore-part was encased in gleaming aluminum leaving exposed only seven tiers of shining black knobs above and five large white pedals below. Behind, however, it lay open, and within there ran crossings and recrossings of finer wires in incredibly complicated paths.

'A curious thing, this,' remarked the Earthman.

The Martian joined him on the dais, 'It's an expensive instrument. It cost me ten thousand Martian credits.'

'How does it work?'

'Not so differently from a Terrestrial piano. Each of the upper knobs controls a different electric circuit. Singly and together an expert *portwem* player could, by manipulating the knobs, form any conceivable pattern of electric current. The pedals below control the strength of the current.'

Fields nodded absently and ran his fingers over the knobs at random. Idly, he noticed the small galvanometer located just above the keys kick violently each time he depressed a knob. Aside from that, he sensed nothing.

'Is the instrument really playing?'

The Martian smiled, 'Yes, it is. And a set of unbelievably atrocious discords too.'

He took a seat before the instrument and with a murmured 'Here's how!' his fingers skimmed rapidly and accurately over the gleaming buttons.

The sound of a reedy Martian voice crying out in strident accents broke in upon him, and Garth Jan ceased in sudden embarrassment. 'This is Novi Lon,' he said hastily to Fields, 'As usual, he does not like my playing.'

Fields rose to meet the newcomer. He was bent of shoulder and evidently of great age. A fine tracing of wrinkles, especially about eyes and mouth, covered his face.

'So this is the young Earthman,' he cried, in strongly-accented English. 'I disapprove your rashness but sympathize with your desire to attend a *portwem*. It is a great pity you can own our sense for no more than five minutes. Without it no one can truly be said to live.'

Garth Jan laughed, 'He exaggerates, Lincoln. He's one of the greatest musicians of Mars, and thinks anyone doomed to damnation who would not rather attend a *portwem* than breathe.' He hugged the older man warmly, 'He was my teacher in my youth and many were the long hours in which he struggled to teach me the proper combinations of circuits.'

'And I have failed after all, you dunce,' snapped the old Martian. 'I heard your attempt at playing as I entered. You still have not learned the proper *fortgass* combination. You were desecrating the soul of the great Bar Danin. My pupil! Bah! It is a disgrace!'

The entrance of the third Martian, Done Vol, prevented Novi Lon from continuing his tirade. Garth, glad of the reprieve, approached the physician hastily.

'Is all ready?'

'Yes,' growled Vol surlily, 'and a particularly uninteresting experiment this will be. We know all the results beforehand.' His eyes fell upon the Earthman, whom he eyed contemptuously. 'Is this the one who wishes to be inoculated?'

Lincoln Fields nodded eagerly and felt his throat and mouth go dry suddenly. He eyed the newcomer uncertainly and felt uneasy at the sight of a tiny bottle of clear liquid and a hypodermic which the physician had extracted from a case he was carrying.

'What are you going to do?' he demanded.

'He'll merely inoculate you. It'll take a second,' Garth Jan assured him. 'You see, the sense-organs in this case are several groups of cells in the cortex of the brain. They are activated by a hormone, a synthetic preparation of which is used to stimulate the dormant cells of the occasional Martian who is born – er – "blind". You'll receive the same treatment.'

'Oh! – then Earthmen possess those cortex cells?'

'In a very rudimentary state. The concentrated hormone will activate them, but only for five minutes. After that time, they are literally blown out as a result of their unwonted activity. After that, they can't be re-activated under *any* circumstances.'

Done Vol completed his last-minute preparations and approached Fields. Without a word, Fields extended his right arm and the hypodermic plunged in.

With the, operation completed, the Terrestrial waited a moment or two and then essayed a shaky laugh, 'I don't feel any change.'

'You won't for about ten minutes,' explained Garth. 'It takes time. Just sit back and relax. Novi Lon has begun Bar Danin's "Canals in the Desert" – it is my favorite – and when the hormone begins its work you will find yourself in the very middle of things.'

Now that the die was cast irrevocably, Fields found himself stonily calm. Novi Lon played furiously, and Garth Jan, at the Earthman's right, was already lost in the composition. Even Done Vol, the fussy doctor, had forgotten his peevishness for the nonce.

Fields snickered under his breath. The Martians listened attentively but to him the room was devoid of sound and – almost – of all other sensation as well. What – no, it was impossible, of course – but what if it were just an elaborate practical joke? He stirred uneasily and put the thought from his mind angrily.

The minutes passed; Novi Lon's fingers flew; Garth Jan's expression was one of unfeigned delight.

Then Lincoln Fields blinked his eyes rapidly. For a moment a nimbus of color seemed to surround the musician and his instrument. He couldn't identify it – but it was, there. It grew and spread until the room was full of it. Other hues came to join it and still others. They wove and wavered; expanding and contracting; changing with lightning speed and yet staying the same. Intricate patterns of brilliant tints formed and faded, beating in silent bursts of color upon the young man's eyeballs.

Simultaneously, there came the impression of sound. From a whisper it rose into a glorious, ringing shout that wavered up and down the scale in quivering tremolos. He seemed to hear every instrument from fife to bass viol simultaneously, and yet, paradoxically, each rang in his ear in solitary clearness.

And together with this, there came the more subtle sensation of odor. From a suspicion, a mere trace, it waxed into a phantasmal field of flowers. Delicate spicy scents followed each other in ever stronger succession; in gentle wafts of pleasure.

Yet all this was nothing. Fields knew that. Somehow, he *knew* that what he saw, heard, and smelt were mere delusions – mirages of a brain that frantically attempted to interpret an entirely new conception in the old, familiar ways.

Gradually, the colors and the sounds and the scents died. His brain was beginning to realize that that which beat upon it was something hitherto unexperienced. The effect of the hormone became stronger, and suddenly – in one burst – Fields realized what it was he sensed.

He didn't see it – nor hear it – nor smell it – nor taste it – nor feel it. He knew what it was but he couldn't think of the word for it. Slowly, he realized that there wasn't any word for it. Even more slowly, he realized that there wasn't even any *concept* for it.

Yet he knew what it was.

There beat upon his brain something that consisted of pure waves of enjoyment – something that lifted him out of himself and pitched him headlong into a universe unknown to him earlier. He was falling through an endless eternity of – something. It wasn't sound or sight but it was – something. Something that enfolded him and hid his surroundings from him – that's what it was. It was endless and infinite in its variety, and with each crashing wave, he glimpsed a farther horizon, and the wonderful cloak of sensation became thicker – and softer – and more beautiful.

Then came the discord. Like a little crack at first – marring a perfect beauty. Then spreading and branching and growing wider, until, finally, it split apart thunderously – though without a sound.

Lincoln Fields, dazed and bewildered, found himself back in the concert room again.

He lurched to his feet and grasped Garth Jan by the arm violently, 'Garth! Why did he stop? Tell him to continue! Tell him!'

Garth Jan's startled expression faded into pity, 'He is still playing, Lincoln.'

The Earthman's befuddled state showed no signs of understanding. He gazed about him with unseeing eyes. Novi Lon's fingers sped across the keyboard as nimbly as ever; the expression on his face was as rapt as ever. Slowly, the truth seeped in, and the Earthman's empty eyes filled with horror.

He sat down, uttering one hoarse cry, and buried his head in his hands.

The five minutes had passed! There could be no return!

Garth Jan was smiling – a smile of dreadful malice, 'I had pitied you just a moment ago, Lincoln, but now I'm glad – glad! You forced this out of me – you made me do this. I hope you're satisfied, because I certainly am. For the rest of your life,' his voice sank to a sibilant whisper, 'you'll remember these five minutes and know what it is you're missing – what it is you can never have again. You are blind, Lincoln – blind!'

The Earthman raised a haggard face and grinned, but it was no more than a horrible baring of the teeth. It took every ounce of willpower he possessed to maintain an air of composure.

He did not trust himself to speak. With wavering step, he marched out of the room, head held high to the end.

And within, that tiny, bitter voice, repeating over and over again, 'You entered a normal man! You leave blind – *blind* – BLIND.'

Homo Sol

The seven thousand and fifty-fourth session of the Galactic Congress sat in solemn conclave in the vast semicircular hall on Eon, second planet of Arcturus.

Slowly, the president delegate rose to his feet. His broad Arcturian countenance flushed slightly with excitement as he surveyed the surrounding delegates. His sense of the dramatic caused him to pause a moment or so before making the official announcement – for, after all, the entrance of a new planetary system into the great Galactic family is not a thing likely to happen twice in any one man's lifetime.

A dead silence prevailed during that pause. The two hundred and eighty-eight delegates – one from each of the two hundred and eighty-eight oxygen-atmosphere, water-chemistry worlds of the System – waited patiently for him to speak.

Beings of every manlike type and shape were there. Some were tall and polelike, some broad and burly, some short and stumpy. There were those with long, wiry hair, those with scanty gray fuzz covering head and face, others with thick, blond curls piled high, and still others entirely bald. Some possessed long, hair-covered trumpets

of ears, others had tympanum membranes flush with their temples.
There were those present with large gazelle-like eyes of a deep-purple
luminosity, others with tiny optics of a beady black. There was a delegate with green skin, one with an eight-inch proboscis and one with a
vestigial tail. Internally, variation was almost infinite.

But all were alike in two things.

They were all Humanoid. They all possessed intelligence.

The president delegate's voice boomed out then: 'Delegates! The
system of Sol has discovered the secret of interstellar travel and by
that act becomes eligible for entrance into the Galactic Federation.'

A storm of approving shouts arose from those present and the
Arcturian raised a hand for silence.

'I have here,' he continued, 'the official report from Alpha Centauri, on whose fifth planet the Humanoids of Sol have landed. The
report is entirely satisfactory and so the ban upon travel into and
communication with the Solarian System is lifted. Sol is free, and
open to the ships of the Federation. Even now, there is in preparation an expedition to Sol, under the leadership of Joselin Arn of
Alpha Centauri, to tender that System the formal invitation into the
Federation.'

He paused, and from two hundred and eighty-eight throats came
the stentorian shout: 'Hail, Homo Sol! Hail, Homo Sol! *Hail!*'

It was the traditional welcome of the Federation for all new
worlds.

Tan Porus raised himself to his full height of five feet two – he was tall
for a Rigellian – and his sharp, green eyes snapped with annoyance.

'There it is, Lo-fan. For six months that damned freak squid from
Beta Draconis IV has stumped me.'

Lo-fan stroked his forehead gently with one long finger, and one
hairy ear twitched several times. He had traveled eighty-five light
years to be here on Arcturus II with the greatest psychologist of the
Federation – and, more specifically, to see this strange mollusk whose
reactions had stumped the great Rigellian.

He was seeing it now: a puffy, dull-purple mass of soft flesh that writhed its tentacular form in placid unconcern through the huge tank of water that held it. With unruffled serenity, it fed on the green fronds of an underwater fern.

'Seems ordinary enough,' said Lo-fan.

'Ha!' snorted Tan Porus. 'Watch this.'

He drew the curtain and plunged the room into darkness. Only a dim blue light shone upon the tank, and in the murk the Draconian squid could barely be discerned.

'Here goes the stimulus,' grunted Porus. The screen above his head burst into soft green light, focused directly upon the tank. It persisted a moment and gave way to a dull red and then almost at once to a brilliant yellow. For half a minute it shot raggedly through the spectrum and then, with a final glare of glowing white, a clear bell-like tone sounded.

And as the echoes of the note died away, a shudder passed over the squid's body. It relaxed and sank slowly to the bottom of the tank.

Porus pulled aside the curtain. 'It's *sound* asleep,' he growled. 'Hasn't failed yet. Every specimen we've ever had drops as if shot the moment that note sounds.'

'Asleep, eh? That's strange. Have you got the figures on the stimulus?'

'Certainly! Right here. The exact wave lengths of the lights required are listed, plus the length of duration of each light unit, plus the exact pitch of the sounded note at the end.'

The other surveyed the figures dubiously. His forehead wrinkled and his ears rose in surprise. From an inner pocket, he drew forth a slide rule.

'What type nervous system has the animal?'

'Two-B. Plain, simple, ordinary Two-B. I've had the anatomists, physiologists, and ecologists check that until they were blue in the face. Two-B is all they get. Damn fools!'

Lo-fan said nothing, but pushed the center bar of the rule back and forth carefully. He stopped and peered closely, shrugged his shoulders, and reached for one of the huge volumes on the shelf above his head. He leafed through the pages and picked out numbers from among the close print. Again the slide rule.

Finally he stopped. 'It doesn't make sense,' he said helplessly.

'I know that! I've tried six times in six different ways to explain that reaction – and I failed each time. Even if I rig up a system that will explain its going to sleep, I can't get it to explain the specificity of the stimulus.'

'It's highly specific?' questioned Lo-fan, his voice reaching the higher registers.

'That's the worst part of it,' shouted Tan Porus. He leaned forward and tapped the other on the knee. 'If you shift the wave length of any of the light units by fifty angstroms either way – any *one* of them – it doesn't sleep. Shift the length of duration of a light unit two seconds either way – it doesn't sleep. Shift the pitch of the tone at the end an eighth of an octave either way – it doesn't sleep. *But* get the right combination, and it goes straight into a coma.'

Lo-fan's ears were two hairy trumpets, stiffly erect. 'Galaxy!' he whispered. 'How did you ever stumble on the combination?'

'I didn't. It happened at Beta Draconis. Some hick college was putting its freshmen through a lab period on light-sound reactions of molluscoids – been doing it for years. Some student runs through his light-sound combinations and his blasted specimen goes to sleep. Naturally, he's scared out of his wits and brings it to the instructor. The instructor tries it again on another squid – it goes to sleep. They shift the combination – nothing happens. They go back to the original – it goes to sleep. After they fooled around with it long enough to know they couldn't make head or tail of it, they sent it to Arcturus and wished it on me. It's six months since *I* had a real night's sleep.'

A musical note sounded and Porus turned impatiently.

'What is it?'

'Messenger from the president delegate of Congress, sir,' came in metallic tones from the telecaster on his desk.

'Send him up.'

The messenger stayed only long enough to hand Porus an impressively sealed envelope and to say in hearty tone: 'Great news, sir. The system of Sol has qualified for enhance.'

'So what?' snorted Porus beneath his breath as the other left. 'We all knew it was coming.'

He ripped off the outer sheath of cello-fiber from the envelope and removed the sheaf of papers from within. He glanced through them and grimaced.

'Oh, *Rigel!*'

'What's wrong?' asked Lo-fan.

'Those politicians keep bothering me with the most inconsequential things. You'd think there wasn't another psychologist on Eron. Look! We've been expecting the Solarian System to solve the principle of the hyperatomo any century now. They've finally done it and an expedition of theirs landed on Alpha Centauri. At once, there's a politicians' holiday! We must send an expedition of our own to ask them to join the Federation. And, of course, we must have a psychologist along to ask them in a nice way so as to be sure of getting the right reaction, because, to be sure, there isn't a man in the army that ever gets proper training in psychology.'

Lo-fan nodded seriously. 'I know, I know. We have the same trouble out our way. They don't need psychology until they get into trouble and then they come running.'

'Well, it's a cinch *I'm* not going to Sol. This sleeping squid is too important to neglect. It's a routine job, anyway – this business of raking in new worlds; a Type A reaction that any sophomore can handle.'

'Whom will you send?'

'I don't know. I've got several good juniors under me that can do this sort of thing with their eyes closed. I'll send one of them. And meanwhile, I'll be seeing you at the faculty meeting tomorrow, won't I?'

'You will – and hearing me, too. I'm making a speech on the finger-touch stimulus.'

'Good! I've done work on it, so I'll be interested in hearing what you have to say. Till tomorrow, then.'

Left alone, Porus turned once more to the official report on the Solarian System which the messenger had handed him. He leafed through it leisurely, without particular interest, and finally put it down with a sigh.

'Lor Haridin could do it,' he muttered to himself. 'He's a good kid – deserves a break.'

He lifted his tiny bulk out of the chair and, with the report under his arm, left his office and trotted down the long corridor outside. As he stopped before a door at the far end, the automatic flash blazed up and a voice within called out to him to enter.

The Rigellian opened the door and poked his head inside. 'Busy, Haridin?'

Lor Haridin looked up and sprang to his feet at once. 'Great space, boss, no! I haven't had anything to do since I finished work on anger reactions. You've got something for me, maybe?'

'I have – if you think you're up to it. You've heard of the Solarian System, haven't you?'

'Sure! The visors are full of it. They've got interstellar travel, haven't they?'

'That's right. An expedition is leaving Alpha Centauri for Sol in a month. They'll need a psychologist to do the fine work, and I was thinking of sending you.'

The young scientist reddened with delight to the very top of his hairless dome. 'Do you mean it, boss?'

'Why not? That is – if you think you can do it.'

'Of course I can.' Haridin drew himself up in offended hauteur. 'Type A reaction! I can't miss.'

'You'll have to learn their language, you know, and administer the stimulus in the Solarian tongue. It's not always an easy job.'

Haridin shrugged. 'I still can't miss. In a case like this, translation need only be seventy-five percent effective to get ninety-nine and six tenths percent of the desired result. That was one of the problems I had to solve on my qualifying exam. So you can't trip me up that way.'

Porus laughed. 'All right, Haridin, I know you can do it. Clean up everything here at the university and sign up for indefinite leave. And if you can, Haridin, write some sort of paper on these Solarians. If it's any good, you might get senior status on the basis of it.'

The junior psychologist frowned. 'But, boss, that's old stuff. Humanoid reactions are as well known as . . . as— You *can't* write anything on them.'

'There's always something if you look hard enough, Haridin. Nothing is well known; remember that. If you'll look at Sheet 25 of the report, for instance, you'll find an item concerning the care with which the Solarians armed themselves on leaving their ship.'

The other turned to the proper page. 'That's reasonable,' said he. 'An entirely normal reaction.'

'Certainly. But they insisted on retaining their weapons throughout their stay, even when they were greeted and welcomed by fellow Humanoids. *That's* quite a perceptible deviation from the normal. Investigate it – it might be worth while.'

'As you say, boss. Thanks a lot for the chance you're giving me. And say – how's the squid coming along?'

Porus wrinkled his nose. 'My sixth try folded up and died yesterday. It's disgusting.' And with that, he was gone.

Tan Porus of Rigel trembled with rage as he folded the handful of papers he held in two and tore them across. He plugged in the telecaster with a jerk.

'Get me Santins of the math department immediately,' he snapped.

His green eyes shot fire at the placid figure that appeared on the visor almost at once. He shook his fist at the image.

'What on Eron's the idea of that analysis you sent me just now, you Betelgeusian slime worm?'

The image's eyebrows shot up in mild surprise. 'Don't blame

me, Porus. They were your equations, not mine. Where did you get them?'

'Never mind where I got them. That's the business of the psychology department.'

'All right! And solving them is the business of the mathematics department. That's the seventh set of the damnedest sort of screwy equations I've ever seen. It was the worst yet. You made at least seventeen assumptions which you had no right to make. It took us two weeks to straighten you out, and finally we boiled it down—'

Porus jumped as if stung. 'I know what you boiled it down to. I just tore up the sheets. You take eighteen independent variables in twenty equations, representing two months of work, and solve them out at the bottom of the last, last page with that gem of oracular wisdom – "a" equals "a". All that work – and all I get is an identity.'

'It's still not my fault, Porus. You argued in circles, and in mathematics that means an identity and there's nothing you can do about it.' His lips twitched in a slow smile. 'What are you kicking about, anyway? "A" does equal "a", doesn't it?'

'Shut *up!*' The telecaster went dead, and the psychologist closed his lips tightly and boiled inwardly. The light signal above the telecaster flashed to life again.

'What do you want now?'

It was the calm, impersonal voice of the receptionist below that answered him. 'A messenger from the government, sir.'

'Damn the government! Tell them I'm dead.'

'It's important, sir. Lor Haridin has returned from Sol and wants to see you.'

Porus frowned. 'Sol? What Sol? Oh, I remember. Send him up, but tell him to make it snappy.'

'Come in, Haridin,' he said a little later, voice calmer, as the young Arcturian, a bit thinner, a bit more weary than he had been six months earlier when he left the Arcturian System, entered.

'Well, young man? Did you write the paper?'

The Arcturian gazed intently upon his fingernails. 'No, sir!'

'Why not?' Porus' green eyes peered narrowly at the other. 'Don't tell me you've had trouble.'

'Quite a bit, boss.' The words came with an effort. 'The psychological board itself has sent for you after hearing my report. The fact of the matter is that the Solarian System has . . . has refused to join the Federation.'

Tan Porus shot out of his chair like a jack-in-the-box and landed, purely by chance, on his feet.

'What!!'

Haridin nodded miserably and cleared his throat.

'Now, by the Great Dark Nebula,' swore the Rigellian, distractedly, 'if this isn't one sweet day! First, they tell me that "a" equals "a", and then you come in and tell me you muffed a Type A reaction – *muffed it completely!*'

The junior psychologist fired up. 'I didn't muff it. There's something wrong with the Solarians themselves. They're not normal. When I landed they went wild over us. There was a fantastic celebration – entirely unrestrained. Nothing was too good for us. I delivered the invitation before their parliament in their own language – a simple one which they call Esperanto. I'll stake my life that my translation was ninety-five percent effective.'

'Well? And then?'

'I can't understand the rest, boss. First, there was a neutral reaction and I was a little surprised, and then' – he shuddered in retrospect – 'in seven days – only seven days, boss – the entire planet had reversed itself completely. I couldn't follow their psychology, not by a hundred miles. I've brought home copies of their newspapers of the time in which they objected to joining with "alien monstrosities" and refused to be "ruled by inhumans of worlds parsecs away." I ask you, does that make sense?

'And that's only the beginning. It was light years worse than that. Why, good Galaxy, I went all the way into Type G reactions, trying to figure them out, and couldn't. In the end, we *had* to leave. We were in actual *physical* danger from those . . . those Earthmen, as they call themselves.'

Tan Porus chewed his lip a while. 'Interesting! Have you your report with you?'

'No. The psychological board has it. They've been going over it with a microscope all day.'

'And what do they say?'

The young Arcturian winced. 'They don't say it openly, but they leave a strong impression of thinking the report an inaccurate one.'

'Well, I'll decide about that after I've read it. Meanwhile, come with me to Parliamentary Hall and you can answer a few questions on the way.'

Joselin Arn of Alpha Centauri rubbed stubbled jaws with his huge, six-fingered hand and peered from under beetling brows at the semicircle of diversified faces that stared down upon him. The psychological board was, composed of psychologists of a score of worlds, and their united gaze was not the easiest thing in the world to withstand.

'We have been informed,' began Frian Obel, head of the board and native of Vega, home of the green-skinned men, 'that those sections of the report dealing with Sol's military state are *your* work.'

Joselin Arn inclined his head in silent agreement.

'And you are prepared to confirm what you have stated here, in spite of its inherent improbability? You are no psychologist, you know.'

'No! But I'm a soldier!' The Centaurian's jaws set stubbornly as his bass voice rumbled through the hall. 'I don't know equations and I don't know graphs – but I *do* know spaceships. I've seen theirs and I've seen ours, and theirs are better. I've seen their first interstellar ship. Give them a hundred years and they'll have a better hyper-atomos than we have. I've seen their weapons. They've got almost everything we have, at a stage in their history millennia before us. What they haven't got – they'll get, and soon. What they have got, they'll improve.

'I've seen their munitions plants. Ours are more advanced, but theirs are more efficient. I've seen their soldiers – and I'd rather fight with them than against them.

'I've said all that in the report. I say it again now.'

His brusque sentences came to an end and Frian Obel waited for the murmur from the men about him to cease.

'And the rest of their science; medicine, chemistry, physics? What of them?'

'I'm not the best judge of those. You have the report there of those who know, however, and to the best of my knowledge I confirm them.'

'And so these Solarians are true Humanoids?'

'By the circling worlds of Centauri, yes!'

The old scientist drew himself back in his chair with a peevish gesture and cast a rapid, frowning glance up and down the length of the table.

'Colleagues,' he said, 'we make little progress by rehashing this mess of impossibilities. We have a race of Humanoids of a superlatively technological turn; possessing at the same time an intrinsically unscientific belief in supernatural forces, an incredibly childish predilection toward individuality, singly and in groups, and, worst of all, lack of sufficient vision to embrace a galaxy-wide culture.'

He glared down upon the lowering Centaurian before him. 'Such a race must exist if we are to believe the report – and fundamental axioms of psychology must crumble. But I, for one, refuse to believe any such – to be vulgar about it – comet gas. This is plainly a case of mismanagement to be investigated by the proper authorities. I hope you all agree with me when I say that this report be consigned to the scrap heap and that a second expedition led by an expert in his line, not by an inexperienced junior psychologist or a soldier—'

The drone of the scientist's voice was buried suddenly in the crash of an iron fist against the table. Joselin Arn, his huge bulk writhing in anger, lost his temper and gave vent to martial wrath.

'Now, by the writhing spawn of Templis, by the worms that crawl and the gnats that fly, by the cesspools and the plague spots, and by the hooded death itself, *I wont allow this*. Are you to sit there with your theories and your long-range wisdom and deny what I have seen with my eyes? Are my eyes' – and they flashed fire as he spoke – 'to deny themselves because of a few wriggling marks your palsied hands trace on paper?

'To the core of Centauri with these armchair wise men, say I – and the psychologists first of all. Blast these men who bury themselves in their books and their laboratories and are blind to what goes on in the living world outside. Psychology, is it? Rotten, putrid—'

A tap on his belt caused him to whirl, eyes staring, fists clenched. For a moment, he looked about vainly. Then, turning his gaze downward, he found himself looking into the enigmatic green eyes of a pygmy of a man, whose piercing stare seemed to drench his anger with ice water.

'I know you, Joselin Arn,' said Tan Porus slowly, picking his words carefully. 'You're a brave man and a good soldier, but you don't like psychologists, I see. That is wrong of you, for it is on psychology that the political success of the Federation rests. Take it away and our Union crumbles, our great Federation melts away, the Galactic System is shattered.' His voice descended into a soft, liquid croon. 'You have sworn an oath to defend the System against all its enemies, Joselin Arn – and you yourself have now become its greatest. You strike at its foundations. You dig at its roots. You poison it at its source. You are dishonored. You are disgraced. You are a traitor.'

The Centaurian soldier shook his head helplessly. As Porus spoke, deep and bitter remorse filled him. Recollection of his words of a moment ago lay heavy on his conscience. When the psychologist finished, Arn bent his head and wept. Tears ran down those lined, war-scarred cheeks, to which for forty years now they had been a stranger.

Porus spoke again, and this time his voice boomed like a thunderclap: 'Away with your mewling whine, you coward. Danger is at hand. *Man the guns!*'

Joselin Arn snapped to attention; the sorrow that had filled him a bare second before was gone as if it had never existed.

The room rocked with laughter and the soldier grasped the situation. It had been Porus' way of punishing him. With his complete knowledge of the devious ins and outs of the Humanoid mind, he had only to push the proper button, and—

The Centaurian bit his lip in embarrassment, but said nothing.

But Tan Porus, himself, did not laugh. To tease the soldier was one thing; to humiliate him, quite another. With a bound, he was on a chair and laid his small hand on the other's massive shoulder.

'No offense, my friend – a little lesson, that is all. Fight the sub-humanoids and the hostile environments of fifty worlds. Dare space in a leaky rattletrap of a ship. Defy whatever dangers you wish. But never, *never* offend a psychologist. He might get angry in *earnest* the next time.'

Arn bent his head back and laughed – a gigantic roar of mirth that shook the room with its earthquake-like lustiness.

'Your advice is well taken, psychologist. Burn me with an atomo, if I don't think you're right.' He strode from the room with his shoulders still heaving with suppressed laughter.

Porus hopped off the chair and turned to face the board.

'This is an interesting race of Humanoids we have stumbled upon, colleagues.'

'Ah,' said Obel, dryly, 'the great Porus feels bound to come to bis pupil's defense. Your digestion seems to have improved, since you feel yourself capable of swallowing Haridin's report.'

Haridin, standing, head bowed, in the corner, reddened angrily, but did not move.

Porus frowned, but his voice kept to its even tone. 'I do, and the report, if properly analyzed, will give rise to a revolution in the science. It is a psychological gold mine; and Homo Sol, the find of the millenium.'

'Be specific, Tan Porus,' drawled someone. 'Your tricks are all very well for a Centaurian blockhead, but we remain unimpressed.'

The fiery little Rigellian emitted a gurgle of anger. He shook one tiny fist in the direction of the last speaker.

'I'll be more specific, Inar Tubal, you hairy space bug.' Prudence and anger waged a visible battle within him. 'There is more to a Humanoid than you think – certainly far more than you mental cripples can understand. Just to show you what you don't know, you desiccated group of fossils, I'll undertake to show you a bit of psychotechnology that'll knock the guts right out of you. Panic, morons, panic! Worldwide *panic!*'

There was an awful silence. 'Did you say world-wide panic?' stuttered Frian Obel, his green skin turning gray. 'Panic?'

'Yes, you parrot. Give me six months and fifty assistants and I'll show you a world of Humanoids in panic.'

Obel attempted vainly to answer. His mouth worked in a heroic attempt to remain serious – and failed. As though by signal, the entire board dropped its dignity and leaned back in a single burst of laughter.

'I remember,' gasped Inar Tubal of Sirius, his round face streaked with tears of pure joy, 'a student of mine who once claimed to have discovered a stimulus that would induce world-wide panic. When I checked his results, I came across an exponent with a misplaced decimal point. He was only ten orders of magnitude out of the way. How many decimal points have you misplaced, Colleague Porus?'

'What of Kraut's Law, Porus, which says you can't panic more than five Humanoids at a time? Shall we pass a resolution repealing it? And maybe the atomic theory as well, while we're about it?' and Semper Gor of Capella cackled gleefully.

Porus climbed onto the table and snatched Obel's gavel. 'The next one who laughs is getting this over his empty head.' There was sudden silence.

'I'm taking fifty assistants,' shouted the green-eyed Rigellian, 'and Joselin Arn is taking me to Sol. I want five of you to come with me – Inar Tubal, Semper Gor and any three others – so that I can watch their stupid faces when I've done what I said I would.' He hefted the gavel, threateningly. 'Well?'

Frian Obel gazed at the ceiling placidly. 'All right, Porus. Tubal, Gor, Helvin, Prat, and Winson can go with you. At the end of the specified time, we'll witness world-wide panic which will be very gratifying – or we'll watch you eat your words, and how much more gratifying *that* would be.' And with that, he chuckled very quietly to himself.

Tan Porus stared thoughtfully out the window. Terrapolis, capital city of Earth, sprawled beneath him to the very edge of the horizon. Its muted roar reached even to the half-mile height at which he stood.

There was something over that city, invisible and intangible but none the less real. Its presence was only too evident to the small psychologist. The choking cloak of dank fear that spread over the metropolis beneath was one of his own weaving – a horrible cloak of dark uncertainty, that clutched with clammy fingers at the hearts of Mankind and stopped short – just short – of actual panic.

The roar of the city had voices in it, and the voices were tiny ones of fear.

The Rigellian turned away in disgust. 'Hey, Haridin,' he roared.

The young Arcturian turned away from the televisor. 'Calling me, boss?'

'What do you think I'm doing? Talking to myself? What's the latest from Asia?'

'Nothing new. The stimuli just aren't strong enough. The yellow men seem to be more stolid of disposition than the white dominants of America and Europe. I've sent out orders not to increase the stimuli, though.'

'No, they mustn't,' agreed Porus. 'We can't risk *active* panic.' He ruminated in silence. 'Listen, we're about through. Tell them to hit a few of the big cities – they're more susceptible – and quit.'

He turned to the window again. 'Space, what a world – what a world! An entirely new branch of psychology has opened up – one we never dreamed of. Mob psychology, Haridin, mob psychology.' He shook his head impressively.

'There's lots of suffering, though, boss,' muttered the younger man. 'This passive panic has completely paralyzed trade and commerce. The business life of the entire planet is stagnant. The poor government is helpless – they don't know what's wrong.'

'They'll find out – when I'm ready. And, as for the suffering – well, I don't like it, either, but it's all a means to an end, a damned important end.'

There followed a short silence, and then Porus' lips twitched into a nasty smile. 'Those five nitwits returned from Europe yesterday, didn't they?'

Haridin smiled in turn and nodded vigorously. 'And hopping sore! Your predictions have checked to the fifth decimal place. They're fit to be tied.'

'Good! I'm only sorry I can't see Obel's face right now, after the last message I sent him. And, incidentally' – his voice dropped lower – 'what's the latest on *them?*'

Haridin raised two fingers. 'Two weeks, and they'll be here.'

'Two weeks . . . two weeks,' gurgled Porus jubilantly. He rose and made for the door. 'I think I'll find my dear, dear colleagues and pass the time of day.'

The five scientists of the board looked up from their notes and fell into an embarrassed silence as Porus entered.

The latter smiled impishly. 'Notes satisfactory, gentlemen? Found some fifty or sixty fallacies in my fundamental assumptions, no doubt?'

Hybron Prat of Alpha Cepheus rumpled the gray fuzz he called hair. 'I don't trust the unholy tricks this crazy mathematical notation of yours plays.'

The Rigellian emitted a short bark of laughter. 'Invent a better, then. So far, it's done a good job of handling reactions, hasn't it?'

There was an unmusical chorus of throat-clearings but no definite answer.

'Hasn't it?' thundered Porus.

'Well, what if it has,' returned Kim Winson, desperately. 'Where's your panic? All this is well and good. These Humanoids are cosmic freaks, but where's the big show you were going to put on? Until you break Kraut's Law, this entire exhibition of yours isn't worth a pinhead meteor.'

'You're beaten, gentlemen, you're beaten,' crowed the small master psychologist. 'I've proven my point – this passive panic is as impossible according to classic psychology as the active form. You're trying to deny facts and save face now, by harping on a technicality. Go home; go home, gentlemen, and hide under the bed.'

Psychologists are only human. They can analyze the motives that drive them, but they are the slave of those motives just as much as the commonest mortal of all. These galaxy-famous psychologists writhed under the lash of wounded pride and shattered vanity, and their blind stubbornness was the mechanical reaction due therefrom. They knew it was and they knew Porus knew it was – and that made it all the harder.

Inar Tubal stared angrily from red-rimmed eyes. 'Active panic or nothing, Tan Porus. That's what you promised, and that's what we'll have. We want the letter of the bond or, by space and time, we'll balk at any technicality. Active panic or we report failure!'

Porus swelled ominously and, with a tremendous effort, spoke quietly. 'Be reasonable, gentlemen. We haven't the equipment to handle active panic. We've never come up against this superform they have here on Earth. What if it gets beyond control?' He shook his head violently.

'Isolate it, then,' snarled Semper Gor. 'Start it up and put it out. Make all the preparations you want, but do it!'

'If you can,' grunted Hybron Prat.

But Tan Porus had *his* weak point. His brittle temper lay in splintered shards about him. His agile tongue blistered the atmosphere and inundated the sullen psychologist with wave after wave of concentrated profanity.

'Have your way, vacuumheads! Have your way and to outer space with you!' He was breathless with passion. 'We'll set it off right here in Terrapolis as soon as all the men are back home. Only you'd all better get from under!'

And with one last parting snarl, he stalked from the room.

Tan Porus parted the curtains with a sweep of his hand, and the five psychologists facing him averted their eyes. The streets of Earth's capital were deserted of civilian population. The ordered tramp of the military patrolling the highways of the city sounded like a dirge. The wintry sky hung low over a scene of strewn bodies – and silence; the silence that follows an orgy of wild destruction.

'It was touch and go for a few hours there, colleagues.' Porus' voice was tired. 'If it had passed the city limits, we could never have stopped it.'

'Horrible, horrible!' muttered Hybron Prat. 'It was a scene a psychologist would have given his right arm to witness – and his life to forget.'

'And these are Humanoids!' groaned Kim Winson.

Semper Gor rose to his feet in sudden decision. 'Do you see the significance of this, Porus? These Earthmen are sheer uncontrolled atomite. They can't be handled. Were they twice the technological geniuses they are, they would be useless. With their mob psychology, their mass panics, their superemotionalism, they simply won't fit into the Humanoid picture.'

Porus raised an eyebrow. 'Comet gas! Individually, we are as emotional as they are. They carry it into mass action and we don't; that's the only difference.'

'And that's enough!' exclaimed Tubal. 'We've made our decision, Porus. We made it last night, at the height of the . . . the . . . of it. The Solar System is to be left to itself. It is a plague spot and we want none of it. As far as the Galaxy is concerned, Homo Sol will be placed in strict quarantine. That is final!'

The Rigellian laughed softly. 'For the Galaxy, it may be final. But for Homo Sol?'

Tubal shrugged. 'They don't concern us.'

Porus laughed again. 'Say, Tubal. Just between the two of us, have you tried a time integration of Equation 128 followed by expansion with Karolean tensors?'

'No-o. I can't say I have.'

'Well, then, just glance up and down these calculations and enjoy yourself.'

The five scientists of the board grouped themselves about the sheets of paper Porus had handed them. Expressions changed from interest to bewilderment and then to something approaching panic.

Naru Helvin tore the sheets across with a spasmodic movement. 'It's a lie,' he screeched.

'We're a thousand years ahead of them now, and by that time we'll be advanced another two hundred years!' Tubal snapped. 'They won't be able to do anything against the mass of the Galaxy's people.'

Tan Porus laughed in a monotone, which is hard to do, but very unpleasant to hear. 'You still don't believe mathematics. That's in your behavior pattern, of course. All right, let's see if experts convince you – as they should, unless contact with these off-normal Humanoids has twisted you. Joselin – Joselin Arn – come in here!'

The Centaurian commander came in, saluted automatically, and looked expectant.

'Can one of your ships defeat one of the Sol ships in battle, if necessary?'

Arn grinned sourly. 'Not a chance, sir. These Humanoids break Kraut's Law in panic – and also in fighting. We have a corps of experts manning our ships; these people have a single crew that functions as a unit, without individuality. They manifest a form of fighting – panic, I imagine, is the best word. Every individual on a ship becomes an organ of the ship. With us, as you know, that's impossible.

'Furthermore, this world's a mass of mad geniuses. They have, to my certain knowledge, taken no less than twenty-two interesting but useless gadgets they saw in the Thalsoon Museum when they visited us, turned 'em inside out, and produced from them some of the most unpleasant military devices I've seen. You know of Julmun Thill's gravitational line tracer? Used – rather ineffectively – for spotting ore deposits before the modern electric potential method came in?

'They've turned it – somehow – into one of the deadliest automatic fire directors it's been my displeasure to see. It will automatically lay a gun or projector on a completely invisible target in space, air, water or rock, for that matter.'

'We,' said Tan Porus, gleefully, 'have far greater fleets than they. We could overwhelm them, could we not?'

Joselin Arn shook his head. 'Defeat them now – probably. It wouldn't be overwhelming, though, and I wouldn't bet on it too heavily. Certainly wouldn't invite it. The trouble is, in a military way, this collection of gadget maniacs invent things at a horrible rate. Technologically, they're as unstable as a wave in water; our civilization is more like a sanddune. I've seen their ground-car plants install a complete plant of machine tools for production of a new model of automobile – and rip it out in six months because it's completely obsolete!

'Now we've come in contact with their civilization briefly. We've learned the methods of one new civilization to add to our previous two hundred and eighty-odd – a small percentage advantage. They've added one new civilization to their previous one – a one-hundred-percent advance!'

'How about,' Porus asked gently, 'our military position if we simply ignore them completely for two hundred years?'

Joselin Arn gave an explosive little laugh. '*If* we could – which means *if* they'd let us – I'd answer offhand and with assurance. They're all I'd care to tackle right now. Two hundred years of exploring the new hacks suggested by their brief contact with us and they'd be doing things I can't imagine. Wait two hundred years and there won't be a battle; there'll be an annexation.'

Tan Porus bowed formally. 'Thank you, Joselin Arn. That was the result of my mathematical work.'

Joselin Arn saluted and left the room.

Turning to the five thoroughly paralyzed scientists, Porus went on: 'And I hope these learned gentlemen still react in a vaguely Humanoid way. Are you convinced that it is not up to us to decide to end all intercourse with this race? We may – but they won't!

'Fools' – he spat out the word – 'do you think I'm going to waste time arguing with you? I'm laying down the law, do you understand? Homo Sol *shall* enter the Federation. They are going to be trained into maturity in two hundred years. And I'm not asking you; *I'm telling you!*' The Rigellian stared up at them truculently.

'Come with me!' he growled brusquely.

They followed in tame submission and entered Tan Porus' sleeping quarters. The little psychologist drew aside a curtain and revealed a life-size painting.

'Make anything of that?'

It was the portrait of an Earthman, but of such an Earthman as none of the psychologists had yet seen. Dignified and sternly handsome, with one hand stroking a regal beard, and the other holding the single flowing garment that clothed him, he seemed personified majesty.

'That's Zeus,' said Porus. 'The primitive Earthmen created him as the personification of storm and lightning.' He whirled upon the bewildered five. 'Does it remind you of anybody?'

'Homo Canopus?' ventured Helvin uncertainly.

For a moment, Porus' face relaxed in momentary gratification and then it hardened again. 'Of course,' he snapped. 'Why do you hesitate about it? That's Canopus to the life, down to the full yellow beard.'

Then: 'Here's something else.' He drew another curtain.

The portrait was of a female, this time. Full-bosomed and widehipped she was. An ineffable smile graced her face and her hands seemed to caress the stalks of grain that sprang thickly about her feet.

'Demeter!' said Porus. 'The personification of agricultural fertility. The idealized mother. Whom does *that* remind you of?'

There was no hesitation this time. Five voices rang out as one: 'Homo Betelgeuse!'

Tan Porus smiled in delight. 'There you have it. Well?'

'Well?' said Tubal.

'Don't you see?' The smile faded. 'Isn't it clear? Nitwit! If a hundred Zeuses and a hundred Demeters were to land on Earth as part of a "trade mission", and turned out to be trained psychologists— *Now* do you see?'

Semper Gor laughed suddenly. 'Space, time, and little meteors. Of course! The Earthmen would be putty in the hands of their own personifications of storm and motherhood come to life. In two hundred years – why, in two hundred years, we could do anything.'

'But this so-called trade mission of yours, Porus,' interposed Prat. 'How would you get Homo Sol to accept it in the first place?'

Porus cocked his head to one side. 'Dear Colleague Prat,' he murmured, 'do you suppose that I created the passive panic just for the show – or just to gratify five woodenheads? This passive panic paralyzed industry, and the Terrestrial government is faced with revolution – another form of mob action that could use investigation. Offer them Galactic trade and eternal prosperity and do you think they'd jump at it? Has matter mass?'

The Rigellian cut short the excited babble that followed with an impatient gesture. 'If you've nothing more to ask, gentlemen, let's begin our preparations to leave. Frankly, I'm tired of Earth, and, more than that, I'm blasted anxious to get back to that squid of mine.'

He opened the door and shouted down the corridor: 'Hey, Haridin! Tell Arn to have the ship ready in six hours. We're leaving.'

'But . . . but—' The chorus of puzzled objections crystallized into sudden action as Semper Gor dashed at Porus and snatched him back as he was on the point of leaving. The little Rigellian struggled vainly in the other's powerful grasp.

'Let go!'

'We've endured enough, Porus,' said Gor, 'and now you'll just calm down and behave like a Humanoid. Whatever you say, we're not leaving until we're finished. We've got to arrange with the Terrestrial government concerning the trade mission. We've got to secure approval of the board. We've got to pick our psychologist. We've got to—'

Here Porus, with a sudden jerk, freed himself. 'Do you suppose for one moment that I would wait for your precious board to start to begin to commence to consider doing something about the situation in two or three decades?

'Earth agreed to my terms unconditionally a month ago. The squad of Canopans and Betelgeusans set sail five months ago, and landed day before yesterday. It was only with their help that we managed to stop yesterday's panic – though you never suspected it. You probably thought you did it yourself. Today, gentlemen, they have the situation in full control and your services are no longer needed. We're going home.'

Half-Breeds On Venus

The damp, somnolent atmosphere stirred violently and shrieked aside. The bare plateau shook three times as the heavy eggshaped projectiles shot down from outer space. The sound of the landing reverberated from the mountains on one side to the lush forest on the other, and then all was silent again.

One by one, three doors clanged open, and human figures stepped out in hesitant single file. First slowly, and then with impatient turbulence, they set first foot upon the new world, until the space surrounding the ships was crowded.

A thousand pairs of eyes gazed upon the prospect and a thousand mouths chattered excitedly. And in the other-world wind, a thousand crests of foot-high white hair swayed gracefully.

The Tweenies had landed on Venus!

Max Scanlon sighed wearily, 'Here we are!'

He turned from the porthole and slumped into his own special arm-chair. 'They're as happy as children – and I don't blame them. We've got a new world – one all for ourselves – and that's a great thing. But just the same, there are hard days ahead of us. I am almost afraid! It is a project so lightly embarked upon, but one so hard to carry out to completion.'

A gentle arm stole about his shoulder and he grasped it tightly, smiling into the soft, blue eyes that met his. 'But *you're* not afraid, are you, Madeline?'

'Certainly not!' And then her expression grew sadder, 'If only father had come with us. You – you know that he meant more to us than to the others. We were the – the first he took under his wing, weren't we?'

There was a long silence after that as each fell into deep thought. Max sighed, 'I remember him that day forty years ago – old suit, pipe, everything. He took me in. *Me*, a despised half-breed! And – and he found you for me, Madeline!'

'I know,' there were tears in her eyes. 'But he's still with us, Max, and always will be – here, and there.' Her hand crept first to her own heart and then to Max's.

'Hey, there, Dad, catch her, catch her!'

Max whirled at the sound of his elder son's voice, just in time to catch up the little bundle of flying arms and legs that catapulted into him.

He held her gravely up before him, 'Shall I give you to your papa, Elsie? He wants you.'

The little girl kicked her legs ecstatically. 'No, no. I want *you*, grand-daddy. I want you to give me a piggy-back and come out with grandmamma to see how nice everything is.'

Max turned to his son, and motioned him sternly away, 'Depart, despised father, and let old grand-dad have a chance.'

Arthur laughed and mopped a red face, 'Keep her, for Heaven's sake. She's been leading me and the wife a merry chase outside. We had to drag her back by the dress to keep her from running off into the forest. Didn't we, Elsie?'

Elsie, thus appealed to, suddenly recalled a past grievance. 'Grand-daddy, tell him to let me see the pretty trees. He doesn't want me to.'

She wriggled from Max's grasp and ran to the porthole. 'See them, grand-daddy, see them. It's all trees outside. It's not black anymore. I hated it when it was black, didn't you?'

Max leaned over and ruffled the child's soft, white hair gravely, 'Yes, Elsie, I hated it when it was black. But it isn't black anymore, and it won't ever be black again. Now go run to grandmamma. She'll get some cake specially for you. Go ahead, run!'

He followed the departing forms of his wife and granddaughter with smiling eyes, and then, as they turned to his son, they became serious once more.

'Well, Arthur?'

'Well, dad, what now?'

'There's no time to waste, son. We've got to start building immediately – underground!'

Arthur snapped into an attentive attitude, 'Underground!' He frowned his dismay.

'I know, I know. I said nothing of this previously, but it's got to be done. At all costs we must vanish from the face of the System. There are Earthmen on Venus – purebloods. There aren't many, it's true, but there are some. They mustn't find us – at least, not until we are prepared for whatever may follow. *That* will take years.'

'But father, *underground!* To live like moles, hidden from light and air. I don't like that.'

'Oh, nonsense. Don't overdramatize. We'll *live* on the surface – but the city; the power-stations, the food and water reserves, the laboratories – all that must be below and impregnable.'

The old Tweenie gestured the subject away with impatience, 'Forget that, anyway. I want to talk about something else – something we've discussed already.'

Arthur's eyes hardened and he shifted his glance to the ceiling. Max rose and placed his hands upon his son's brawny shoulders.

'I'm past sixty, Arthur. How long I have yet to live, I don't know. In any case, the best of me belongs to the past and it is better that I yield the leadership to a younger, more vigorous person.'

'Dad, that's sentimental bosh and you know it. There isn't one of us that's fit to wipe your shoes and no one is going to listen for a second to any plan of appointing a successor while you're still alive.'

'I'm not going to ask them to listen. It's done – and you're the new leader.'

The younger man shook his head firmly, 'You can't make me serve against my will.'

Max smiled whimsically, 'I'm afraid you're dodging responsibility, son. You're leaving your poor old father to the strains and hardships of a job beyond his aged strength.'

'Dad!' came the shocked retort. 'That's not so. You know it isn't. You – '

'Then prove it. Look at it this way. Our race needs *active* leadership, and I can't supply it. I'll always be here – while I live – to advise you and help you as best I can, but from now on, *you* must take the initiative.'

Arthur frowned and the words came from him reluctantly, 'All right, then. I take the job of field commander. But remember, *you're* commander-in-chief.'

'Good! And now let's celebrate the occasion.' Max opened a cupboard and withdrew a box, from which he abstracted a pair of cigars. He sighed, 'The supply of tobacco is down to the vanishing point and we won't have any more until we grow our own, but – we'll smoke to the new leader.'

Blue smoke curled upwards and Max frowned through it at his son, 'Where's Henry?'

Arthur grinned, 'Dunno! I haven't seen him since we landed. I can tell you with whom he is, though.'

Max grunted, 'I know that, too.'

'The kid's making hay while the sun shines. It won't be many years now, Dad, before you'll be spoiling a second set of grandchildren.'

'If they're as good as the three of my first set, I only hope I live to see the day.'

And father and son smiled affectionately at each other and listened in silence to the muted sound of happy laughter from the hundreds of Tweenies outside.

Henry Scanlon cocked his head to one side, and raised his hand for silence, 'Do you hear running water, Irene?'

The girl at his side nodded, 'Over in that direction.'

'Let's go there, then. A river flashed by just before we landed and maybe that's it.'

'All right, if you say so, but I think we ought to be getting back to the ships.'

'What for?' Henry stopped and stared. 'I should think you'd be glad to stretch your legs after weeks on a crowded ship.'

'Well, it might be dangerous.'

'Not here in the highlands, Irene. Venusian highlands are practically a second Earth. You can see this is forest and not jungle. Now if we were in the coastal regions – ' He broke off short, as if he had just remembered something. 'Besides, what's there to be afraid of? *I'm* with you, aren't I?' And he patted the Tonite gun at his hip.

Irene repressed a sudden smile and shot an arch glance at her strutting companion, 'I'm quite aware that you're with me. *That's* the danger.'

Henry's chest deflated with an audible gasp. He frowned. '*Very* funny— And I on my best behavior, too.' He drifted away, brooded sulkily awhile, and then addressed the trees in a distant manner, 'Which reminds me that tomorrow is Daphne's birthday. I've promised her a present.'

'Get her a reducing belt,' came the quick retort. 'Fat thing!'

'Who's fat? Daphne? Oh – I wouldn't say so.' He considered matters carefully, one thoughtful eye upon the young girl at his side. 'Now my description of her would be – shall we say – "pleasingly plump", or, maybe, "comfortably upholstered".'

'She's *fat*,' Irene's voice was suddenly a hiss, and something very like a frown wrinkled her lovely face, 'and her eyes are green.' She swung on ahead, chin high, and superbly conscious of her own little figure.

Henry hastened his steps and caught up, 'Of course, I prefer skinny girls any day.'

Irene whirled on him and her little fists clenched, 'I'm not skinny, you incredibly stupid ape.'

'But Irene, who said I meant you?' His voice was solemn, but his eyes were laughing.

The girl reddened to the ears and turned away, lower lip trembling. The smile faded from Henry's eyes and was replaced by a look of concern. His arm shot out hesitantly and slipped about her shoulder.

'Angry, Irene?'

The smile that lit her face of a sudden was as brilliant as the sparkling sheen of her silvery hair in the bright sun.

'No,' she said.

Their eyes met and, for a moment, Henry hesitated – and found that he who hesitates is lost; for with a sudden twist and a smothered laugh, Irene was free once more.

Pointing through a break in the trees, she cried, 'Look, a lake!' and was off at a run.

Henry scowled, muttered something under his breath, and ran after.

The scene was truly Earthly. A rapids-broken stream wound its way through banks of slender-trunked trees and then spread into a placid lake some miles in width. The brooding quiet was unbroken save by the muffled beat that issued from the throat-bags of the frilled lizards that nested in the upper reaches of the trees.

The two Tweenies – boy and girl – stood hand in hand upon the bank and drank in the beauty of the scene.

Then there was a muffled splash near by and Irene shrank into the encircling arms of her companion.

'What's the matter?'

'N-nothing. Something moved in the water, I think.'

'Oh, imagination, Irene.'

'No. I *did* see something. It came up and – oh, goodness, Henry, don't squeeze so tightly—'

She almost lost her balance as Henry suddenly dropped her altogether and jerked at his Tonite gun.

Immediately before them, a dripping green head lifted out of the water and regarded them out of wide-set, staring goggle-eyes. Its broad lipless mouth opened and closed rapidly, but not a sound issued forth.

Max Scanlon stared thoughtfully at the rugged foot-hills ahead and clasped his hands behind his back.

'You think so, do you?'

'Certainly, Dad,' insisted Arthur, enthusiastically. 'If we burrow under these piles of granite, all Earth couldn't get at us. It wouldn't take two months to form the entire cavern, with our unlimited power.'

'Hmph! It will require care!'

'It will get it!'

'Mountainous regions are quake regions.'

'We can rig up enough stat-rays to hold up all Venus, quakes or no quakes.'

'Stat-rays eat up energy wholesale, and a breakdown that will leave us energyless would mean the end.'

'We can hook up five separate power-houses – as foolproof as we can make them. All five won't break down at once.'

The old Tweenie smiled, 'All right, son. I see you've got it planned thoroughly. Go ahead! Start whenever you want – and remember, it's all up to you.'

'Good! Let's get back to the ships.' They picked their way gingerly down the rocky slope.

'You know, Arthur,' said Max, stopping suddenly, 'I've been thinking about those stat-beams.'

'Yes?' Arthur offered his arm, and the two resumed their walk.

'It's occurred to me that if we could make them two-dimensional in extent and curve them, we'd have the perfect defense, as long as our energy lasted – a stat-field.'

'You need four-dimensional radiation for that, Dad – nice to think about but can't be done.'

'Oh, is that so? Well, listen to this—'

What Arthur was to listen to remained hidden, however – for that day at least. A piercing shout ahead jerked both their heads upward. Up towards them came the bounding form of Henry Scanlon, and following him, at a goodly distance and a much more leisurely pace, came Irene.

'Say, Dad, I had a devil of a time finding you. Where were you?'

'Right here, son. Where were you?'

'Oh, just around. Listen, Dad. You know those amphibians the explorers talk about as inhabiting the highland lakes of Venus, don't you? Well, we've located them, lots of them, a regular convoy of them. Haven't we, Irene?'

Irene paused to catch her breath and nodded her head, 'They're the cutest things, Mr Scanlon. All green.' She wrinkled her nose laughingly.

Arthur and his father exchanged glances of doubt. The former shrugged. 'Are you sure you haven't been seeing things? I remember once, Henry, when you sighted a meteor in space, scared us all to death, and then had it turn out to be your own reflection in the port glass.'

Henry, painfully aware of Irene's snicker, thrust out a belligerent lower lip, 'Say, Art, I guess you're looking for a shove in the face. And I'm old enough to give it to you, too.'

'Whoa there, quiet down,' came the peremptory voice of the elder Scanlon, 'and you, Arthur, had better learn to respect your younger brother's dignity. Now here, Henry, all Arthur meant was that these amphibians are as shy as rabbits. No one's ever caught more than a glimpse of them.'

'Well, we have, Dad. Lots of them. I guess they were attracted by Irene. No one can resist her.'

'I know *you* can't,' and Arthur laughed loudly.

Henry stiffened once more, but his father stepped between. 'Grow up, you two. Let's go and see these amphibians.'

*

'This is amazing,' exclaimed Max Scanlon. 'Why, they're as friendly as children. I can't understand it.'

Arthur shook his head, 'Neither can I, Dad. In fifty years, no explorer has ever gotten a good look at one, and here they are – thick as flies.'

Henry was throwing pebbles into the lake. 'Watch this, all of you.'

A pebble curved its way into the water, and as it splashed six green forms turned a back somersault and slid smoothly below the surface. With no time for a breath between, one was up again and the pebble arced back to fall at Henry's feet.

The amphibians were crowding closer in ever increasing numbers now, approaching the very edge of the lake, where they grasped at the coarse reeds on the bank and stared goggle-eyed at the Tweenies. Their muscular webbed legs could be seen below the surface of the water, moving back and forth with lazy grace. Without cessation, the lipless mouths opened and closed in a queer, uneven rhythm.

'I think they're talking, Mr Scanlon,' said Irene, suddenly.

'It's quite possible,' agreed the old Tweenie, thoughtfully. 'Their brain-cases are fairly large, and they may possess considerable intelligence. If their voice boxes and ears are tuned to sound waves of higher or lower range than our own, we would be unable to hear them – and that might very well explain their soundlessness.'

'They're probably discussing us as busily as we are them,' said Arthur.

'Yes, and wondering what sort of freaks we are,' added Irene.

Henry said nothing. He was approaching the edge of the lake with cautious steps. The ground grew muddy beneath his feet, and the reeds thick. The group of amphibians nearest turned anxious eyes toward him, and one or two loosened their hold and slipped silently away.

But the nearest held his ground. His wide mouth was clamped tight; his eyes were wary – but he did not move.

Henry, paused, hesitated, and then held out his hand, 'Hiya, Phib!'

The 'Phib' stared at the outstretched hand. Very cautiously, his own webbed forelimb stretched out and touched the Tweenie's fingers. With a jerk, they were drawn back, and the Phib's mouth worked in soundless excitement.

'Be careful,' came Max's voice from behind. 'You'll scare him that way. His skin is terribly sensitive and dry objects must irritate him. Dip your hand in the water.'

Slowly, Henry obeyed. The Phib's muscles tensed to escape at the slightest sudden motion, but none came. Again the Tweenie's hand was held out, dripping wet this time.

For a long minute, nothing happened, as the Phib seemed to debate within itself the future course of action. And then, after two false starts and hasty withdrawals, fingers touched again.

'Ataphib,' said Henry, and clasped the green hand in his own.

A single, startled jerk followed and then a lusty return of pressure to an extent that numbed the Tweenie's fingers. Evidently encouraged by the first Phib's example, his fellows were crowding close now, offering hosts of hands.

The other three Twennies slushed up through the mud now, and offered wetted hands in their turn.

'That's funny,' said Irene. 'Everytime I shake hands I seem to keep thinking of hair.'

Max turned to her, 'Hair?'

'Yes, ours. I get a picture of long, white hair, standing straight up and shining in the sun.' Her hand rose unconsciously to her own smooth tresses.

'Say!' interrupted Henry suddenly, 'I've been noticing that, too, now that you mention it. Only when I shake hands, though.'

'How about you, Arthur?' asked Max.

Arthur nodded once, his eyebrows climbing.

Max smiled and pounded fist into palm. 'Why, it's a primitive sort of telepathy – too weak to work without physical contact and even then capable of delivering only a few simple ideas.'

'But why hair, dad?' asked Arthur.

'Maybe it's our hair that attracted them in the first place. They've never seen anything like it and – and – well, who can explain their psychology?'

He was down on his knees suddenly, splashing water over his high crest of hair. There was a frothing of water and a surging of green bodies as the Phibs pressed closer. One green paw passed gently through the stiff white crest, followed by excited, if noiseless, chattering. Struggling amongst themselves for favored vantage-points, they competed for the privilege of touching the hair until Max, for sheer weariness, was forced to rise again.

'They're probably our friends for life now,' he said. 'A pretty queer set of animals.'

It was Irene, then, who noticed the group of Phibs a hundred yards from shore. They paddled quietly, making no effort to approach closer, 'Why don't *they* come?' she asked.

She turned to one of the foremost Phibs and pointed, making frantic gestures of dubious meaning. She received only solemn stares in return.

'That's not the way, Irene,' admonished Max, gently. He held out his hand, grasped that of a willing Phib and stood motionless for a moment. When he loosed his grip, the Phib slid into the water and disappeared. In a moment, the laggard Phibs were approaching shore slowly.

'How did you do it?' gasped Irene.

'Telepathy! I held on tightly and pictured an isolated group of Phibs and a long hand stretching out over the water to shake theirs.' He smiled gently, 'They are quite intelligent, or they would not have understood so readily.'

'Why, they're females,' cried Arthur, in sudden breathless astonishment. 'By all that's holy – they suckle their young!'

The newcomers were slenderer and lighter in color than the others. They advanced shyly, urged on by the bolder males and held out timid hands in greeting.

'Oh-h,' Irene cried in sudden delight. 'Look at this!'

She was down on her knees in the mud, arms outstretched to the nearest female. The other three watched in fascinated silence as the nervous she-Phib clasped its tiny armful closer to its breast.

But Irene's arms made little inviting gestures, 'Please, please. It's so cute. I won't hurt him.'

Whether the Phib mother understood is doubtful, but with a sudden motion, she held out a little green bundle of squirming life and deposited it in the waiting arms.

Irene rose, squealing with delight. Little webbed feet kicked aimlessly and round frightened eyes stared at her. The other three crowded close and watched it curiously.

'It's the *dearest* little thing, it is. Look at its funny little mouth. Do you want to hold it, Henry?'

Henry jumped backwards as if stung, 'Not on your life! I'd probably drop it.'

'Do you get any thought images, Irene?' asked Max, thoughtfully.

Irene considered and frowned her concentration, 'No-o. It's too young, mayb— oh, *yes!* It's – it's—' She stopped, and tried to laugh. 'It's *hungry!*'

She returned the little baby Phib to its mother, whose mouth worked in transports of joy and whose muscular arms clasped the little mite close. The tiny Phib swiveled its little green head to bend one last goggling look at the creature that had held it for an instant.

'Friendly creatures,' said Max, 'and intelligent. They can keep their lakes and rivers. We'll take the land and won't interfere with them.'

A lone Tweenie stood on Scanlon Ridge and his field-glass pointed at the Divide ten miles up the hills. For five minutes, the glass did not waver and the Tweenie stood like some watchful statue made of the same rock as formed the mountains all about.

And then the field-glass lowered, and the Tweenie's face was a pale thin-lipped picture of gloom. He hastened down the slope to the guarded, hidden entrance to Venustown.

He shot past the guards without a word and descended into the lower levels where solid rock was still being puffed into nothingness and shaped at will by controlled blasts of super-energy.

Arthur Scanlon looked up and with a sudden premonition of disaster, gestured the Disintegrators to a halt.

'What's wrong, Sorrell?'

The Tweenie leant over and whispered a single word into Arthur's ear.

'Where?' Arthur's voice jerked out hoarsely.

'On the other side of the ridge. They're coming through the Divide now in our direction. I spotted the blaze of sun on metal and—' he held up his field-glass significantly.

'Good Lord!' Arthur rubbed his forehead distractedly and then turned to the anxiously-watching Tweenie at the controls of the Disinto. 'Continue as planned! No change!'

He hurried up the levels to the entrance, and snapped out hurried orders, 'Triple the guard immediately. No one but me or those with me, are to be permitted to leave. Send out men to round up any stragglers outside immediately and order them to keep within shelter and make no unnecessary sound.'

Then, back again through the central avenue to his father's quarters.

Max Scanlon looked up from his calculations and his grave forehead smoothed out slowly.

'Hello, son. Is anything wrong? Another resistant stratum?'

'No, nothing like that.' Arthur closed the door carefully lowered his voice. 'Earthmen!'

For a moment, Max made no movement. The expression on his face froze for an instant, and then, with a sudden exhalation, he slumped in his chair and the lines in his forehead deepened wearily.

'Settlers?'

'Looks so. Sorrell said women and children were among them, There were several hundred in all, equipped for a stay – and headed in this direction.'

Max groaned, 'Oh, the luck, the luck! All the vast of Venus to choose and they come here. Come, let's get a look at this.'

They came through the Divide in a long, snaky line. Hard-bitten pioneers with their pinched work-worn women and their carefree, half-barbarous, wilderness-bred children. The low, broad 'Venus Vans' joggled clumsily over the untrodden ways, loaded down with amorphous masses of household necessities.

The leaders surveyed the prospect and one spoke in clipped, jerky syllables, 'Almost through, Jem. We're out among the foot-hills now.'

And the other replied slowly, 'And there's good new growing-land ahead. We can stake out farms and settle down.' He sighed, 'It's been tough going this last month. I'm glad it's over!'

And from a ridge ahead – the last ridge before the valley – the Scanlons, father and son, unseen dots in the distance, watched the newcomers with heavy hearts.

'The one thing we could not prepare for – and it's happened.'

Arthur spoke slowly and reluctantly, 'They are few and unarmed. We can drive them out in an hour.' With sudden fierceness, 'Venus is *ours!*'

'Yes, we can drive them out in an hour – in ten minutes. But they would return, in thousands, and armed. We're not ready to fight all Earth, Arthur.'

The younger man bit his lip and words were muttered forth half in shame, 'For the sake of the race, Father – we could kill them all.'

'Never!' exclaimed Max, his old eyes flashing. '*We* will not be the first to strike. If we kill, we can expect no mercy from Earth; and we will deserve none.'

'But, father, what else? We can expect no mercy from Earth as it is. If we're spotted – if they ever suspect our existence, our whole hegira becomes pointless and we lose out at the very beginning.'

'I know. I know.'

'We can't change now,' continued Arthur, passionately. 'We've spent months preparing Venustown. How could we start over?'

'We can't,' agreed Max, tonelessly. 'To even attempt to move would mean sure discovery. We can only—'

'Live like moles after all. Hunted fugitives! Frightened refugees! Is that it?'

'Put it any way you like – but we must hide, Arthur, and bury ourselves.'

'Until—?'

'Until I – or we – perfect a curved two-dimensional stat-beam. Surrounded by an impermeable defense, we can come out into the open. It may take years; it may take one week. I don't know.'

'And every day we run the risk of detection. Any day the swarms of purebloods can come down upon us and wipe us out. We've got to hang by a hair day after day, week after week, month after month—'

'We've *got* to.' Max's mouth was clamped shut, and his eyes were a frosty blue.

Slowly, they went back to Venustown.

Things were quiet in Venustown, and eyes were turned to the top-most level and the hidden exits. Out there was air and the sun and space – and Earthmen.

They had settled several miles up the river-bed. Their rude houses were springing up. Surrounding land was being cleared. Farms were being staked out. Planting was taking place.

And in the bowels of Venus, eleven hundred Tweenies shaped their home and waited for an old man to track down the elusive equations that would enable a stat-ray to spread in two dimensions and curve.

Irene brooded somberly as she sat upon the rocky ledge and stared ahead to where the dim gray light indicated the existence of an exit to the open. Her shapely legs swung gently back and forth and Henry Scanlon, at her side, fought desperately to keep his gaze focussed harmlessly upon air.

'You know what, Henry?'

'What?'

'I'll bet the Phibs could help us.'

'Help us do what, Irene?'

'Help us get rid of the Earthmen.'

Henry thought it over carefully, 'What makes you think that?'

'Well, they're pretty clever – cleverer than we think. Their minds are altogether different, though, and maybe they could fix it. Besides – I've just got a feeling.' She withdrew her hand suddenly, 'You don't have to hold it, Henry.'

Henry swallowed, 'I-I thought you had a sort of unsteady seat there – might fall, you know.'

'Oh!' Irene looked down the terrific three-foot drop. 'There's something in what you say. It does look pretty high here.'

Henry decided he was in the presence of a hint, and acted accordingly. There was a moment's silence while he seriously considered the possibility of her feeling a bit chilly – but before he had quite decided that she probably was, she spoke again.

'What I was going to say, Henry, was this. Why don't we go out and see the Phibs?'

'Dad would take my head off if I tried anything like that.'

'It would be a lot of fun.'

'Sure, but it's dangerous. We can't risk anyone seeing us.'

Irene shrugged resignedly, 'Well, if you're afraid, we'll say no more about it.'

Henry gasped and reddened. He was off the ledge in a bound, 'Who's afraid? When do you want to go?'

'Right now, Henry. Right this very minute.' Her cheeks flushed with enthusiasm.

'All right then. Come on.' He started off at a half-run, dragging her along. —And then a thought occurred to him and he stopped short.

He turned to her fiercely, '*I'll* show you if I'm afraid.' His arms were suddenly about her and her little cry of surprise was muffled effectively.

'Goodness,' said Irene, when in a position to speak once more. 'How thoroughly *brutal!*'

'Certainly. I'm a very well-known brute,' gasped Henry, as he uncrossed his eyes and got rid of the swimming sensation in his head. 'Now let's get to those Phibs; and remind me, when I'm president, to put up a memorial to the fellow who invented kissing.'

Up through the rock-lined corridor, past the backs of outward-gazing sentries, out through the carefully camouflaged opening, and they were upon the surface.

The smudge of smoke on the southern horizon was grim evidence of the presence of man, and with that in mind, the two young Twee-nies slithered through the underbrush into the forest and through the forest to the lake of the Phibs.

Whether in some strange way of their own the Phibs sensed the presence of friends, the two could not tell, but they had scarcely reached the banks when approaching dull-green smudges beneath water told of the creatures' coming.

A wide, goggle-eyed head broke the surface, and, in a second, bobbing frogheads dotted the lake.

Henry wet his hand and seized the friendly forelimb outstretched to him.

'Hi there, Phib.'

The grinning mouth worked and made its soundless answer.

'Ask him about the Earthmen, Henry,' urged Irene. Henry motioned impatiently.

'Wait a while. It takes time. I'm doing the best I can.'

For two slow minutes, the two, Tweenie and Phib, remained motionless and stared into each other's eyes. And then the Phib broke away and, at some silent order, every lake-creature vanished, leaving the Tweenies alone.

Irene stared for a moment, nonplussed, 'What happened?'

Henry shrugged, 'I don't know. I pictured the Earthmen and he seemed to know who I meant. Then I pictured Earthmen fighting us and killing us – and he pictured a lot of us and only a few of them and another fight in which we killed them. But then I pictured us killing them and then a lot more of *them* coming – hordes and hordes – and killing us and then—'

But the girl was holding her hands to her tortured ears, 'Oh, my goodness. No wonder the poor creature didn't understand. I wonder he didn't go crazy.'

'Well, I did the best I could,' was the gloomy response. 'This was all your nutty idea, anyway.'

Irene got no further with her retort than the opening syllable, for in a moment the lake was crowded with Phibs once more. 'They've come back,' she said instead.

A Phib pushed forward and seized Henry's hand while the others crowded around in great excitement. There were several moments of silence and Irene fidgeted.

'Well?' she said.

'Quiet, please. I don't get it. Something about big animals, or monsters, or—' His voice trailed away, and the furrow between his eyes deepened into painful concentration.

He nodded, first abstractedly, then vigorously.

He broke away and seized Irene's hands. 'I've got it – and it's the perfect solution. We can save Venustown all by ourselves, Irene, with the help of the Phibs – if you want to come to the Lowlands with me tomorrow. We can take along a pair of Tonite pistols and food supplies and if we follow the liver, it oughtn't to take us more than two or three days there and the same time back. What do you say, Irene?'

Youth is not noted for forethought. Irene's hesitation was for effect only, 'Well – maybe we shouldn't go ourselves, but – but I'll go – with you.' There was the lightest accent on the last word.

Ten seconds later, the two were on their way back to Venustown, and Henry was wondering, if on the whole, it weren't better to put up *two* memorials to the fellow who invented kissing.

The flickering red-yellow of the fire sent back ruddy highlights from Henry's lordly crest of hair and cast shifting shadows upon his brooding face.

It was hot in the Lowlands, and the fire made it worse, yet Henry huddled close and kept an anxious eye upon the sleeping form of Irene on the other side. The teeming life of the Venusian jungle respected fire, and the flames spelt safety.

They were three days from the plateau now. The stream had become a lukewarm, slowly-moving liver, the shores of which were covered with the green scum of algae. The pleasant forests had given way to the tangled, vine-looped growths of the jungle. The mingled sounds of life had grown in volume and increased to a noisy crescendo. The air became warmer and damper; the ground swampier; the surroundings more fantastically unfamiliar.

And yet there was no real danger – of that, Henry was convinced. Poisonous life was unknown on Venus, and as for the tough-skinned monsters that lorded the jungles, the fire at night and the Phibs during day would keep them away.

Twice the ear-splitting shriek of a Centosaur had sounded in the distance and twice the sound of crashing trees had caused the two Tweenies to draw together in fear. Both times, the monsters had moved away again.

This was the third night out, and Henry stirred uneasily. The Phibs seemed confident that before morning they could start their return trip, and somehow the thought of Venustown was rather attractive. Adventure and excitement are fine and with every passing hour the glory of his scintillating bravery grew in Irene's eyes – which was wonderful – but still Venustown and the friendly Highlands were nice to think about.

He threw himself on his stomach and gazed morosely into the fire, thinking of his twenty years of age – almost twenty years.

'Why, heck,' he tore at the rank grass beneath. 'It's about time I was thinking of getting *married*.' And his eye strayed involuntarily to the sleeping form beyond the fire.

As if in response, there was a flickering of eyelids and a vague stare out of deep blue eyes.

Irene sat up and stretched.

'I can't sleep at all,' she complained, brushing futilely at her white hair. 'It's so hot.' She stared at the fire distastefully.

Henry's good humor persisted. 'You slept for hours – and snored like a trombone.'

Irene's eyes snapped wide open, 'I did not!' Then, with a voice vibrant with tragedy, 'Did I?'

'No, of course not!' Henry howled his laughter, stopping only at the sudden, sharp contact between the toe of Irene's shoe and the pit of his own stomach. 'Ouch,' he said.

'Don't speak to me anymore, *Mister* Scanlon!' was the girl's frigid remark.

It was Henry's turn to look tragic. He rose in panicky dismay and took a single step towards the girl. And then he froze in his tracks at the ear-piercing shriek of a Centosaur. When he came to himself, he found his arms full of Irene.

Reddening, she disentangled herself, and then the Centosaurian shriek sounded again, from another direction – and there she was, right back again.

Henry's face was pale, in spite of his fair armful. 'I think the Phibs have snared the Centosaurs. Come with me and I'll ask them.'

The Phibs were dim blotches in the gray dawn that was breaking. Rows and rows of strained, abstracted individuals were all that met the eye. Only one seemed to be unoccupied and when Henry rose from the handclasp, he said, 'They've got three Centosaurs and that's all they can handle. We're starting back to. the Highlands right now.'

The rising sun found the party two miles up the river. The Tweenies, hugging the shore, cast wary eyes towards the bordering jungle. Through an occasional clearing, vast gray bulks could be made out. The noise of the reptilian shrieks was almost continuous.

'I'm sorry I brought you, Irene,' said Henry. 'I'm not so sure now that the Phibs can take care of the monsters.'

Irene shook her head. 'That's all right, Henry. I *wanted* to come.

Only – I wish we had thought of letting the Phibs bring the beasts themselves. They don't need us.'

'Yes, they do! If a Centosaur gets out of control, it will make straight for the Tweenies and they'd never get away. We've got the Tonite guns to kill the 'saurs with if the worst comes to the worst—' His voice trailed away and he glanced at the lethal weapon in his hand and derived but cold comfort therefrom.

The first night was sleepless for both Tweenies. Somewhere, unseen in the blackness of the river, Phibs took shifts and their tele-pathic control over the tiny brains of the gigantic, twenty-legged Centosaurs maintained its tenuous hold. Off in the jungle, three hundred-ton monsters howled impatiently against the force that drove them up the river side against their will and raved impotently against the unseen barrier that prevented them from approaching the stream.

By the side of the fire, a pair of Tweenies, lost between moun-tainous flesh on one side and the fragile protection of a telepathic web on the other, gazed longingly towards the Highlands some forty miles off.

Progress was slow. As the Phibs tired, the Centosaurs grew balkier. But gradually, the air grew cooler. The rank jungle growth thinned out and the distance to Venustown shortened.

Henry greeted the first signs of familiar temperate-zone forest with a tremulous sigh of relief. Only Irene's presence prevented him from discarding his role of heroism.

He felt pitifully eager for their quixotic journey to be over, but he only said, 'It's practically all over but the shouting. And you can bet there'll be shouting, Irene. We'll be heroes, you and I.'

Irene's attempt at enthusiasm was feeble. 'I'm tired, Henry. Let's rest.' She sank slowly to the ground, and Henry, after signalling the Phibs, joined her.

'How much longer, Henry?' Almost without volition, she found her head nestling wearily against his shoulder.

'One more day, Irene. Tomorrow this time, we'll be back.' He looked wretched, 'You think we shouldn't have tried to do this our-selves, don't you?'

'Well, it seemed a good idea at the time.'

'Yes, I know,' said Henry. 'I've noticed that I get lots of ideas that seem good at the time, but sometimes they turn sour.' He shook his head philosophically, 'I don't know why, but that's the way it is.'

'All I know,' said Irene, 'is that I don't care if I never move another step in my life. I wouldn't get up now—'

Her voice died away as her beautiful blue eyes stared off towards the right. One of the Centosaurs stumbled into the waters of a small tributary to the stream they were following. Wallowing in the water, his huge serpentine body mounted on the ten stocky pairs of legs, glistened horribly. His ugly head weaved towards the sky and his ter-rifying call pierced the air. A second joined him.

Irene was on her feet. 'What are you waiting for, Henry. Let's go! Hurry!'

Henry gripped his Tonite gun tightly and followed.

Arthur Scanlon gulped savagely at his fifth cup of black coffee and, with an effort, brought the Audiomitter into optical focus. His eyes, he decided, were becoming entirely too balky. He rubbed them into red-rimmed irritation and cast a glance over his shoulder at the rest-lessly sleeping figure on the couch.

He crept over to her and adjusted the coverlet.

'Poor Mom,' he whispered, and bent to kiss the pale lips. He turned to the Audiomitter and clenched a fist at it, 'Wait till I get you, you crazy nut.'

Madeline stirred, 'Is it dark yet?'

'No,' lied Arthur with feeble cheerfulness. 'He'll call before sundown, Mom. You just sleep and let me take care of things. Dad's upstairs working on the stat-field and he says he's making progress. In a few days everything will be all right.' He sat silently beside her and grasped her hand tightly. Her tired eyes closed once more.

The signal light blinked on and, with a last look at his mother, he stepped out into the corridor, 'Well!'

The waiting Tweenie saluted smartly, 'John Barno wants to say that it looks as if we are in for a storm.' He handed over an official report.

Arthur glanced at it peevishly, 'What, of that? We've had plenty so far, haven't we? What do you expect of Venus?'

'This will be a particularly bad one, from all indications. The barometer has fallen unprecedentedly. The ionic concentration of the upper atmosphere is at an unequaled maximum. The Beulah River has overflowed its banks and is rising rapidly.'

The other frowned, 'There's not an entrance to Venustown that isn't at least filty yards above river level. As for rain – our drainage system is to be relied upon.' He grimaced suddenly, 'Go back and tell Barno that it can storm for my part – for forty days and forty nights if it wants to. Maybe it will drive the Earthmen away.'

He turned away, but the Tweenie held his ground, 'Beg pardon sir, but that's not the worst. A scouting party today—'

Arthur whirled. 'A scouting party? Who ordered one to be sent out?'

'Your father, sir. They were to make contact with the Phibs – I don't know why.'

'Well, go on.'

'Sir, the Phibs could not be located.'

And now, for the first time, Arthur was startled out of his savage ill-humor, 'They were gone?'

The Tweenie nodded, 'It is thought that they have sought shelter from the coming storm. It is that which causes Barno to fear the worst.'

'They say rats desert a sinking ship,' murmured Arthur. He buried his head in trembling hands. 'God! Everything at once! Everything at once!'

The darkening twilight hid the pall of blackness that lowered over the mountains ahead and emphasized the darting flashes of lightning that flickered on and off continuously.

Irene shivered, 'It's getting sort of windy and chilly, isn't it?'

'The cold wind from the mountains. We're in for a storm, I guess,' Henry assented absently. 'I think the river is getting wider.'

A short silence, and then, with sudden vivacity, 'But look, Irene, only a few more miles to the lake and then we're practically at the Earth village. It's almost over.'

Irene nodded, 'I'm glad for all of us – and the Phibs, too.'

She had reason for the last statement. The Phibs were swimming slowly now. An additional detachment had arrived the day before from upstream, but even with those reinforcements, progress had slowed to a walk. Unaccustomed cold was nipping the multi-legged reptiles and they yielded to superior mental force more and more reluctantly.

The first drops fell just after they had passed the lake. Darkness had fallen, and in the blue glare of the lightning the trees about them were ghostly specters reaching swaying fingers towards the sky. A sudden flare in the distance marked the funeral pyre of a lightning-hit tree.

Henry paled. 'Make for the clearing just ahead. At a time like this, trees are dangerous.'

The clearing he spoke of composed the outskirts of the Earth village. The rough-hewn houses, crude and small against the fury of the elements, showed lights here and there that spoke of human occupancy. And as the first Centosaur stumbled out from between splintered trees, the storm suddenly burst in all its fury.

The two Tweenies huddled close. 'It's up to the Phibs,' screamed Henry, dimly heard above the wind and rain. 'I hope they can do it.'

The three monsters converged upon the houses ahead. They moved more rapidly as the Phibs called up every last bit of mental power.

Irene buried her wet head in Henry's equally wet shoulder, 'I can't look! Those houses will go like matchsticks. Oh, the poor people!'

'No, Irene, no. They've stopped!'

The Centosaurs pawed vicious gouges out of the ground beneath and their screams rang shrill and clear above the noise of the storm. Startled Earthmen rushed from their cabins.

Caught unprepared – most having been roused from sleep – and faced with a Venusian storm and nightmarish Venusian monsters, there was no question of organized action. As they stood, carrying nothing but their clothes, they broke and ran.

There was the utmost confusion. One or two, with dim attempts at presence of mind, took wild, ineffectual pot-shots at the mountains of flesh before them – and then ran.

And when it seemed that all were gone, the giant reptiles surged forward once more and where once had been houses, there were left only mashed splinters.

'They'll never come back, Irene, they'll never come back.' Henry was breathless at the success of his plan. 'We're heroes now, and—' His voice rose to a hoarse shriek, 'Irene, get back! Make for the trees!'

The Centosaurian howls had taken on a deeper note. The nearest one reared onto his two hindmost pairs of legs and his great head, two hundred feet above ground, was silhouetted horribly against the lightning. With a rumbling thud, he came down on all feet again and made for the river – which under the lash of the storm was now a raging flood.

The Phibs had lost control!

Henry's Tonite gun flashed into quick action as he shoved Irene away. She, however, backed away slowly and brought her own gun into line.

The ball of purple light that meant a hit blazed into being and the nearest Centosaur screamed in agony as its mighty tail threshed aside the surrounding trees. Blindly, the hole where once a leg had been gushing blood, it charged.

A second glare of purple and it was down with an earth-shaking thud, its last shriek reaching a crescendo of shrill frightfulness.

But the other two monsters were crashing towards them. They blundered blindly towards the source of the power that had held them captive almost a week; driving violently with all the force of their mindless hate to the river. And in the path of the Juggernauts were the two Tweenies.

The boiling torrent was at their backs. The forest was a groaning wilderness of splintered trees and ear-splitting sound.

Then, suddenly, the reports of Tonite guns sounded from the distance. Purple glares – a flurry of threshing-spasmodic shrieking – and then a silence in which even the wind, as if overawed by recent events, held its peace momentarily.

Henry yelled his glee and performed an impromptu war-dance. 'They've come from Venustown, Irene,' he shouted. 'They've got the Centosaurs and everything's finished! We've saved the Tweenies!'

It happened in a breath's time. Irene had dropped her gun and sobbed her relief. She was running to Henry and then she tripped and the river had her.

'Henry!' The wind whipped the sound away.

For one dreadful moment, Henry found himself incapable of motion. He could only stare stupidly, unbelievingly, at the spot where Irene had been, and then he was in the water. He plunged into the surrounding blackness desperately.

'Irene!' He caught his breath with difficulty. The current drove him on.

'*Irene!*' No sound but the wind. His efforts at swimming were futile. He couldn't even break surface for more than a second at a time, his lungs were bursting.

'*Irene!*' There was no answer. Nothing but rushing water and darkness.

And then something touched him. He lashed out at it instinctively, but the grip tightened. He felt himself borne up into the air. His tortured lungs breathed in gasps. A grinning Phib face stared into his and after that there were nothing but confused impressions of cold, dark wetness.

He became aware of his surroundings by stages. First, that he was sitting on a blanket under the trees, with other blankets wrapped tightly about him. Then, he felt the warm radiation of the heatlamps upon him and the illumination of Atomo bulbs. People were crowding close and he noticed that it was no longer raining.

He stared about him hazily and then, 'Irene!'

She was beside him, as wrapped up as he, and smiling feebly, 'I'm all right, Henry. The Phibs dragged me back, too.'

Madeline was bending over him and he swallowed the hot coffee placed to his lips. 'The Phibs have told us of what you two have helped them do. We're all proud of you, son – you and Irene.'

Max's smile transfigured his face into the picture of paternal pride, 'The psychology you used was perfect. Venus is too vast and has too many friendly areas to expect Earthmen to return to places that have shown themselves to be infested with Centosaurs – not for a good long while. And when they *do* come back, we shall have our stat-field.'

Arthur Scanlon hurried up out of the gloom. He thwacked Henry on the shoulder and then wrung Irene's hand. 'Your guardian and I,' he told her, 'are fixing up a celebration for day after tomorrow, so get good and rested. It's going to be the greatest thing you ever saw.'

Henry spoke up, 'Celebration, huh? Well, I'll tell you what you can do. After it's over, you can announce an engagement.'

'An engagement?' Madeline sat up and looked interested. 'What do you mean?'

'An engagement – to be married,' came the impatient answer. 'I'm old enough, I suppose. Today proves it!'

Irene's eyes bent in furious concentration upon the grass, 'With whom, Henry?'

'Huh? With *you*, of course. Gosh, who else could it be?'

'But you haven't asked me.' The words were uttered slowly and with great firmness.

For a moment Henry flushed, and then his jaws grew grim, 'Well, I'm not going to. I'm telling you! And what are you going to do about it?'

He leaned close to her and Max Scanlon chuckled and motioned the others away. On tip-toes, they left.

A dim shape hobbled into view and the two Tweenies separated in confusion. They had forgotten the others.

But it wasn't another Tweenie. 'Why – why, it's a Phib!' cried Irene.

He limped his ungainly way across the wet grass, with the inexpert aid of his muscular arms. Approaching, he flopped wearily on his stomach and extended his forearms.

His purpose was plain. Irene and Henry grasped a hand apiece. There was silence a moment or two and the Phib's great eyes glinted solemnly in the light of the Atomo lamps. Then there was a sudden squeal of embarrassment from Irene and a shy laugh from Henry. Contact was broken.

'Did you get the same thing I did?' asked Henry.

Irene was red, 'Yes, a long row of little baby Phibs, maybe fifiteen—'

'Or twenty,' said Henry.

'—with *long white hair!*'

The Imaginary

The telecaster flashed its fitful signal, while Tan Porus sat by complacently. His sharp, green eyes glittered their triumph, and his tiny body was vibrant with excitement. Nothing could have better indicated the greatness of the occasion than his extraordinary position – Tan Porus had his feet on the desk!

The 'caster glowed into life and a broad Arcturian countenance frowned fretfully out at the Rigellian psychologist.

'Do you have to drag me here straight from bed, Porus? It's the middle of the night!'

'It's broad daylight in this part of the world, Final. But I've got something to tell you that'll make you forget all about sleep.'

Gar Final, editor of the *J.G.P.* – *Journal of Galactic Psychology* – allowed a look of alertness to cross his face. Whatever Tan Porus's faults – and Arcturus knew they were many – he had never issued a false alarm. If he said something great was in the air, it was not merely great – it was colossal!

It was quite evident that Porus was enjoying himself. 'Final,' he said, 'the next article I send to your rag is going to be the greatest thing you've ever printed.'

Final was impressed. 'Do you really mean what you say?' he asked idiotically.

'What kind of a stupid question is that? Of course I do. Listen—' There followed a dramatic silence, while the tenseness on Final's face reached painful proportions. Then came Porus's husky whisper – 'I've solved the problem of the squid!'

Of course the reaction was exactly what Porus had expected. There was a blow-up at the other end, and for thirty interesting seconds the Rigellian was surprised to learn that the staid and respectable Final had a blistering vocabulary.

Porus's squid was a by-word throughout the galaxy. For two years now, he had been fussing over an obscure Draconian animal that persisted in going to sleep when it wasn't supposed to. He had set up equations and torn them down with a regularity that had become a standing joke with every psychologist in the Federation – and none had explained the unusual reaction. Now Final had been dragged from bed to be told that the solution had been reached – and that was all.

Final ripped out a concluding phrase that all but put the 'caster out of commission.

Porus waited for the storm to pass and then said calmly, 'But do you know how I solved it?'

The other's answer was an indistinct mumble.

The Rigellian began speaking rapidly. All traces of amusement had left his face and, after a few sentences, all traces of anger left Final's.

The Arcturian's expression became one of wide-eyed interest. 'No?' he gasped.

'Yes!'

When Porus had finished, Final raced madly to put in rush calls to the printers to delay publication of the coming issue of the J.G.P. for two weeks.

Furo Santins, head of the math department of the University of Arcturus, gazed long and steadily at his Sirian colleague.

'No, no, you're wrong! His equations were legitimate. I checked them myself.'

'Mathematically, yes,' retorted the round-faced Sirian. 'But psychologically they had no meaning.'

Santins slapped his high forehead. 'Meaning! Listen to the mathematician talk. Great space, man, what have mathematics to do with meaning? Mathematics is a tool and as long as it can be manipulated to give proper answers and to make correct predictions, actual meaning has no significance. I'll say this for Tan Porus – most psychologists don't know enough mathematics to handle a slide-rule efficiently, but he knows his stuff.'

The other nodded doubtfully, 'I guess *so*. I guess so. But using imaginary quantities in psychological equations stretches my faith in science just a little bit. Square root of minus one!'

He shuddered . . .

The seniors' lounge in Psychology Hall was crowded and a-buzz with activity. The rumor of Porus's solution to the now-classic problem of the squid had spread fast, and conversation touched on nothing else.

At the center of the thickest group was Lor Haridin. He was young, with but newly acquired Senior status. But as Porus's assistant he was, under present conditions, master of the situation.

'Look, fellows – just exactly what it's all about I don't know. That's the old man's secret. All I can tell you is that I've got the general idea as to how he solved it.'

The others squeezed closer. 'I hear he had to make up a new mathematical notation for the squid,' said one, 'like that time we had trouble with the humanoids of Sol.'

Lor Haridin shook his head. 'Worse! What made him think of it, I can't imagine. It was either a brainstorm or a nightmare, but anyway he introduced imaginary quantities – the square root of minus one.'

There was an awful silence and then someone said, 'I don't believe it!'

'Fact!' was the complacent reply.

'But it doesn't make sense. What can the square root of minus one represent, psychologically speaking? Why, that would mean—' he was doing rapid calculation in his head, as were most of the others— 'that the neural synapses were hooked up in neither more nor less than four dimensions!'

'Sure,' broke in another. 'I suppose that if you stimulate the squid today, it will react yesterday. That's what an imaginary would mean. Comet gas! That's what *I* say.'

'That's why you're not the man Tan Porus is,' said Haridin. 'Do you suppose he cares how many imaginaries there are in the intermediate steps if they all square out into minus one in the final solution. All he's interested in is that they give him the proper sign in the answer – an answer which will explain that sleep business. As for its physical significance, what matter? Mathematics is only a tool, anyway.'

The others considered silently and marveled.

Tan Porus sat in his stateroom aboard the newest and most luxurious interstellar liner and gazed at the young man before him happily. He was in amazing good humor and, for perhaps the first time in his life, did not mind being interviewed by the keen, efficient employees of the Ether Press.

The Ethereporter on his side wondered in silence at the affability of the scientist. From bitter experience, he had found out that scientists, as a whole, detested reporters – and that psychologists, in particular, thought it fun to practice a bit of applied psych on them and to induce killingly amusing – to others – reactions.

He remembered the time that the old fellow from Canopus had convinced him that arboreal life was the greatest good. It had taken twenty men to drag him down from the tree-tops and an expert psychologist to bring him back to normal.

But here was the greatest of them all, Tan Porus, actually answering questions like a normal human being.

'What I would like to know now, Professor,' said the reporter, 'is just what this imaginary quantity is all about. That is,' he interposed hastily, 'not the mathematics of it – we'll take your word on that – but just a general idea that the ordinary humanoid can picture. For instance, I've heard that the squid has a four-dimensional mind.'

Porus groaned, 'Oh, Rigel! Four-dimensional poppycock! To tell the honest truth, that imaginary I used – which seems to have caught the popular fancy – probably indicates nothing more than some abnormality in the squid's nervous system, but just what, I don't know. Certainly, to the gross methods of ecology and micro-physiology, nothing unusual has been found. No doubt, the answer would lie in the atomic physics of the creature's brain, but there I have no hope.' There was a trace of disdain in his voice. 'The atomic physicists are too far behind the psychologists to expect them to catch up at this late date.'

The reporter bore down furiously on his stylus. The next day's headline was clear in his mind: *Noted Psychologist Blasts Atomic Physicists!*

Also, the headline of the day after: *Indignant Physicists Denounce Noted Psychologist!*

Scientific feuds were great stuff for the Ether Press, particularly that between psychologists and physicists, who, it was well known, hated each other's guts.

The reporter glanced up brightly. 'Say, Professor, the humanoids of the galaxy are very interested, you know, in the private lives of you scientists. I hope you don't mind if I ask you a few questions about your trip home to Rigel IV.'

'Go ahead,' said Porus, genially. 'Tell them it's the first time I'm getting home in two years. I'm sort of looking forward to it. Arcturus is just a bit too yellow for my eyes and the furniture you have here is too big.'

'It's true, isn't it, that you have a wife at home?'

Porus coughed. 'Hmm, yes. Sweetest little woman in the galaxy. I'm looking forward to seeing her, too. Put that down.'

The reporter put it down. 'How is it you didn't bring her to Arcturus with you?'

Some of the geniality left the Rigellian's face. 'I like to be alone when I work. Women are all right – in their place. Besides, my idea of a vacation is one by myself. Don't put that down.'

The reporter didn't put it down. He gazed at the others little form with open admiration. 'Say, Prof, how did you ever get her to stay home, though? I wish you'd tell me the secret.' Then, with a wealth of feeling he added, 'I could use it!'

Porus laughed. 'I tell you, son. When you're an ace psychologist, you're master in your own home!'

He motioned the interview to an end and then suddenly grasped the other by the arm. His green eyes were piercingly sharp. 'And listen, son, that last remark doesn't go into the story, you know.'

The reporter paled and backed away. 'No, sir; no, sir! We've got a little saying in our profession that goes: "Never monkey around with a psychologist, or he'll make a monkey of *you*."'

'Good! I can do it literally, you know, if I have to.'

The young press employee ducked out hastily after that, wiped the cold perspiration from his brow and left with his story. For a moment, towards the last, he had felt himself hanging on the ragged edge. He made a mental note to refuse all future interviews with psychologists – unless they raised his pay.

Tens of billions of miles out, the pure white orb of Rigel had reached Porus's eyes, and something in his heart uplifted him.

Type B reaction – nostalgia; conditioned reflex through association of Rigel with happy scenes of youth—

Words, phrases, equations spun through his keen brain, but he was happy in spite of them. And in a little while, the human triumphed over the psychologist and Porus abandoned analysis for the superior joy of uncritical happiness.

He sat up past the middle of the sleep period two nights before the landing to catch first glimpse of Hanlon, fourth planet of Rigel, his home world. Some place on that world, on the shores of a quiet sea, was a little two-story house. A little house – not those giant structures fit only for Arcturians and other hulking humanoids.

It was the summer season now and the house would be bathed in the pearly light of Rigel, and after the harsh yellow-red of Arcturus, how restful that would be.

And – he almost shouted in his joy – the very fust night he was going to insist on gorging himself with broiled *tryptex*. He hadn't tasted it for two years, and his wife was the best hand at *tryptex* in the system.

He winced a little at the thought of his wife. It *had* been a dirty trick, getting her to stay home the last two years, but it had had to be done. He glanced over the papers before him once more. There was just a little nervousness in his fingers as they shuffled the sheets. *Re* had spent a full day in calculating her reactions at fust seeing him after two years' absence and they were not pleasant.

Nina Porus was a woman of untamed emotions, and he would have to work quickly and efficiently.

He spotted her quickly in the crowd. He smiled. It was nice to see her, even if his equations did predict long and serious storms. He ran over his initial speech once more and made a last-minute change.

And then she saw him. She waved frantically and broke from the forefront of the crowd. She was on Tan Porus before he was aware of it and, in the grip of her affectionate embrace, he went limp with surprise.

That wasn't the reaction to be expected at all! Something was wrong!

She was leading him dexterously through the crowd of reporters to the waiting stratocar, talking rapidly along the way.

'Tan Porus, I thought I'd never live to see you again. It's so good to have you with me again; you have absolutely no idea. Everything here at home is just fine, of course, but it isn't quite the same without you.'

Porus's green eyes were glazed. This speech was entirely

uncharacteristic of Nina. To the sensitive ears of a psychologist, it sounded little short of the ravings of a maniac. He had not even the presence of mind to grunt at proper intervals. Frozen mutely in his seat, he watched the ground rush downwards and heard the air shriek backwards as they headed for their little house by the sea.

Nina Porus prattled on gaily – the one normal aspect of her conversation being her ability to uphold both ends of a dialogue with smooth efficiency.

'And, of course, dear, I've fixed up an entire *tryptex*, broiled to a turn, garnished with *sarnees*. And, of yes, about that affair last year with that new planet – Earth, do you call it? I was so proud of you when I heard about it. I said—'

And so on and on, until her voice degenerated into a meaningless conglomeration of sounds.

Where were her tears? Where were the reproaches, the threats, the impassioned self pity?

Tan Porus roused himself to one great effort at dinner. He stared at the steaming dish of *tryptex* before him with an odd lack of appetite and said, 'This reminds me of the time at Arcturus when I dined with the President Delegate—'

He went into details, dilating on the gayety and abandon of the affair, waxing lyrical over his own enjoyment of it, stressing, almost unsubtly, the fact that he had not missed his wife, and finally, in one last wild burst of desperation, mentioning casually the presence of a surprising number of Rigellian females in the Arcturian system.

And through it all, his wife sat smiling. 'Wonderful, darling,' she'd say. 'I'm so glad you enjoyed yourself. Eat your *tryptex*.'

But Porus did not eat his *tryptex*. The mere thought of food nauseated him. With one lingering stare of dismay at his wife, he arose with what dignity he could muster and left for the privacy of his room.

He tore up the equations furiously and hurled himself into a chair. He seethed with anger, for evidently something had gone wrong with Nina. Terribly wrong! Even interest in another man – and for just a moment that had occurred to him as a possible explanation – would not cause such a revolution in character.

He tore at his hair. There was some hidden factor more startling than that – but what it was he had no idea. At that moment Tan Porus would have given the sum total of his worldly possessions to have his wife enter and make one – just one – attempt to snatch his scalp off, as of old.

And below, in the dining room, Nina Porus allowed a crafty gleam to enter her eye.

Lor Haridin put down his pen and said, 'Come in!'

The door opened, and his friend, Eblo Ranin, entered, brushed off a corner of the desk and sat down.

'Haridin, I've got an idea.' His voice was uncommonly like a guilty whisper.

Haridin gazed at him suspiciously.

'Like the time,' he said, 'you set up the booby trap for old man Obel?'

Ranin shuddered. He had spent two days hiding in the ventilator shaft after that brilliant piece of work. 'No, this is legitimate. Listen, Porus left you in charge of the squid, didn't he?'

'Oh, I see what you're getting at. It's no go. I can feed the squid, but that's all. If I as much as clapped my hands at it to induce a color-change tropism, the boss would throw a fit.'

'To space with him! He's parsecs away, anyway.' Ranin drew forth a two-month old copy of the J.G.P. and folded the cover back. 'Have you been following Livell's experiments at Procyon U.? You know – magnetic fields applied with and without ultra-violet radiation.'

'Out of my field,' grunted Haridin. 'I've heard of it, but that's all. What about it?'

'Well, it's a type E reaction which gives, believe it or not, a strong Fimbal Effect in practically every case, especially in the higher invertebrates.'

'Hmm!'

'Now, if we could try it on this squid, we could—'

'No, no, no, no!' Haridin shook his head violently. 'Porus would break me. Great stars and little meteors, *how* he would break me!'

'Listen, you nut – Porus can't tell you what to do with the squid. It's Frian Obel that has final say. He's head of the Psychological Board, not Porus. All you have to do is to apply for his permission and you'll get it. Just between us, since that Homo Sol affair last year, he can't stand the sight of Porus anyway.'

Haridin weakened. 'You ask him.'

Ranin coughed. 'No. On the whole, perhaps I'd better not. He's sort of got a suspicion that I set that booby trap, and I'd rather keep out of his way.'

'Hmm. Well – all right!'

Lor Haridin looked as if he had not slept well for a week – which shows that sometimes appearances are not deceiving. Eblo Ranin regarded him with patient kindliness and sighed.

'Look! Will you please sit down? Santin said he would have the final results in today, didn't he?'

'I know, I know, but it's humiliating. I spent seven years on higher math. And now I make a stupid mistake and can't even find it!'

'Maybe it's not there to find.'

'Don't be silly. The answer is just impossible. It must be impossible. It must be.' His high forehead creased. 'Oh, I don't know what to think.'

He continued his concentrated attempt to wear out the nap of the rug beneath and mused bitterly. Suddenly he sat down.

'It's those time integrals. You can't work with them, I tell you. You look 'em up in a table, taking half an hour to find the proper entry, and they give you seventeen possible answers. You have to pick the one that makes sense, and – Arcturus help me! – either they all do, or none do! Run up against eight of them, as we do in this problem, and we've got enough permutations to last us the rest of our life. Wrong answer! It's a wonder I lived through it at all.'

The look he gave the fat volume of Helo's *Tables of Time Integrals* did not sear the binding, to Ranin's great surprise.

The signal light flashed, and Haridin leaped to the door.

He snatched the package from the messenger's hand and ripped open the wrappings frantically.

He turned to the last page and stared at Santin's final note:

> Your calculations are correct. Congratulations – and won't this knock Porus's head right off his shoulders! Better get in touch with him at once.

Ranin read it over the other's shoulder, and for one long minute the two gazed at each other.

'I was right,' whispered Haridin, eyes bulging. 'We've found something in which the imaginary doesn't square out, We've got a predicted reaction which includes an imaginary quantity!'

The other swallowed and brushed aside his stupefaction with an effort. 'How do you interpret it?'

'Great space! How in the galaxy should I know? We've got to get Porus, that's all.'

Ranin snapped his fingers and grabbed the other by the shoulders. 'Oh, no, we won't. This is our big chance. If we can carry this through, we're made for life.' He stuttered in his excitement. 'Arcturus! Any psychologist would sell his life twice over to have our opportunity right now.'

The Draconian squid crawled placidly about, unawed by the huge solenoid that surrounded its tank. The mass of tangled wires, the current leads, the mercury-vapor lamp up above meant nothing to it. It nibbled contentedly at the fronds of the sea fern about it and was at peace with the world.

Not so the two young psychologists. Eblo Ranin scurried through the complicated set-up in a last-minute effort at checking everything. Lor Haridin helped him in intervals between nail-biting.

'Everything's set,' said Ranin, and swabbed wearily at his damp brow. 'Let her shoot!'

The mercury-vapor lamp went on and Haridin pulled the window curtains together. In the cold red-less light, two green-tinted faces watched the squid closely. It stirred restlessly, its warm pink changing to a dull black in the mercury light.

'Turn on the juice,' said Haridin hoarsely.

There was a soft click, and that was all.

'No reaction?' questioned Ranin, half to himself. And then he held his breath as the other bent closer.

'Something's happening to the squid. It seems to glow a bit – or is it my eyes?'

The glow became perceptible and then seemed to detach itself from the body of the animal and take on a spherical shape of itself. Long minutes passed.

'It's emitting some sort of radiation, field, force – whatever you want to call it – and there seems to be expansion with time.'

There was no answer, and none was expected. Again they waited and watched.

And then Ranin emitted a muffled cry and grasped Haridin's elbow tightly. 'Crackling comets, what's it doing?'

The globular glowing sphere of whatever it was had thrust out a pseudopod. A gleaming little projection touched the swaying branch of the sea-fern, and where it touched the leaves turned brown and withered!

'Shut off the current!'

The current clicked off; the mercury-vapor lamp went out; the shades were parted and the two stared at each other nervously.

'What was it?'

Haridin shook his head. 'I don't know. It was something definitely insane. I never saw anything like it.'

'You never saw an imaginary in a reaction equation before, either, did you? As a matter of fact, I don't think that expanding field was any known form of energy at—'

His breath came out in one long whistling exhalation and he retreated slowly from the tank containing the squid. The mollusc was motionless, but around it half the fern in the tank hung sere and withered.

Haridin gasped. He pulled the shades and in the gloom, the globe of glowing haze bulked through half the tank. Little curving tentacles of light reached toward the remaining fern and one pulsing thread extended through the glass and was creeping along the table.

That fright in Ranin's voice rendered it a cracked, scarcely-understood sound.

'It's a lag reaction. Didn't you test it by Wilbon's Theorem?'

'How could I?' The other's heart pumped madly and his dry lips fought to form words. 'Wilbon's Theorem didn't make sense with an imaginary in the equation. I let it go.'

Ranin sped into action with feverish energy. He left the room and was back in a moment with a tiny, squealing, squirrel-like animal from his own lab. He dropped it in the path of the thread of light stealing along the table, and held it there with a yard rule.

The glowing thread wavered, seemed to sense the presence of life in some horribly blind way, and lunged towards it. The little rodent squealed once, a high-pitched shriek of infinite torture, and went limp. In two seconds it was a shriveled, shrunken travesty of its former self.

Ranin swore and dropped the rule with a sudden yell, for the thread of light – a bit brighter, a bit thicker – began creeping up the wood toward him.

'Here,' said Haridin, 'let's end this!' He yanked a drawer open and withdrew the chromium-plated Tonite gun within. Its sharp thin beam of purple light lunged forward towards the squid and exploded in blazing, soundless fury against the edge of the sphere of force. The psychologist shot again and again, and then compressed the trigger to form one continuous purple stream of destruction that ceased only when power failed.

And the glowing sphere remained unharmed. It engulfed the entire tank. The ferns were brown masses of death.

'Get the Board,' yelled Ranin. 'It's beyond us entirely!'

There was no confusion – humanoids in the mass are simply not subject to panic, if you don't count the half-genius, half-humanoid inhabitants of the planets of Sol – and the evacuation of the University grounds was carried out smoothly.

'One fool,' said old Mir Deana, ace physicist of Arcturus U., 'can ask more questions than a thousand wise men can answer.' He fingered his scraggly beard and his button nose sniffed loudly in disdain.

'What do you mean by that?' questioned Frian Obel sharply. His green Vegan skin darkened angrily.

'Just that, by analogy, one cosmic fool of a psychologist can make a bigger mess than a thousand physicists can clear up.'

Obel drew in his breath dangerously. He had his own opinion of Haridin and Ranin, but no lame-brain physicist could—

The plump figure of Qual Wynn, university president, came charging down upon them. He was out of breath and spoke between puffs.

'I've gotten in touch with the Galactic Congress and they're arranging for evacuation of all Eron, if necessary.' His voice became pleading. 'Isn't there anything that can be done?'

Mir Deana sighed, 'Nothing – yet! All we know is this: the squid is emitting some sort of pseudo-living radiatory field which is not electromagnetic in character. Its advance cannot be stopped by anything we have yet tried, material or vacuum. None of our weapons affect it, for within the field the ordinary attributes of space-time apparently don't hold.'

The president shook a worried head. 'Bad, bad! You've sent for Porus, though?' He sounded as though he were clutching at a last straw.

'Yes,' scowled Frian Obel. 'He's the only one that really knows that squid. If he can't help us, no one can.' He stared off toward the gleaming white of the university buildings, where the grass over half the campus was brown stubble and the trees blasted ruins.

'Do you think,' said the president, turning to Deana once more, 'that the field can span interplanetary space?'

'Sizzling novae, I don't know what to think!' Deana exploded, and he turned pettishly away.

There was a thick silence of utter gloom.

Tan Porus was sunk in deep apathy. He was unaware of the brilliant coruscations of color overhead. He didn't hear a sound of the melodious tones that filled the auditorium.

He knew only one thing – that he had been talked into attending a concert. Concerts above all were anathema to him, and in twenty years of married life he had steered clear of them with a skill and ease that only the greatest psychologist of them all could have shown. And now—

He was startled out of his stupor by the sudden discordant sounds that arose from the rear.

There was a rush of ushers to the exit where the disturbance originated, a waving of protesting uniformed arms and then a strident voice: 'I am here on urgent business direct from the Galactic Congress on Eron, Arcturus. Is Tan Porus in the audience?'

Tan Porus was out of his seat with a bound. Any excuse to leave the auditorium was nothing short of heaven-sent.

He ripped open the communication handed him by the messenger and devoured its contents. At the second sentence, his elation left him. When he was finished, he raised a face in which only his darting green eyes seemed alive.

'How soon can we leave?'

'The ship is waiting now.'

'Come, then.'

He took one step forward and stopped. There was a hand on his elbow.

'Where are you going?' asked Nina Porus. There was hidden steel in her voice.

Tan Porus felt stifled for a moment. He foresaw what would happen. 'Darling, I must go to Eron immediately. The fate of a world, of the whole galaxy perhaps, is at stake. You don't know how important it is. I tell you—'

'All right, go! And I'll go with you.'

The psychologist bowed his head.

'Yes, dear!' he said. He sighed.

The psychological board hemmed and hawed as one man and then stared dubiously at the large-scale graph before them.

'Frankly, gentlemen,' said Tan Porus, 'I don't feel too certain about it myself, but – well, you've all seen my results, and checked them too. And it is the only stimulus that will yield a canceling reaction.'

Frian Obel fingered his chin nervously. 'Yes, the mathematics is clear. Increase in hydrogen-ion activity past pH_3 would set up a Demane's Integral and that— But listen, Porus, we're not dealing with space-time. The math might not hold – perhaps nothing will hold.'

'It's our only chance. If we were dealing with normal space-time, we could just dump in enough acid to kill the blasted squid or fry it with a Tonite. As it is, we have no choice but to take our chances with—'

Loud voices interrupted him. 'Let me through, I say! I don't care if there are ten conferences going on!'

The door swung open and Qual Wynn's portly figure made its entrance. He spied Porus and bore down upon him. 'Porus, I tell you I'm going crazy. Parliament is holding me, as university president, responsible for all this, and now Deana says that—' He sputtered into silence and Mir Deana, standing composedly behind him, took up the tale.

'The field now covers better than one thousand square miles and its rate of increase is growing steadily. There seems to be no doubt now that it can span interplanetary space if it wishes to do so – interstellar as well, if given the time.'

'You hear that? You hear that?' Wynn was fairly dancing in his anxiety. 'Can't you do something? The galaxy is doomed, I tell you, doomed!'

'Oh, keep your tunic on,' groaned Porus, 'and let *us* handle this.' He turned to Deana. 'Didn't your physicist stooges conduct some clumsy investigations as to the speed of penetration of the field through various substances?'

Deana nodded stiffly.

'Penetration varies, in general, inversely with density. Osmium, iridium and platinum are the best. Lead and gold are fair.'

'Good! That checks! What I'll need then is an osmium-plated suit with a lead-glass helmet. And make both plating and helmet good and thick.'

Qual Wynn stared horrified. 'Osmium plating! Osmium! By the great nebula, think of the expense.'

'I'm thinking,' said Porus frostily.

'But they'll charge it to the university; they'll—' He recovered with difficulty as the somber stares of the assembled psychologists fastened themselves upon him. 'When do you need it?' he muttered weakly.

'You're really going, yourself?'

'Why not?' asked Porus, clambering out of the suit.

Mir Deana said, 'The lead-glass headpiece will hold off the field not longer than an hour and you'll probably be getting partial penetration in much shorter time. I don't know if you can do it.'

'*I'll* worry about that.' He paused, and then continued uncertainly. 'I'll be ready in a few minutes. I'd like to speak to my wife first – alone.'

The interview was a short one. It was one of the very few occasions that Tan Porus forgot that he was a psychologist, and spoke as his heart moved him, without stopping to consider the natural reaction of the one spoken to.

One thing he did know – by instinct rather than thought – and that was that his wife would not break down or go sentimental on him; and there he was right. It was only in the last few seconds that her eyes fell and her voice quavered. She tugged a handkerchief from her wide sleeve and hurried from the room.

The psychologist stared after her and then stooped to pick up the thin book that had fallen as she had removed the handkerchief. Without looking at it, he placed it in the inner pocket of his tunic.

He smiled crookedly. 'A talisman!' he said.

Tan Porus's gleaming one-man cruiser whistled into the 'death field.' The clammy sensation of desolation impressed itself upon him at once.

He shrugged. 'Imagination! Mustn't get nervy now.'

There was the vaguest glitter – a sparkle that was felt rather than seen – in the air about him. And then it invaded the ship itself, and, looking up, the Rigellian saw the five Eronian ricebirds he had brought with him lying dead on the floor of their cage, huddled masses of bedraggled feathers.

'The "death field" is in,' he whispered. It had penetrated the steel hull of the cruiser.

The cruiser bumped to a rather unskillful landing on the broad university athletic field, and Tan Porus, an incongruous figure in the bulky osmium suit, stepped out. He surveyed his depressing surroundings. From the brown stubble underfoot to the glimmering haze that hid the normal blue of the sky, all seemed – dead.

He entered Psychology Hall.

His lab was dark; the shades were still drawn. He parted them and studied the squid's tank. The water replenisher was still working, for the tank was full. However, that was the only normal thing about it. Only a few dark-brown, ragged strands of rot were left of what had once been sea-fern. The squid itself lay inertly upon the floor of the tank.

Tan Porus sighed. He felt tired and numbed. His mind was hazy and unclear. For long minutes he stared about him unseeingly.

Then, with an effort, he raised the bottle he held and glanced at the label – 12 molar hydrochloric acid.

He mumbled vaguely to himself. 'Two hundred cc. Just dump the whole thing in. That'll force the pH down – if only hydrogen ion activity means something here.'

He was fumbling with the glass stopper, and – suddenly – laughing. He had felt exactly like this the one and only time he had ever been drunk.

He shook the gathering cobwebs from his brain. 'Only got a few minutes to do – to do what? I don't know – something anyway. Dump this thing in. Dump it in. Dump! Dump! Dumpety-dump!' He was mumbling a silly popular song to himself as the acid gurgled its way into the open tank.

Tan Porus felt pleased with himself and he laughed. He stirred the water with his mailed fist and laughed some more. He was still singing that song.

And then he became aware of a subtle change in environment. He fumbled for it and stopped singing. And then it hit him with the suddenness of a downpour of cold water. *The glitter in the atmosphere had gone!*

With a sudden motion, he unclasped the helmet and cast it off. He drew in long breaths of air, a bit musty, but unkilling.

He had acidified the water of the tank, and destroyed the field at its source. Chalk up another victory for the pure mathematics of psychology!

He stepped out of his osmium suit and stretched. The pressure on his chest reminded him of something. Withdrawing the booklet his wife had drnpped, he said, 'The talisman came through!' and smiled indulgently at his own whimsy.

The smile froze as he saw for the first time the title upon the book. The title was *Intermediate Course in Applied Psychology – Volume 5*.

It was as if something large and heavy had suddenly fallen onto Porus's head and driven understanding into it. *Nina had been boning up on applied psych for two whole years.*

This was the missing factor. He could allow for it. He would have to use triple time integrals, but—

He threw the communicator switch and waited for contact.

'Hello! This is Porus! Come on in, all of you! The death field is gone! I've beaten the squid.' He broke contact and added triumphantly, '—and my wife!'

Strangely enough – or, perhaps, not so strangely – it was the latter feat that pleased him more.

Heredity

Dr Stefansson fondled the thick sheaf of typewritten papers that lay before him, 'It's all here, Harvey – twenty-five years of work.'

Mild-mannered Professor Harvey puffed idly at his pipe, 'Well, your part is over – and Markey's, too, on Ganymede. It's up to the twins, themselves, now.'

A short ruminative silence, and then Dr Stefansson stirred uneasily, 'Are you going to break the news to Allen soon?'

The other nodded quietly, 'It will have to be done before we get to Mars, and the sooner the better.' He paused, then added in a tightened voice, 'I wonder how it feels to find out after twenty-five years that one has a twin brother whom one has never seen. It must be a damned shock.'

'How did George take it?'

'Didn't believe it at first, and I don't blame him. Markey had to work like a horse to convince him it wasn't a hoax. I suppose I'll have as hard a job with Allen.' He knocked the dottle from his pipe and shook his head.

'I have half a mind to go to Mars just to see those two get together,' remarked Dr Stefansson wistfully.

'You'll do no such thing, Stef. This experiment's taken too long and means too much to have you ruin it by any such fool move.'

'I know, I know! Heredity versus environment! Perhaps at last the definite answer.' He spoke half to himself, as if repeating an old, familiar formula, 'Two identical twins, separated at birth; one brought up on old, civilized Earth, the other on pioneer Ganymede. Then, on their twenty-fifth birthday brought together for the first time on Mars – God! I wish Carter had lived to see the end of it. They're *his* children.'

'Too bad! – But we're alive, and the twins. To carry the experiment to its end will be our tribute to him.'

There is no way of telling, at first seeing the Martian branch of Medicinal Products, Inc., that it is surrounded by anything but desert. You can't see the vast underground caverns where the native fungi of Mars are artificially nurtured into huge blooming fields. The intricate transportation system that connects all parts of the square miles of fields to the central building is invisible. The irrigation system; the air-purifiers; the drainage pipes, are all hidden.

And what one sees is the broad squat red-brick building and Martian desert, rusty and dry, all about.

That had been all George Carter had seen upon arriving via rocket taxi, but him, at least, appearances had not deceived. It would have been strange had it done so, for his life on Ganymede had been oriented in its every phase towards eventual general managership of that very concern. He knew every square inch of the caverns below as well as if he had been born and raised in them himself.

And now he sat in Professor Lemuel Harvey's small office and allowed just the slightest trace of uneasiness to cross his impassive countenance. His ice-blue eyes sought those of Professor Harvey.

'This – this twin brother o' mine. He'll be here soon?'

Professor Harvey nodded, 'He's on his way over right now.'

George Carter uncrossed his knees. His expression was almost wistful, 'He looks a lot like me, d'ya rackon?'

'Quite a lot. You're identical twins, you know.'

'Hmm! Rackon so! Wish I'd known him all the time – on Ganny!' He frowned, 'He's lived on Airth all's life, huh?'

An expression of interest crossed Professor Harvey's face. He said briskly, 'You dislike Earthmen?'

'No, not exactly,' came the immediate answer. 'It's just the Airth-men are tanderfeet. All of 'm I know are.'

Harvey stifled a grin, and conversation languished.

The door-signal snapped Harvey out of his reverie and George Carter out of his chair at the same instant. The professor pressed the desk-button and the door opened.

The figure on the threshold crossed into the room and then stopped. The twin brothers faced each other.

It was a tense, breathless moment, and Professor Harvey sank into his soft chair, put his finger-tips together and watched keenly.

The two stood stiffly erect, ten feet apart, neither making a move to lessen the distance. They made a curious contrast – a contrast all the more marked because of the vast similarity between the two.

Eyes of frozen blue gazed deep into eyes of frozen blue. Each saw a long, straight nose over full, red lips pressed firmly together. The high cheekbones were as prominent in one as in the other, the jutting, angular chin as square. There was even the same, odd half-cock of one eyebrow in twin expressions of absorbed, part-quizzical interest.

But with the face, all resemblance ended. Allen Carter's clothes bore the New York stamp on every square inch. From his loose blouse, past his dark purple knee breeches, salmon-colored cellulite stockings, down to the glistening sandals on his feet, he stood a living embodiment of latest Terrestrial fashion.

For a fleeting moment, George Carter was conscious of a feeling of ungainliness as he stood there in his tight-sleeved, close-necked shirt of Ganymedan linen. His unbuttoned vest and his voluminous trousers with their ends tucked into high-laced, heavy-soled boots were clumsy and provincial. Even *he* felt it – for just a moment.

From his sleeve-pocket Allen removed a cigarette case – it was the first move either of the brothers had made – opened it, withdrew a slender cylinder of paper-covered tobacco that spontaneously glowed into life at the first puff.

George hesitated a fraction of a second and his subsequent action was almost one of defiance. His hand plunged into his inner vest pocket and drew therefrom the green, shriveled form of a cigar made of Ganymedan greenleaf. A match flared into flame upon his thumbnail and for a long moment, he matched, puff for puff, the cigarette of his brother.

And then Allen laughed – a queer, high-pitched laugh, 'Your eyes are a little closer together, I think.'

'Rackon 'tis, maybe. Y'r hair's fixed sort o' different.' There was faint disapproval in his voice. Allen's hand went self-consciously to his long, light-brown hair, carefully curled at the ends, while his eyes flickered over the carelessly-bound queue into which the other's equally long hair was drawn.

'I suppose we'll have to get used to each other. —I'm willing to try.' The Earth twin was advancing now, hand outstretched.

George smiled, 'Y' bet. 'At goes here, too.'

The hands met and gripped.

'Y'r name's All'n, huh?' said George.

'And yours is George, isn't it?' answered Allen.

And then for a long while they said nothing more. They just looked – and smiled as they strove to bridge the twenty-five year gap that separated them.

George Carter's impersonal gaze swept over the carpet of low-growing purple blooms that stretched in plot-path bordered squares into the misty distance of the caverns. The newspapers and feature writers might rhapsodize over the 'Fungus Gold' of Mars – about the purified extracts, in yields of ounces to acres of blooms, that had become indispensable to the medical profession of the System. Opiates, purified vitamins, a new vegetable specific against pneumonia – the blooms were worth their weight in gold, almost.

But they were merely blooms to George Carter – blooms to be forced to full growth, harvested, baled, and shipped to the Aresopolis labs hundreds of miles away.

He cut his little ground car to half-speed and leant furiously out the window, 'Hi y' mudcat there. Y' with the dairty face. Watch what y'r doing – keep the domned water in the channel.'

He drew back and the ground car leapt ahead once more. The Ganymedan muttered viciously to himself, 'These domned men about here are wairse than useless. So many machines t' do their wairk for 'm they give their brains a pairmenent vacation, I rackon.'

The ground car came to a halt and he clambered out. Picking his way between the fungus plots, he approached the clustered group of men about the spider-armed machine in the plotway ahead.

'Well, here I am. What is 't, All'n?'

Allen's head bobbed up from behind the other side of the machine. He waved at the men about him, 'Stop it for a second!' and leaped toward his twin.

'George, it works. It's slow and clumsy, but it works. We can improve it now that we've got the fundamentals down. And in no time at all, we'll be able to—'

'Now wait a while, All'n. On Ganny, we go slow. Y' live long, that way. What y' got there?'

Allen paused and swabbed at his forehead. His face shone with grease, sweat, and excitement. 'I've been working on this thing ever since I finished college. It's a modification of something we have on Earth – but it's no end improved. It's a mechanical bloom picker.'

He had fished a much-folded square of heavy paper from his pocket and talked steadily as he spread it on the plotway before them, 'Up to now, bloom-picking has been the bottleneck of production, to say nothing of the 15 to 20% loss due to picking under- and over-ripe blooms. After all, human eyes are only human eyes, and the blooms— Here, look!'

The paper was spread flat and Allen squatted before it. George leaned over his shoulder, with frowning watchfulness.

'You see. It's a combination of fluoroscope and photo-electric cell. The ripeness of the bloom can be told by the state of the spores within. This machine is adjusted so that the proper circuit is tripped upon the impingement of just that combination of light and dark formed by ripe spores within the bloom. On the other hand, this second circuit – but look, it's easier to show you.'

He was up again, brimming with enthusiasm. With a jump, he was in the low seat behind the picker and had pulled the lever.

Ponderously, the picker turned towards the blooms and its 'eye' traveled sideways six inches above the ground. As it passed each fungus bloom, a long spidery arm shot out, lopping it cleanly half an inch from the ground and depositing it neatly in the downwardsloping slide beneath. A pile of blooms formed behind the machine.

'We can hook on a binder, too, later on. Do you notice those blooms it doesn't touch? Those are unripe. Just wait till it comes to an over-ripe one and see what it does.'

He yelled in triumph a moment later when a bloom was torn out and dropped on the spot.

He stopped the machine, 'You see? In a month, perhaps, we can actually start putting it to work in the fields.'

George Carter gazed sourly upon his twin, 'Take more 'n a month, I rackon. It'll take foraver, more likely.'

'What do you mean, forever. It just has to be sped up—'

'I don't care if 't just has t' be painted pairple. 'Tisn't going t' appear on *my* fields.'

'*Your* fields?'

'Yup, mine,' was the cool response. 'I've got veto pow'r here same as you have. Y' can't do anything 'thout my say-so – and y' won't get it f'r this. In fact, I want y' t' clear that thing out o' here, altogether. Got no use f'r 't.'

Allen dismounted and faced his brother, 'You agreed to let me have this plot to experiment on, veto-free, and I'm holding you to that agreement.'

'All right, then. But keep y'r damned machine out o' the rest o' the fields.'

The Earthman approached the other slowly. There was a dangerous look in his eyes. 'Look, George, I don't like your attitude – and I don't like the way you're using your veto power. I don't know what you're used to running on Ganymede, but you're in the big time now, and there are a lot of provincial notions you'll have to get out of your head.'

'Not unless I want to. And if y' want t' have 't out with me, we'd batter go t' y'r office. Spatting before the men 'd be bad for discipline.'

The trip back to Central was made in ominous silence. George whistled softly to himself while Allen folded his arms and stared with ostentatious indifference at the narrow, twisting plotway ahead. The silence persisted as they entered the Earthman's office. Allen gestured shortly towards a chair and the Ganymedan took it without a word. He brought out his ever-present green-leaf cigar and waited for the other to speak.

Allen hunched forward upon the edge of his seat and leaned both elbows on his desk. He began with a rush.

'There's lots to this situation, George, that's a mystery to me. I don't know why they brought up you on Ganymede and me on Earth, and I don't know why they never let us know of each other, or made us co-managers now with veto-power over one another – but I do know that the situation is rapidly growing intolerable.

'This corporation needs modernization, and you know that. Yet you've been wielding that veto-power over every trifling advance I've tried to initiate. I don't know just what your viewpoint is, but I've a suspicion that you think you're still living on Ganymede. If you're still in the sticks – I'm warning you – get out of them fast. I'm from Earth, and this corporation is going to be run with Earth effciency and Earth organization. Do you understand?'

George puffed odorous tobacco at the ceiling before answering, but when he did, his eyes came down sharply, and there was a cutting edge to his voice.

'Airth, is it? Airth efficiency, no less? Well, All'n, I like ye. I can't help it. Y'r so much like me, that disliking y' would be like disliking myself, I rackon. I hate t' say this, but y'r upbringing's all wrong.'

His voice became sternly accusatory, 'Y'r an Airthman. Well, look at y'. An Airthman's but half a man at best, and naturally y' lean on machines. But d' y' suppose *I* want the corporation to be run by machines – just *machines?* What're the *men* t' do?'

'The men run the machines,' came the clipped, angry response.

The Ganymedan rose, and a fist slammed down on the desk, 'The machines run the men, and y' know it. Fairst, y' use them; then y' depend on them; and finally y'r slaves t' them. Over on y'r pracious Airth, it was machines, machines, machines – and as a result, what *are* y'? I'll tell y'. Half a man!'

He drew himself up, 'I still like y'. I like y' well enough t' wish y'd lived on Gannie with me. By Jupe 'n' domn, 'twould have made a man o' y'.'

'Finished?' said Allen.

'Rackon so!'

'Then I'll tell you something. There's nothing wrong with you that a life time on a decent planet wouldn't have fixed. As it is, however, you belong on Ganymede. I'd advise you to go back there.'

George spoke very softly, 'Y'r not thinking o' taking a punch at me, are y'?'

'No. I couldn't fight a mirror image of myself, but if your face were only a little different, I would enjoy splashing it about the premises a bit.'

'Think y' could do it – an Airthman like you? Here, sit down. We're both getting a bit too excited, I rackon. Nothing'll be settled *this* way.'

He sat down once more, puffed vainly at his dead cigar, and tossed it into the incinerator chute in disgust.

'Where's y'r water?' he grunted.

Allen grinned with sudden delight, 'Would you object to having a machine supply it?'

'Machine? What d' y' mean?' The Ganymedan gazed about him suspiciously.

'Watch! I had this installed a week ago.' He touched a button on his desk and a low click sounded below. There was the sound of pouring water for a second or so and then a circular metal disk beside the Earthman's right hand slid aside and a cup of water lifted up from below.

'Take it,' said Allen.

George lifted it gingerly and drank it down. He tossed the empty cup down the incinerator shaft, then stared long and thoughtfully at his brother, 'May I see this water feeder o' y'rs?'

'Surely. It's just under the desk. Here, I'll make room for you.'

The Ganymedan crawled underneath while Allen watched uncertainly. A brawny hand was thrust out suddenly and a muffled voice said, 'Hand me a screwdriver.'

'Here! What are you going to do?'

'Nothing. Nothing 't all. Just want t' investigate this contraption.'

The screw-driver was handed down and for a few minutes there was no other sound than an occasional soft scraping of metal on metal. Finally, George withdrew a flushed face and adjusted his wrinkled collar with satisfaction.

'Which button do I press for the water?'

Allen gestured and the button was pressed. The gurgling of water sounded. The Earthman stared in mystification from his desk to his brother and back again. And then he became aware of a moistness about his feet.

He jumped, looked downwards, and squawked in dismay, 'Why, damn you, what have you done?' A snaky stream of water wriggled blindly out from under the desk and the pouring sound of water still continued.

George made leisurely for the door, 'Just short-caircuited it. Here's y'r screw-driver; fix 't up again.' And just before he slammed the door, 'So much f'r y'r pracious machines. They go wrong at the wrong times.'

*

The sounder was buzzily insistent and Allen Carter opened one eye peevishly. It was still dark.

With a sigh, he lifted one arm to the head of his bed and put the Audiomitter into commission.

The treble voice of Amos Wells of the night shift squawked excitedly at him. Allen's eyes snapped open and he sat up.

'You're crazy!' But he was plunging into his breeches even as he spoke. In ten seconds, he was careening up the steps three at a time. He shot into the main office just behind the charging figure of his twin brother.

The place was crowded – its occupants in a jitter.

Allen brushed his long hair out of his eyes, 'Turn on the turret searchlight!'

'It's on,' said someone helplessly.

The Earthman rushed to the window and looked out. The yellow beam reached dimly out a few feet and ended in a muddy murkiness. He pulled at the window and it lifted upwards grittily a few inches. There was a whistle of wind and a tornado of coughing from within the room. Allen slammed it down again and his hands went at once to his tear-filled eyes.

George spoke between sneezes, 'Were not located in the sandstorm zone. This can't be one.'

'It is,' asserted Wells in a squeak. 'It's the worst I've ever seen. Started full blast from scratch just like that. It caught me flatfooted. By the time I closed off all exits to above, it was too late.'

'Too late!' Allen withdrew his attention from his sand-filled eyes and snapped out the words, 'Too late for what?'

'Too late for our rolling stock. Our rockets got it worst of all. There isn't one that hasn't its propulsives clogged with sand. And that goes for our irrigation pumps and the ventilating system. The generators below are safe but everything else will have to be taken apart and put together again. We're stalled for a week at least. Maybe more.'

There was a short, pregnant silence, and then Allen said, 'Take charge, Wells. Put the men on double shift and tackle the irrigation pumps first. They've got to be in working order inside of twenty-four hours, or half the crop will dry up and die on us. Here – wait, I'll go with you.'

He turned to leave, but his first footstep froze in midair at the sight of Michael Anders, communications officer, rushing up the stairs.

'What's the matter?'

Anders spoke between gasps, 'The damned planet's gone crazy. There's been the biggest quake in history with its center not ten miles from Aresopolis.'

There was a chorus of 'What?' and a ragged follow-up of blistering imprecations. Men crowded in anxiously – many had relatives and wives in the Martian metropolis.

Anders went on breathlessly, 'It came all of a sudden. Aresopolis is in ruins and fires have started. There aren't any details but the transmitter at our Aresopolis labs went dead five minutes ago.'

There was a babel of comment. The news spread out into the furthest recesses of Central, and excitement waxed to dangerously panicky proportions. Allen raised his voice to a shout.

'Quiet, everyone. There's nothing we can do about Aresopolis. We've got our own troubles. This freak storm is connected with the quake some way – and that's what *we* have to take care of. Everyone back to his work now – and work fast. They'll be needing us at Aresopolis damned soon.' He turned to Anders, 'You! Get back to that receiver and don't knock off until you've gotten in touch with Aresopolis again. Coming with me, George?'

'No, rackon not,' was the response. 'Y' tend t' y'r machines. I'll go down with Anders.'

Dawn was breaking, a dusky, lightless dawn, when Allen Carter returned to Central. He was weary – weary in mind and body – and looked it. He entered the radio room.

'Things are a mess. If—'

There was a 'Shhh' and George waved frantically. Allen fell silent. Anders bent over the receiver, turning tiny dials with nervous fingers.

Anders looked up, 'It's no use, Mr Carter. Can't get them.'

'All right. Stay here and keep y'r ears open. Let me know if anything turns up.'

He walked out, hooking an arm underneath his brother's and dragging the latter out.

'When c'n we get out the next shipment, All'n?'

'Not for at least a week. We haven't a thing that'll either roll or fly for days, and it will be even longer before we can start harvesting again.'

'Have we any supplies on hand now?'

'A few tons of assorted blooms – mainly the red-purples. The Earth shipment last Tuesday took off almost everything.'

George fell into a reverie.

His brother waited a moment and said sharply, 'Well, what's on your mind? What's the news from Aresopolis?'

'Domned bad! The quake's leveled three-fourths o' Aresopolis and the rest's pretty much gutted with fire, I rackon. There 're fifty thousand that'll have t' camp out nights. —That's no fun in Martian autumn weather with the Airth gravity system broken down.'

Allen whistled, 'Pneumonia!'

'And common colds and influenza and any o' half doz'n diseases t' say nothing o' people bairnt. —Old Vincent is raising cain.'

'Wants blooms?'

'He's only got a two-day supply on hand. He's *got* t' have more.'

Both were speaking quietly, almost with indifference, with the vast understatement that is all that makes great crises bearable.

There was a pause and then George spoke again, 'What's the best we c'n do?'

'Not under a week – not if we kill ourselves to do it. If they could send over a ship as soon as the storm dies down, we might be able to send what we have as a temporary supply until we can get over with the rest.'

'Silly even t' think o' that. The Aresopolis port is just ruins. They haven't a ship t' their names.'

Again silence. Then Allen spoke in a low, tense voice, 'What are you waiting for? What's that look on your face for?'

'I'm waiting f'r y' t' admit y'r domned machines have failed y' in the fairest emairgency we've had t' meet.'

'Admitted,' snarled the Earthman.

'Good! And now it's up t' me t' show y' what human ingenuity can do.' He handed a sheet of paper to his brother, 'There's a copy of the message I sent Vincent.'

Allen looked long at his brother and slowly read the penciled scribbling.

'Will deliver all we have on hand in thirty-six hours. Hope it will keep you going the few days until we can get a real shipment out. Things are a little rough out here.'

'How are you going to do it?' demanded Allen, upon finishing.

'I'm trying to show y',' answered George, and Allen realized for the first time that they had left Central and were out in the caverns.

George led the way for five minutes and stopped before an object bulking blackly in the dimness. He turned on the section lights and said, 'Sand truck!'

The sand truck was not an imposing object. With the low driving car in front and the three squat, open-topped freight-cars behind, it presented a picture of obsolete decrepitude. Fifteen years ago, it had been relegated to the dust-heap by the sand-sleds and rocket-freights.

The Ganymedan was speaking, 'Checked it an hour ago, m'self, and 'tis still in wairking order. It has shielded bearings, air condition-ing unit f'r the driving car, and an intairnal combustion engine.'

The other looked up sharply. There was an expresson of distaste on his face. 'You mean it burns chemical fuel.'

'Yup! Gas'line. That's why I like it. Reminds me o Ganymede. On Gannie, I had a gas engine that—'

'But wait a while. We haven't any of that gasoline.'

'No, rackon not. But we gots lots o' liquid hydrocarbons round the place. How about Solvent D? That's mostly octane. We've got tanks o' it.'

Allen said, 'That's so – but the truck holds only two.'

'I know it. I'm one.'

'And I'm the other.'

George grunted, 'I rackond y'd say that – but this isn't going t' be a push-button machine job. Rackon y'r up t' it – Airthman?'

'I reckon I am – Gannie.'

The sun had been up some two hours before the sand-truck's engine whirred into life, but outside, the murk had become, if anything, thicker.

The main driveway within the caverns was ahum with activity. Grotesque figures with eyes peering through the thick glass of improvised air-helmets stepped back as the truck's broad, sand-adapted wheels began their slow turn. The three cars behind had been piled high with purple blooms, canvas covers had been thrown over them and bound down tightly – and now the signal was given to open the doors.

The lever was jerked downwards and the double doors separated with sand-clogged protests. Through a gray whirl of inblown sand, the truck made its way outwards, and behind it sand-coated figures brushed at their air-helmets and closed the doors again.

George Carter, inured by long Ganymedan custom, met the sudden gravity change as they left the protective Gravitor fields of the caverns, with a single long-drawn breath. His hands held steady upon the wheels. His Terrestrial brother, however, was in far different condition. The hard nauseating knot into which his stomach tied itself loosened only very gradually, and it was a long time before his irregular stertorous breathing approached anything like normality again.

And throughout, the Earthman was conscious of the other's sidelong glance and of just a trace of a smile about the other's lips.

It was enough to keep the slightest moan from issuing forth, though his abdominal muscles cramped and icy perspiration bathed his face.

The miles clicked off slowly, but the illusion of motionlessness was almost as complete as that in space. The surroundings were gray – uniform, monotonous and unvarying. The noise of the engine was a harsh purr and the clicking of the air-purifier behind like a drowsy tick. Occasionally, there was an especially strong gust of wind, and a patter of sand dashed against the window with a million tiny, separate pings.

George kept his eye strictly upon the compass before him. The silence was almost oppressive.

And then the Ganymedan swiveled his head, and growled, 'What's wrong with the domned vent'lator?'

Allen squeezed upward, head against the low top, and then turned back, pale-faced, 'It's stopped.'

'It'll be hours 'fore the storm's over. We've got t' have air till then. Crawl in back there and start it again.' His voice was flat and final.

'Here,' he said, as the other crawled over his shoulder into the back of the car. 'Here's the tool-kit. Y'v got 'bout twenty minutes 'fore the air gets too foul t' breathe. 'Tis pretty bad now.'

The clouds of sand hemmed in closer and the dim yellow light above George's head dispelled only partially the darkness within.

There was the sound of scrambling from behind him and then Allen's voice, 'Damn this rope. What's it doing here?' There was a hammering and then a disgusted curse.

'This thing is choked with rust.'

'Anything else wrong?' called out the Ganymedan.

'Don't know. Wait till I clear it out.' More hammering and an almost continuous harsh, scraping sound followed.

Allen backed into his seat once more. His face dripped rusty perspiration and a swab with the back of an equally damp, rust-covered hand did it no good.

'The pump is leaking like a punctured kettle, now that the rust's been knocked loose. I've got it going at top speed, but the only thing between it and a total breakdown is a prayer.'

'Start praying,' said George, brusquely. 'Pray for a button to push.'

The Earthman frowned, and stared ahead in sullen silence.

At four in the afternoon, the Ganymedan drawed, 'Air's beginning t' thin out, looks like.'

Allen snapped to alertness. The air was foul and humid within. The ventilator behind swished sibilantly between each click and the clicks were spacing themselves further apart. It wouldn't hold out much longer now.

'How much ground have we covered?'

''Bout a thaird o' the distance,' was the reply. 'How 'r y' holding out?'

'Well enough,' Allen snapped back. He retired once more into his shell.

Night came and the first brilliant stars of a Martian night peeped out when with a last futile and long-sustained swi-i-i-s-s-sh, the ventilator died.

'Domn!' said George. 'I can't breathe this soup any longer, anyway. Open the windows.'

The keenly cold Martian wind swept in and with it the last traces of sand. George coughed as he pulled his woolen cap over his ears and turned on the heaters.

'Y' can still taste the grit.'

Allen looked wistfully up into the skies, 'There's Earth – with the moon hanging right onto her tail.'

'Airth?' repeated George with fine contempt. His finger pointed horizonwards, 'There's good old Jupe for y'.'

And throwing back his head, he sang in a full-throated baritone:

> 'When the golden orb o' Jove
> Shines down from the skies above,
> Then my spirit longs to go
> To that happy land I know,
> Back t' good, old *Ganyme-e-e-e-ede*.'

The last note quavered and broke, and quavered and broke again and still again in an ever increasing rapidity of tempo until its vibrating ululation pierced the air about ear-shatteringly.

Allen stared at his brother wide-eyed, 'How did you do that?'

George grinned, 'That's the Gannie quaver. Didn't y' ever hear it before?'

The Earthman shook his head, 'I've heard *of* it, but that's all.'

The other became a bit more cordial, 'Well, o' course y' can only do it in a thin atmosphere. Y should hear me on Gannie. I c'd shake y' right off y'r chair when I'm going good. Here! Wait till I gulp down some coffee, and then I'll sing y' vairse twenty-four o' the "Ballad o' Ganymede".'

He took a deep breath:

> 'There's a fair-haired maid I love
>   Standing in the light o' Jove
>   And she's waiting there for me-e-e-e-e.

Then—'

Allen grasped him by the arm and shook him. The Ganymedan choked into silence.

'What's the matter?' he asked sharply.

'There was a thumping sound on the roof just a second ago. There's something up there.'

George stared upwards, 'Grab the wheel. I'll go up.'

Allen shook his head, 'I'm going myself. I wouldn't trust myself running this primitive contraption.'

He was out on the running board the next instant.

'Keep her going,' he shouted, and threw one foot up onto the roof.

He froze in that position when he became aware of two yellow slits of eyes staring hard into his. It took not more than a second for him too realize that he was face to face with a *keazel*, a situation which for discomfort is about on a par with the discovery of a rattlesnake in one's bed back on Earth.

There was little time for mental comparisons of his position with Earth predicaments, however, for the *keazel* lunged forward, its poisonous fangs agleam in the starlight.

Allen ducked desperately and lost his grip. He hit the sand with a slow-motion thud and the cold, scaly body of the Martian reptile was upon him.

The Earthman's reaction was almost instinctive. His hand shot out and clamped down hard upon the creature's narrow muzzle.

In that position, beast and man stiffened into breathless statuary. The man was trembling and within him his heart pounded away with hard rapidity. He scarcely dared move. In the unaccustomed Martian gravity, he found he could not judge the movements of his limbs. Muscles knotted almost of their own accord and legs swung when they ought not to.

He tried to lie still – and think.

The *keazel* squirmed, and from its lips, clamped shut by Earth muscles, issued a tremulous whine. Allen's hand grew slick with perspiration and he could feel the beast's muzzle turn a bit within his palm. He clamped harder, panic-stricken. Physically, the *keazel* was no match for an Earthman, even a tired, frightened, gravity-unaccustomed Earthman – but one bite, anywhere, was all that was needed.

The *keazel* jerked suddenly; its back humped and its legs threshed. Allen held on with both hands and *could* not let go. He had neither gun nor knife. There was no rock on the level desert sands to crack its skull against. The sand-truck had long since disappeared into the Martian night, and he was alone – alone with a *keazel*.

In desperation, he twisted. The *keazel*'s head bent. He could hear its breath whistling forth harshly – and again there was that low whine.

Allen writhed above it and clamped knees down upon its cold, scaly abdomen. He twisted the head, further and further. The *keazel* fought desperately, but Allen's Earthly biceps maintained their hold. He could almost sense the beast's agony in the last stages, when he called up all his strength – and something snapped.

And the beast lay still.

He rose to his feet, half-sobbing. The Martian night wind knifed into him and the perspiration froze on his body. He was alone in the desert.

Reaction set in. There was an intense buzzing in his ears. He found it difficult to stand. The wind was biting – but somehow he didn't feel it any more.

The buzzing in his ears resolved itself into a voice – a voice calling weirdly through the Martian wind.

'All'n, where are y'? Domn y', y' tanderfoot, where are y'? All'n! *All'n!*'

New life swept into the Earthman. He tossed the *keazel*'s carcass onto his shoulders and staggered on towards the voice.

'Here I am, G-Gannie. Right here.'

He stumbled blindly into his brother's arms.

George began harshly, 'Y' blasted Airthman, can't y' even keep y'r footing on a sandtruck moving at ten miles per? Y' might've—'

His voice died away in a semi-gurgle.

Allen said tiredly, 'There was a *keazel* on the roof. He knocked me off. Here, put it somewhere. There's a hundred dollar bonus for every *keazel* skin brought in to Aresopolis.'

He had no clear recollection of anything for the next half hour. When things straightened out, he was in the truck again with the taste of warm coffee in his mouth. The engine was rumbling once more and the pleasant warmth of the heaters surrounded him.

George sat next to him silently, eyes fixed on the desert ahead. But once in a while, he cleared his throat and shot a lightning glance at his brother. There was a queer look in his eyes.

Allen said, 'Listen, I've got to keep awake – and you look half dead yourself – so how about teaching me that "Gannie quaver" of yours. That's bound to wake the dead.'

The Ganymedan stared even harder and then said gruffly, 'Sure, watch m' Adam's apple while I do 't again.'

*

The sun was half-way to zenith when they reached the canal.

An hour before dawn there had come the crackling sound of hoarfrost beneath the heavy wheels and that signified the end of the desert area and the approach of the canal oasis. With the rising of the sun, the crackling disappeared and the softening mud underneath slowed the sand-adapted truck. The pathetic clumps of gray-green scrub that dotted the flat landscape were the first variant to eternal red sand since the two had started on their journey.

And then Allen had leaned forward and grasped his brother by the arm, 'Look, there's the canal itself right ahead.'

The 'canal' – a small tributary of the mighty Jefferson Canal – contained a mere trickle of water at this season of the year. A dirty winding line of dampness, it was, and little more. Surrounding it on both sides were the boggy areas of black mud that were to fill up into a rushing ice-cold current an Earth-year hence.

The sand-truck nosed gingerly down the gentle slope, weaving a tortuous path among the sparsely-strewn boulders brought down by the springs torrents and left there as the sinking waters receded.

It slopped through the mud and splashed clumsily through the puddles. It jounced noisily over rocks, muddied itself past the hubs as it made its way through the murky mid-stream channel and then settled itself for the upward pull out.

And then, with a suddenness that tossed the two drivers out of their seats, it sideslipped, made one futile effort to proceed onwards, and thereafter refused to budge.

The brothers scrambled out and surveyed the situation. George swore lustily, voice more thickly accented than ever.

'B' Jupe 'n' domn, we're in a pickled situation f'r fair. 'Tis wallowing in the mud there like a blasted pig.'

Allen shoved his hair back wearily, 'Well, don't stand there looking at it. We're still a hundred miles or better from Aresopolis. We've got to get it out of there.'

'Sure, but how?' His imprecations dropped to sibilant breathings as he reached into the truck for the coil of rope in the back. He looked at it doubtfully.

'Y' get in here, All'n, and when I pull, press down with y'r foot on that pedal.'

He was tying the rope to the front axle even as he spoke. He played it out behind him as he slogged out through ankle-deep mud, and stretched it taut.

'All right, now, *give!*' he yelled. His face turned purple with effort as his back muscles ridged. Allen, within the car, pressed the indicated pedal to the floor, heard a loud roar from the engine and a spinning whir from the back wheels. The truck heaved once, and then sank back.

'Tis no use,' George called. 'I can't get a footing. If the ground were dry, I c'd do it.'

'If the ground were dry, we wouldn't be stuck,' retorted Allen. 'Here, give me that rope.'

'D' y' think y' can do it, if *I* can't?' came the enraged cry, but the other had already left the car.

Allen had spied the large, deep-bedded boulder from the truck, and it was with relief that he found it to be within reaching distance of the rope. He pulled it taut and tossed its free end about the boulder. Knotting it clumsily, he pulled, and it held.

His brother leaned out of the car window, as he made his way, back, with one lumped Ganymedan fist agitating the air.

'Hi, y' nitwit. What're y' doing? D' y' expect that overgrown rock t' pull us out?'

'Shut up,' yelled back Allen, 'and feed her the gas when I pull.'

He paused midway between boulder and truck and seized the rope.

'*Give!*' he shouted in his turn, and with a sudden jerk pulled the rope towards him with both hands.

The truck moved; its wheels caught hold. For a moment it hesitated with the engine blasting ahead full speed, and George's hands trembling upon the wheel. And then it went over. And almost simultaneously, the boulder at the other end of the taut rope lifted out of the mud with a liquid smacking sound and went over on its side.

Allen slipped the noose off it and ran for the truck

'Keep her going,' he shouted, and hopped onto the running board, rope trailing.

'How did y' do that?' asked George, eyes round with awe.

'I haven't got the energy to explain it now. When we get to Aresopolis and after we've had a good sleep, I'll draw the triangle of forces for you, and show you what happened. No muscles were involved. Don't look at me as if I were Hercules.'

George withdrew his gaze with an effort, 'Triangle o' forces, is it? I never heard o' it, but if *that's* what it c'n do, education's a great thing.'

'Comet-gas! Is any coffee left?' He stared at the last thermos-bottle, shook it near his ear dolefully, and said, 'Oh, well, let's practice the quaver. It's almost as good and I've practically got it perfected.'

He yawned prodigiously, 'Will we make it by nightfall?'

'Maybe!'

The canal was behind them now.

The reddening sun was lowering itself slowly behind the Southern Range. The Southern Range is one of the two 'mountain chains' left on Mars. It is a region of hills; ancient, time-worn, eroded hills behind which lies Aresopolis.

It possesses the only scenery worth mentioning on all Mars and also the golden attribute of being able, through the updrafts along its sides, to suck an occasional rain out of the desiccated Martian atmosphere.

Ordinarily, perhaps, a pair from Earth and Ganymede might have idled through this picturesque area, but this was definitely not the case with the Carter twins.

Eyes, puffed for lack of sleep, glistened once more at the sight of hills on the horizon. Bodies, almost broken for sheer weariness, tensed once more when they rose against the sky.

And the truck leaped ahead – for just behind the hills lay Aresopolis. The road they traveled was no longer a rule-edge straight one, guided by the compass, over table-top-flat land. It followed narrow, twisting trails over rocky ground.

They had reached Twin Peaks, then, when there was a sudden sputter from the motor, a few halting coughs and then silence.

Allen sat up and there was weariness and utter disgust in his voice, 'What's wrong with this everlastingly-to-be-damned machine now?'

His brother shrugged, 'Nothing that I haven't been expecting for the last hour. We're out o' gas. Doesn't matter at all. We're at Twin Peaks – only ten miles fr'm the city. We c'n get there in an hour, and then they c'n send men out here for the blooms.'

'Ten miles in an hour!' protested Allen. 'You're crazy.' His face suddenly twisted at an agonizing thought, 'My God! We can't do it under three hours and it's almost night. No one can last that long in a Martian night. George, we're—'

George was pulling him out of the car by main force, 'By Jupe 'n' domn, All'n, don't let the tenderfoot show through *now*. We c'n do it in an hour, I tell y'. Didn't y' ever try running under sub-normal gravity? It's like flying. Look at me.'

He was off, skimming the ground closely, and proceeding in ground-covering leaps that shrank him to a speck up the mountain side in a moment.

He waved, and his voice came thinly, 'Come on!'

Allen started – and sprawled at the third wild stride, arms flailing and legs straddled wide. The Ganymedan's laughter drifted down in heartless gusts.

Allen rose angrily and dusted himself. At an ordinary walk, he made his way upwards.

'Don't get sore, All'n,' said George. 'It's just a knack, and I've had practice on Gannie. Just pretend y'r running along a feather bed. Run rhythmically – a sort o' very slow rhythm – and run close t' the ground; don't leap high. Like this. Watch me!'

The Earthman tried it, eyes on his brother. His first few uncertain strides became surer and longer. His legs stretched and his arms swung as he matched his brother, step for step.

George shouted encouragement and speeded his pace, 'Keep lower t' the ground, All'n. Don't leap 'fore y'r toes hit the ground.'

Allen's eyes shone and, for the moment, weariness was forgotten, 'This is great! It *is* like flying – or like springs on your shoes.'

'Y' ought t' have lived on Gannie with me. We've got special fields f'r subgravity races. An expairt racer c'n do forty miles an hour at times – and I c'n do thirty-five myself. —O' course, the gravity there's a bit lower than here on Mars.'

Long hair streamed backwards in the wind and skin reddened at the bitter cold air that blew past. The ruddy patches of sunlight traveled higher and higher up the slopes, lingered briefly upon the very summits and went out altogether. The short Martian twilight started upon its rapidly darkening career. The Evening Star – Earth – was already glimmering brightly, its attendant moon somewhat closer than the night previous.

The passing minutes went unheeded by Allen. He was too absorbed by the wonderful new sensation of sub-gravity running, to do anything more than follow his brother. Even the increasing chilliness scarcely registered upon his consciousness.

It was George, then, upon whose countenance a tiny, puckered uneasiness grew into a vast, panicky frown.

'Hi, All'n, hold up!' he called. Leaning backward, he brought himself to a short, hopping halt full of grace and ease. Allen tried to do likewise, broke his rhythm, and went forward upon his face. He rose with loud reproaches.

The Ganymedan turned a deaf ear to them. His gaze was sombre in the dusk, 'D' y' know where we are, All'n?'

Allen felt a cold constriction about his windpipe as he stared about him quickly. Things looked different in semi-darkness, but they looked more different than they ought. It was impossible for things to be *so* different.

'We should've sighted Old Baldy by now, shouldn't we have?' he quavered.

'We sh'd've sighted him long ago,' came the hard answer. 'Tis that domned quake. Landslides must've changed the trails. The peaks themselves must've been screwed up—' His voice was thin-edged, 'Allen, 'tisn't any use making believe. We're dead lost.'

For a moment, they stood silently – uncertainly. The sky was purple and the hills retreated into the night. Allen licked blue-chilled lips with a dry tongue.

'We can't be but a few miles away. We're bound to stumble on the city if we look.'

'Consider the situation, Airthman,' came the savage, shouted answer, ''Tis night, Martian night. The temperature's down past zero and plummeting every minute. We haven't any time t' look – we've got t' go straight there. If we're not there in half an hour, we're not going t' get there at all.'

Allen knew that well, and mention of the cold increased his consciousness of it. He spoke through chattering teeth as he drew his heavy, fur-lined coat closer about him.

'We might build a fire!' The suggestion was a half-hearted one, muttered indistinctly, and fallen upon immediately by the other.

'With what?' George was beside himself with sheer disappoinment and frustration. 'We've pulled through this far, and now we'll prob'ly freeze t' death within a mile o' the city. C'mon, keep running. It's a hundred-t'-one chance.'

But Allen pulled him back. There was a feverish glint in the Earthman's eye, 'Bonfires!' he said irrelevantly. 'It's a possibility. Want to take a chance that might do the trick?'

'Nothin else t' do,' growled the other. 'But hurry. Every minute I—'

'Then run with the wind and keep going.'

'Why?'

'Never mind why. Do what I say – run with the wind!'

There was no false optimism in Allen as he bounded through the dark, stumbling over loose stones, sliding down declivities – always with the wind at his back. George ran at his side, a vague, formless blotch in the night.

The cold was growing more bitter, but it was not quite as bitter as the freezing pang of apprehension gnawing at the Earthman's vitals.

Death is unpleasant!

And then they topped the rise, and from George's throat came a loud 'B' Jupe 'n' domn!' of triumph.

The ground before them, as far as the eye could see, was dotted by bonfires. Shattered Aresopolis lay ahead, its homeless inhabitants making the night bearable by the simple agency of burning wood.

And on the hilly slopes, two weary figures slapped each other on the backs, laughed wildly, and pressed half-frozen, stubbly cheeks together for sheer, unadulterated joy.

They were there at last!

The Aresopolis lab, on the very outskirts of the city, was one of the few structures still standing. Within, by makeshift light, haggard chemists were distilling the last drops of extract. Without, the city's police-force remnants were clearing desperate way for the precious flasks and vials as they were distributed to the various emergency medical centers set up in various regions of the bonfire-pocked ruins that were once the Martian metropolis.

Old Hal Vincent supervised the process and his faded eyes ever and again peered anxiously into the hills beyond, watching hopefully but doubtfully for the promised cargo of blooms.

And then two figures reeled out of the darkness and collapsed to a halt before him.

Chill anxiety clamped down upon him, 'The blooms! Where are they? Have you got them?'

'At Twin Peaks,' gasped Allen. 'A ton of them and better in a sand-truck. Send for them.'

A group of police ground-cars set off before he had finished, and Vincent exclaimed bewilderedly, 'A sand-truck? Why didn't you send it in a ship? What's wrong with you out there, anyway? Earthquake—'

He received no direct answer. George had stumbled towards the nearest bonfire with a beatific expression on his worn face.

'Ahhh, 'tis warm!' Slowly, he folded and dropped, asleep before he hit the ground.

Allen coughed gaspingly, 'Huh! The Gannie tenderfoot! Couldn't – ulp – take it!'

And the ground came up and hit him in the face.

Allen woke with the evening sun in his eyes and the odor of frying bacon in his nostrils. George shoved the frying pan towards him and said between gigantic, wolfing mouthfuls, 'Help yourself.'

He pointed to the empty sand-truck outside the labs, 'They got the stuff all right.'

Allen fell to, quietly. George wiped his lips with the back of his hand and said, 'Say, All'n, how 'd y' find the city? I've been sitting here trying t' figure it all out.'

'It was the bonfires,' came the muffled answer. 'It was the only way they could get heat, and fires over square miles of land create a whole section of heated air, which rises, causing the cold surrounding air of the hills to sweep in.' He suited his words with appropriate gestures. 'The wind in the hills was heading for the city to replace warm air and we followed the wind. —Sort of a natural compass, pointing to where we wanted to go.'

George was silent, kicking with embarrassed vigor at the ashes of the bonfire of the night before.

'Lis'n, All'n, I've had y' a'wrong. Y' were an Airthman tanderfoot t' me till—' He paused, drew a deep breath and exploded with, 'Well, by Jupe 'n' domn, y'r my twin brother and I'm proud o' it. All Airth c'dn't drown out the Carter blood in y'.'

The Earthman opened his mouth to reply but his brother clamped one palm over it, 'Y' keep quiet, till I'm finished. After we get back, y' can fix up that mechanical picker or anything else y' want. I drop my veto. If Airth and machines c'n tairn out y'r kind o' man, they're all right. But just the same,' there was a trace of wistfulness in his voice, 'y' got t' admit that everytime the machines broke down – from irrigation-trucks and rocket-ships to ventilators and sand-trucks – 'twas men who had t' pull through in spite o' all that Mars could do.'

Allen wrenched his face from out behind the restraining palm.

'The machines do their best,' he said, but not too vehemently.

'Sure, but that's all they *can* do. When the emairgency comes, a man's got t' do a damn lot better than his best or he's a goner.'

The other paused, nodded, and gripped the other's hand with sudden fierceness, 'Oh, we're not so different. Earth and Ganymede are plastered thinly over the outside of us, but inside—'

He caught himself.

'Come on, let's give out with that old Gannie quaver.'

And from the two fraternal throats tore forth a shrieking eldritch yell such as the thin, cold Martian air had seldom before carried.

History

Ullen's lank arm pushed the stylus carefully and painstakingly across the paper; his near-sighted eyes blinked through thick lenses. The signal light flashed twice before he answered.

He turned a page, and called out, 'Is dat you, Johnnie? Come in, please.'

He smiled gently, his thin, Martian face alight with pleasure.

'Sit down, Johnnie – but first lower de window-shade. De glare of your great Eard sun is annoying. Ah, dat's good, and now sid down and be very, very quiet for just a little while, because I am busy.'

John Brewster shifted a pile of ill-stacked papers and seated himself. He blew the dust from the edges of an open book in the next chair and looked reproachfully on the Martian historian.

'Are you still poking around these musty old things? Don't you get tired?'

'Please, Johnnie,' Ullen did not look up, 'you will lose de page. Dat book dere is William Stewart's "Hitlerian Era" and it is very hard to read. So many words he uses which he doesn't explain.'

His expression as it focussed upon Johnnie was one of frowning petulance, *'Never* do dey explain deir terms. It is so unscientific. On

Mars, before we even start, we say, "Dis is a list of all definitions of terms to be used." How oderwise can people talk sensibly? Hmp! You *crazy* Eardmen.'

'Oh, nuts, Ullen – forget it. Why don't you *look* at me. Don't you even notice anything?'

The Martian sighed, removed his glasses, cleaned them thoughtfully, and carefully replaced them. He stared impersonally at Johnnie, 'Well, I think it is new clothes you are wearing. Is it not so?'

'New clothes! Is *that* all you can say, Ullen? This is a *uniform*. I'm a member of the Home Defense.' He rose to his feet, a picture of boyish exuberance.

'What is dis "Home Defense"?' asked Ullen languidly.

Johnnie gulped and sat down helplessly, 'You know, I really think you haven't heard that Earth and Venus have been at war for the last week. I'll bet money you haven't.'

'I've been busy.' He frowned and pursed his thin, bloodless lips, 'On Mars, dere is no war – at least, dere isn't any more. Once, we used to fight, but dat was long ago. Once we were scientists, too, and *dat* was long ago. Now, dere are only a few of us – and we do not fight. Dere is no happiness dat way.' He seemed to shake himself, and spoke more briskly, 'Tell me, Johnnie, do you know where it is I can find what it means, dis "national honor"? It holds me back. I can't go furder unless I can understand it.'

Johnnie rose to his full height and glittered in the spotless green of the Terrestrial Service. He laughed with fond indulgence, 'You're hopeless, Ullen, you old coot. Aren't you going to wish me luck? I'm hitting space tomorrow.'

'Oh, is dere danger?'

There was a squawk of laughter, 'Danger? What do you think?'

'Well, den, to seek danger – it is foolish. Why do you do it?'

'You wouldn't understand, Ullen. Just wish me luck and say you hope I come through whole.'

'Cer-tain-ly! I don't want *anyone* to die.' He slipped his hand into the strong fist held out to him. 'Take care of yourself, Johnnie – and wait, before you go, bring me Stewart's book. Everything is so heavy here on Eard. Heavy, heavy – and de words have no definitions.'

He sighed, and was back at his books as Johnnie slipped quietly out of the room.

'Dese barbarous people,' he muttered sleepily to himself. 'War! Dey clink dat by killing—' His voice died away and merged into a slurred mumble as his eyes followed creeping finger across the page.

'From the very moment of the union of the Anglo-Saxon world into a single governmental entity and even as far back as the spring of 1941, it was evident that the doom of—'

'Dese crazy Eardmen!'

Ullen leaned heavily upon his crutches on the steps of the University library and one thin hand shielded his watering eyes from the terrible Earthly sun.

The sky was blue, cloudless – undisturbed. Yet somewhere up above, beyond the planet's airy blanket, steel-sided ships were veering and sparking in vicious combat. And down upon the city were falling the tiny 'Drops of Death,' the highly-publicized radioactive bombs that noiselessly and inexorably ate out a fifteen foot crater wherever they fell.

The city's population was herding into the shelters and burying themselves inside the deep-set leaden cells. Upstaring, silent, anxious, they streamed past Ullen. Uniformed guards invested some sort of order into the gigantic flight, steering the stragglers and speeding the laggards.

The air was filled with barked orders.

'Hit the shelter, Pop. Better get going. You can't stand there, you know.'

Ullen turned to the guard who addressed him and slowly brought his wandering thoughts to bear upon the situation.

'I am sorry, Eardman – but I cannot move very fast on your huge world.' He tapped one crutch upon the marble flags beneath. 'Dings are so heavy. If I were to crowd in wid de rest, I would be crushed.'

He smiled gently down from his lank height, and the guard rubbed a stubby chin, 'All right, pop, I can fix that. It *is* tough on you Marsies at that. —Here, hold those crutches up out of the way.'

With a heave, he cradled the Martian, 'Hold your legs close to my body, because we're going to travel fast.'

His bulky figure pressed through the line of Earthmen. Ullen shut his eyes as the rapid motion under supernormal gravity stirred his stomach into rebellion. He opened them once again in the dim recesses of the low-ceilinged shelter.

The guard set him down carefully and adjusted the crutches beneath Ullen's armpits, 'O.K. Pop. Take care of yourself.'

Ullen took in his surroundings and hobbled to one of the low benches at the near end of the shelter. From behind him came the sombre clang of the thick, leaden door.

The Martian historian fished a worn tablet from his pocket and scribbled slow notes. He disregarded the excited babble that arose about him and the scraps of heated talk that filled the air thickly.

And then he scratched at his furrowed forehead with the stub end of his pencil, meeting the staring eyes of the man sitting next to him. He smiled abstractedly and returned to his notes.

'You're a Martian, aren't you?' His neighbor spoke in quick, squeaky tones. 'I don't like foreigners much, but I've got nothing special against Marsies. These Veenies, now, they—'

Ullen's soft tones interrupted him. 'Hate is all wrong, I dink. Dis war is a great annoyance – a great one. It interferes wid my work and you Eardmen ought to stop it. Is it not so?'

'You can bet your hide we're going to stop it,' came the emphatic reply. 'We're going to bash their planet inside out – and the dirty Veenies with it.'

'You mean attack deir cities like dis?' The Martian blinked owlishly in thought, 'You dink dat would be best?'

'Damn it, yes. It—'

'But look.' Ullen placed a skeleton finger in one palm and

continued in gentle argument. 'Would it not be easier to get de ships demselves by de fall-apart weapon? Don't you dink so? Or is it dat de Venus people, dey have de screens?'

'What weapon, did you say?'

Ullen ruminated carefully, 'I suppose dat isn't de name *you* call it by – but I don't know about weapons, anyway. We call it on Mars de *"skellingbeg"* and dat means in English "fall-apart weapon". Now you know?'

There was no direct answer unless a vague under-breath mutter could be called one. The Earthman pushed away from his companion and stared at the opposite wall in a fidget.

Ullen sensed the rebuff and shrugged one shoulder wearily, 'It is not dat I care much about de whole ding. It is only dat de war is a big bodder. It should be ended.' He sighed, 'But I don't care!'

His fingers had just begun manipulating the pencil once more in its travels across the open tablet on his lap, when he looked up again.

'Tell me, please, what is de name of dat country where Hitler died. Your Eard names, dey are so complicated sometimes. I dink it begins wid an M.'

His neighbor ripped him open with a stare and walked away. Ullen's eyes followed him with a puzzled frown.

And then the all-clear signal sounded.

'Oh, yes,' said Ullen. 'Madagascar! Such a silly name!'

Johnnie Brewster's uniform was war-worn now; a bit more wrinkled about the neck and shoulders, a trace more worn at knees and elbows.

Ullen ran his finger along the angry scar that ran the length of Johnnie's right fore-arm, 'It hurts no more, Johnnie?'

'Nuts! A scratch! I got the Veenie that did that. He's chasing dreams in the moon now.'

'You were in de hospital long, Johnnie?'

'A week!' He lit a cigarette, pushed some of the mess off the Martian's desk and seated himself. 'I've spent the rest of the time with my family, though I did get around to visiting you, you see.'

He leaned over and poked an affectionate hand at the Martians leathery cheek, 'Aren't you going to say you're glad to see me?'

Ullen removed his glasses and peered at the Earthman, 'Why, Johnnie, are you so uncertain dat I am glad to see you, dat you require I should say it in words?' He paused, 'I'll make a note of dat. You silly Eardmen must always be telling each oder dese simple dings – and den you don't believe it anyway. On Mars—'

He was rubbing his glasses methodically, as he spoke, and now he replaced them, 'Johnnie, don't you Eardmen have de "fall-apart" weapon? I met a person once in de raid shelter and he didn't know what I was talking about.'

Johnnie frowned, 'I don't either, for that matter. Why do you ask?'

'Because it seems strange dat you should have to fight so hard dese Venus men, when dey don't seem to have de screens to stop it wid. Johnnie, I want de war should be over. It makes me all de time stop my work to go to a shelter.'

'Hold on, now, Ullen. Don't sputter. What is this "fall-apart" weapon? A disintegrator? What do you know about it?'

'I? I know nodding about it at all. I dought *you* knew – dat's why I asked. Back on Mars, in our histories, dey talk about using dat kind of weapon in our old wars. But we don't know nodding about weapons any more. Anyway, dey're so silly, because de oder side always dinks of someding which protects against it, and den everyding is de same as always. Johnnie, do you suppose you could go down to de desk and ask for a copy of Higginboddam's "Beginnings of Space Travel"?'

The Earthman clenched his fists and shook them impotently, 'Ullen, you damned Martian pedant – don't you understand that this is important? Earth is at war! War! War! *War!*'

'Well, den, stop de war.' There was irritation in Ullen's voice. 'Dere is no peace and quiet anywheres on Eard. I wish I had dis library – Johnnie, be careful. Please, what are you doing? You're hurting me.'

'I'm sorry, Ullen, but you've got to come with me. We're going to see about this.' Johnny had the feebly protesting Martian wedged into the wheel-chair and was off with a rush, before he had finished the sentence.

A rocket-taxi was at the bottom of the Library steps, and together chauffeur and Spaceman lifted the chair inside. With a comet-tail of smoke, they were off.

Ullen moaned softly at the acceleration, but Johnnie ignored him. 'Washington in twenty minutes, fellow,' he said to the driver, 'and ignore the signal beams.'

The starched secretary spoke in a frozen monotone, 'Admiral Korsakoff will see you now.'

Johnnie wheeled and stamped out the last cigarette butt. He shot a hasty glance at his watch and grunted.

At the motion of the wheel-chair, Ullen roused himself out of a troubled sleep. He adjusted his glasses, 'Did dey let us in finally, Johnnie?'

'Shhh!'

Ullen's impersonal stare swept over the rich furnishings of the room, the huge maps of Earth and Venus on the wall, the imposing desk in the center. It lingered upon the pudgy, bearded figure behind this desk and then came to rest upon the lanky, sandyhaired man at his side.

The Martian attempted to rise from the chair in sudden eagerness, 'Aren't you Dr Dorning? I saw you last year at Princeton. You remember me, don't you? Dey gave me at dat time, my honorary degree.'

Dr Thorning had advanced and shook hands vigorously, 'Certainly. You spoke then on Martian historical methods, didn't you?'

'Oh, you remember. I'm glad! But dis is a great opportunity for me, meeting you. Tell me, as a scientist, what would be your opinion of my deory dat de social insecurity of de Hitlerian Era was de direct cause for de lag—'

Dr Thorning smiled, 'I'll discuss it with you later, Dr Ullen. Right now, Admiral Korsakoff wants information from you, with which we hope to end the war.'

'Exactly,' Korsakoff spoke in clipped tones as he met Ullen's mild gaze. 'Although a Martian, I presume you favor the victory of the principles of freedom and justice over the foul practices of Venusian tyranny.'

Ullen stared uncertainly, 'Dat sounds familiar – but I don't dink about it much. You mean, maybe, de war should end?'

'With victory, yes.'

'Oh, "victory", dat is just a silly word. History proves dat a war decided on military superiority only lays de groundwork for future wars of retaliation and revenge. I refer you to a very good essay on de subject by a James Calkins. It was published all de way back in 2050.'

'My dear sir!'

Ullen raised his voice in bland indifference to Johnnie's urgent whisperings. 'Now to end de war – really end it – you should say to de plain people of Venus, "It is unnecessary to fight. Let us just talk"—'

There was the slam of fist on desk and a muttered oath of frightful import. 'For God's sakes, Thorning, get what you want out of him. I give you five minutes.'

Thorning stifled his chuckle, 'Dr Ullen, we want you to tell us what you know about the disintegrator.'

'Disintegrator?' Ullen put a puzzled finger to his cheek.

'The one you told Lieutenant Brewster of.'

'Ummmm— Oh! You mean de "fall-apart" weapon. I don't know nodding about it. De Martian historians mention it some times, but none of dem *know* about it – de technical side, dat is.'

The sandy-haired physicist nodded patiently, 'I know, I know. But what do they say? What kind of a weapon is it?'

'Well, de way dey talk about it, it makes de metals to fall to pieces. What is it you call de ding dat holds metals togedder, now?'

'Intra-molecular forces?'

Ullen frowned and then spoke thoughtfully, 'Maybe. I forgot

what de Martian word is – except dat it's long. Anyway, dis weapon, it makes dis force dat holds de metals togedder not to exist anymore and it all falls apart in a powder. But it only works on de dree metals, Iron, cobalt, and – uh – de odder one!'

'Nickel,' prompted Johnnie, softly.

'Yes, yes, nickel!'

Thorning's eyes glittered, 'Aha, the ferromagnetic elements. There's an oscillating magnetic field mixed up in this, or I'm a Veenie. How about it, Ullen?'

The Martian sighed, 'Such crazy Eard words. Let's see now, most of what I know about de weapon is from de work of Bogel Beg. It was – I'm pretty sure – in his "Cultural and Social History of de Dird Empire." It was a huge work in twenty-four volumes, but I always dought it was radder mediocre. His technique in de presentation of—'

'Please,' said Thorning, 'the weapon—'

'Oh, yes, *dat!*' He hitched himself higher in his chair and grimaced with the effort. 'He talks about electricity and it goes back and ford very fast – *very* fast, and its pressure—' He paused hopelessly, and regarded the scowling visage of the bearded Admiral naively, 'I *dink* de word is pressure, but I don't know, because it is hard to translate. De Martian word is *"cranstad"*. Does dat help?'

'I think you mean "potential", Dr Ullen!' Thorning sighed audibly.

'Well, if you say so. Anyway, dis "potential" changes also *very* fast and de two changes are synchronized somehow along wid magnetism dat – uh – shifts and dat's all I know about it.' He smiled uncertainly, 'I would like to go back now. It would be all right now, wouldn't it?'

The Admiral vouchsafed no answer, 'Do you make anything out of that mess, Doctor?'

'Damned little,' admitted the physicist, 'but it gives me a lead or two. We might try getting hold of this Beg's book, but there's not much hope. It will simply repeat what we've just heard. Dr Ullen, are there any scientific works on your planet?'

The Martian saddened, 'No, Dr Dorning, dey were all destroyed during de Kalynian reaction. On Mars, we doroughly disbelieve in science. History has shown dat it comes from science no happiness.' He turned to the young Earthman at his side, 'Johnnie, let us go now, please.'

Korsakoff dismissed the two with a wave of the hand.

Ullen bent carefully over the closely-typed manuscript and inserted a word. He glanced up brightly at Johnnie Brewster, who shook his head and placed a hand on the Martian's arm. His brow furrowed more deeply.

'Ullen,' he said harshly, 'You're in trouble.'

'Eh? I? In trouble? Why, Johnnie, dat is not so. My book is coming along famously. De whole first volume, it is completed and, but for a bit of polishing, is ready for de printers.'

'Ullen, if you can't give the government definite information on the disintegrator, I won't answer for the consequences.'

'But I told all I knew—'

'It won't do. It's not enough. You've got to remember more, Ullen, you've *got* to.'

'But knowledge where dere is none is impossible to have – dat is an axiom.' Ullen sat upright in his seat, propping himself on a crutch.

'I know it,' Johnnie's mouth twisted in misery, 'but you've got to understand.

'The Venusians have control of space; our Asteroid garrisons have been wiped out, and last week Phobos and Deimos fell. Communications between Earth and Luna are broken and God knows how long the Lunar squadron can hold out. Earth itself is scarcely secure and their bombings are becoming more serious— Oh, Ullen, don't you understand?'

The Martian's look of confusion deepened, 'Eard is losing?'

'God, yes!'

'Den give up. Dat is de logical ding to do. Why did you start at all – you stupid Eardmen.'

Johnnie ground his teeth, 'But if we have the disintegrator, we won't lose.'

Ullen shrugged, 'Oh, Johnnie, it gets wearisome to listen to de same old story. You Eardmen have one-track minds. Look, wouldn't it make you feel better to have me read you some of my manuscript? It would do your intellect good.'

'All right, Ullen, you've asked for it, and here's everything right out. If you don't tell Thorning what he wants to know, you're going to be arrested and tried for treason.'

There was a short silence, and then a confused stutter, 'T-treason. You mean dat I betray—' The historian removed his glasses and wiped them with shaking hand, 'It's not true. You're trying to frighten me.'

'Oh, no, I'm not. Korsakoff thinks you know more than you're telling. He's sure that you're either holding out for a price or, more likely, that you've sold out to the Veenies.'

'But Dorning—'

'Thorning isn't any too secure himself. He has his own skin to think of. Earth governments in moments of stress are not famous for being reasonable.' There were sudden tears in his eyes, 'Ullen, there must be something you can do. It's not only you – it's for Earth.'

Ullen's breathing whistled harshly, 'Dey tink I would *sell* my scientific knowledge. Is dat de kind of insult dey pay my sense of eddics; my scientific integrity?' His voice was thick with fury and for the first time since Johnnie knew him, he lapsed into guttural Martian. 'For dat, I say not a word,' he finished. 'Let dem put me in prison or shoot me, but dis insult I cannot forget.'

There was no mistaking the firmness in his eyes, and Johnnie's shoulders sagged. The Earthman didn't move at the glare of the signal light.

'Answer de light, Johnnie,' said the Martian, softly, 'Dey are coming for me.'

*

In a moment, the room was crowded with green uniforms. Dr Thorning and the two with him were the only ones present in civilian clothes.

Ullen struggled to his feet, 'Gentlemen, say nodding. I have heard dat it is dought dat I am selling what I know – *selling for money*.' He spat the words. 'It is a ding never before said of me – a ding I have not deserved. If you wish you can imprison me immediately, but I shall say nodding more – nor have anyding furder to do wid de Eard government.'

A green-garbed official stepped forward immediately, but Dr Thorning waved him back.

'Whoa, there, Dr Ullen,' he said jovially, 'don't jump too soon. I've just come to ask if there isn't a single additional fact that you remember. Anything, no matter how insignificant—'

There was stony silence. Ullen leant heavily on his crutches but remained stolidly erect.

Dr Thorning seated himself imperturbably upon the historian's desk, picked up the high stack of type-written pages, 'Ah, is this the manuscript young Brewster was telling me about.' He gazed at it curiously, 'Well, of course, you realize that your attitude will force the government to confiscate all this.'

'Eh?' Ullen's stern expression melted into dismay. His crutch slipped and he dropped heavily into his seat.

The physicist warded off the other's feeble clutch, 'Keep your hands off, Dr Ullen, I'm taking care of this.' He leafed through the pages with a rustling noise. 'You see, if you are arrested for treason, your writings become subversive.'

'Subversive!' Ullen's voice was hoarse, 'Dr Dorning, you don't know what you are saying. It is my – my great labor.' His voice caught huskily, 'Please, Dr Dorning, give me my manuscript.'

The other held it just beyond the Martian's shaking fingers.

'*If*—' he said.

'But I don't know!'

The sweat stood out on the historian's pale face. His voice came thickly. 'Time! Give me time! But let me dink – and don't, please don't harm dis manuscript.'

The other's fingers sank painfully into Ullen's shoulder, 'So help me, I burn your manuscript in five minutes, if—'

'Wait, I'll tell you. Somewhere – I don't know where – it was said dat in de weapon dey used a special metal for some of de wiring. I don't know what metal, but water spoiled it and had to be kept away – also air. It—'

'Holy jumping *Jupiter*,' came the sudden shout from one of Thorning's companions. 'Chief, don't you remember Aspartier's work on sodium wiring in argon atmosphere five years ago—'

Dr Thorning's eyes were deep with thought, 'Wait-wait-wait-*Damn!* It was staring us in the face—'

'I know,' shrieked Ullen suddenly. 'It was in Karisto. He was discussing de fall of Gallonie and dat was one of de minor causes – de lack of dat metal – and den he mentioned—'

He was talking to an empty room, and for a while he was silent in puzzled astonishment.

And then, 'My manuscript!' He salvaged it from where it lay scattered over the floor, hobbling painfully about, smoothing each wrinkled sheet with care.

'De barbarians – to treat a great scientific work so!'

Ullen opened still another drawer and scrabbled through its contents. He closed it and looked about peevishly, 'Johnnie, where did I put dat bibliography? Did you see it?'

He looked toward the window, 'Johnnie!'

Johnnie Brewster said, 'Wait a while, Ullen. Here they come now.'

The streets below were a burst of color. In a long, stiffly-moving line the Green of the Navy paraded down the avenue, the air above them snow-thick with confetti, hail-thick with ticker-tape. The roar of the crowd was dull, muted.

'Ah, de foolish people,' mused Ullen. 'Dey were happy just like dis when de war started and dere was a parade just like dis – and now anodder one. Silly!' He stumped back to his chair.

Johnnie followed, 'The government is naming a new museum after you, isn't it?'

'Yes,' was the dry reply. He peered helplessly about under the desk, 'De Ullen War Museum – and it will be filled wid ancient weapons, from stone larife to anti-aircraft gun. Dat is your queer Eard sense of de fitness of dings. *Where* in dunderation is dat bibliography?'

'Here,' said Johnnie, withdrawing the document from Ullen's vest pocket. 'Our victory was due to your weapon, ancient to you, so it *is* fit in a way.'

'Victory! Sure! Until Venus rearms and reprepares and refights for revenge. All history shows – but never mind. It is useless, dis talk.' He settled himself deeply in his chair, 'Here, let me show you a real victory. Let me read you some of de first volume of my work. It's already in print, you know.'

Johnnie laughed, 'Go ahead, Ullen. Right now I'm even willing to listen to you read your entire twelve volumes – word for word.'

And Ullen smiled gently. 'It would be good for your intellect,' he said.

Christmas on Ganymede

Olaf Johnson hummed nasally to himself and his china-blue eyes were dreamy as he surveyed the stately fir tree in the corner of the library. Though the library was the largest single room in the Dome, Olaf felt it none too spacious for the occasion. Enthusiastically he dipped into the huge crate at his side and took out the first roll of red-and-green crêpe paper.

What sudden burst of sentiment had inspired the Ganymedan Products Corporation, Inc. to ship a complete collection of Christmas decorations to the Dome, he did not pause to inquire. Olaf's was a placid disposition, and in his self-imposed job as chief Christmas decorator, he was content with his lot.

He frowned suddenly and muttered a curse. The General Assembly signal light was flashing on and off hysterically. With a hurt air Olaf laid down the tack-hammer he had just lifted, then the roll of crêpe paper, picked some tinsel out of his hair and left for officers quarters.

Commander Scott Pelham was in his deep armchair at the head of the table when Olaf entered. His stubby fingers were drumming unrhythmically upon the glass-topped table. Olaf met the commander's hotly furious eyes without fear, for nothing had gone wrong in his department in twenty Ganymedan revolutions.

The room filled rapidly with men, and Pelham's eyes hardened as he counted noses in one sweeping glance.

'We're all here. Men, we face a crisis!'

There was a vague stir. Olaf's eyes sought the ceiling and he relaxed. Crises hit the Dome once a revolution, on the average. Usually they turned out to be a sudden rise in the quota of oxite to be gathered, or the inferior quality of the last batch of karen leaves. He stiffened, however, at the next words.

'In connection with the crisis, I have one question to ask.' Pelham's voice was a deep baritone, and it rasped unpleasantly when he was angry. 'What dirty imbecilic troublemaker has been telling those blasted Ossies fairy tales?'

Olaf cleared his throat nervously and thus immediately became the center of attention. His Adam's apple wobbled in sudden alarm and his forehead wrinkled into a washboard. He shivered.

'I-I—' he stuttered, quickly fell silent. His long fingers made a bewildered gesture of appeal. 'I mean I was out there yesterday, after the last – uh – supplies of karen leaves, on account the Ossies were slow and—'

A deceptive sweetness entered Pelham's voice. He smiled.

'Did you tell those natives about Santa Claus, Olaf?'

The smile looked uncommonly like a wolfish leer and Olaf broke down. He nodded convulsively.

'Oh, you did? Well, well, you told them about Santa Claus! He comes down in a sleigh that flies through the air with eight reindeer pulling it, huh?'

'Well – er – doesn't he?' Olaf asked unhappily.

'And you drew pictures of the reindeer, just to make sure there was no mistake. Also, he has a long white beard and red clothes with white trimmings.'

'Yeah, that's right,' said Olaf, his face puzzled.

'And he has a big bag, chock full of presents for good little boys and girls, and he brings it down the chimney and puts presents inside stockings.'

'Sure.'

'You also told them he's about due, didn't you? One more revolution and he's going to visit us.'

Olaf smiled weakly. 'Yeah, Commander, I meant to tell you. I'm fixing up the tree and—'

'Shut up!' The commander was breathing hard in a whistling sort of way. 'Do you know what those Ossies have thought of?'

'No, Commander.'

Pelham leaned across the table toward Olaf and shouted:

'They want Santa Claus to visit *them!*'

Someone laughed and changed it quickly into a strangling cough at the commander's raging stare.

'And if Santa Claus doesn't visit them, the Ossies are going to quit work!' He repeated, 'Quit cold – strike!'

There was no laughter, strangled or otherwise, after that. If there were more than one thought among the entire group, it didn't show itself. Olaf expressed that thought:

'But what about the quota?'

'Well, what about it?' snarled Pelham. 'Do I have to draw pictures for you? Ganymedan Products has to get one hundred tons of wolf-ramite, eighty tons of karen leaves and fifty tons of oxite every year, or it loses its franchise. I suppose there isn't anyone here who doesn't know that. It so happens that the current year ends in two Ganymedan revolutions, and we're five percent behind schedule as it is.'

There was pure, horrified silence.

'And now the Ossies won't work unless they get Santa Claus. No work, no quota, no franchise – no jobs! Get that, you low-grade morons. When the company loses its franchise, we lose the best-paying jobs in the System. Kiss them good-bye, men, unless—'

He paused, glared steadily at Olaf, and added:

'Unless, by next revolution, we have a flying sleigh, eight reindeer and a Santa Claus. And by every cosmic speck in the rings of Saturn, we're going to have just that, especially a Santa!'

Ten faces turned ghastly pale.

'Got someone in mind, Commander?' asked someone in a voice that was three-quarters croak.

'Yes, as a matter of fact, I have.'

He sprawled back in his chair. Olaf Johnson broke into a sudden sweat as he found himself staring at the end of a pointing forefinger.

'Aw, Commander!' he quavered.

The pointing finger never moved.

Pelham tramped into the foreroom, removed his oxygen nosepiece and the cold cylinders attached to it. One by one he cast off thick woolen outer garments and, with a final, weary sigh, jerked off a pair of heavy knee-high space boots.

Sim Pierce paused in his careful inspection of the latest batch of karen leaves and cast a hopeful glance over his spectacles.

'Well?' he asked.

Pelham shrugged. 'I promised them Santa. What else could I do? I also doubled sugar rations, so they're back on the job – for the moment.'

'You mean till the Santa we promised doesn't show up.' Pierce straightened and waved a long karen leaf at the commander's face for emphasis. 'This is the silliest thing I ever heard of. It can't be done. There ain't no Santa Claus!'

'Try telling that to the Ossies.' Pelham slumped into a chair and his expression became stonily bleak. 'What's Benson doing?'

'You mean that flying sleigh he says he can rig up?' Pierce held a leaf up to the light and peered at it critically. 'He's a crackpot, if you ask me. The old buzzard went down to the sub-level this morning and he's been there ever since. All I know is that he's taken the spare lectro-dissociator apart. If anything happens to the regular, it just means that we're without oxygen.'

'Well,' Pelham rose heavily, 'for my part I hope we *do* choke. It would be an easy way out of this whole mess. I'm going down below.'

He stumped out and slammed the door behind him.

In the sub-level he gazed about in bewilderment, for the room was littered with gleaming chrome-steel machine parts. It took him some time to recognize the mess as the remains of what had been a compact, snugly built lectro-dissociator the day before. In the center, in anachronistic contrast, stood a dusty wooden sleigh atop rust-red runners. From beneath it came the sound of hammering.

'Hey, Benson!' called Pelham.

A grimy, sweat-streaked face pushed out from underneath the sleigh, and a stream of tobacco juice shot toward Benson's ever-present cuspidor.

'What are you shouting like that for?' he complained. 'This is delicate work.'

'What the devil is that weird contraption?' demanded Pelham.

'Flying sleigh. My own idea, too.' The light of enthusiasm shone in Benson's watery eyes, and the quid in his mouth shifted from cheek to cheek as he spoke. 'The sleigh was brought here in the old days, when they thought Ganymede was covered with snow like the other Jovian moons. All I have to do is fix a few gravo-repulsors from the dissociator to the bottom and that'll make it weightless when the current's on. Compressed air-jets will do the rest.'

The commander chewed his lower lip dubiously.

'Will it work?'

'Sure it will. Lots of people have thought of using repulsors in air travel, but they're inefficient, especially in heavy gravity fields. Here on Ganymede, with a field of one-third gravity and a thin atmosphere, a child could run it. Even Johnson could run it, though I wouldn't mourn if he fell off and broke his blasted neck.'

'All right, then, look here. We've got lots of this native purple-wood. Get Charlie Finn and tell him to put that sleigh on a platform of it. He's to have it extend about twenty feet or more frontward, with a railing around the part that projects.'

Benson spat and scowled through the stringy hair over his eyes.

'What's the idea, Commander?'

Pelham's laughter came in short, harsh barks.

'Those Ossies are expecting reindeer, and reindeer they're going to have. Those animals will have to stand on something, won't they?'

'Sure . . . But wait, hold on! There aren't any reindeer on Ganymede.'

Commander Pelham paused on his way out. His eyes narrowed unpleasantly as they always did when he thought of Olaf Johnson.

'Olaf is out rounding up eight spinybacks for us. They've got four feet, a head on one end and a tail on the other. That's close enough for the Ossies.'

The old engineer chewed this information and chuckled nastily.

'Good! I wish the fool joy of his job.'

'So do I,' gritted Pelham.

He stalked out as Benson, still leering, slid underneath the sleigh.

The commander's description of a spinyback was concise and accurate, but it left out several interesting details. For one thing, a spinyback has a long, mobile snout, two large ears that wave back and forth gently, and two emotional purple eyes. The males have pliable spines of a deep crimson color along the backbone that seem to delight the female of the species. Combine these with a scaly, muscular tail and a brain by no means mediocre, and you have a spinyback—or at least you have one if you can catch one.

It was just such a thought that occurred to Olaf Johnson as he sneaked down from the rocky eminence toward the herd of twenty-five spinybacks grazing on the sparse, gritty undergrowth. The nearest spinies looked up as Olaf, bundled in fur and grotesque with attached oxygen nosepiece, approached. However, spinies have no natural enemies, so they merely gazed at the figure with languidly disapproving eyes and returned to their crunchy but nourishing fare.

Olaf's notions on bagging big game were sketchy. He fumbled in his pocket for a lump of sugar, held it out and said:

'Here, pussy, pussy, pussy, pussy, pussy!'

The ears of the nearest spinie twitched in annoyance. Olaf came closer and held out the sugar again.

'Come, bossy! Come, bossy!'

The spinie caught sight of the sugar and rolled his eyes at it. His snout twitched as he spat out his last mouthful of vegetation and ambled over. With neck stretched out, he sniffed. Then, using a rapid, expert motion, he struck at the outheld palm and flipped the lump into his mouth. Olaf's other hand whistled down upon nothingness.

With a hurt expression, Olaf held out another piece.

'Here, Prince! Here, Fido!'

The spinie made a low, tremulous sound deep in his throat. It was a sound of pleasure. Evidently this strange monstrosity before him, having gone insane, intended to feed him these bits of concentrated succulence forever. He snatched and was back as quickly as the first time. But, since Olaf had held on firmly this time, the spinie almost bagged half a finger as well.

Olaf's yell lacked a bit of the nonchalance necessary at such times. Nevertheless, a bite that can be felt through thick gloves is a *bite!*

He advanced boldly upon the spinie. There are some things that stir the Johnson blood and bring up the ancient spirit of the Vikings. Having one's finger bitten, especially by an unearthly animal, is one of these.

There was an uncertain look in the spinie's eyes as he backed slowly away. There weren't any white cubes being offered any more and he wasn't quite sure what was going to happen now. The uncertainty vanished with a suddenness he did not expect, when two glove-muffled hands came down upon his ears and jerked. He let out a high-pitched yelp and charged forward.

A spinie has a certain sense of dignity. He doesn't like to have his ears pulled, particularly when other spinies, including several unattached females, have formed a ring and are looking on.

The Earthman went over backward and remained in that position for awhile. Meantime, the spinie backed away a few feet in a gentlemanly manner and allowed Johnson to get to his feet.

The old Viking blood frothed still higher in Olaf. After rubbing the hurt spot where he had landed on his oxygen cylinder, he jumped, forgetting to allow for Ganymedean gravity. He sailed five feet over the spinie's back.

There was awe in the animal's eye as he watched Olaf, for it was a stately jump. But there was a certain amount of bewilderment as well. There seemed to be no purpose to the maneuver.

Olaf landed on his back again and got the cylinder in the same place. He was beginning to feel a little embarrassed. The sounds that came from the circle of onlookers were remarkably like snickers.

'Laugh!' he muttered bitterly. 'I haven't even begun to fight yet.'

He approached the spinie slowly, cautiously. He circled, watching for his opening. So did the spinie. Olaf feinted and the spinie ducked. Then the spinie reared and Olaf ducked.

Olaf kept remembering new profanity all the time. The husky 'Ur-r-r-r' that came out the spinie's throat seemed to lack the brotherly spirit that is usually associated with Christmas.

There was a sudden, swishing sound. Olaf felt something collide with his skull, just behind his left ear. This time he turned a back somersault and landed on the nape of his neck. There was a chorused whinny from the onlookers, and the spinie waved his tail triumphantly.

Olaf got rid of the impression that he was floating through a star-studded unlimited space and wavered to his feet.

'Listen,' he objected, 'using your tail is a foul!'

He leaped back as the tail shot forward again, then flung himself forward in a diving tackle. He grabbed at the spinie's feet and felt the animal come down on his back with an indignant yelp.

Now it was a case of Earth muscles against Ganymedan muscles, and Olaf became a man of brute strength. He struggled up, and the spinie found himself slung over the stranger's shoulders.

The spinie objected vociferously and tried to prove his objections by a judicious whip of the tail. But he was in an inconvenient position and the stroke whistled harmlessly over Olaf's head.

The other spinies made way for the Earthman with saddened expressions. Evidently they were all good friends of the captured animal and hated to see him lose a fight. They returned to their meal in philosophic resignation, plainly convinced that it was kismet.

On the other side of the rocky ledge, Olaf reached his prepared cave. There was the briefest of scrambling struggles before he managed to sit down hard on the spinie's head and put enough knots into rope to hold him there.

A few hours later, when he had corralled his eighth spinyback, he possessed the technique that comes of long practice. He could have given a Terrestrial cowboy valuable pointers on throwing a maverick. Also, he could have given a Terrestrial stevedore lessons in simple and compound swearing.

'Twas the night before Christmas – and all through the Ganymedan Dome there was deafening noise and bewildering excitement, like an exploding nova equipped for sound. Around the rusty sleigh, mounted on its huge platform of purplewood, five Earthmen were staging a battle royal with a spinie.

The spinie had definite views about most things, and one of his stubbornest and most definite views was that he would never go where he didn't want to go. He made that clear by flailing one head, one tail, three spines and four legs in every possible direction, with all possible force.

But the Earthmen insisted, and not gently. Despite loud, agonized squeaks, the spinie was lifted onto the platform, hauled into place and harnessed into hopeless helplessness.

'Okay!' Peter Benson yelled. 'Pass the bottle.'

Holding the spinie's snout with one hand, Benson waved the bottle under it with the other. The spinie quivered eagerly and whined tremulously. Benson poured some of the liquid down the animal's throat. There was a gurgling swallow and an appreciative whinny. The spinie's neck stretched out for more.

Benson sighed. 'Our best brandy, too.'

He up-ended the bottle and withdrew it half empty. The spinie, eyes whirling in their sockets rapidly, did what seemed an attempt at a gay jig. It didn't last long, however, for Ganymedan metabolism is almost immediately affected by alcohol. His muscles locked in a drunken rigor and, with a loud hiccup, he went out on his feet.

'Drag out the next!' yelled Benson.

In an hour the eight spinybacks were so many cataleptic statues. Forked sticks were tied around their heads as antlers. The effect was crude and sketchy, but it would do.

As Benson opened his mouth to ask where Olaf Johnson was, that worthy showed up in the arms of three comrades, and he was putting up as stiff a fight as any spinie. His objections, however, were highly articulate.

'I'm not going anywhere in this costume!' he roared, gouging at the nearest eye. 'You hear me?'

There certainly was cause for objection. Even at his best, Olaf had never been a heart-throb. But in his present condition, he resembled a hybrid between a spinie's nightmare and a Picassian conception of a patriarch.

He wore the conventional costume of Santa. His clothes were as red as red tissue paper sewed onto his space coat could make it. The 'ermine' was as white as cotton wool, which it was. His beard, more cotton wool glued into a linen foundation, hung loosely from his ears. With that below and his oxygen nosepiece above, even the strongest were forced to avert their eyes.

Olaf had not been shown a mirror. But, between what he could see of himself and what his instinct told him, he would have greeted a good, bright lightning bolt like a brother.

By fits and starts, he was hauled to the sleigh. Others pitched in to help, until Olaf was nothing but a smothered squirm and muffled voice.

'Leggo,' he mumbled. 'Leggo and come at me one by one. Come on!'

He tried to spar a bit, to point his dare. But the multiple grips upon him left him unable to wriggle a finger.

'Get in!' ordered Benson.

'You go to hell!' gasped Olaf. 'I'm not getting into any patented short cut to suicide, and you can take your bloody flying sleigh and—'

'Listen,' interrupted Benson, 'Commander Pelham is waiting for you at the other end. He'll skin you alive if you don't show up in half an hour.'

'Commander Pelham can take the sleigh sideways and—'

'Then think of your job! Think of a hundred and fifty a week. Think of every other year off with pay. Think of Hilda, back on Earth, who isn't going to marry you without a job. Think of all that!'

Johnson thought, snarled. He thought some more, got into the sleigh, strapped down his bag and turned on the gravo-repulsors. With a horrible curse, he opened the rear jet.

The sleigh dashed forward and he caught himself from going backward, over and out of the sleigh, by two-thirds of a whisker. He held onto the sides thereafter, watching the surrounding hills as they rose and fell with each lurch of the unsteady sleigh.

As the wind rose, the undulations grew more marked. And when Jupiter came up, its yellow light brought out every jag and crag of the rocky ground, toward every one of which, in turn, the sleigh seemed headed. And by the time the giant planet had shoved completely over the horizon, the curse of drink – which departs from the Ganymedan organism just as quickly as it descends – began removing itself from the spinies.

The hindmost spinie came out of it first, tasted the inside of his mouth, winced and swore off drink. Having made that resolution, he took in his immediate surroundings languidly. They made no immediate impression on him. Only gradually was the fact forced upon him that his footing, whatever it was, was not the usual stable one of solid Ganymede. It swayed and shifted, which seemed very unusual.

Yet he might have attributed this unsteadiness to his recent orgy, had he not been so careless as to drop his glance over the railing to which he was anchored. No spinie ever died of heart-failure, as far as is recorded, but, looking downward, this one almost did.

His agonized screech of horror and despair brought the other spinies into full, if headachy, consciousness. For a while there was a confused blur of squawking conversation as the animals tried to get the pain out of their heads and the facts in. Both aims were achieved and a stampede was organized. It wasn't much of a stampede, because the spinies were anchored tightly. But, except for the fact that they got nowhere, they went through all the motions of a full gallop. And the sleigh went crazy.

Olaf grabbed his beard a second before it let go of his ears.

'Hey!' he shouted.

It was something like saying 'Tut, tut' to a hurricane.

The sleigh kicked, bucked and did a hysterical tango. It made sudden spurts, as if inspired to dash its wooden brains out against Ganymede's crust. Meanwhile Olaf prayed, swore, wept and jiggled all the compressed air jets at once.

Ganymede whirled and Jupiter was a wild blur. Perhaps it was the spectacle of Jupiter doing the shimmy that steadied the spinies. More likely it was the fact that they just didn't give a hang any more. Whatever it was, they halted, made lofty farewell speeches to one another, confessed their sins and waited for death.

The sleigh steadied and Olaf resumed his breathing once more. Only to stop again as he viewed the curious spectacle of hills and solid ground up above, and black sky and swollen Jupiter down below.

It was at this point that he, too, made his peace with the eternal and awaited the end.

'Ossie' is short for ostrich, and that's what native Ganymedans look like, except that their necks are shorter, their heads are larger, and their feathers look as if they were about to fall out by the roots. To this, add a pair of scrawny, feathered arms with three stubby fingers apiece. They can speak English, but when you hear them, you wish they couldn't.

There were fifty of them in the low purplewood structure that was their 'meeting hall.' On the mound of raised dirt in the front of the room – dark with the smoky dimness of burning purplewood torches fetid to boot – sat Commander Scott Pelham and five of his men. Before them strutted the frowziest Ossie of them all, inflating his huge chest with rhythmic, booming sounds.

He stopped for a moment and pointed to a ragged hole in the ceiling.

'Look!' he squawked. 'Chimney. We make. Sannycaws come in.'

Pelham grunted approval. The Ossie clucked happily. He pointed to the little sacks of woven grass that hung from the walls.

'Look! Stockies. Sannycaws put presets!'

'Yeah,' said Pelham unenthusiastically. 'Chimney and stockings. Very nice.' He spoke out of the corner of his mouth to Sim Pierce, who sat next to him: 'Another half-hour in this dump will kill me. When is that fool coming?'

Pierce stirred uneasily.

'Listen,' he said, 'I've been doing some figuring. We're safe on everything but the karen leaves, and we're still four tons short on that. If we can get this fool business over with in the next hour, so we can start the next shift and work the Ossies at double, we can make it.' He leaned back. 'Yes, I think we can make it.'

'Just about,' replied Pelham gloomily. 'That's if Johnson gets here without pulling another bloomer.'

The Ossie was talking again, for Ossies like to talk. He said:

'Every year Kissmess comes. Kissmess nice, evvybody friendly. Ossie like Kissmess. You like Kissmess?'

'Yeah, fine,' Pelham snarled politely. 'Peace on Ganymede, good will toward men – especially Johnson. Where the devil is that idiot, anyhow?'

He fell into an annoyed fidget, while the Ossie jumped up and down a few times in a thoughtful sort of manner, evidently for the exercise of it. He continued the jumping, varying it with little hopping dance steps, till Pelham's fists began making strangling gestures. Only an excited squawk from the hole in the wall dignified by the term 'window' kept Pelham from committing Ossie-slaughter.

Ossies swarmed about and the Earthmen fought for a view.

Against Jupiter's great yellowness was outlined a flying sleigh, complete with reindeers. It was only a tiny thing, but there was no doubt about it. Santa Claus was coming.

There was only one thing wrong with the picture. The sleigh, 'reindeer' and all, while plunging ahead at a terrific speed, was flying upside down.

The Ossies dissolved into squawking cacophony.

'Sannycaws! Sannycaws! Sannycaws!'

They scrambled out the window like so many animated dust-mops gone mad. Pelham and his men used the low door.

The sleigh was approaching, growing larger, lurching from side to side and vibrating like an off-center flywheel. Olaf Johnson was a tiny figure holding on desperately to the side of the sleigh with both hands.

Pelham was shouting wildly, incoherently, choking on the thin atmosphere every time he forgot to breathe through his nose. Then he stopped and stared in horror. The sleigh, almost life-size now, was dipping down. If it had been an arrow shot by William Tell, it could not have aimed between Pelham's eyes more accurately.

'Everybody down!' he shrieked, and dropped.

The wind of the sleigh's passage whistled keenly and brushed his face. Olaf's voice could be heard for an instant, high-pitched and indistinct. Compressed air spurted, leaving tracks of condensing water vapor.

Pelham lay quivering, hugging Ganymede's frozen crust. Then, knees shaking like a Hawaiian hula-girl, he rose slowly. The Ossies who had scattered before the plunging vehicle had assembled again. Off in the distance, the sleigh was veering back.

Pelham watched as it swayed and hovered, still rotating. It lurched toward the dome, curved off to one side, turned back, and gathered speed.

Inside that sleigh, Olaf worked like a demon. Straddling his legs wide, he shifted his weight desperately. Sweating and cursing, trying hard not to look 'downward' at Jupiter, he urged the sleigh into wilder and wilder swings. It was wobbling through an angle of 180 degrees now, and Olaf felt his stomach raise strenuous objections.

Holding his breath, he leaned hard with his right foot and felt the sleigh swing far over. At the extremity of that swing, he released the gravo-repulsor and, in Ganymede's weak gravity, the sleigh jerked downward. Naturally, since the vehicle was bottom-heavy due to the metal gravo-repulsor beneath, it righted itself as it fell.

But this was little comfort to Commander Pelham, who found himself once more in the direct path of the sleigh.

'Down!' he yelled, and dropped again.

The sleigh *whi-i-ished* overhead, came up against a huge boulder with a *crack*, bounced twenty-five feet into the air, came down with a *rush* and a *bang*, and Olaf fell over the railing and out.

Santa Claus had arrived.

With a deep, shuddering breath, Olaf swung his bag over his shoulders, adjusted his beard and patted one of the silently suffering spinies on the head. Death might be coming – in fact, Olaf could hardly wait – but he was going to die on his feet nobly, like a Johnson.

Inside the shack, into which the Ossies had once more swarmed, a *thump* announced the arrival of Santa's bag on the roof, and a second *thud* the arrival of Santa himself. A ghastly face appeared through the makeshift hole in the ceiling.

'Merry Christmas!' it croaked, and tumbled through.

Olaf landed on his oxygen cylinders, as usual, and got them in the usual place.

The Ossies jumped up and down like rubber balls with the itch.

Olaf limped heavily toward the first stocking and deposited the garishly colored sphere he withdrew from his bag, one of the many that had originally been intended as a Christmas tree ornament. One by one he deposited the rest in every available stocking.

Having completed his job, he dropped into an exhausted squat, from which position he watched subsequent proceedings with a glazed and fishy eye. The jolliness and belly-shaking good humor, traditionally characteristic of Santa Claus, were absent from this one with remarkable thoroughness.

The Ossies made up for it by their wild ecstasy. Until Olaf had deposited the last globe, they had kept their silence and their seats. But when he had finished, the air heaved and writhed under the stresses of the discordant screeches that arose. In half a second the hand of each Ossie contained a globe.

They chattered among themselves furiously, handling the globes carefully and hugging them close to their chests. Then they compared one with another, flocking about to gaze at particularly good ones.

The frowziest Ossie approached Pelham and plucked at the commander's sleeve. 'Sannycaws good,' he cackled. 'Look, he leave eggs!' He stared reverently at his sphere and said: 'Pittier'n Ossie eggs. Must be Sannycaws eggs, huh?'

His skinny finger punched Pelham in the stomach. 'No!' yowled Pelham vehemently. 'Hell, no!'

But the Ossie wasn't listening. He plunged the globe deep into the warmth of his feathers and said:

'Pitty colors. How long take for little Sannycaws come out? And what little Sannycaws eat?' He looked up. 'We take good care. We teach little Sannycaws, make him smart and full of brain like Ossie.'

Pierce grabbed Commander Pelham's arm.

'Don't argue with them,' he whispered frantically. 'What do you care if they think those are Santa Claus eggs? Come on! If we work like maniacs, we can still make the quota. Let's get started.'

'That's right,' Pelham admitted. He turned to the Ossie. 'Tell everyone to get going.' He spoke clearly and loudly. 'Work now. Do you understand? Hurry, hurry, hurry! Come on!'

He motioned with his arms. But the frowzy Ossie had come to a sudden halt. He said slowly:

'We work, but Johnson say Kissmess come every year.'

'Isn't one Christmas enough for you?' Pelham rasped.

'No!' squawked the Ossie. 'We want Sannycaws next year. Get more eggs. And next year more eggs. And next year. And next year, And next year. More eggs. More little Sannycaws eggs. If Sannycaws not come, we not work.'

'That's a long time off,' said Pelham. 'We'll talk about it then. By that time I'll either have gone completely crazy, or you'll have forgotten all about it.'

Pierce opened his mouth, closed it, opened his mouth, closed it, opened it, and finally managed to speak.

'Commander, they want him to come every year.'

'I know. They won't remember by next year, though.'

'But you don't get it. A year to them is one Ganymedan revolution around Jupiter. In Earth time, that's seven days and three hours. They want Santa Claus to come every *week*.'

'Every week!' Pelham gulped. 'Johnson told them—'

For a moment everything turned sparkling somersaults before his eyes. He choked, and automatically his eye sought Olaf.

Olaf turned cold to the marrow of his bones and rose to his feet apprehensively, sidling toward the door. There he stopped as a sudden recollection of tradition hit him. Beard a-dangle, he croaked:

'Merry Christmas to all, and to all a good night!'

He made for the sleigh as if all the imps of Hades were after him. The imps weren't, but Commander Scott Pelham was.

The Little Man on the Subway
(with James MacCreigh)

Subway stations are places where people usually get out, so when no one left the first car at Atlantic Avenue station, Conductor Cullen of the I.R.T. began to get worried. In fact, no one had left the first car from the time the run to Flatbush had begun – though dozens were getting on all the time.

Odd! Very odd! It was the kind of proposition that made well-bred conductors remove their caps and scratch their heads. Conductor Cullen did so. It didn't help, but he repeated the process at Bergen Street, the next station, where again the first car lost not one of its population. And at Grand Army Plaza, he added to the headscratching process a few rare old Gaelic words that had passed down from father to son for hundreds of years. They ionized the surrounding atmosphere, but otherwise did not affect the situation.

At Eastern Parkway, Cullen tried an experiment. He carefully refrained from opening the first car's doors at all. He leaned forward eagerly, twisted his head and watched – and was treated to nothing short of a miracle. The New York subway rider is neither shy, meek, nor modest, and doors that do not open immediately or sooner are helped on their way by sundry kicks. But this time there was not a kick, not a shriek, not even a modified yell. Cullen's eyes popped.

He was getting angry. At Franklin Avenue, where he again contacted the Express, he flung open the doors and swore at the crowd. Every door spouted commuters of both sexes and all ages, except that terrible first car. At those doors, three men and a very young girl got on, though Cullen could plainly see the slight bulging of the walls that the already super-crowded condition of the car had caused.

For the rest of the trip to Flatbush Avenue, Cullen ignored the first car completely, concentrating on that last stop where everyone would *have* to get off. Everyone! President, Church, and Beverly Road were visited and passed, and Cullen found himself counting the stations to the Flatbush terminus.

They seemed like such a nice bunch of passengers, too. They read their newspapers, stared into the whirling blackness out the window, or at the girl's legs across the way, or at nothing at all, quite like ordinary people. Only, they didn't want to get out. They didn't even want to get into the next car, where empty seats filled the place. Imagine New Yorkers resisting the impulse to pass from one car to the other, and missing the chance to leave the doors open for the benefit of the draft.

But it was Flatbush Avenue! Cullen rubbed his hands, slammed the doors open and yelled in his best unintelligible manner, 'Lasstop!' He repeated it two or three times hoarsely and several in that damned first car looked up at him. There was reproach in their eyes. Have you never heard of the Mayor's anti-noise campaign, they seemed to say.

The last other passenger had come out of the train, and the scattered new ones were coming in. There were a few curious looks at the jammed car, but not too many. The New Yorker considers everything he cannot understand a publicity stunt.

Cullen fell back on his Gaelic once more and dashed up the platform toward the motorman's booth. He needed moral assistance. The motorman should have been out of his cab, preparing for his next trip, but he wasn't. Cullen could see him through the glass of the door, leaning on the controls and staring vacantly at the bumper-stop ahead.

'Gus!' cried Cullen. 'Come out! There's a hell of—'

At that point, his tongue skidded to a halt, because it wasn't Gus. It was a little old man, who smiled politely and twiddled his fingers in greeting.

Patrick Cullen's Irish soul rebelled. With a yelp, he grabbed the edge of the door and tried to shove it open. He should have known that wouldn't work. So, taking a deep breath and commending said Irish soul to God, he made for the open door and ploughed into the mass of haunted humans in that first car. Momentum carried him six feet, and then there he stuck. Behind him, those he had knocked down picked themselves up from the laps of their fellow-travelers, apologized with true New York courtesy (consisting of a growl, a grunt, and a grimace) and returned to their papers.

Then, caught helplessly, he heard the Dispatcher's bell. It was time for his own train to be on its way. Duty called! With a superhuman effort, he inched towards the door, but it closed before he could get there, and the train commenced to move.

It occurred to Cullen that he had missed a report for the first time, and he said, 'Damn!' After the train had traveled some fifty feet, it came to him that they were going the wrong way, and this time he said nothing.

After all, what was there to say – even in the purest of Gaelic.

How *could* a train go the wrong way at Flatbush Ave. There were no further tracks. There was no further tunnel. There was a bumper-stop to prevent eccentric motormen from trying to bore one. It was absurd. Even the Big Deal couldn't do it.

But there they were!

There were stations in this new tunnel, too – cute little small ones just large enough for one car. But that was all right, because only one car was travelling. The rest had somehow become detached, presumably to make the routine trip to Bronx Park.

There were maybe a dozen stations on the line – with curious names. Cullen noticed only a few, because he found it difficult to keep his eyes from going out of focus. One was Archangel Boulevard; another Seraph Road; still another Cherub Plaza.

And then, the train slid into a monster station, that looked uncommonly like a cave, and stopped. It was huge, about three hundred feet deep, and almost spherical. The tracks ran to the exact center, without trusses, and the platform at its side likewise rested comfortably upon air.

The conductor was the only person left in the car, the rest having mostly gotten off at Hosannah Square. He hung limply from the porcelain hand-grip, staring fixedly at a lip-stick advertisement. The door of the motorman's cabin opened and the little man came out. He glanced at Cullen, turned away, then whirled back.

'Hey,' he said, 'who are you?'

Cullen rotated slowly, still clutching the hand-grip. 'Only the conductor. Don't mind me. I'm quitting anyway. I don't like the work.'

'Oh, dear, dear, this is unexpected.' The little man waggled his head and tch-tched. 'I'm Mr Crumley,' he explained. 'I steal things. People mostly. Sometimes subway cars – but they're such big, clumsy things, don't you think?'

'Mister,' groaned Cullen. 'I quit thinking two hours ago. It didn't get me anywhere. Who are you, anyway?'

'I told you – I'm Mr Crumley. I'm practicing to be a god.'

'A gob?' said Cullen. 'You mean a sailor?'

'Dear, no,' frowned Mr Crumley. 'I said, "god", as in Jehovah. Look!' He pointed out the window to the wall of the cave. Where his finger pointed, the rock billowed and rose. He moved his finger and there was a neat ridge of rock describing a reversed, lower case 'h'.

'That's my symbol,' said Crumley modestly. 'Mystic, isn't it? But that's nothing. Wait till I really get things organized. Dear, dear, will I give them miracles!'

Cullen's head swiveled between the raised-rock symbol and the simpering Mr Crumley, until he began to get dizzy, and then he stopped.

'Listen,' he demanded hoarsely. 'How did you get that car out of Flatbush Avenue? Where did that tunnel come from? Are some of them foreigners—'

'Oh, my, no!' answered Mr Crumley. 'I made that myself and willed it so that no one would notice. It was quite difficult. It just wears the ectoplasm right out of me. Miracles with people mixed up in it are much harder than the other kind, because you have to fight their wills. Unless you have lots of Believers, you can't do it. Now that I've got over a hundred thousand, I can do it, but there was a time,' he shook his head reminiscently, 'when I couldn't even have levitated a baby – or healed a leper. Oh, well, we're wasting time. We ought to be at the nearest factory.'

Cullen brightened. 'Factory' was more prosaic. 'I once had a brother,' he said, 'who worked in a sweater factory, but—'

'Oh, goodness, Mr Cullen. I'm referring to my Believers' Factories. I have to educate people to believe in me, don't I, and preaching is such slow work. I believe in mass production. Some day I intend to be called the Henry Ford of Utopia. Why, I've got twelve Factories in Brooklyn alone and when I manufacture enough Believers, I'll just cover the world with them.'

He sighed, 'Gracious me, if I only had enough Believers. I've got to have a million before I can let things progress by themselves and until then I have to attend to every little detail myself. It is so boring! I even have to keep reminding my Believers who I am – even the Disciples. Incidentally, Cullen – I read your mind, by the way, so that's how I know your name – you want to be a Believer, of course.'

'Well, now,' said Cullen nervously.

'Oh, come now. *Some* gods would have been angry at your intrusion and done away with you,' he snapped his fingers, 'like that. Not I, though, because I think killing people is messy and inconsiderate. Just the same, you'll have to be a Believer.'

Now Patrick Cullen was an intelligent Irishman. That is to say, he admitted the existence of banshees, leprechauns, and the Little Folk, and kept an open mind on poltergeists, werewolves, vampires and such-like foreign trash. At mere supernaturalities, he was too well-educated to sneer. Still, Cullen did not intend to compromise his religion. His theology was weak, but for a mortal to claim godship smacked of heresy, not to say sacrilege and blasphemy, even to him.

'You're a faker,' he cried boldly, 'and you're headed straight for Hell the way you're going.'

Mr Crumley clicked his tongue, 'What terrible language you use. And so unnecessary! Of course you Believe in me.'

'Oh, yeah?'

'Well, then, if you are stubborn, I'll pass a minor miracle. It's inconvenient, but now,' he made vague motions with his left hand, 'you Believe in me.'

'Certainly,' said Cullen, hurt. 'I always did. How do I go about worshipping you? I want to do this properly.'

'Just Believe in me, and that's enough. Now you must go to the factories and then we'll send you back home – they'll never know you were gone – and you can live your life like a Believer.'

The conductor smiled ecstatically, 'Oh, happy life! I *want* to go to the factories.'

'Of course you would,' replied Mr Crumley. 'You'd be a fine Crumleyite otherwise, wouldn't you? Come!' He pointed at the door of the car, and the door slid open. They walked out and Crumley kept on pointing. Rock faded away in front, and bit down again behind. Through the wall Cullen walked, following that little figure who was his god.

That *was* a god, thought Cullen. Any god that could do that was one hell of a damn good god to believe in.

And then he was at the factory – in another cave, only smaller. Mr Crumley seemed to like caves.

Cullen didn't pay much attention to his surroundings. He couldn't see much anyway on account of the faint violet mist that blurred his vision. He got the impression of a slowly-moving conveyor belt, with men stationed at intervals along it. Disciples, he thought. And the parts being machined on that belt were probably non-Believers, or such low trash.

There was a man watching him, smiling. A Disciple, Cullen thought, and quite naturally made the sign to him. He had never made it before, but it was easy. The Disciple replied in kind.

'He told me you were coming,' said the Disciple. 'He made a special miracle for you, he said. That's quite a distinction. Do you want me to show you around the belt?'

'You bet.'

'Well, this is Factory One. It's the nerve center of all the factories of the country. The others give preliminary treatment only; and make only Believers. *We* make Disciples.'

Oh, boy, Disciples! 'Am I going to be a Disciple?' asked Cullen eagerly.

'After being miraculated by *him*. Of course! You're a *somebody*, you know. There are only five other people he ever took personal charge of.'

This was a glorious way to do things. Everything Mr Crumley did was glorious. What a god! What a god! 'You started that way, too.'

'Certainly,' said the Disciple, placidly, 'I'm an important fellow, too. Only I wish I were more important, even.'

'What for?' said Cullen, in a shocked tone of voice. 'Are you murmuring against the dictates of Mr Crumley? (may he prosper). This is sacrilege.'

The Disciple shifted uncomfortably, 'Well, I've got ideas, and I'd like to try them out.'

'You've got ideas, huh?' muttered Cullen balefully. 'Does Mr Crumley (may he live forever) know?'

'Well – frankly, no! But just the same,' the Disciple looked over each shoulder carefully and drew closer, 'I'm not the only one. There are lots of us that think Mr Crumley (on whom be blessings) is just a trifle old-fashioned. For instance, take the lights in this place.'

Cullen stared upwards. The lights were the same type as those in the terminal-cave. They might have been stolen from any line of the I.R.T subway. Perfect copies of the stop-and-go signals and the exit markers.

'What's wrong?' he asked.

The Disciple sneered, 'They lack originality. You'd think a grade A god would do something new. When he takes people, he does it through the subway, and he obeys subway rules. He waits for the Dispatcher to tell him to go; he stops at every station; he uses crude electricity and so on. What we need,' the Disciple was waving his hands wildly and shouting, 'is more enterprise, more git-and-go. We've got to speed up things and run them with efficiency and vim.'

Cullen stared hotly, 'You are a heretic,' he accused. 'You are doomed to damnation.' He looked angrily about for a bell, whistle, gong, or drum wherewith to summon the great Crumley, but found nothing.

The other blinked in quick thought. 'Say,' he said, bluffly, 'look at what time it is. I'm behind schedule. You better get on the belt for your first treatment.'

Cullen was hot about the slovenly assistance Mr Crumley was getting from this inferior Disciple, but a treatment is a treatment, so making the sign devoutly, he got on. He found it fairly comfortable despite its jerky motion. The Disciple motioned to Cullen's first preceptor – another Disciple – standing beside a sort of blackboard. Cullen had watched others while discussing Crumley and he had noticed the question and answer procedure that had taken place. He had noticed it particularly.

Consequently, he was surprised, when the second Disciple, instead of using his heavy pointer to indicate a question on the board, reversed it and brought it down upon his head.

The lights went out!

When he came to, he was under the belt, at the very bottom of the cave. He was tied up, and the Rebellious Disciple and three others were talking about him.

'He couldn't be persuaded,' the Disciple was saying. 'Crumley must have given him a double treatment or something.'

'It's the last double treatment Crumley'll ever give,' said the fat little man.

'Let's hope so. How's it coming?'

'Very well. Very well, indeed. We teleported ourselves to Section Four about two hours ago. It was a perfect miracle.'

The Disciple was pleased. 'Fine! How're they doing at Four?'

The fat little man clucked his lips. 'Well, now, not so hot. For some reason, they're getting odd effects over there. Miracles are just happening. Even ordinary Crumleyites can pass them, and sometimes they just happen. It's extremely annoying.'

'Hmm, that's bad. If there are too many hitches, Crumley'll get suspicious. If he investigates there first, he can reconvert all of them in a jiffy, before he comes here and then without their support we might not be strong enough to stand up against him.'

'Say, now,' said the fat man apprehensively, 'we're not strong enough *now*, you know. None of this going off half-cocked.'

'We're strong enough,' pointed out the Disciple stiffly, 'to weaken him long enough to get us a new god started, and after that—'

'A new god, eh?' said another. He nodded wisely.

'Sure,' said the Disciple. 'A new god, created by us, can be destroyed by us. He'd be completely under our thumb and then instead of this one-man tyranny, we can have a sort of – er – council.'

There were general grins and everyone looked pleased.

'But we'll discuss that further some other time,' continued the Disciple briskly. 'Let's Believe just a bit. Crumley isn't stupid, you know, and we don't want him to observe any slackening. Come on, now. All together.'

They closed their eyes, concentrated a bit, and then opened them with a sigh.

'Well,' said the little, fat man, *'that's* over. I'd better be getting back now.'

From under the belt, Cullen watched him. He looked singularly like a chicken about to take off for a tree as he flexed his knees and stared upwards. Then he added to the resemblance not a little when he spread his arms, gave a little hop and fluttered away.

Cullen could follow his flight only by watching the eyes of the three remaining. Those eyes turned up and up, following the fat man to the very top of the cave, it seemed. There was an air of selfsatisfaction about those eyes. They were very happy over their miracles.

Then they all went away and left Cullen to his holy indignation. He was shocked to the very core of his being at this sinful rebellion, this apostasy – this – this— There weren't any words for it, even when he tried Gaelic.

Imagine trying to create a god that would be under the thumbs of the creators. It was anthropomorphic heresy (where had he heard that word, now?) and struck at the roots of all religion. Was he going to lie there and watch anything strike at the roots of all religion? Was he going to submit to having Mr Crumley (may he swim through seas of ecstasy) deposed?

Never!

But the ropes thought otherwise, so there he stayed.

And then there was an interruption in his thoughts. There came a low, booming sound – a sound which would have been a voice if it had not been pitched so incredibly low. There was a menace to it that got immediate attention. It got attention from Cullen, who quivered in his bonds; from the others in the cave, who quivered even harder, not being restrained by ropes; from the belt itself, which stopped dead with a jerk, and quivered mightily.

The Rebellious Disciple dropped to his knees and quivered more than any of them.

The voice came again, this time in a recognizable language, 'WHERE IS THAT BUM, CRUMLEY?' it roared.

There was no wait for an answer. A cloud of shadow gathered in the center of the hall and spat a black bolt at the belt. A spot of fire leaped out from where the bolt had touched and spread slowly outward. Where it passed, the belt ceased to exit. It was far from

Cullen, but there were humans nearer, and among those scurrying pandemonium existed.

Cullen wanted very much to join the flight, but unfortunately the Disciple who had trussed him up had evidently been a Boy Scout. Jerking, twisting, and writhing had no effect upon the stubborn ropes, so he fell back upon Gaelic and wishing. He wished he were free. He wished he weren't tied. He wished he were far away from that devouring flame. He wished lots of things, some unprintable, but mainly those.

And with that he felt a gentle slipping pressure and down at his feet was an untidy pile of hempen fibre. Evidently the forces liberated by the rebellion were getting out of control here as well as in Section Four. What had the little fat man said? 'Miracles are just happening. Even ordinary Crumleyites can pass them, and sometimes they – just happen.'

But why waste time? He ran to the rock wall and howled a wish at it to dissolve into nothing. He howled several times, with Gaelic modifications, but the wall didn't even slightly soften. He stared wildly and then saw the hole. It was on the side of the cave, diametrically across from Cullen's position at the bottom of the hall, and about three loops of the belt up. The upward spiral passed just below it.

Somehow he made the leap that grabbed the lower lip of the spiral, wriggled his way onto it and jumped into a run. The fire of disintegration was behind him and plenty far away, but it was making time. Up the belt to the third loop he ran, not taking time to be dizzy from the circular trip. But when he got there, the hole, large, black and inviting, was just the tiniest bit higher than he could jump. He leaned against the wall panting. The spot of fire was now two spots, crawling both ways from a twenty foot break in the belt. Everyone in the cavern, some two hundred people, was in motion, and everyone made some sort of noise.

Somehow, the sight stimulated him. It nerved him to further efforts to get into the hole. Wildly, he tried walking up the sheer wall, but this didn't work.

And then Mr Crumley stuck his head out of the hole and said,

'Oh, mercy me, what a perfectly terrible mess. Dear, dear! Come up here, Cullen! Why do you stay down there!'

A great peace descended upon Cullen. 'Hail, Mr Crumley,' he cried. 'May you sniff the essence of roses forever.'

Mr Crumley looked pleased, 'Thank you, Cullen.' He waved his hand, and the conductor was beside him – a simple matter of levitation. Once again, Cullen decided in his inmost soul that here was a *god*.

'And now,' said Mr Crumley, 'we must hurry, hurry, hurry. I've lost most of my power when the Disciples rebelled, and my subway car is stuck half-way. I'll need your help. Hurry!'

Cullen had no time to admire the tiny subway at the end of the tunnel. He jumped off the platform on Crumley's heels and dashed about a hundred feet down the tube to where the car was standing idle. He wafted into the open front door with the grace of a chorus-boy. Mr Crumley took care of that.

'Cullen,' said Mr Crumley, 'start this thing and take it back to the regular line. And be careful; *he* is waiting for me.'

'Who?'

'He, the new god. Imagine those fools – no, idiots – thinking they could create a controllable god, when the very essence of godship is uncontrollability. Of course, when they made a god to destroy me, they made a Destroyer, and he'll just destroy everything in sight that I created, including my Disciples.'

Cullen worked quickly. He knew how to start car 30990; any conductor would. He raced to the other end of the car for the control lever, snatched it off, and returned at top speed. That was all he needed. There was power in the rail; the lights were on; and there were no stop signals between him and God's Country.

Mr Crumley lay himself down on a seat, 'Be very quiet. *He* may let you get past him. I'm going to blank myself out, and maybe he won't notice me. At any rate, he won't harm you – I *hope*. Dear, dear, since this all started in section four, things are *such* a mess.'

Eight stations passed before anything happened and then came Utopia Circle station and – well, nothing really *happened*. It was just an impression – an impression of people all around him for a few seconds watching him closely with a virulent hostility. It wasn't exactly people, but a person. It wasn't exactly a person either, but just a huge eye, watching – watching – watching.

But it passed, and almost immediately Cullen saw a black and white 'Flatbush Avenue' sign at the side of the tunnel. He jammed on his brakes in a hurry, for there was a train waiting there. But the controls didn't work the way they should have, and the car edged up until it was in contact with the cars before. With a soft click, it coupled and 30990 was just the last car of the train.

It was Mr Crumley's work, of course. Mr Crumley stood behind him, watching. 'He didn't get you, did he? No – I see he didn't.'

'Is there any more danger?' asked Cullen, anxiously.

'I don't think so,' responded Mr Crumley sadly. 'After he has destroyed all my creation, there will be nothing left for him to destroy, and, deprived of a function, he will simply cease to exist. That's the result of this nasty, slipshod work. I'm disgusted with human beings.'

'Don't say that,' said Cullen.

'I will,' reported Mr Crumley savagely, 'Human beings aren't fit to be god of. They're too much trouble and worry. It would give any self-respecting god gray hairs and I suppose you think a god looks very dignified all gray. Darn all humans! They can get along without me. From now on, I'm going to go to Africa and try the chimpanzees. I'll bet they make *much* better material.'

'But wait,' wailed Cullen. 'What about me? I *believe* in you.'

'Oh, dear, that would never do. Here! Return to normal.'

Mr Crumley's hand caressed the air, and Cullen, once more a Godfearing Irishman, let loose a roar in the purest Gaelic and made for him.

'Why, you blaspheming spalpeen—'

But there was no Mr Crumley. There was only the Dispatcher, asking very impolitely – in English – what the blankety-blank hell was the matter with him.

Super-Neutron

It was at the seventeenth meeting of the Honorable Society of Ananias that we got the greatest scare of our collective lives and consequently elected Gilbert Hayes to the office of Perpetual President.

The Society is not a large one. Before the election of Hayes there were only four of us: John Sebastian, Simon Murfree, Morris Levin and myself. On the first Sunday of every month we met at luncheon, and on these monthly occasions justified our Society's title by gambling the dinner check on our ability to lie.

It was quite a complicated process, with strict Parliamentary rules. One member spun a yarn each meeting as his turn came up, and two conditions had to be adhered to. His story had to be an outrageous, complicated, fantastic lie; *and*, it had to sound like the truth. Members were allowed to – and did – attack any and every point of the story by asking questions or demanding explanations.

Woe to the narrator who did not answer any questions immediately, or who, in answering, involved himself in a contradiction. The dinner-check was his! Financial loss was slight; but the disgrace was great.

And then came that seventeenth meeting – and Gilbert Hayes. Hayes was one of several non-members who attended occasionally to listen to the after-dinner whopper, paying his own check, and, of course, being forbidden to participate; but on this occasion he was the only one present aside from the regular members.

Dinner was over, I had been voted into the chair (it was my regular turn to preside), and the minutes had been read, when Hayes leaned forward and said quietly, 'I'd like a chance today, gentlemen.'

I frowned, 'In the eyes of the Society you are non-existent, Mr Hayes. It is impossible for you to take part.'

'Then just let me make a statement,' he rejoined. 'The Solar System is coming to an end at exactly seventeen and a half minutes after two this afternoon.'

There was a devil of a stir, and I looked at the electric clock over the television receiver. It was 1:14 p.m.

I said hesitantly, 'If you have anything to substantiate that extraordinary statement, it should be most interesting. It is Mr Levin's turn today, but if he is willing to waive it, and if the rest of the Society agrees—'

Levin smiled and nodded, and the others joined in.

I banged the gavel, 'Mr Hayes has the floor.'

Hayes lit his cigar and gazed at it pensively. 'I have little more than an hour, gentlemen, but I'll start at the beginning – which is about fifteen years ago. At that time, though I've resigned since, I was an astrophysicist at Yerkes Observatory – young, but promising. I was hot on the trail of the solution to one of the perennial puzzles of astrophysics – the source of the cosinic rays – and full of ambition.'

He paused, and continued in a different tone, 'You know, it is strange that with all our scientific advance in the last two centuries we have never found either that mysterious source or the equally mysterious reason for the explosion of a star. They are the two enternal puzzles and we know as little about them today as we did in the days of Einstein, Eddington, and Millikan.

'Still, as I say, I thought I had the cosmic ray by the tail, so I set out to check my ideas by observation, and for that I had to go out in space. It wasn't, however, as easy as all that. It was in 2129, you see, just after the last war, and the Observatory was about broke – as weren't we all?

'I made the best of it. I hired an old second-hand '07 model, piled my apparatus in, and set out alone. What's more, I had to sneak out of port without clearance papers, not wishing to go through the red tape the occupation army would have put me through. It was illegal, but I wanted my data – so I headed out at a right angle to the ecliptic, in the direction of the South Celestial Pole, approximately, and left Sol a billion miles behind me.

'The voyage I made, and the data I collected are unimportant. I never reported one or the other. It was the planet I found that makes the story.'

At this point, Murfree raised those bushy eyebrows of his and grunted, 'I would like to warn the gentleman, Mr Chairman. No member has yet escaped with his skin with a phony planet.'

Hayes smiled grimly, 'I'll take my chance. —To continue; it was on the eighteenth day of my trip that I first detected the planet, as a little orange disc the size of a pea. Naturally, a planet in that region of space is something of a sensation. I headed for it; and immediately discovered that I had not even scratched the surface of that planet's queerness. To exist there at all was phenomenal – but it likewise possessed absolutely no gravitational field.'

Levin's wine-glass crashed to the floor. 'Mr Chairman,' he gasped, 'I demand the gentleman's immediate disqualification. No mass can exist without distorting the space in its neighborhood and thus creating a gravitational field. He has made an impossible statement, and should therefore be disqualified.' His face was an angry red.

But Hayes held his hand up, 'I demand time, Mr Chairman. The explanation will be forthcoming in due course. To make it now would only complicate things. Please, may I continue?'

I considered, 'In view of the name of your story, I am disposed to be lenient. Delay is granted, but please remember that an explanation will be required eventually. You will lose without it.'

'All right,' said Hayes. 'For the present, you will have to accept my statement that the planet had no gravity *at all*. That is definite, for I had complete astronomical equipment upon my ship, and though my instruments were very sensitive, they registered a dead zero.

'It worked the other way around as well, for the planet was not affected by the gravity of other masses. Again, I stress the point that it was not affected *at all*. This I was not able to determine at the time, but subsequent observation over a period of years, showed that the planet was traveling in a straight-line orbit and at a constant speed. As it was well within the sun's influence, the fact that its orbit was neither elliptical nor hyperbolic, and that, though approaching the sun, it was not accelerating, showed definitely that it was independent of solar gravity.'

'Wait a while, Hayes.' Sebastian scowled till his gold premolar gleamed. 'What held this wonderful planet together? Without gravity, why didn't it break up and drift apart?'

'Sheer inertia, for one thing!' was the immediate retort. 'There was nothing to *pull* it apart. A collision with another body of comparable size might have done it – leaving out of consideration the possibility of the existence of some other binding force peculiar to the planet.'

He sighed and continued, 'That doesn't finish the properties of the body. Its red-orange color and its low reflective power, or albedo, set me on another track, and I made the astonishing discovery that the planet was entirely transparent to the whole electro-magnetic spectrum from radio waves to cosmic rays. It was only in the region of the red and yellow portion of the visible-light octave that it was reasonably opaque. Hence, its color.'

'Why was this?' demanded Murfree.

Hayes looked at me, 'That is an unreasonable question, Mr Chairman. I maintain that I might as well be asked to explain why glass is entirely transparent to anything above or below the ultra-violet region, so that heat, light, and X-rays pass through, while it remains opaque to ultra-violet light itself. This sort of thing is a property of the substance itself and must be accepted as such without explanation.'

I whacked my gavel, 'Question declared improper!'

'I object,' declared Murfree. 'Hayes missed the point. Nothing is perfectly transparent. Glass of sufficient thickness will stop even cosmic rays. Do you mean to say that blue light would pass through an entire planet, or heat, for instance?'

'Why not?' replied Hayes. 'That perfect transparency does not exist in your experience does not mean it does not exist altogether. There is certainly no scientific law to that effect. This planet was perfectly transparent except for one small region of the spectrum. That's a definite fact of observation.'

My gavel thumped again, 'Explanation declared sufficient. Continue, Hayes.'

His cigar had gone out and he paused to relight. Then, 'In other respects, the planet was normal. It was not quite the size of Saturn – perhaps half way in diameter between it and Neptune. Subsequent experiments showed it to possess mass, though it was hard to find out how much – certainly more than twice Earth's. With mass, it possessed the usual properties of inertia and momentum – but no gravity.'

It was 1:35 now.

Hayes followed my eyes and said, 'Yes, only three-quarters of an hour is left. I'll hurry! . . . Naturally, this queer planet set me to thinking, and that, together with the fact that I had already been evolving certain theories concerning cosmic rays and novae, led to an interesting solution.'

He drew a deep breath, 'Imagine – if you can – our cosmos as a cloud of – well, super-atoms which—'

'I beg your pardon,' exclaimed Sebastian, rising to his feet, 'are you intending to base any of your explanation on drawing analogies between stars and atoms, or between solar systems and electronic orbits?'

'Why do you ask?' questioned Hayes, quietly.

'Because if you do, I demand immediate disqualification. The belief that atoms are miniature solar systems is in a class with the Ptolemaic scheme of the universe. The idea has never been accepted by responsible scientists even at the very dawn of the atomic theory.'

I nodded, 'The gentleman is correct. No such analogy will be permitted as part of the explanation.'

'*I* object,' said Hayes. 'In your school course in elementary physics or chemistry, you will remember that in the study of the properties of gases, it was often pretended, for the sake of illustrating a point, that the gas molecules were tiny billiard balls. Does that mean that gas molecules *are* billiard balls?'

'No,' admitted Sebastian.

'It only means,' drove on Hayes, 'that gas molecules act similarly to billiard balls in some ways. Therefore the actions of one are better visualized by studying the actions of the other. —Well, then, I am only trying to point out a phenomenon in our universe of stars, and for the sake of ease of visualization, I compare it to a similar, and better-known, phenomenon in the world of atoms. That does not mean that stars are magnified atoms.'

I was won over. 'The point is well-taken,' I said. 'You may continue with your explanation, but if it is the judgment of the chair that the analogy becomes a false one, you will be disqualified.'

'Good,' agreed Hayes, 'but we'll pass on to another point for a moment. Do any of you remember the first atomic power plants of a hundred and seventy years ago and how they operated?'

'I believe,' muttered Levin, 'that they used the classical uranium fission method for power. They bombarded uranium with slow neutrons and split it up into masurium, barium, gamma rays and more neutrons, thus establishing a cyclic process.'

'That's right! Well, imagine that the stellar universe acted in ways – mind you, this is a metaphor, and not to be taken literally – like a body composed of uranium atoms, and imagine this stellar universe to be bombarded from without by objects which might act in some ways similar to the way neutrons act on an atomic scale.

'Such a super-neutron, hitting a sun, would cause that sun to explode into radiation and more super-neutrons. In other words, you would have a nova.' He looked around for disagreement.

'What justification have you for that idea?' demanded Levin.

'Two; one logical, and one observational. Logic first. Stars are essentially in matter-energy equilibrium, yet suddenly, with no observable change, either spectral or otherwise, they occasionally explode. An explosion indicates instability, but where? Not within the star, for it had been in equilibrium for millions of years. Not from a point within the universe, for novae occur in even concentration throughout the universe. Hence, by elimination, only from a point *outside* the universe.

'Secondly, observation. I came across one of these super-neutrons!'

Said Murfree indignantly: 'I suppose you mean that gravitation-less planet you came across?'

'That's right.'

'Then what makes you think it's a super-neutron? You can't use your theory as proof, because you're using the super-neutron itself to bolster the theory. We're not allowed to argue in circles here.'

'I know that,' declared Hayes, stiffly. 'I'll resort to logic again. The world of atoms possesses a cohesive force in the electro-magnetic charge on electrons and protons. The world of stars possesses a cohesive force in gravity. The two forces are only alike in a very general manner. For instance, there are two kinds of electrical charges, positive and negative, but only one kind of gravity – and innumerable minor differences. Still, an analogy this far seems to me to be permissible. A neutron on an atomic scale is a mass without the atomic cohesive force – electric charge. A super-neutron on a stellar scale *ought* to be a mass without the stellar cohesive force – gravity. Therefore, if I find a body without gravity, it seems reasonable to assume it to be a super-neutron.'

'Do you consider that a rigorously scientific proof?' asked Sebastian sarcastically.

'No,' admitted Hayes, 'but it is logical, conflicts with no scientific fact I know of, and works out to form a consistent explanation of novae. That should be enough for our purpose at present.'

Murfree was gazing hard at his fingernails, 'And just where is this super-neutron of yours heading?'

'I see you anticipate,' said Hayes, sombrely. 'It was what I asked myself at the time. At 2:09½ today it hits the sun square, and eight minutes later, the radiation resulting from the explosion will sweep Earth to oblivion.'

'Why didn't you report all this?' barked Sebastian.

'Where was the use? There was nothing to be done about it. We can't handle astronomical masses. All the power available on Earth would not have sufficed to swerve that great body from its path. There was no escape within the Solar System itself, for Neptune and Pluto will turn gaseous along with the other planets, and interstellar travel is as yet impossible. Since man cannot exist independently in space, he is doomed.

'Why tell of all this? What would result after I had convinced them that the death warrant was signed? Suicides, crime waves, orgies, messiahs, evangelists, and everything bad and futile you could think of. And after all, is death by nova so bad? It is instantaneous and clean. At 2:17 you're here. At 2:18 you are a mass of attenuated gas. It is so quick and easy a death, it is almost not death.'

There was a long silence after this. I felt uneasy. There are lies and lies, but this sounded like the real thing. Hayes didn't have that little quirk of the lip or that little gleam in the eye which marks the triumph of putting over a good one. He was deadly, deadly serious. I could see the others felt the same. Levin was gulping at his wine, hand shaking.

Finally, Sebastian coughed loudly, 'How long ago did you discover this super-neutron and where?'

'Fifteen years ago, a billion miles or better from the sun.'

'And all that time it has been approaching the sun?'

'Yes; at a constant speed of two miles per second.'

'Good, I've got you!' Sebastian almost laughed his relief. 'Why haven't the astronomers spotted it in all this while?'

'My God,' responded Hayes, impatiently, 'it's clear you aren't an astronomer. Now, what fool would look to the Southern Celestial Pole for a planet, when they're only found in the ecliptic?'

'But,' pointed out Sebastian, 'the region is studied just the same. It is photographed.'

'Surely! For all I know, the super-neutron has been photographed a hundred times – a thousand times if you like – though the Southern Pole is the most poorly watched region of the sky. But what's to differentiate it from a star? With its low albedo, it never passed eleventh magnitude in brightness. After all, it's hard enough to detect any planets in any case. Uranus was spotted many times before Herschel realized it was a planet. Pluto took years to find even when they were *looking* for it. Remember also that without gravity, it causes no planetary perturbations, and that the absence of these removes the most obvious indication of its presence.'

'But,' insisted Sebastian, desperately, 'as it approached the sun, its apparent size would increase and it would begin to show a perceptible disc through a telescope. Even if its reflected light were very faint, it would certainly obscure the stars behind it.'

'True,' admitted Hayes. 'I will not say that a really thorough mapping of the Polar Region would not have uncovered it, but such mapping has been done long ago, and the present cursory searches for novae, special spectral types, and so on are by no means thorough. Then, as the super-neutron approaches the sun, it begins to appear only in the dawn and twilight – in evening and morning star fashion – so that observation becomes much more difficult. And so, as a matter of fact, it just has not been observed – and it is what should have been expected.'

Again a silence, and I became aware that my heart was pounding. It was two o'clock even, and we hadn't been able to shake Hayes' story. We had to prove it a lie fast, or I'd die of sheer suspense. We were all of us watching the clock.

*

Levin took up the fight. 'It's an awfully queer coincidence that the super-neutron should be heading straight for the sun. What are the chances against it? Remember, that would be the same thing as reciting the chances against the truth of the story.'

I interposed, 'That is an illegitimate objection, Mr Levin. To cite improbability, however great, is not sufficient. Only outright impossibility or citation of inconsistency can serve to disqualify.'

But Hayes waved his hand, 'It's all right. Let me answer. Taking an individual super-neutron and an individual star, the chances of collision, head on, are all but infinitely small. However, statistically, if you shoot enough super-neutrons into the universe, then, given enough time, every star ought to be hit sooner or later. Space must be swarming with super-neutrons – say one every thousand cubic parsecs – so that in spite of the vast distances between the stars and the relative minuteness of the targets, twenty novae occur in our single Galaxy every year – that is, there are twenty collisions between super-neutrons and stars annually.

'The situation is no different really from uranium being bombarded with ordinary neutrons. Only one neutron out of a hundred million may score a hit, but, given time, every nucleus is exploded eventually. If there is an outer-universe intelligence directing this bombardment – pure hypothesis, and *not* part of my argument, please – a year to us is probably an infinitesimal fraction of a second to them. The hits, to them, may be occurring at the rate of billions to their seconds. Energy is being developed, perhaps, to the point where the material this universe composes has become heated to the gaseous state – or whatever passes for the gaseous state there. The universe *is* expanding, you know – like a gas.'

'Still, for the very first super-neutron entering our system to head straight for the sun seems—' Levin ended in a weak stammer.

'Good Lord,' snapped Hayes, 'who told you this *was* the first? Hundreds may have passed through the system in geologic times, One or two may have passed through in the last thousand years or so. How would we know? Even when one is headed straight for the sun, astronomers don't find it. Perhaps this is the only one that's passed through since the telescope was invented, and before then, of course . . . And never forget that, having no gravity, they can go right through the middle of the system, without affecting the planets. Only a hit on the sun registers, and then it's too late.'

He looked at the clock, '2:05! We ought to see it now against the sun.' He stood up and raised the window shade. The yellow sunlight streamed in and I moved away from the dusty shaft of light. My mouth was dry as desert sand. Murfree was mopping his brow, but beads of sweat stood out all along his cheeks and neck.

Hayes took out several slips of exposed film-negative and handed them out, 'I came prepared, you see.' He held one up and squinted at the sun. 'There it is,' he remarked placidly. 'My calculations showed it would be in transit with respect to Earth at the time of collision. Rather convenient!'

I was looking at the sun, too, and felt my heart skip a beat. There, quite clear against the brightness of the sun, was a little, perfectly round, black spot.

'Why doesn't it vaporize?' stammered Murfree. 'It must be almost in the sun's atmosphere.' I don't think he was trying to disprove Hayes' story. He had gone past that. He was honestly seeking information.

'I told you,' explained Hayes, 'that it is transparent to almost all solar radiation. Only the radiation it absorbs can go into heat and that's a very small percentage of all it receives. Besides, it isn't ordinary matter. It's probably much more refractory than anything on Earth, and the Solar surface is only at 6,000 degrees Centigrade.'

He pointed a thumb over his shoulder, 'It's 2:09½, gentlemen. The super-neutron has struck and death is on its way. We have eight minutes.'

We were dumb with something that was just simply unbearable terror. I remember Hayes' voice, quite matter-of-fact, saying, 'Mercury just went!' then a few minutes later, 'Venus has gone!' and lastly, 'Thirty seconds left, gentlemen!'

The seconds crawled, but passed at last, and another thirty seconds, and still another . . .

And on Hayes' face, a look of astonishment grew and spread. He lifted the clock and stared at it, then peered through his film at the sun once more.

'It's gone!' He turned and faced us, 'It's unbelievable. I had thought of it, but I dared not draw the atomic analogy too far. You know that not all atomic nuclei explode on being hit by a neutron. Some, cadmium, for instance, absorb them one after the other like sponges do water. I—'

He paused again, drew a deep breath, and continued musingly, 'Even the purest block of uranium contains traces of all other elements. And in a universe of trillions of stars acting like uranium, what does a paltry million of cadmium-like stars amount to – nothing! Yet the sun is one of them! Mankind never deserved that!'

He kept on talking, but relief had finally penetrated and we listened no longer. In half-hysterical fashion, we elected Gilbert Hayes to the office of Perpetual President by enthusiastic acclamation, and voted the story the whoppingest lie ever told.

But there's one thing that bothers me. Hayes fills his post well; the Society is more successful than ever – but I think he should have been disqualified after all. His story fulfilled the second condition; it sounded like the truth. But I don't think it fulfilled the *first* condition.

I think it *was* the truth!

Legal Rites
(with James MacCreigh)

Already the stars were out, though the sun had just dipped under the horizon, and the sky of the west was a blood-stuck gold behind the Sierra Nevadas.

'Hey!' squawked Russell Harley. 'Come back!'

But the one-lunged motor of the old Ford was making too much noise; the driver didn't hear him. Harley cursed as he watched the old car careen along the sandy ruts on its half-flat tires. Its taillight was saying a red *no* to him. *No*, you can't get away tonight; *no*, you'll have to stay here and fight it out.

Harley grunted and climbed back up the porch stairs of the old wooden house. It was well made, anyhow. The stairs, though half a century old, neither creaked beneath him nor showed cracks.

Harley picked up the bags he'd dropped when he experienced his abrupt change of mind – fake leather and worn out, they were – and carted them into the house. He dumped them on a dust-jacketed sofa and looked around.

It was stifling hot, and the smell of the desert outside had permeated the room. Harley sneezed.

'Water,' he said out loud. 'That's what I need.'

He'd prowled through every room on the ground floor before he stopped still and smote his head. Plumbing – naturally there'd be no plumbing in this hole eight miles out on the desert! A well was the best he could hope for—

If that.

It was getting dark. No electric lights either, of course. He blundered irritatedly through the dusky rooms to the back of the house. The screen door shrieked metallically as he opened it. A bucket hung by the door. He picked it up, tipped it, shook the loose sand out of it. He looked over the 'back yard' – about thirty thousand visible acres of hilly sand, rock and patches of sage and flame-tipped ocotillo.

No well.

The old fool got water from somewhere, he thought savagely. Obstinately he climbed down the back steps and wandered out into the desert. Overhead the stars were blinding, a million billion of them, but the sunset was over already and he could see only hazily. The silence was murderous. Only a faint whisper of breeze over the sand, and the slither of his shoes.

He caught a glimmer of starlight from the nearest clump of sage and walked to it. There was a pool of water, caught in the angle of two enormous boulders. He stared at it doubtfully, then shrugged. It was water. It was better than nothing. He dipped the bucket in the little pool. Knowing nothing of the procedure, he filled it with a quart of loose sand as he scooped it along the bottom. When he lifted it, brimful, to his lips, he spat out the first mouthful and swore violently.

Then he used his head. He set the bucket down, waited a second for the sand grains to settle, cupped water in his hands, lifted it to his lips . . .

Pat. HISS. Pat. HISS. Pat. HISS—

'What the hell!' Harley stood up, looked around in abrupt puzzlement. It sounded like water dripping from somewhere, onto a redhot stove, flashing into sizzling steam. He saw nothing, only the sand and the sage and the pool of tepid, sickly water.

Pat. HISS—

Then he saw it, and his eyes bulged. Out of nowhere it was dripping, a drop a second, a sticky, dark drop that was thicker than water, that fell to the ground lazily, in slow defiance of gravity. And when it struck each drop sizzled and skittered about, and vanished. It was perhaps eight feet from him, just visible in the starlight.

And then, 'Get off my land!' said the voice from nowhere.

Harley got. By the time he got to Rebel Butte three hours later, he was barely managing to walk, wishing desperately that he'd delayed long enough for one more good drink of water, despite all the fiends of hell. But he'd run the first three miles. He'd had plenty of encouragement. He remembered with a shudder how the clear desert air had taken a milky shape around the incredible trickle of dampness and had advanced on him threateningly.

And when he got to the first kerosene-lighted saloon of Rebel Butte, and staggered inside, the saloonkeeper's fascinated stare at the front of his shoddy coat showed him strong evidence that he hadn't been suddenly taken with insanity, or drunk on the unaccustomed sensation of fresh desert air. All down the front of him it was, and the harder he rubbed the harder it stayed, the stickier it got. Blood!

'Whiskey!' he said in a strangled voice, tottering to the bar. He pulled a threadbare dollar bill from his pocket, flapped it onto the mahogany.

The blackjack game at the back of the room had stopped. Harley was acutely conscious of the eyes of the players, the bartender and the tall, lean man leaning on the bar. All were watching him.

The bartender broke the spell. He reached for a bottle behind him without looking at it, placed it on the counter before Harley. He poured a glass of water from a jug, set it down with a shot glass beside the bottle.

'I could of told you that would happen,' he said casually. 'Only you wouldn't of believed me. You had to meet Hank for yourself before you'd believe he was there.'

Harley remembered his thirst and drained the glass of water, then poured himself a shot of the whiskey and swallowed it without waiting for the chaser to be refilled. The whiskey felt good going down, almost good enough to stop his internal shakes.

'What are you talking about?' he said finally. He twisted his body and leaned forward across the bar to partly hide the stains on his coat. The saloonkeeper laughed.

'Old Hank,' he said. 'I knowed who you was right away, even before Tom came back and told me where he'd took you. I knowed you was Zeb Harley's no-good nephew, come to take Harley Hall an' sell it before he was cold in the grave.'

The blackjack players were still watching him, Russell Harley saw. Only the lean man farther along the bar seemed to have dismissed him. He was pouring himself another drink, quite occupied with his task.

Harley flushed. 'Listen,' he said, 'I didn't come in here for advice. I wanted a drink. I'm paying for it. Keep your mouth out of this.'

The saloonkeeper shrugged. He turned his back and walked away to the blackjack table. After a couple of seconds one of the players turned, too, and threw a card down. The others followed suit.

Harley was just getting set to swallow his pride and talk to the saloonkeeper again – he seemed to know something about what Harley'd been through, and might be helpful – when the lean man tapped his shoulder. Harley whirled and almost dropped his glass. Absorbed and jumpy, he hadn't seen him come up.

'Young man,' said the lean one, 'my name's Nicholls. Come along with me, sir, and we'll talk this thing over. I think we may be of service to each other.'

Even the twelve-cylinder car Nicholls drove jounced like a haywagon over the sandy ruts leading to the place old Zeb had – laughingly – named 'Harley Hall'.

Russell Harley twisted his neck and stared at the heap of para-phernalia in the open rumble seat. 'I don't like it,' he complained. 'I never had anything to do with ghosts. How do I know this stuf'll work?'

Nicholls smiled. 'You'll have to take my word for it. I've had deal-ings with ghosts before. You could say that I might qualify as a ghost exterminator, if I chose.'

Harley growled. 'I still don't like it.'

Nicholls turned a sharp look on him. 'You like the prospect of owning Harley Hall, don't you? And looking for all the money your late uncle is supposed to have hidden around somewhere?' Harley shrugged. 'Certainly you do,' said Nicholls, returning his eyes to the road. 'And with good reason. The local reports put the figure pretty high, young man.'

'That's where you come in, I guess,' Harley said sullenly. 'I find the money – that I own anyhow – and give some of it to you. How much?'

'We'll discuss that later,' Nicholls said. He smiled absently as he looked ahead.

'We'll discuss it right now!'

The smile faded from Nicholls' face. 'No,' he said. 'We won't. I'm doing you a favor, young Harley. Remember that. In return – you'll do as I say, all the way!'

Harley digested that carefully, and it was not a pleasant meal. He waited a couple of seconds before he changed the subject.

'I was out here once when the old man was alive,' he said. 'He didn't say nothing about any ghost.'

'Perhaps he felt you might think him – well, peculiar,' Nicholls said. 'And perhaps you would have. When were you here?'

'Oh, a long time ago,' Harley said evasively. 'But I was here a whole day, and part of the night. The old man was crazy as a coot, but he didn't keep any ghosts in the attic.'

'This ghost was a friend of his,' Nicholls said. 'The gentleman in charge of the bar told you that, surely. Your late uncle was something of a recluse. He lived in this house a dozen miles from nowhere, came into town hardly ever, wouldn't let anyone get friendly with him. But he wasn't exactly a hermit. He had Hank for company.'

'Fine company.'

Nicholls inclined his head seriously. 'Oh, I don't know,' he said. 'From all accounts, they got on well together. They played pinochle and chess – Hank's supposed to have been a great pinochle player. He was killed that way, according to the local reports. Caught somebody dealing from the bottom and shot it out with him. He lost. A bullet pierced his throat and he died quite bloodily.' He turned the wheel, putting his weight into the effort, and succeeded in twisting the car out of the ruts of the 'road,' sent it jouncing across unmarked sand to the old frame house to which they were going.

'That,' he finished as he pulled up before the porch, 'accounts for the blood that accompanies his apparition.'

Harley opened the door slowly and got out, looking uneasily at the battered old house. Nicholls cut the motor, got out and walked at once to the back of the car.

'Come on,' he said, dragging things out of the compartment. 'Give me a hand with this. I'm not going to carry this stuff all by myself.'

Harley came around reluctantly, regarded the curious assortment of bundles of dried faggots, lengths of colored cord, chalk pencils, ugly little bunches of wilted weeds, bleached bones of small animals and a couple of less pleasant things without pleasure.

Pat. HISS. Pat. HISS—

'He's here!' Harley yelped. 'Listen! He's someplace around here watching us.'

'Ha!'

The laugh was deep, unpleasant and – bodiless. Harley looked around desperately for the tell-tale trickle of blood. And he found it; from the air it issued, just beside the car, sinking gracefully to the ground and sizzling, vanishing, there.

'I'm watching you, all right,' the voice said grimly. 'Russell, you worthless piece of corruption, I've got no more use for you than you used to have for me. Dead or alive, this is my land! I shared it with your uncle, you young scalawag, but I won't share it with you. Get out!'

Harley's knees weakened and he tottered dizzily to the rear bumper, sat on it. 'Nicholls—' he said confusedly.

'Oh, brace up,' Nicholls said with irritation. He tossed a ball of gaudy twine, red and green, with curious knots tied along it, to Harley. Then he confronted the trickle of blood and made a few brisk passes in the air before it. His lips were moving silently, Harley saw, but no words came out.

There was a gasp and a chopped-off squawk from the source of the blood drops. Nicholls clapped his hands sharply, then turned to young Harley.

'Take that cord you have in your hands and stretch it around the house,' he said. 'All the way around, and make sure it goes right across the middle of the doors and windows. It isn't much, but it'll hold him till we can get the good stuff set up.'

Harley nodded, then pointed a rigid finger at the drops of blood, now sizzling and fuming more angrily than before. 'What about *that?*' he managed to get out.

Nicholls grinned complacently. 'I'll hold him here till the cows come home,' he said. 'Get moving!'

Harley inadvertently inhaled a lungful of noxious white smoke and coughed till the tears rolled down his cheeks. When he recovered he looked at Nicholls, who was reading silently from a green leather book with dog-eared pages. He said, 'Can I stop stirring this now?'

Nicholls grimaced angrily and shook his head without looking at him. He went on reading, his lips contorting over syllables that were not in any language Harley had ever heard, then snapped the book shut and wiped his brow.

'Fine,' he said. 'So far, so good.' He stepped over to windward of the boiling pot Harley was stirring on the hob over the fireplace, peered down into it cautiously.

'That's about done,' he said. 'Take it off the fire and let it cool a bit.'

Harley lifted it down, then squeezed his aching biceps with his left hand. The stuff was the consistency of sickly green fudge.

'Now what?' he asked.

Nicholls didn't answer. He looked up in mild surprise at the sudden squawk of triumph from outside, followed by the howling of a chill wind.

'Hank must be loose,' he said casually. 'He can't do us any harm, I think, but we'd better get a move on.' He rummaged in the dwindled pile of junk he'd brought from the car, extracted a paintbrush. 'Smear this stuff around all the windows and doors. All but the front door. For that I have something else.' He pointed to what seemed to be the front axle of an old Model-T. 'Leave that on the doorsill. Cold iron. You can just step over it, but Hank won't be able to pass it. It's been properly treated already with the very best thaumaturgy.'

'Step over it,' Harley repeated. 'What would I want to step over it for? *He's* out there.'

'He won't hurt you,' said Nicholls. 'You will carry an amulet with you – that one, there – that will keep him away. Probably he couldn't really hurt you anyhow, being a low-order ghost who can't materialize to any great density. But just to take no chances, carry the amulet and don't stay out too long. It won't hold him off forever, not for more than half an hour. If you ever have to go out and stay for any length of time, tie that bundle of herbs around your neck.' Nicholls smiled. 'That's only for emergencies, though. It works on the asafoetida principle. Ghosts can't come anywhere near it – but you won't like it much yourself. It has – ah – a rather definite odor.'

He leaned gingerly over the pot again, sniffing. He sneezed.

'Well, that's cool enough,' he said. 'Before it hardens, get moving. Start spreading the stuff upstairs – and make sure you don't miss any windows.'

'What are you going to do?'

'I,' said Nicholls sharply, 'will be here. Start.'

But he wasn't. When Harley finished his disagreeable task and came down, he called Nicholls' name, but the man was gone. Harley stepped to the door and looked out; the car was gone, too.

He shrugged. 'Oh, well,' he said, and began taking the dust-cloths off the furniture.

II

Somewhere within the cold, legal mind of Lawyer Turnbull, he weighed the comparative likeness of nightmare and insanity.

He stared at the plush chair facing him, noted with distinct uneasiness how the strangely weightless, strangely sourceless trickle of redness disappeared as it hit the floor, but left long, mud-ochre streaks matted on the upholstery. The sound was unpleasant, too; *Pat. HISS. Pat. HISS—*

The voice continued impatiently, 'Damn your human stupidity! I may be a ghost, but heaven knows I'm not trying to haunt you. Friend, you're not that important to me. Get this – I'm here on business.'

Turnbull learned that you cannot wet dry lips with a dehydrated tongue. 'Legal business?'

'Sure. The fact that I was once killed by violence, and have to continue my existence on the astral plane, doesn't mean I've lost my legal rights. Does it?'

The lawyer shook his head in bafflement. He said, 'This would be easier on me if you weren't invisible. Can't you do something about it?'

There was a short pause. 'Well, I could materialize for a minute,' the voice said. 'It's hard work – damn hard, for me. There are a lot of us astral entities that can do it easy as falling out of bed, but— Well, if I have to I shall try to do it once.'

There was a shimmering in the air above the armchair, and a milky, thin smoke condensed into an intangible seated figure. Turnbull took no delight in noting that, through the figure, the outlines of the chair were still hazily visible. The figure thickened. Just as the features took form – just as Turnbull's bulging eyes made out a prominent hooked nose and a crisp beard – it thinned and exploded with a soft pop.

The voice said weakly, 'I didn't think I was that bad. I'm way out of practice. I guess that's the first daylight materialization I've made in seventy-five years.'

The lawyer adjusted his rimless glasses and coughed. *Hell's binges*, he thought, *the worst thing about this is that I'm believing it!*

'Oh, well,' he said aloud. Then he hurried on before the visitor could take offense: 'Just what did you want? I'm just a small-town lawyer, you know. My business is fairly routine—'

'I know all about your business,' the voice said. 'You can handle my case – it's a land affair. I want to sue Russell Harley.'

'Harley?' Turnbull fingered his cheek. 'Any relation to Zeb Harley?'

'His nephew – and his heir, too.'

Turnbull nodded. 'Yes, I remember now. My wife's folks live in Rebel Butte, and I've been there. Quite a coincidence you should come to me—'

The voice laughed. 'It was no coincidence,' it said softly.

'Oh.' Turnbull was silent for a second. Then, 'I see,' he said. He cast a shrewd glance at the chair. 'Lawsuits cost money, Mr – I don't think you mentioned your name?'

'Hank Jenkins,' the voice prompted. 'I know that. Would – let's see. Would six hundred and fifty dollars be sufficient?'

Turnbull swallowed. 'I think so,' he said in a relatively unemotional tone – relative to what he was thinking.

'Then suppose we call that your retainer. I happen to have cached a considerable sum in gold when I was – that is to say, before I became an astral entity. I'm quite certain it hasn't been disturbed. You will have to call it treasure trove, I guess, and give half of it to the state, but there's thirteen hundred dollars altogether.'

Turnbull nodded judiciously. 'Assuming we can locate your trove,' he said, 'I think that would be quite satisfactory.' He leaned back in his chair and looked legal. His aplomb had returned.

And half an hour later he said slowly, 'I'll take your case.'

*

Judge Lawrence Gimbel had always liked his job before. But his thirteen honorable years on the bench lost their flavor for him as he grimaced wearily and reached for his gavel. This case was far too confusing for his taste.

The clerk made his speech, and the packed courtroom sat down en masse. Gimbel held a hand briefly to his eyes before he spoke.

'Is the counsel for the plaintiff ready?'

'I am, your honor.' Turnbull, alone at his table, rose and bowed.

'The counsel for the defendant?'

'Ready, your honor!' Fred Wilson snapped. He looked with a hard flicker of interest at Turnbull and his solitary table, then leaned over and whispered in Russell Harley's ear. The youth nodded glumly, then shrugged.

Gimbel said, 'I understand the attorneys for both sides have waived jury trial in this case of Henry Jenkins versus Russell Joseph Harley.'

Both lawyers nodded. Gimbel continued, 'In view of the unusual nature of this case, I imagine it will prove necessary to conduct it with a certain amount of informality. The sole purpose of this court is to arrive at the true facts at issue, and to deliver a verdict in accord with the laws pertaining to these facts. I will not stand on ceremony. Nevertheless, I will not tolerate any disturbances or unnecessary irregularities. The spectators will kindly remember that they are here on privilege. Any demonstration will result in the clearing of the court.'

He looked severely at the white faces that gleamed unintelligently up at him. He suppressed a sigh as he said, 'The counsel for the plaintiff will begin.'

Turnbull rose quickly to his feet, faced the judge.

'Your honor,' he said, 'we propose to show that my client, Henry Jenkins, has been deprived of his just rights by the defendant. Mr Jenkins, by virtue of a sustained residence of more than twenty years in the house located on Route 22, eight miles north of the town of Rebel Butte, with the full knowledge of its legal owner, has acquired certain rights. In legal terminology we define these as the rights of adverse possession. The layman would call them common-law rights – squatters' rights.'

Gimbel folded his hands and tried to relax. Squatters' rights – for a ghost! He sighed, but listened attentively as Turnbull went on.

'Upon the death of Zebulon Harley, the owner of the house involved – it is better known, perhaps, as Harley Hall – the defendant inherited title to the property. We do not question his right to it. But my client has an equity in Harley Hall; the right to free and full existence. The defendant has forcefully evicted my client, by means which have caused my client great mental distress, and have even endangered his very existence.'

Gimbel nodded. If the case only had a precedent somewhere . . . But it hadn't; he remembered grimly the hours he'd spent thumbing through all sorts of unlikely law books, looking for anything that might bear on the case. It had been his better judgment that he throw the case out of court outright – a judge couldn't afford to have himself laughed at, not if he were ambitious. And public laughter was about the only certainty there was to this case. But Wilson had put up such a fight that the judge's temper had taken over. He never did like Wilson, anyhow.

'You may proceed with your witnesses,' he said.

Turnbull nodded. To the clerk he said, 'Call Henry Jenkins to the stand.'

Wilson was on his feet before the clerk opened his mouth.

'Objection!' he bellowed. 'The so-called Henry Jenkins cannot qualify as a witness!'

'Why not?' demanded Turnbull.

'Because he's dead!'

The judge clutched his gavel with one hand, forehead with the other. He banged on the desk to quiet the courtroom.

Turnbull stood there, smiling. 'Naturally,' he said, 'you'll have proof of that statement.'

Wilson snarled. 'Certainly.' He referred to his brief. 'The so-called Henry Jenkins is the ghost, spirit or specter of one Hank Jenkins, who prospected for gold in this territory a century ago. He was killed by a bullet through the throat from the gun of one Long Tom Cooper, and was declared legally dead on September 14, 1850. Cooper was hanged for his murder. No matter what hocus-pocus you produce for evidence to the contrary now, that status of legal death remains completely valid.'

'What evidence have you of the identity of my client with this Hank Jenkins?' Turnbull asked grimly.

'Do you deny it?'

Turnbull shrugged. 'I deny nothing. I'm not being cross-examined. Furthermore, the sole prerequisite of a witness is that he understand the value of an oath. Herny Jenkins was tested by John Quincy Fitzjames, professor of psychology at the University of Southern California. The results – I have Dr Fitzjames' sworn statement of them here, which I will introduce as an exhibit – show clearly that my client's intelligence quotient is well above normal, and that a psychiatric examination discloses no important aberrations which would injure his validity as a witness. I insist that my client be allowed to testify on his own behalf.'

'But he's dead!' squawked Wilson. 'He's invisible right now!'

'My client,' said Turnbull stiffly, 'is not present just now. Undoubtedly that accounts for what you term his invisibility.' He paused for the appreciative murmur that swept through the court. Things were breaking perfectly, he thought, smiling. 'I have here another affidavit,' he said. 'It is signed by Elihu James and Terence MacRae, who respectively head the departments of physics and biology at the same university. It states that my client exhibits all the vital phenomena of life. I am prepared to call all three of my expert witnesses to the stand, if necessary.'

Wilson scowled but said nothing. Judge Gimbel leaned forward.

'I don't see how it is possible for me to refuse the plaintiff the right to testify,' he said. 'If the three experts who prepared these reports will testify on the stand to the facts contained in them, Henry Jenkins may then take the stand.'

Wilson sat down heavily. The three experts spoke briefly – and dryly. Wilson put them through only the most formal of cross-examinations.

The judge declared a brief recess. In the corridor outside, Wilson and his client lit cigarettes and looked unsympathetically at each other.

'I feel like a fool,' said Russell Harley. 'Bringing suit against a ghost.'

'The ghost brought the suit,' Wilson reminded him. 'If only we'd been able to hold fire for a couple more weeks, till another judge came on the bench, I could've got this thing thrown right out of comt.'

'Well, why couldn't we wait?'

'Because you were in such a damn hurry!' Wilson said. 'You and that idiot Nicholls – so confident that it would never come to trial.'

Harley shrugged, and thought unhappily of their failure in completely exorcizing the ghost of Hank Jenkins. That had been a mess. 'Jenkins had somehow escaped from the charmed circle they'd drawn around him, in which they'd hoped to keep him till the trial was forfeited by non-appearance.'

'That's another thing,' said Wilson. 'Where is Nicholls?'

Harley shrugged again. 'I dunno. The last I saw of him was in your office. He came around to see me right after the deputy slapped the show-cause order on me at the house. He brought me down to you – said you'd been recommended to him. Then you and him and I talked about the case for a while. He went out, after he lent me a little money to help meet your retainer. Haven't seen him since.'

'I'd like to know who recommended me to him,' Wilson said grimly. 'I don't think he'd ever recommend anybody else. I don't like this case – and I don't much like you.'

Harley growled but said nothing. He flung his cigarette away. It tasted of the garbage that hung around his neck – everything did. Nicholls had told no lies when he said Harley wouldn't much like the bundle of herbs that would ward off the ghost of old Jenkins. They smelled.

The court clerk was in the corridor, bawling something, and people were beginning to trickle back in. Harley and his attorney went with them.

When the trial had been resumed, the clerk said, 'Henry Jenkins!'

Wilson was on his feet at once. He opened the door of the judge's chamber, said something in a low tone. Then he stepped back, as if to let someone through.

Pat. HISS. Pat. HISS—

There was a concerted gasp from the spectators as the weirdly appearing trickle of blood moved slowly across the open space to the witness chair. This was the ghost – the plaintiff in the most eminently absurd case in the history of jurisprudence.

'All right, Hank,' Turnbull whispered. 'You'll have to materialize long enough to let the clerk swear you in.'

The clerk drew back nervously at the pillar of milky fog that appeared before him, vaguely humanoid in shape. A phantom hand, half transparent, reached out to touch the Bible. The clerk's voice shook as he administered the oath, and heard the response come from the heart of the cloudpillar.

The haze drifted into the witness chair, bent curiously at about hip-height, and popped into nothingness.

The judge banged his gavel wildly. The buzz of alarm that had arisen from the spectators died out.

'I'll warn you again,' he declared, 'that unruliness will not be tolerated. The counsel for the plaintiff may proceed.'

Turnbull walked to the witness chair and addressed its emptiness. 'Your name?'

'My name is Henry Jenkins.'

'Your occupation?'

There was a slight pause. 'I have none. I guess you'd say I'm retired.'

'Mr Jenkins, just what connection have you with the building referred to as Harley Hall?'

'I have occupied it for ninety years.'

'During this time, did you come to know the late Zebulon Harley, owner of the Hall?'

'I knew Zeb quite well.'

Turnbull nodded. 'When did you make his acquaintance?' he asked.

'In the spring of 1907. Zeb had just lost his wife. After that, you see, he made Harley Hall his year-round home. He became – well, more or less of a hermit. Before that we had never met, since he was only seldom at the Hall. But we became friendly then.'

'How long did this friendship last?'

'Until he died last fall. I was with him when he died. I still have a few keepsakes he left me then.' There was a distinct nostalgic sigh from the witness chair, which by now was liberally spattered with muddy red liquid. The falling drops seemed to hesitate for a second, and their sizzling noise was muted as with a strong emotion.

Turnbull went on, 'Your relations with him were good, then?'

'I'd call them excellent,' the emptiness replied firmly. 'Every night we sat up together. When we didn't play pinochle or chess or cribbage, we just sat and talked over the news of the day. I still have the book we used to keep records of the chess and pinochle games. Zeb made the entries himself, in his own handwriting.'

Turnbull abandoned the witness for a moment. He faced the judge with a smile. 'I offer in evidence,' he said, 'the book mentioned. Also a ring given to the plaintiff by the late Mr Harley, and a copy of the plays of Gilbert and Sullivan. On the flyleaf of this book is inscribed, "To Old Hank", in Harley's own hand.'

He turned again to the empty, blood-leaking witness chair.

He said, 'In all your years of association, did Zebulon Harley ever ask you to leave, or to pay rent?'

'Of course not. Not Zeb!'

Turnbull nodded. 'Very good,' he said. 'Now, just one or two more questions. Will you tell in your own words what occurred, after the death of Zebulon Harley, that caused you to bring this suit?'

'Well, in January young Harley—'

'You mean Russell Joseph Harley, the defendant?'

'Yes. He arrived at Harley Hall on January fifth. I asked him to leave, which he did. On the next day he returned with another man. They placed a talisman upon the threshold of the main entrance, and soon after sealed every threshold and windowsill in the Hall with a substance which is noxious to me. These activities were accompanied by several of the most deadly spells in the Ars Magicorum. He further added an Exclusion Circle with a radius of a little over a mile, entirely surrounding the Hall.'

'I see,' the lawyer said. 'Will you explain to the court the effects of these activities?'

'Well,' the voice said thoughtfully, 'it's a little hard to put in words. I can't pass the Circle without a great expenditure of energy. Even if I did I couldn't enter the building because of the talisman and the seals.'

'Could you enter by air? Through a chimney, perhaps?'

'No. The Exclusion Circle is really a sphere. I'm pretty sure the effort would destroy me.'

'In effect, then, you are entirely barred from the house you have occupied for ninety years, due to the wilful acts of Russell Joseph Harley, the defendant, and an unnamed accomplice of his.'

'That is correct.'

Turnbull beamed. 'Thank you. That's all.'

He turned to Wilson, whose face had been a study in dourness throughout the entire examination. 'Your witness,' he said.

Wilson snapped to his feet and strode to the witness chair.

He said belligerently, 'You say your name is Henry Jenkins?'

'Yes.'

'That is your name now, you mean to say. What was your name before?'

'Before?' There was surprise in the voice that emanated from above the trickling blood-drops. 'Before when?'

Wilson scowled. 'Don't pretend ignorance,' he said sharply. 'Before you *died*, of course.'

'Objection!' Turnbull was on his feet, glaring at Wilson. 'The counsel for the defense has no right to speak of some hypothetical death of my client!'

Gimbel raised a hand wearily and cut off the words that were forming on Wilson's lips. 'Objection sustained,' he said. 'No evidence has been presented to identify the plaintiff as the prospector who was killed in 1850 – or anyone else.'

Wilson's mouth twisted into a sour grimace. He continued on a lower key.

'You say, Mr Jenkins, that you occupied Harley Hall for ninety years.'

'Ninety-two years next month. The Hall wasn't built – in its present form, anyhow – until 1876, but I occupied the house that stood on the site previously.'

'What did you do before then?'

'Before then?' The voice paused, then said doubtfully, 'I don't remember.'

'You're under oath!' Wilson flared.

The voice got firmer. 'Ninety years is a long time,' it said. 'I don't remember.'

'Let's see if I can't refresh your memory. Is it true that ninety-one years ago, in the very year in which you claim to have begun your occupancy of Harley Hall, Hank Jenkins was killed in a gun duel?'

'That may be true, if you say so. I don't remember.'

'Do you remember that the shooting occurred not fifty feet from the present site of Harley Hall?'

'It may be.'

'Well, then,' Wilson thundered, 'is it not a fact that when Hank Jenkins died by violence his ghost assumed existence? That it was then doomed to haunt the site of its slaying throughout eternity?'

The voice said evenly, 'I have no knowledge of that.'

'Do you deny that it is well known throughout that section that the ghost of Hank Jenkins haunts Harley Hall?'

'Objection!' shouted Turnbull. 'Popular opinion is not evidence.'

'Objection sustained. Strike the question from the record.'

Wilson, badgered, lost his control. In a dangerously uneven voice, he said, 'Perjury is a criminal offense. Mr Jenkins, do you deny that you are the ghost of Hank Jenkins?'

The tone was surprised. 'Why, certainly.'

'You *are* a ghost, aren't you?'

Stiffly, 'I'm an entity on the astral plane.'

'That, I believe, is what is called a ghost?'

'I can't help what it's called. I've heard you called a lot of things. Is that proof?'

There was a surge of laughter from the audience. Gimbel slammed his gavel down on the bench.

'The witness,' he said, 'will confine himself to answering questions.'

Wilson bellowed, 'In spite of what you say, it's true, isn't it, that you are merely the spirit of a human being who had died through violence?'

The voice from above the blood drops retorted, 'I repeat that I am an entity of the astral plane. I am not aware that I was ever a human being.'

The lawyer turned an exasperated face to the bench.

'Your honor,' he said, 'I ask that you instruct the witness to cease playing verbal hide-and-seek. It is quite evident that the witness is a ghost, and that he is therefore the relict of some human being, ipso facto. Circumstantial evidence is strong that he is the ghost of the Hank Jenkins who was killed in 1850. But this is a non-essential point. What is definite is that he is the ghost of someone who is dead, and hence is unqualified to act as witness! I demand his testimony be stricken from the record!'

Turnbull spoke up at once. 'Will the counsel for the defense quote his authority for branding my client a ghost – in the face of my client's repeated declaration that he is an entity of the astral plane? What is the legal definition of a ghost?'

Judge Gimbel smiled. 'Counsel for the defense will proceed with the cross-examination,' he said.

Wilson's face flushed dark purple. He mopped his brow with a large bandanna, then glared at the dropping, sizzling trickle of blood.

'Whatever you are,' he said, 'answer me this question. Can you pass through a wall?'

'Why, yes. Certainly.' There was a definite note of surprise in the voice from nowhere. 'But it isn't as easy as some people think. It definitely requires a lot of effort.'

'Never mind that. You can do it?'

'Yes.'

'Could you be bound by any physical means? Would handcuffs hold you? Or ropes, chains, prison walls, a hermetically sealed steel chest?'

Jenkins had no chance to answer. Turnbull, scenting danger, cut in hastily. 'I object to this line of questioning. It is entirely irrelevant.'

'On the contrary,' Wilson cried loudly, 'it bears strongly on the qualifications of the so-called Henry Jenkins as a witness! I demand that he answer the question.'

Judge Gimbel said, 'Objection overruled. Witness will answer the question.'

The voice from the chair said superciliously, 'I don't mind answering. Physical barriers mean nothing to me, by and large.'

The counsel for the defense drew himself up triumphantly.

'Very good,' he said with satisfaction. '*Very* good.' Then to the judge, the words coming sharp and fast, 'I claim, your honor, that the so-called Henry Jenkins has no legal status as a witness in court. There is clearly no value in understanding the nature of an oath if a violation of the oath can bring no punishment in its wake. The statements of a man who can perjure himself freely have no worth. I demand they be stricken from the record!'

Turnbull was at the judge's bench in two strides.

'I had anticipated that, your honor,' he said quickly. 'From the very nature of the case, however, it is clear that my client can be very definitely restricted in his movements – spells, pentagrams, talismans, amulets, Exclusion Circles and what-not. I have here – which I am prepared to deliver to the bailiff of the court – a list of the various methods of confining an astral entity to a restricted area for periods ranging from a few moments to all eternity. Moreover, I have also signed a bond for five thousand dollars, prior to the beginning of the trial, which I stand ready to forfeit should my client be confined and make his escape, if found guilty of any misfeasance as a witness.'

Gimbel's face, which had looked startled for a second, slowly cleared. He nodded. 'The court is satisfied with the statement of the counsel for the plaintiff,' he declared. 'There seems no doubt that the plaintiff can be penalized for any misstatements, and the motion of the defense is denied.'

Wilson looked choleric, but shrugged. 'All right,' he said. 'That will be all.'

'You may step down, Mr Jenkins,' Gimbel directed, and watched in fascination as the blood-dripping column rose and floated over the floor, along the corridor, out the door.

Turnbull approached the judge's bench again. He said, 'I would like to place in evidence these notes, the diary of the late Zebulon Harley. It was presented to my client by Harley himself last fall. I call particular attention to the entry for April sixth, nineteen seventeen, in which he mentions the entrance of the United States into the First World War, and records the results of a series of eleven pinochle games played with a personage identified as "Old Hank". With the court's permission, I will read the entry for that day, and also various other entries for the next four years. Please note the references to someone known variously as "Jenkins", "Hank Jenkins" and – in one extremely significant passage – "Old Invisible".'

Wilson stewed silently during the slow reading of Harley's diary. There was anger on his face, but he paid close attention, and when the reading was over he leaped to his feet.

'I would like to know,' he asked, 'if the counsel for the plaintiff is in possession of any diaries *after* nineteen twenty?'

Turnbull shook his head. 'Harley apparently never kept a diary, except during the four years represented in this.'

'Then I demand that the court refuse to admit this diary as evidence on two counts,' Wilson said. He raised two fingers to tick off the points. 'In the first place, the evidence presented is frivolous. The few vague and unsatisfactory references to Jenkins nowhere specifically describe him as what he is – ghost, astral entity or what you will. Second, the evidence, even were the first point overlooked, concerns only the years up to nineteen twenty-one. The case concerns itself only with the supposed occupation of Harley Hall by the so-called Jenkins in the last twenty years – *since* 'twenty-one. Clearly, the evidence is therefore irrelevant.'

Gimbel looked at Turnbull, who smiled calmly.

'The reference to "Old Invisible" is far from vague,' he said. 'It is a definite indication of the astral character of my client. Furthermore, evidence as to the friendship of my client with the late Mr Zebulon Harley before nineteen twenty-one is entirely relevant, as such a friendship, once established, would naturally be presumed to have continued indefinitely. Unless of course, the defense is able to present evidence to the contrary.'

Judge Gimbel said, 'The diary is admitted as evidence.'

Turnbull said, 'I rest my case.'

There was a buzz of conversation in the courtroom while the judge looked over the diary, and then handed it to the clerk to be marked and entered.

Gimbel said, 'The defense may open its case.'

Wilson rose. To the clerk he said, 'Russell Joseph Harley.'

But young Harley was recalcitrant. 'Nix,' he said, on his feet, pointing at the witness chair. 'That thing's got blood all over it! You don't expect me to sit down in that large puddle of blood, do you?'

Judge Gimbel leaned over to look at the chair. The drip-drop trickle of blood from the apparition who'd been testifying had left its mark. Muddy brown all down the front of the chair. Gimbel found himself wondering how the ghost managed to replenish its supply of the fluid, but gave it up.

'I see your point,' he said. 'Well, it's getting a bit late anyhow. The clerk will take away the present witness chair and replace it. In the interim, I declare the court recessed till tomorrow morning at ten o'clock.'

III

Russell Harley noticed how the elevator boys back registered repulsion and disapproval, and scowled. He was not a popular guest in the hotel, he knew well. Where he made his mistake, though, was in thinking that the noxious bundle of herbs about his neck was the cause of it. His odious personality had a lot to do with the chilly attitude of the management and his fellow guests.

He made his way to the bar, ignoring the heads that turned in surprise to follow the reeking comet-tail of his passage. He entered the red-leather-and-chromium drinking room, and stared about for Lawyer Wilson.

And blinked in surprise when he saw him. Wilson wasn't alone. In the booth with him was a tall, dark figure, with his back to Harley. The back alone was plenty for recognition. Nicholls!

Wilson had seen him. 'Hello, Harley,' he said, all smiles and affability in the presence of the man with the money. 'Come on and sit down. Mr Nicholls dropped in on me a little while ago, so I brought him over.'

'Hello,' Harley said glumly, and Nicholls nodded. The muscles of his cheeks pulsed, and he seemed under a strain, strangely uncomfortable in Harley's presence. Still there was a twinkle in the look he gave young Harley, and his voice was friendly enough – though supercilious – as he said:

'Hello, Harley. How is the trial going?'

'Ask him,' said Harley, pointing a thumb at Wilson as he slid his knees under the booth's table and sat down. 'He's the lawyer. He's supposed to know these things.'

'Doesn't he?'

Harley shrugged and craned his neck for the waitress. 'Oh, I guess so . . . Rye and water!' He watched the girl appreciatively as she nodded and went off to the bar, then turned his attention back to Nicholls. 'The trouble is,' he said, 'Wilson may think he knows, but I think he's all wet.'

Wilson frowned. 'Do you imply—' he began, but Nicholls put up a hand.

'Let's not bicker,' said Nicholls. 'Suppose you answer my question. I have a stake in this, and I want to know. How's the trial going?'

Wilson put on his most open-faced expression. 'Frankly,' he said, 'not too well. I'm afraid the judge is on the other side. If you'd listened to me and stalled till another judge came along—'

'I had no time to stall,' said Nicholls. 'I have to be elsewhere within a few days. Even now, I should be on my way. Do you think we might lose the case?'

Harley laughed sharply. As Wilson glared at him he took his drink from the waitress' tray and swallowed it. The smile remained on his face as he listened to Wilson say smoothly:

'There is a good deal of danger, yes.'

'Hum.' Nicholls looked interestedly at his fingernails. 'Perhaps I chose the wrong lawyer.'

'Sure you did.' Harley waved at the waitress, ordered another drink. 'You want to know what else I think? I think you picked the wrong client, spelled s-t-o-o-g-e. I'm getting sick of this. This damn thing around my neck smells bad. How do I know it's any good, anyhow? Far as I can see, it just smells bad, and that's all.'

'It works,' Nicholls said succinctly. 'I wouldn't advise you to go without it. The late Hank Jenkins is not a very strong ghost – a strong one would tear you apart and chew up your herbs for dessert – but without the protection of what you wear about your neck, you would become a very uncomfortable human as soon as Jenkins heard you'd stopped wearing it.'

He put down the glass of red wine he'd been inhaling without drinking, looked intently at Wilson. 'I've put up the money in this,' he said. 'I had hoped you'd be able to handle the legal end. I see I'll have to do more. Now listen intently, because I have no intention of repeating this. There's an angle to this case that's got right by your blunted legal acumen. Jenkins claims to be an astral entity, which he undoubtedly is. Now, instead of trying to prove him a ghost, and legally dead, and therefore unfit to testify, which you have been doing, suppose you do this . . .'

He went on to speak rapidly and to the point.

And when he left them a bit later, and Wilson took Harley up to his room and poured him into bed, the lawyer felt happy for the first time in days.

Russell Joseph Harley, a little hung over and a lot nervous, was called to the stand as first witness in his own behalf.

Wilson said, 'Your name?'

'Russell Joseph Harley.'

'You are the nephew of the late Zebulon Harley, who bequeathed the residence known as Harley Hall to you?'

'Yes.'

Wilson turned to the bench. 'I offer this copy of the late Mr Zebulon Harley's will in evidence. All his possessions are left to his nephew and only living kin, the defendant.'

Turnbull spoke from his desk. 'The plaintiff in no way disputes the defendant's equity in Harley Hall.'

Wilson continued, 'You passed part of your childhood in Harley Hall, did you not, and visited it as a grown man on occasion?'

'Yes.'

'At any time, has anything in the shape of a ghost, specter or astral entity manifested itself to you in Harley Hall?'

'No. I'd remember it.'

'Did your late uncle ever mention any such manifestation to you?'

'Him? No.'

'That's all.'

Turnbull came up for the cross-examination.

'When, Mr Harley, did you last see your uncle before his death?'

'It was in nineteen thirty-eight. In September, some time – around the tenth or eleventh of the month.'

'How long a time did you spend with him?'

Harley flushed unaccountably. 'Ah – just one day,' he said.

'When before that did you see him?'

'Well, not since I was quite young. My parents moved to Pennsylvania in nineteen twenty.'

'And since then – except for that one-day visit in nineteen thirty-eight – has any communication passed between your uncle and yourself?'

'No, I guess not. He was a rather queer duck – solitary. A little bit balmy, I think.'

'Well, you're a loving nephew. But in view of what you've just said, does it sound surprising that your uncle never told you of Mr Jenkins? He never had much chance to, did he?'

'He had a chance in nineteen thirty-eight, but he didn't,' Harley said defiantly.

Turnbull shrugged. 'I'm finished,' he said.

Gimbel began to look bored. He had anticipated something more in the way of fireworks. He said, 'Has the defense any further witnesses?'

Wilson smiled grimly. 'Yes, your honor,' he said. This was his big moment, and he smiled again as he said gently, 'I would like to call Mr Henry Jenkins to the stand.'

In the amazed silence that followed, Judge Gimbel leaned forward. 'You mean you wish to call the plaintiff as a witness for the defense?'

Serenely, 'Yes, your honor.'

Gimbel grimaced. 'Call Henry Jenkins,' he said wearily to the clerk, and sank back in his chair.

Turnbull was looking alarmed. He bit his lip, trying to decide whether to object to this astonishing procedure, but finally shrugged as the clerk bawled out the ghost's name.

Turnbull sped down the corridor, out the door. His voice was heard in the anteroom, then he returned more slowly. Behind him came the trickle of blood drops: *Pat. HISS. Pat. HISS—*

'One moment,' said Gimbel, coming to life again. 'I have no objection to your testifying, Mr Jenkins, but the State should not be subjected to the needless expense of reupholstering its witness chair every time you do. Bailiff, find some sort of a rug or something to throw over the chair before Mr Jenkins is sworn in.'

A tarpaulin was hurriedly procured and adjusted to the chair; Jenkins materialized long enough to be sworn in, then sat.

'Tell me, Mr Jenkins,' he said, 'just how many "astral entities" – I believe that is what you call yourself – are there?'

'I have no way of knowing. Many billions.'

'As many, in other words, as there have been human beings to die by violence?'

Turnbull rose to his feet in sudden agitation, but the ghost neatly evaded the trap. 'I don't know. I only know there are billions.'

The lawyer's cat-who-ate-canary smile remained undimmed. 'And all these billions are constantly about us, everywhere, only remaining invisible. Is that it?'

'Oh, no. Very few remain on Earth. Of those, still fewer have anything to do with humans. Most humans are quite boring to us.'

'Well, how many would you say are on Earth? A hundred thousand?'

'Even more, maybe. But that's a good guess.'

Turnbull interrupted suddenly. 'I would like to know the significance of these questions. I object to this whole line of questioning as being totally irrelevant.'

Wilson was a study in legal dignity. He retorted, 'I am trying to elicit some facts of major value, your honor. This may change the entire character of the case. I ask your patience for a moment or two.'

'Counsel for the defense may continue,' Gimbel said curtly.

Wilson showed his canines in a grin. He continued to the blood-dripping before him. 'Now, the contention of your counsel is that the late Mr Harley allowed an "astral entity" to occupy his home for twenty years or more, with his full knowledge and consent. That strikes me as being entirely improbable, but shall we for the moment assume it to be the case?'

'Certainly! It's the truth.'

'Then tell me, Mr Jenkins, have you fingers?'

'Have I – what?'

'You heard me!' Wilson snapped. 'Have you fingers, flesh-and-blood fingers, capable of making an imprint?'

'Why, no. I—'

Wilson rushed on. 'Or have you a photograph of yourself – or specimens of your handwriting – or any sort of material identification? Have you any of these?'

The voice was definitely querulous. 'What do you mean?'

Wilson's voice became harsh, menacing. 'I mean, can you prove that *you* are the astral entity alleged to have occupied Zebulon Harley's home. Was it you – or was it another of the featureless, faceless, intangible unknowns – one of the hundreds of thousands of them that, by your own admission, are all over the face of the earth, rambling where they choose, not halted by any locks or bars? Can you prove that *you* are anyone in particular?'

'Your honor!' Turnbull's voice was almost a shriek as he found his feet at last. 'My client's identity was never in question!'

'It is now!' roared Wilson. 'The opposing counsel has presented a personage whom he styles "Henry Jenkins". Who is this Jenkins? What is he? Is he even an individual – or a corporate aggregation of these mysterious "astral entities" which we are to believe are everywhere, but which we never see? If he is an individual, is he *the* individual? And how can we know that, even if he says he is? Let him produce evidence – photographs, a birth certificate, fingerprints. Let him bring in identifying witnesses who have known both ghosts, and are prepared to swear that these ghosts are the same ghost. Failing this, there is no case! Your honor, I demand the court declare an immediate judgment in favor of the defendant!'

Judge Gimbel stared at Turnbull. 'Have you anything to say?' he asked. 'The argument of the defense would seem to have every merit with it. Unless you can produce some sort of evidence as to the identity of your client, I have no alternative but to find for the defense.'

For a moment there was a silent tableau. Wilson triumphant, Turnbull furiously frustrated.

How could you identify a ghost?

And then came the quietly amused voice from the witness chair.

'This thing has gone far enough,' it said above the sizzle and splatter of its own leaking blood. 'I believe I can present proof that will satisfy the court.'

Wilson's face fell with express-elevator speed. Turnbull held his breath, afraid to hope.

Judge Gimbel said, 'You are under oath. Proceed.'

There was no other sound in the courtroom as the voice said, 'Mr Harley, here, spoke of a visit to his uncle in nineteen thirty-eight. I can vouch for that. They spent a night and a day together. They weren't alone. I was there.'

No one was watching Russell Harley, or they might have seen the sudden sick pallor that passed over his face.

The voice, relentless, went on. 'Perhaps I shouldn't have eavesdropped as I did, but old Zeb never had any secrets from me anyhow. I listened to what they talked about. Young Harley was working for a bank in Philadelphia at the time. His first big job. He needed money, and needed it bad. There was a shortage in his department. A woman named Sally—'

'Hold on!' Wilson yelled. 'This has nothing to do with your identification of yourself. Keep to the point!'

But Turnbull had begun to comprehend. He was shouting, too, almost too excited to be coherent. 'Your honor, my client must be allowed to speak. If he shows knowledge of an intimate conversation between the late Mr Harley and the defendant, it would be certain proof that he enjoyed the late Mr Harley's confidence, and thus, Q.E.D., that he is no other than the astral entity who occupied Harley Hall for so long!'

Gimbel nodded sharply. 'Let me remind counsel for the defense that this is his own witness. Mr Jenkins, continue.'

*

The voice began again, 'As I was saying, the woman's name—'

'Shut up, damn you!' Harley yelled. He sprang upright, turned beseechingly toward the judge. 'He's twisting it! Make him stop! Sure, I knew my uncle had a ghost. He's it, all right, curse his black soul! He can have the house if he wants it – I'll clear out. I'll clear out of the whole damned state!'

He broke off into babbling and turned about wildly. Only the intervention of a marshal kept him from hurtling out of the courtroom.

Banging of the gavel and hard work by the court clerk and his staff restored order in the courtroom. When the room had returned almost to normalcy, Judge Gimbel, perspiring and annoyed, said. 'As far as I am concerned, identification of the witness is complete. Has the defense any further evidence to present?'

Wilson shrugged morosely. 'No, your honor.'

'Counsel for the plaintiff?'

'Nothing, your honor. I rest my case.'

Gimbel plowed a hand through his sparse hair and blinked. 'In that case,' he said, 'I find for the plaintiff. An order is entered hereby that the defendant, Russell Joseph Harley, shall remove from the premises of Harley Hall all spells, pentagrams, talismans and other means of exorcism employed; that he shall cease and desist from making any attempts, of whatever nature, to evict the tenant in the future; and that Henry Jenkins, the plaintiff, shall be permitted to full use and occupancy of the premises designated as Harley Hall for the full term of his natural – ah – existence.'

The gavel banged. 'The case is closed.'

'Don't take it so hard,' said a mild voice behind Russell Harley. He whirled surlily. Nicholls was coming up the street after him from the courthouse, Wilson in tow.

Nicholls said, 'You lost the case, but you've still got your life. Let me buy you a drink. In here, perhaps.'

He herded them into a cocktail lounge, sat them down before

they had a chance to object. He glanced at his expensive wrist watch. 'I have a few minutes,' he said. 'Then I really must be off. It's urgent.'

He hailed a barman, ordered for all. Then he looked at young Harley and smiled broadly as he dropped a bill on the counter to pay for the drinks.

'Harley,' he said, 'I have a motto that you would do well to remember at times like these. I'll make you a present of it, if you like.'

'What is it?'

'The worst is yet to come.'

Harley snarled and swallowed his drink without replying. Wilson said, 'What gets me is, why didn't they come to us before the trial with that stuff about this charmingly illicit client you wished on me? We'd have had to settle out of court.'

Nicholls shrugged. 'They had their reasons,' he said. 'After all, one case of exorcism, more or less, doesn't matter. But lawsuits set precedents. You're a lawyer, of sorts, Wilson; do you see what I mean?'

'Precedents?' Wilson looked at him slackjawed for a moment; then his eyes widened.

'I see you understand me.' Nicholls nodded. 'From now on in this state – and by virtue of the full-faith-and-credence clause of the Constitution, in *every* state of the country – a ghost has a legal right to haunt a house!'

'Good lord!' said Wilson. He began to laugh, not loud, but from the bottom of his chest.

Harley stared at Nicholls. 'Once and for all,' he whispered, 'tell me – what's your angle on all this?'

Nicholls smiled again.

'Think about it a while,' he said lightly. 'You'll begin to understand.' He sniffed his wine once more, then sat the glass down gently—

And vanished.

Time Pussy

This was told me long ago by old Mac, who lived in a shack just over the hill from my old house. He had been a mining prospector out in the Asteroids during the Rush of '37, and spent most of his time now in feeding his seven cats.

'What makes you like cats so much, Mr Mac?' I asked him.

The old miner looked at me and scratched his chin. 'Well,' he said, 'they reminds me o' my leetle pets on Pallas. *They* was something like cats – same kind of head, sort o' – and the cleverest leetle fellers y' ever saw. All dead!'

I felt sorry and said so. Mac heaved a sigh.

'Cleverest leetle fellers,' he repeated. 'They was four-dimensional pussies.'

'Four-dimensional, Mr Mac? But the fourth dimension is time.' I had learned that the year before, in the third grade.

'So you've had a leetle schooling, hey?' He took out his pipe and filled it slowly. 'Sure, the fourth dimension is time. These pussies was about a foot long and six inches high and four inches wide and stretched somewheres into middle o' next week. That's four dimensions, ain't it? Why, if you petted their heads, they wouldn't wag their tails till next day, mebbe. Some o' the big ones wouldn't wag till day after. Fact!'

I looked dubious, but didn't say anything.

Mac went on: 'They was the best leetle watchdogs in all creation, too. They had to be. Why, if they spotted a burglar or any suspicious character, they'd shriek like a banshee. And when one saw a burglar today, he'd shriek yesterday, so we had twenty-four hours' notice every time.'

My mouth opened. 'Honest?'

'Cross my heart! Y' want to know how we used to feed them? We'd wait for them to go to sleep, see, and then we'd know they was busy digesting their meals. These leetle time pussies, they always digested their meals exactly three hours before they ate it, on account their stomachs stretched that far back in time. So when they went to sleep, we used to look at the time, get their dinner ready and feed it to them exactly three hours later.'

He had lit his pipe now and was puffing away. He shook his head sadly. 'Once, though, I made a mistake. Poor leetle time pussy. His name was Joe, and he was just about my favorite, too. He went to sleep one morning at nine and somehow I got the idea it was eight. Naturally, I brought him his feed at eleven. I looked all over for him, but I couldn't find him.'

'What had happened, Mr Mac?'

'Well, no time pussy's insides could be expected to handle his breakfast only *two* hours after digesting it. It's too much to expect. I found him finally under the tool kit in the outer shed. He had crawled there and died of indigestion an hour before. Poor leetle feller! After that, I always set an alarm, so I never made that mistake again.'

There was a short, mournful silence after that, and I resumed in a respectful whisper: 'You said they all died, before. Were they all killed like that?'

Mac shook his head solemnly. 'No! They used to catch colds from us fellers and just die anywhere from a week to ten days before they caught them. They wasn't too many to start with, and a year after the miners hit Pallas they wasn't but about ten left and them ten sort o' weak and sickly. The trouble was, leetle feller, that when they died, they went all to pieces; just rotted away fast. Especially the little four-dimensional jigger they had in their brains which made them act the way they did. It cost us all millions o' dollars.'

'How was that, Mr Mac?'

'Y' see, some scientists back on Earth got wind of our leetle time pussies, and they knew they'd all be dead before they could get out there next conjunction. So they offered us all a million dollars for each time pussy we preserved for them.'

'And did you?'

'Well, we tried, but they wouldn't keep. After they died, they were just no good any more, and we had to bury them. We tried packing them in ice, but that only kept the outside all right. The inside was a nasty mess, and it was the inside the scientists wanted.

'Naturally, with each dead time pussy costing us a million dollars, we didn't want that to happen. One of us figured out that if we put a time pussy into hot water when it was about to die, the water would soak all through it. Then, after it died, we could freeze the water so it would just be one solid chunk o' ice, and *then* it would keep.'

My lower jaw was sagging. 'Did it work?'

'We tried and we tried, son, but we just couldn't freeze the water fast enough. By the time we had it all iced, the four-dimensional jigger in the time pussy's brain had just corrupted away. We froze the water faster and faster but it was no go. Finally, we had only one time pussy left, and he was just fixing to die, too. We was desperate – and then one of the fellers thought o' something. He figured out a complicated contraption that would freeze all the water just like that – in a split second.

'We picked up the last leetle feller and put him into the hot water and hooked on the machine. The leetle feller gave us a last look and made a funny leetle sound and died. We pressed the button and iced the whole thing into a solid block in about a quarter of a second.' Here Mac heaved a sigh that must have weighed a ton. 'But it was no use. The time pussy spoiled inside o' fifteen minutes and we lost the last million dollars.'

I caught my breath. 'But Mr Mac, you just said you iced the time pussy in a quarter of a second. It didn't have *time* to spoil.'

'That's just it, leetle feller,' he said heavily. 'We did it *too* doggoned fast. The time pussy didn't keep because we froze that hot water so derned fast that *the ice was still warm!*'

No Connection

Raph was a typical American of his times. Remarkably ugly, too, by American standards of our times. The bony structure of his jaws was tremendous and the musculature suited it. His nose was arched and wide and his black eyes were small and forced wide apart by the span of said nose. His neck was thick, his body broad, his fingers spatulate, with strongly curved nails.

If he had stood erect, on thick legs with large, well-padded feet, he would have topped two and a half yards. Standing or sitting, his mass neared a quarter of a ton.

Yet his forehead rose in an unrestricted arc and his cranial capacity did not stint. His enormous hand dealt delicately with a pen, and his mind droned comfortably on as he bent over his desk.

In fact, his wife and most of his fellow-Americans found him a fine-looking fellow.

Which shows the alchemy of a long displacement along the time-axis.

Raph, Junior, was a smaller edition of our typical American. He was adolescent and had not yet lost the hairy covering of childhood. It spread in a dark, close-curled mat across his chest and back, but it was already thinning and perhaps within the year he would first don the adult shirt that would cover the proudly-naked skin of manhood.

But, meanwhile, he sat in breeches alone, and scratched idly at a favorite spot just above the diaphragm. He felt curious and just a little bored. It wasn't bad to come with his father to the museum when people were there. Today was a Closed-Day, however, and the empty corridors rang lonesomely when he walked along them.

Besides, he knew everything in it – mostly bones and stones.

Junior said: 'What's that thing?'

'What thing?' Raph lifted his head and looked over his shoulder. Then he looked pleased. 'Oh, that's something quite new. That's a reconstruction of Primate Primeval. It was sent to me from the North River Grouping. Isn't it a nice job, though?' And he returned to his work, in the grip of a momentary twinge of pleasure. Private Primeval wasn't to go on exhibition for a week at least – not until he prepared an honorable place for it with suitable surroundings, but, for the moment, it was in his office and his own private darling.

Raph looked at the 'nice job' with quite other emotions, however. What he saw was a spindly figure of contemptuous size, with thin legs and arms, hair-covered and owning an ugly, small-featured face with large, protruding eyes.

He said: 'Well, what *is* it, Pa?'

Raph stirred impatiently: 'It's a creature that lived many millions of years ago, we think. That's the way we think it looks.'

'Why?' insisted the youngster.

Raph gave up. Apparently, he would have to root out the subject and do away with it.

'Well, for one thing we can tell about the muscles from the shape of the bones, and the positions where the tendons would fit and where some of the nerves would go. From the teeth we can tell the type of digestive system the animal would have, and from the footbones, what type of posture it would have. For the rest, we go by the principle of Analogy, that is, by the outside appearance of creatures that exist today that have the same kind of skeleton. For instance, that's why he's covered with red hair. Most of the Primates today – they're little insignificant creatures, practically extinct – are red-haired, have barn callosities on the rump—'

Junior scurried behind the figure and satisfied himself on that score.

'—have long, fleshy probosces, and short, shriveled ears. Their diets are unspecialized, hence the rather all-purpose teeth, and they are nocturnal, hence the large eyes. It's all simple, really. Now, does that dispose of you, youngster?'

And then Junior, having thought and thought about it, came out with a disparaging: 'He looks just like an Eekah to me, though. Just like an ugly, old Eekah.'

Raph stared at him. Apparently he had missed a point: 'An Eekah?' he said, 'What's an Eekah? Is that an imaginary creature you've been reading about?'

'Imaginary! Say, Pa, don't you *ever* stop at the Recorder's?'

This was an embarrassing question to answer, for 'Pa' never did, or at least, never since his maturity. As a child, the Recorder, as custodian of the world's spoken, written, and recorded fiction, had, of course, had an unfailing fascination. But he had grown up—

He said, tolerantly: 'Are there new stories about Eekahs? I remember none when I was young.'

'You don't get it, Pa.' One would almost suppose that the young Raph was on the very verge of an exasperation he was too cautious to express. He explained in wounded fashion: 'The Eekahs are real things. They come from the Other World. Haven't you heard about *that*? We've been hearing about it in school, even, and in the Group Magazine. They stand upside down in their country, only they don't know it, and they look just like Ol' Primeval there.'

Raph collected his astonished wits. He felt the incongruity of cross-examining his half-grown child for archeological data and he hesitated a moment. After all, he had heard *some* things. There *had* been word of vast continents existing on the other hemisphere of Earth. It seemed to him that there were reports of life on them. It was all hazy – perhaps it wasn't always wise to stick so closely to the field of one's own interest.

He asked Junior: 'Are there Eekahs here among the Groupings?'

Junior nodded rapidly: 'The Recorder says they can think as good as us. They got machines that go through the air. That's how they got here.'

'Junior!' said Raph severely.

'I ain't lying,' Junior cried with aggrieved virtue. 'You ask the Recorder and see what *he* says.'

Raph slowly gathered his papers together. It was Closed-Day, but he could find the Recorder at his home, no doubt.

The Recorder was an elderly member of the Red River Gurrow Grouping and few alive could remember a time when he was not. He had succeeded to the post by general consent and filled it well, for he was Recorder for the same reason that Raph was curator of the museum. He liked to be, he wanted to be, and he could conceive no other life.

The social pattern of the Gurrow Grouping is difficult to grasp unless born into it, but there was a looseness about it that almost made the word 'pattern' incongruous. The individual Gurrow took whatever job he felt an aptitude for, and such work as was left over and needed to be done was done either in common, or consecutively by each according to an order determined by lot. Put so, it sounds too simple to work, but actually the traditions that had gathered with the five thousand years since the first Voluntary Grouping of Gurrahs was supposed to have been established, made the system complicated, flexible – and workable.

The Recorder was, as Raph had anticipated, at his home, and there was the embarrassment of renewing an old and unjustly neglected acquaintanceship. He had made use of the Recorder's reference library, of course, but always indirectly – yet he had once been a child, an intimate learner at the feet of accumulated wisdom, and he had let the intimacy lapse.

The room he now entered was more or less choked with recordings and, to a lesser degree, with printed material. The Recorder interspersed greetings with apologies.

'Shipments have come from some of the other Groupings,' he said. 'It needs time for cataloguing, you know, and I can't seem to find the time I used to.' He lit a pipe and puffed strongly. 'Seems to me I'll have to find a full-time assistant. What about your son, Raph? He clusters about here the way you did twenty years ago.'

'You remember those times?'

'Better than you do, I think. Think your son would like that?'

'Suppose you talk to him. He might like to. I can't honestly say he's fascinated by archaeology.' Raph picked up a recording at random and looked at the identification tag: 'Um-m-m – from the Joquin Valley Grouping. That's a long way from here.'

'A long way.' The Recorder nodded. 'I have sent them some of ours, of course. The works of our own Grouping are highly regarded throughout the continent,' he said, with proprietary pride. 'In fact' – he pointed the stem of his pipe at the other – 'your own treatise on extinct primates has been distributed everywhere. I've sent out two thousand copies and there are still requests. That's pretty good – for archaeology.'

'Well, archaeology is why I am here – that and what my son says you've been telling him.' Raph had a little trouble starting: 'It seems you have spoken of creatures called Eekahs from the Antipodes, and I would like to have such information as you have on them.'

The Recorder looked thoughtful: 'Well, I could tell you what I know offhand, or we could go to the Library and look up the references.'

'Don't bother opening the Library for me. It's a Closed-Day. Just give me some notion of things and I'll search the references later.'

The Recorder bit at his pipe, shoved his chair back against the wall and de-focused his eyes thoughtfully. 'Well,' he said, 'I suppose it starts with the discovery of the continents on the other side. That was five years ago. You know about that, perhaps?'

'Only the fact of it. I know the continents exist, as everyone does now. I remember once speculating on what a shining new field it would be for archaeological research, but that is all.'

'Ah, then there is much else to tell you of. The new continents were never discovered by us directly, you know. It was five years ago that a group of non-Gurrow creatures arrived at the East Harbor Grouping in a machine that flew – by definite scientific principles, we found out later, based essentially on the buoyancy of air. They spoke a language, were obviously intelligent, and called themselves Eekahs. The Gurrows, of the East Harbor Grouping, learned their language – a simple one though full of unpronounceable sounds – and I have a grammar of it, if you're interested—'

Raph waved that away.

The Recorder continued: 'The Gurrows of the Grouping, with the aid of those of the Iron Mountain Grouping – which specialize in steel works, you know – built duplicates of the flying machine. A flight was made across the ocean, and I should say there are several dozens of volumes on all that – volumes on the flying machine, on a new science called aerodynamics, new geographies, even a new system of philosophy based on the plurality of intelligences. All produced at the East Harbor and Iron Mountain Groupings. Remarkable work for only five years, and all are available here.'

'But the Eekahs – are they still at the East Harbor Groupings?'

'Um-m-m. I'm pretty certain they are. They refused to return to their own continents. They call themselves "political refugees".'

'Politi . . . *what?*'

'It's their own language,' said the Recorder, 'and it's the only translation available.'

'Well, why *political* refugees? Why not geological refugees, or oompah refugees. I should think a translation ought to make sense.'

The Recorder shrugged: 'I refer you to the books. They're not criminals, they claim. I know only what I tell you.'

'Well, then, what do they look like? Do you have pictures?'

'At the Library.'

'Did you read my "Principles of Archaeology"?'

'I looked through it.'

'Do you remember the drawings of Primate Primeval?'

'I'm afraid not.'

'Then, look, let's go down to the Library, after all.'

'Well, sure.' The Recorder grunted as he rose.

The Administrator of the Red River Gurrow Grouping held a position in no way different in essentials from that of the Museum Curator, the Recorder or any other voluntary job holder. To expect a difference is to assume a society in which executive ability is rare.

Actually, all jobs in a Gurrow Grouping – where a 'job' is defined as regular work, the fruits of which adhere to others in addition to the worker himself – are divided into two classes: one, Voluntary Jobs, and the other, Involuntary or Community Jobs. All of the first classification are equal. If a Gurrow enjoys the digging of useful ditches, his bent is to be respected and his job to be honored. If no one enjoys such burrowing and yet it is found necessary for comfort, it becomes a Community Job, done by lot, or rotation according to convenience – annoying but unavoidable.

And so it was that the Administrator lived in a house no more ample and luxurious than others, sat at the head of no tables, had no particular title other than the name of his job, and was neither envied, hated, nor adored.

He liked to arrange Inter-Group trade, to supervise the common finances of the Group, and to judge the infrequent disagreements that arose. Of course, he received no additional food or energy privileges for doing what he liked.

It was not, therefore, to obtain permission, but to place his accounts in decent order, that Raph stopped in to see the Administrator. The Closed-Day had not yet ended. The Administrator sat peacefully in his after-dinner armchair, with an after-dinner cigar in his mouth, and an after-dinner book in his hand. Although there was something rather timeless about six children and a wife, even they had an after-dinner air about them.

Raph received a multiple greeting upon entering, and raised two hands to his ears, for if the various Administrators (Only applicable title. Author.) had a job, it was noisemaking. Certainly, it was what they liked to do, and certainly others reaped most of the fruits therefrom, for their own eardrums were apparently impervious.

The Administrator shooed them.

Raph accepted a cigar.

'I intend leaving the Grouping for a time, Lahr,' he said. 'My job necessitates it.'

'We won't enjoy your going, Raph. I hope it will not be for long.'

'I hope not. What have we in Common Units?'

'Oh, ample for your purposes, I'm sure. Where do you intend going?'

'To the East Harbor Grouping.'

The Administrator nodded and blew out a thoughtful puff of smoke: 'Unfortunately, East Harbor has a surplus in their favor registered in our books – I can verify that, if you wish – but the Common Units of Exchange on hand will take care of transportation and necessary expenses.'

'Well, that's fine. But tell me, what is my status on the Community Job Roster?'

'Um-m-m – I'll have to get the rolls. You'll excuse me a moment.' He trundled away, heaving his great weight across the room and out into the hallway. Raph paused to poke at the youngest of the children who rolled up to him, growling in mock ferocity with gleaming teeth – a black little bundle of thick fur, with the long, childish snout that had not yet broadened away from the shape of the animal ancestry of half a million years earlier.

The Administrator returned with a heavy ledger and large spectacles. He opened the ledger meticulously, riffled the pages to the proper place and then drew a careful finger down the columns.

He said: 'There's only the question of the water supply, Raph.

You're due on the Maintenance gang for this next week. There's nothing else due for at least two months.'

'I'll be back before then. Is there any chance of someone subbing for me on the Water Maintenance?'

'Um-m-m – I'll get someone. I can always send my oldest. He's getting to job age and he might as well taste everything. He may like working on the dam.'

'Yes? You tell me if he does, then. He can replace me, regularly.'

The Administrator smiled gently: 'Don't plan on that, Raph. If he can figure out a way of making sleeping useful to all of us, he'll certainly take it up as a job. And why are you going to East Harbor Grouping, by the way, if it's something you care to talk about?'

'You'll laugh, perhaps, but I have just found out that there exist such things as Eekahs.'

'Eekahs? Yes, I know.' The Administrator pointed a finger. 'Creatures from across the sea! Right?'

'Right! But that's not all. I've come from the Library. I've seen trimensional reproductions, Lahr, and they're *Primate Primeval*, or almost. They're primates, anyway, *intelligent* primates. They've got small eyes, flat noses, and completely different jawbones – but they're at least second cousins. I've *got* to see them, Lahr.'

The Administrator shrugged. He felt no interest in the matter himself. 'Why? I ask out of ignorance, Raph. Does it matter, your seeing them?'

'Matter?' Raph was obviously appalled at the question. 'Don't you know what's been going on these last years? Have you read my archaeology book?'

'No,' said the Administrator, definitely, 'I wouldn't read it to save myself a turn at Garbage Disposal.'

Raph said: 'Which probably proves you more suited to Garbage Disposal than archaeology. But never mind. I've been fighting single-handed for nearly ten years in favor of my theory that Primate Primeval was an intelligent creature with a developed civilization. I have nothing on my side so far but logical necessity, which is the last thing most archaeologists will accept. They want something solid. They want the remains of a Grouping, or artifacts, structures, books – get it. All I can give them is a skeleton with a huge brain-pan. Stars above, Lahr, what do they expect to survive in ten million years? Metal dies. Paper dies. Film dies.

'Only stone lasts, Lahr. And bone that's turned to stone. I've got that. A skull with room for a brain. And stone, too, old sharpened knives. Ground flints.'

'Well,' said Lahr, 'there are your artifacts.'

'Those are called eoliths, dawn stones. They won't accept them. They call them natural products, fortuitously shaped by erosion into the shapes they have, the idiots.'

Then he grinned with a scientific ferocity: 'But if the Eekahs are intelligent primates, I've practically proven my case.'

Raph had traveled before, but never eastward, and the decline of agriculture on the road impressed him. In early history, the Gurrow Groupings had been entirely unspecialized. Each had been self-sufficient, and trade was a gesture of friendliness rather than a matter of necessity.

And so it was still in most Groupings. His own Grouping, the Red River, was perhaps typical. Some five hundred miles inland, set in lush farm land, agriculture remained centric. The river yielded some fish and there was a well-developed dairy industry. In fact, it was food exports that provided cause for the healthy state of the store of Common Units.

As they traveled eastward, however, the Groupings through which they passed paid less and less mind to the shallowing soil and more and more to the smoking factory structures.

In the East Harbor Grouping, Raph found a trading center which depended for its prosperity primarily upon ships. It was a more populous Grouping than the average, more densely packed, with houses, on occasion, within a hundred yards of each other.

Raph felt an uncomfortable prickling at the thought of living in such close quarters. The docks were even worse, with Gurrows engaged at the huge Community Jobs of loading and unloading.

The Administrator of this East Harbor Grouping was a young man, new at his job, overwhelmed with the joy of his work, and beside himself with the pleasure of welcoming a distinguished stranger.

Raph sat through an excellent meal, and was treated to a long discourse as to the exact derivation of each dish. To his provincial ears, beef from the Prairie Grouping, potatoes from the Northeast Woods Grouping, coffee from the Isthmus Grouping, wine from the Pacific Grouping, and fruit from the Central Lakes Grouping were something strange and wonderful.

Over the cigars – South Island Grouping – he brought up the subject of the Eekahs. The East Harbor Administrator grew solemn and a little uneasy.

'The man you want to see is Lernin. He'll be glad to help you all he can. You say you know something of these Eekahs?'

'I say I would *like* to know something. They resemble an extinct species of animal I am familiar with.'

'Then *that* is your field of interest. I see.'

'Perhaps you can tell me some of the details of their arrival, Administrator,' suggested Raph, politely.

'I was not Administrator at the time, friend, so that I lack first-hand information, but the records are plain. This group of Eekahs that arrived in their flying-machine . . . you've heard about these aeronautical devices?'

'Yes, yes.'

'Yes. Well . . . apparently they were fugitives.'

'So I have heard. Yet they claim not to be criminals. Isn't that so?'

'Yes. Queer, isn't it? They admitted that they had been condemned – this was after long and skillful questioning, once we had learned their language – but denied that they were evildoers. Apparently, they had disagreed with their Administrator on principles of policy.'

Raph nodded his head knowingly: 'Ah, and refused to abide by the common decision. Is that it?'

'More confusing than that. They insist there was no common decision. They claim that the Administrator decided on policy of his own accord.'

'And was not replaced?'

'Apparently those who believe he should are considered criminals – as these were.'

There was a frank pause of disbelief. Then Raph said: 'Does that sound reasonable to you?'

'No, I merely relay to you their words. Of course, the Eekah language is quite a barrier. Some of the sounds can't be pronounced: words have different meanings according to position in the sentence and according to tiny differences in inflection. And it happens often that Eekah words even when best translated are a complete puzzle.'

'They must have been surprised to find Gurrows here,' suggested Raph, 'if they are members of a different genus.'

'Surprised!' The Administrator's voice sank: 'I'll say they were surprised. Now, this information has not been generally published for obvious reasons, so I hope you remember that it's confidential. These Eekahs killed five Gurrows before they could be disarmed. They had an instrument that expelled metal pellets at high speed by means of a controlled explosive chemical reaction. We have duplicated it since. Naturally, under the circumstances, we are not branding them criminals, for it is reasonable to assume that they did not realize we were intelligent beings. Apparently,' and the Administrator smiled ruefully, 'we resemble certain animals in their world. Or so they say.'

But Raph was galvanized into a sudden enthusiasm: 'Stars above! They said that, did they? Did they go into details? What kind of animals?'

The Administrator was taken back: 'Well, I don't know. They give names in their language. What meaning has that? They called us giant "bears".'

'Giant what?'

'Bears. I haven't the slightest idea what they are, except presumably that they look like us. I know of no such in America.'

'Bears. Bears.' Raph stumbled over the word. 'That's interesting. It's more than interesting. It's stupendous. Do you know, Administrator, that there is a great dispute among us as to the ancestry of Gurrows? Living animals related to Gurrow sapiens would be of immense importance.' Raph rubbed his huge hands with pleasure.

The Administrator was pleased at the sensation he had caused. He said: 'And a puzzling thing in addition is that they call themselves by two names.'

'Two names?'

'Yes. No one knows the distinction yet, no matter how much the Eekahs explain it to us, except that one is a more general name, and one a more specific. The basis of the difference escapes us.'

'I see. Which is "Eekah"?'

'That is the specific one. The general one is' – the Administrator stumbled slowly over the harsh syllables – 'Chim-pan-zee. There, that's it. There are a group called Eekahs and there are other groups with other names. But they are all called Chim . . . what I said before.'

The Administrator sought through his mind for other juicy items of miscellany with which he was acquainted, but Raph interrupted him.

'May I see Lernin tomorrow?'

'Of course.'

'Then I shall do so. Thank you for your courtesy, Administrator.'

Lernin was a slight individual. It is doubtful if he weighed more than two hundred and fifty. There was also an imperfection in his walk, a slight lameness. But neither of these facts made much of an impression on Raph once the conversation had begun, for Lernin was a thinker who could impose his vigor upon others.

It was Raph whose eagerness dominated the first half of the conversation, and Lernin's comments were as luminous and as brief as lightning flashes. And then, there was a sudden whirl of the center of gravity, and Lernin took over.

'You will excuse me, learned friend,' Lernin said with a

characteristic stiffness that he could make so amiable, 'if I find your problem unimportant. No, no' – he lifted a long-fingered hand – 'not, in the uncomplicated talk of the times, merely unimportant *to* myself because my interest lies elsewhere, but unimportant to the Grouping of all the Groupings – to every single Gurrow from end to end of the world.'

The concept was staggering. For a moment, Raph was offended; offended deep in his sense of individuality. It showed in his face.

Lernin added quickly: 'It may sound impolite, crude, uncivilized. But I must explain. I must explain because you are primarily a social scientist and will understand – perhaps better than we ourselves.'

'My life-interest,' said Raph angrily, 'is important to myself. I cannot assume those of others in preference.'

'What I talk about should be the life-interest of all – if only because it may be the means of saving the lives of all of us.'

Raph was beginning to suspect all sorts of things from a queer form of joking to the unbalance of mind that sometimes came with age. Yet Lernin was not old.

Lernin said, with an impressive fervor: 'The Eekahs of the other world are a danger to us, for they are not friendly to us.'

And Raph replied naturally: 'How do you know?'

'No one other than myself, my friend, has lived more closely with these Eekahs who have arrived here, and I find them people with minds of emotional content strange to us. I have collected queer facts which we find difficult to interpret, but which point, at any rate, in disquieting directions.

'I'll list a few: Eekahs in organized groups kill one another periodically for obscure reasons. Eekahs find it impossible to live in manner other than those of ants – that is, in huge conglomerate societies – yet find it impossible to allow for the presence of one another. Or, to use the terminology of the social scientists, they are gregarious without being social, just as we Gurrows are social without being gregarious. They have elaborate codes of behavior, which, we are told, are taught to the young, but which are disobeyed in universal practice, for reasons obscure to us. Et cetera. Et cetera. Et cetera.'

'I am an archaeologist,' said Raph, stiffly. 'These Eekahs are of interest to me biologically only. If the curvature of the thigh bone is known to me, I care little for the curvature of their cultural processes. If I can follow the shape of the skull, it is immaterial to me that the shape of their ethics is mysterious.'

'You don't think that their insanities may affect us here?'

'We are six thousand miles apart, or more, along either ocean,' said Raph. 'We have our world. They have theirs. There is no connection between us.'

'No connection,' mused Lernin, 'so others have said. No connection at all. Yet Eekahs have reached us, and others may follow. We are told that the other world is dominated by a few, who are in turn dominated by their queer need for security which they confuse with an Eekah word called "power", which, apparently, means the prevailing of one's own will over the sum of the will of the community. What if this "power" should extend to us?'

Raph bent his mind to the task. The matter was utterly ridiculous. It seemed impossible to picture the strange concepts.

Lernin said: 'These Eekahs say that their world and ours in the long past were closer together. They say that there is a well-known scientific hypothesis in their world of a continental drift. That may interest you, since otherwise you might find it difficult to reconcile the existence of fossils of Primate Primeval closely related to living Eekahs six thousand miles away.'

And the mists cleared from the archaeologist's brain as he glanced up with a live interest untroubled by insanities: 'Ah, you should have said this sooner.'

'I say it now as an example of what you may achieve for yourself by joining us and helping us. There is another thing. These Eekahs are physical scientists, like ourselves here in East Harbor, but with a difference dictated by their own cultural pattern. Since they live in hives, they think in hives, and their science is the result of an ant-society. Individually, they are slow and unimaginative; collectively, each supplies a crumb different from that supplied by his fellow – so that a vast structure is erected quickly. Here the individual is infinitely brighter, but he works alone. You, for instance, know nothing of chemistry, I imagine.'

'A few of the fundamentals, but nothing else,' admitted Raph. 'I leave that, naturally, to the chemist.'

'Yes, naturally. But I *am* a chemist. Yet these Eekahs, though my mental inferiors, and no chemists in their own world, know more chemistry than I. For instance, did you know that there exist elements that spontaneously disintegrate?'

'Impossible,' exploded Raph. 'Elements are eternal, changeless—'

Lernin laughed: 'So you have been taught. So I have been taught. So I taught others. Yet the Eekahs are right, for in my laboratories I have checked them, and in every detail they are right. Uranium gives lise to a spontaneous radiation. You've heard of uranium, of course? And furthermore, I have detected radiations of energy beyond that produced by uranium which must be due to traces of elements unknown to us but described by the Eekahs. And these missing elements fit well into the so-called Periodic Tables some chemists have tried to foist upon the science. Though I do wrong to use the word "foist" now.'

'Well,' said Raph, 'why do you tell me this? Does this, too, help me in my problem?'

'Perhaps,' said Lernin, ironically, 'you will yet find it a royal bribe. You see, the energy production of uranium is absolutely constant. No known outward change in environment can affect it – and as a result of the loss in energy, uranium slowly turns to lead at an *absolutely constant rate*. A group of our men is even now using this fact as a basis for a method of determining the age of the earth. You see, to determine the age of a stratum of rock in the earth, then, it is but necessary to discover a region in it containing a trace of uranium – a widely spread element – and to determine about it the quantity of lead – and

I might here add that the lead produced from uranium differs from ordinary lead and can be easily characterized – and it is then simple to determine the length of time in which that stratum has been solid. And of course, if a fossil is found in that stratum, it is of the same age, am I not correct?'

'Stars above,' and Raph rose to his feet in a tremble, 'you do not deceive me? It is really possible to do this?'

'It is possible. It is even easy. I tell you that our great defense, even at this late date, is co-operation in science. We are a group now of many, my friend, from many Groupings, and we want you among us. If you join us, it would be a simple matter to extend our earth age project to such regions as you may indicate – regions rich in fossils. What do you say?'

'I will help you.'

It is doubtful if the Gurrow Groupings had ever before seen a community venture of such breadth as now took place. East Harbor Grouping, as has been remarked, was a shipping center, and certainly a trans-Atlantic vessel was not beyond the capacity of a Grouping that traded along the full lengths of both coasts of the Americas. What *was* unusual was the vastness of the co-operation of Gurrows from many Groupings, Gurrows of many interests.

Not that they were all happy.

Raph, for instance, on the particular morning that now concerns us, six months from the date of his first arrival in East Harbor, was searching anxiously for Lernin.

Lernin, for his part, was searching for nothing but greater speed. They met on the docks, where Lernin, biting the end off a cigar and leading the way to a region where smoking was permitted, said: 'And you, my friend, seem concerned. Not, certainly, about the progress of our ocean liner?'

'I am concerned,' said Raph, gravely, 'about the reports I have received of the expedition testing the age of the rocks.'

'Oh— And you are unhappy about it?'

'Unhappy!' exploded Raph. 'Have you seen them?'

'I have received a copy. I have looked at it. I have even read parts of it. But I have had little time and most of it bounced off. Will you please enlighten me?'

'Certainly. In the last several months, three of the regions I have indicated as being fossiliferous have been tested. The first region was in the area of East Harbor Grouping itself. Another was in the Pacific Bay Grouping, and a third in the Central Lakes Grouping. I purposely asked that those be done first because they are the richest areas and because they are widely separated. Do you know, for instance, what age they tell me the rocks upon which we stand are?'

'Two billion years, I think, is the oldest figure I noticed.'

'And that's the figure for the oldest rocks – the basic igneous stratum of basalt. The upper strata, however – the recent sedimentary layers containing dozens of fossils of Primate Primeval – how old do you think *these* are supposed to be? Five – hundred – trillion – years! How is that? Do you understand?'

'Trillion?' Lernin squinted upwards and shook his head. 'That's strange.'

'I'll add to it. The Pacific Coast Grouping is one hundred trillion years old – so I am told – and Central Lakes almost eighty trillion years old.'

Lernin said: 'And the other measurements? The ones that did not involve your strata?'

'That is the most peculiar thing of all. Most of the chosen investigations were carried on in strata that were not particularly fossiliferous. They had their own criteria of choice based on geological reasoning – and they got consistent results – one million to two billion years depending upon the depth and geological history of the particular region tested. Only *my* areas give these strange and impossible vagaries.'

And Lernin said, 'But what do the geologists say about all this? Can there be some error?'

'Undoubtedly. But they have fifty decent, reasonable measurements. For themselves, they have proved the method and are happy. There are three anomalies, to be sure, but they view them with equanimity as involving some unknown factors. I don't see it that way. These three measurements mean everything.' Raph interrupted himself fiercely: 'How sure are you that radioactivity is an absolute constant?'

'Sure? Can one ever be sure? Nothing we know of so far affects it, and such is likewise the definite testimony of our Eekahs. Besides, my friend, if you are implying that radioactivity was more extensive in the past than in the present, why only in your fossil regions? Why not everywhere?'

'Why, indeed? It's another aspect of a problem which is growing more important daily. Consider. We have regions which show a past of abnormal radioactivity. We have regions which show abnormal fossil frequencies. Why should these regions coincide, Lernin?'

'One obvious answer suggests itself, my friend. If your Primate Primeval existed at a time when certain regions were highly radioactive, certain individuals would wander into them and die. Radioactive radiation is deadly in excess, of course. Radioactivity and fossils, there you are.'

'Why not other creatures,' demanded Raph. 'Only Primate Primeval occurs in excess, and he was intelligent. He would not be trapped by dangerous radiation.'

'Perhaps he was not intelligent. That is, after all, only your theory and not a proven fact.'

'Certainly, then, he was more intelligent than his small-brained contemporaries.'

'Perhaps not even that. You romanticize too much.'

'Perhaps I do.' Raph spoke in half a whisper. 'It seems to me that I can conjure up visions of a great civilization of a million years back – or more. A great power; a great intelligence – that has vanished completely, except for the tiny whispers of ossified bones which retain that huge cavity in which a brain once existed, and a bony

five-fingered hand curving into slender signs of manipulative skill –
with an opposing thumb. They *must* have been intelligent.'

'Then, what killed them?' Lernin shrugged: 'Several million species of living things have survived.'

Raph looked up, half in anger: 'I cannot accompany your group,
Lernin, on a Voluntary basis. To go to the other world would be
useful, yes, if I could engage in my own studies. For your purposes,
it can be only a Community Job to me. I cannot give my heart to it.'

But Lernin's jaw was set: 'That arrangement would not be fair.
There are many of us, my friend, who are sacrificing our own interests. If we all placed them first and investigated the other world in
terms of our own particular provincialisms only, our great purpose
would be destroyed. My friend, there is not one of our men that we
can spare. We must all work as if our lives depended on our instant
solution of the Eekah problem, which, believe me, it does.'

Raph's jaws twisted in distaste. 'On your side, you have a vague
apprehension of these weak, stupid little creatures. On my side I
have a definite problem of great intellectual attraction to myself.
And between the two I can see no connection – no possible connection at all.'

'Nor can I. But listen to me a moment A small group of our most
trusted men returned last week from a visit to the other world. It was
not official, as ours will be. It made no contacts. It was a frank piece
of espionage, which I am telling you about now. I ask your discretion
on the matter.'

'Naturally.'

'Our men possessed themselves of Eekah event-sheets.'

'Pardon me?'

'It is a created name to describe the objects. Printed records are
issued daily in the various centers of Eekah population of events and
occurrences of the day, and what passes for literary efforts as well.'

Raph was momentarily interested: 'It strikes me as an excellent idea.'

'Yes, in its essence. The Eekah notion of interesting events, however, appears to consist entirely of antisocial events. However, leave that be. My point is that the existence of the Americas is well-known there these days – and it is universally spoken of as a "new land of opportunity." The various divisions of Eekahs eye it with a universal desire. The Eekahs are many, they are crowded, their economy is irrational. They want new land, and that is what this is to them – new and empty land.'

'Not empty,' pointed out Raph, mildly.

'Empty to them,' insisted Lernin terribly. 'That is the vast danger. Lands occupied by Gurrows are to them empty and they mean to take it, all the more so since they have often enough striven to take the lands of one another.'

Raph shrugged: 'Even so, they—'

'Yes. They are weak and stupid. You said that, and so they are. But only singly. They will unite for a purpose. To be sure, they will fall apart when the purpose is done – but momentarily they will join and become strong, which we perhaps cannot do, witness yourself. And their weapons of war have been keened in the fire of conflict. Their flying machines, for instance, are superb war weapons.'

'But we have duplicated it—'

'In quantity? We have also duplicated their chemical explosives, but only in the laboratory, and their firing tubes and armored vehicles, but only in experimental plants. And yet there is more – something developed within the last five years, for our own Eekahs know nothing about it.'

'And what is that?'

'We don't know. Their event-sheets speak of it – the names applied to it mean nothing to us – but the context implies the terror of it, even on the part of these kill-mad Eekahs. There seems no evidence that it has been used, or that all the Eekah groups have it – but it is used as a supreme threat. It will perhaps be clearer to you when all the evidence is presented once our voyage is under way.'

'But what is it? You talk of it as if it were a bogey.'

'Why, *they* talk of it as if it were a bogey. And what *could* be a bogey to an Eekah? That is the most frightening aspect of it. So far, we know only that it involves the bombardment of an, element they call plutonium – of which we have never heard and of which our own Eekahs have never heard either – by objects called neutrons, which our Eekahs say are subatomic particles without charge, which seems to us completely ridiculous.'

'And that is all?'

'All. Will you suspend judgment till we show you the sheets?'

Raph nodded reluctantly: 'Very well.'

Raph's leaden thoughts revolved in their worn groove as he stood there alone.

Eekahs and Primate Primeval. A living creature of erratic habits and a dead creature that must have aspired to heights. A sordid present of explosives and neutron bombardments and a glorious, mysterious past—

No connection! No connection!

Copyright information

UNLOCK THE SECRETS OF ROBOTICS AND ARTIFICIAL INTELLIGENCE WITH ISAAC ASIMOV'S GROUNDBREAKING STORIES.

ROBOT STORIES AND NOVELS

I, Robot

The Rest of the Robots

The Complete Robot

The Caves of Steel

The Naked Sun

The Robots of Dawn

Robots and Empire

VENTURE INTO THE COSMOS WITH ISAAC ASIMOV'S EPIC TALES.

THE GALACTIC EMPIRE NOVELS

The Currents of Space

The Stars, Like Dust

Pebble in the Sky

The End of Eternity

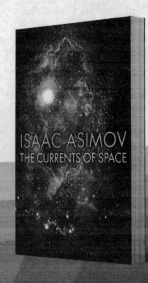

EMBARK ON A JOURNEY THROUGH ISAAC ASIMOV'S UNIVERSE AND DIVE INTO THE SAGA THAT DEFINES SCIENCE FICTION STORYTELLING.

THE FOUNDATION SAGA

Prelude to Foundation

Forward the Foundation

Foundation

Foundation and Empire

Second Foundation

Foundation's Edge

Foundation and Earth

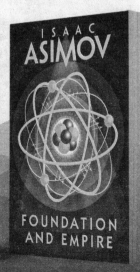

HARPER
Voyager

STEP INTO WORLDS OF WONDER WITH ISAAC ASIMOV'S CAPTIVATING SHORT STORY COLLECTIONS.

SHORT STORY COLLECTIONS

The Complete Stories:

Living Space: And Other Stories

Nightfall: And Other Stories

The Martian Way: And Other Stories

The Bicentennial Man: And Other Stories

Ring Around the Sun: And Other Stories

Mother Earth: And Other Stories

Gold: The Final Science Fiction Collection

Magic: The Final Fantasy Collection

HARPER
Voyager